MISSION TARGET

MARK NOLAN

Copyright © 2023 by Mark Nolan

All rights reserved.

No part of this book may be reproduced in any form or by any electronic or mechanical means, including information storage and retrieval systems, without written permission from the author, except for the use of brief quotations in a book review.

This book is a work of fiction. Names, characters, places, events, incidents, and dialogue are all products of the author's imagination or are used fictitiously. Any resemblance to actual persons, living or dead, businesses, companies, organizations, events or locales is entirely coincidental.

CHAPTER 1

"If an injury has to be done to a man,
it should be so severe that his vengeance need not be feared."
—Machiavelli

Key West, Florida

As Jake Wolfe drove his rented SUV along Caroline Street, he received orders from Washington D.C.

Orders to assassinate a high-value target.

His phone buzzed with a text message from Secret Service Agent Shannon McKay. *May I ask you a favor? No obligation and no compensation.*

Jake pulled over and parked. He knew that when orders began with a coded inquiry, it meant the details were top secret and on a need-to-know basis. He replied in a similar code. *Yes, go ahead and ask, but I can't make any promises.*

There was a momentary pause. *Could you help your uncle solve an impossible problem tonight? It's vitally important.*

He thought it over. This was bad timing. There had to be

someone else who could solve the problem for Uncle Sam. *Sorry, but I have a flight home to California scheduled on a friend's private jet this evening.*

Another pause. Finally, she replied. *I'll ask your friend to wait, and tell him it's an urgent matter.*

Jake knew she meant an urgent matter of national security and that his patriotic and wealthy attorney friend, Gregory "Bart" Bartholomew, would often grant a favor to the Secret Service agent. Jake was visiting Key West because when any client of Bart's law firm purchased an expensive sailboat or motor yacht, Jake acted as their trusted advisor and used his expertise with boats to help them make a wise investment.

As a weariness settled into his bones, Jake felt the need for peace and quiet at Juanita Yacht Harbor in Sausalito, California. He yearned to take his motor yacht, *Far Niente*, out on the ocean—far away from people and their problems. It was the best way for him to heal from his lingering PTSD.

However, he also felt the weight of duty to America on his shoulders. He loved his country and would move mountains to protect her from terrorists and crime syndicates who saw every city full of US citizens as a target-rich environment. His Russian assassin friend, Dmitry, told him the *Russkaya Mafiya* called America "the big store," where they could steal anything they wanted from trusting people.

He texted McKay. *Is this confirmed as a credible threat?*

She replied. *Yes. A clear and present danger that requires your particular skills.*

He took a deep breath. *You're sure my friend will delay the flight?*

McKay answered without hesitation. *Affirmative. I guarantee it.*

Jake wondered how she could be so sure. Perhaps she'd

already agreed to pay Bart's costly fee to charter his twenty-million-dollar Gulfstream G550 jet and its crew.

If he agreed to McKay's last-minute request to assassinate a high-value target tonight, he would be risking not only his own life but also that of his adopted war dog, Cody. Few things in this world could scare him after all he'd been through, but he was fiercely protective of his beloved golden retriever.

When Jake had served in the Marines as a war dog handler on deployments overseas, he and his IED-detector dog named Duke had been targeted and ambushed by terrorists. They'd had a price on their heads. Jake nearly died from a bullet wound to his right thigh, and he never got over the death of his faithful dog. Just thinking about Duke caused the familiar post-traumatic stress anger to begin simmering, and he made a conscious effort to keep it under control.

Can I work alone and not involve my K-9?

McKay replied in the affirmative. *Yes, he can remain behind in your hotel room or rental car.*

With that reassurance, Jake made his decision. Although he'd already checked out of his hotel, Cody could wait in the vehicle.

In that case, yes, my uncle can rely on me tonight.

He kept it specific. He'd never say, *My uncle can always rely on me.* Every mission was a negotiation.

McKay didn't push him for more or provide any details. *Thank you. Stand by in Key West until sundown.*

Jake replied. *Roger that.*

Pocketing his phone, he wondered what the mission he'd volunteered for would entail. The violent death of a high-value terrorist target—but who, when, where, how and why? Knowing the sun would set in about an hour, he drove to one of his favorite restaurants for dinner. If there was a chance he might be eating his last meal, he wanted it to be a good one.

Jake managed to find a parking space in the busy lot next door, and then he and Cody walked over to the humble little Airstream trailer that served as a taco truck. It was a hidden gem in the backyard of a house turned into a bar. Typical Key West "Conch" life.

A teenaged male employee at the window told a customer, "I'm sorry, your card was declined."

The female customer had a young son with her who might've been seven years old. Jake thought they both looked hungry and worried.

"Please try it again," the woman said, gazing at the two red serving baskets filled with cheeseburgers.

Cody lifted his nose and smelled the food.

Jake displayed some folding money to the cashier. "No worries. I'm buying. Please add their order to my tab. And I'm Jake. I called mine in."

The mother blinked at him. "Thank you so much."

"It's my pleasure, ma'am," Jake said. "I had good luck and won some money playing poker with friends. Now I'm simply paying it forward."

The mother and son carried their burger baskets and bottles of apple juice to an outdoor table, sat down, and tore into the food like they hadn't eaten in a while.

Jake paid for his usual taco trio that included a fish taco, a shrimp taco, and a BBQ beef taco. Surf and turf. For Cody, the catch of the day, two filets of dorado/mahi-mahi grilled with butter and no spices. For his new friends, he added two slices of key lime pie.

Jake set down the slices of pie and a hundred-dollar bill in front of the happily surprised mother and son. "Have a good evening."

The boy said, "Thank you, sir."

Jake smiled kindly. "Such good manners. Am I right, Cody?"

Cody barked once, as he'd been trained to when he heard that question.

The mother and son stared at the dog in wonder.

Jake carried his dinners to the SUV, fed Cody the filets, poured him a bowl of water, and then sat and enjoyed his dinner.

As he ate, his thoughts turned to Agent McKay, who often worked overtime at her office in the Catacombs, the secret tunnels below the White House. She was in charge of an off-the-books shadowy group that protected American citizens from deadly threats the general public never heard about. The operation's existence was denied by the US government.

Jake had recently been disavowed and removed from the top-secret team for going rogue and taking matters into his own hands to protect the greater good. He'd left a trail of destruction in his wake, but saved countless lives, had no regrets, and would do it again without hesitation.

A congressional committee that investigated the unusual events and resulting fallout hadn't seen it that way. They wanted answers. They wanted a scapegoat to interrogate. They wanted to know top-secret intel.

Jake didn't answer to clueless bureaucrat pencil-pushers on either side of the aisle. He walked alone. They could kiss his butt every day of the week and twice on Tuesday. Pucker up, buttercup.

Despite Jake's nonactive status, Agent McKay had contacted him on his highly-encrypted phone. Now he knew why she'd allowed him to keep the unusual and costly device.

After dinner, Jake drove to Higgs Beach Dog Park and let Cody off leash to get some exercise on the sun-bleached sand before the cross-country flight they'd catch if Jake survived the impromptu mission. They would both sleep through the night on Bart's jet and arrive on the West Coast in the early morning where Jake's girlfriend, Sarah, patiently waited for their return.

This work for the government always cut into his private life. Sarah was the only woman who'd been able to handle the danger. She was protective of Cody and understanding with Jake.

Jake tossed a Frisbee for his retriever to fetch again and again as the sun sank into the Gulf of Mexico and put on a beautiful light show display. He waited for the rare and fabled green flash, but it didn't appear. Most people who claimed to have seen it were liars telling sea stories, but that was part of the island life and Keys lore that everyone loved.

Once the sun had set, he received another text from the DC phone number. *I'm calling you now.*

His phone buzzed in a specific pattern, indicating a call from McKay. He answered the secure video link using software that resembled FaceTime and Skype, but with stronger encryption to Department of Defense specifications.

"Sitrep?"

"This information is classified top secret," McKay said.

Jake replied, "Understood. Stand by one moment."

CHAPTER 2

Taking a seat in his SUV along with Cody, Jake turned on the engine and AC, and played a radio talk show for background noise. He held the phone down below window height and looked at McKay's worried face on the screen. She wore her usual dark-gray suit, white blouse, and quiet tie.

"This mission was requested by four-star General Lloyd Clemens of the United States Marine Corps," McKay said.

Jake sat up straighter. "You're still working with the Marine Recapture Tactics Teams?"

Most Americans never thought about how some Marines were allowed to fight on US soil. They protected the president and flew his helicopter, protected nuclear weapons on Navy bases and ships, and protected very important people from kidnapping attempts.

According to the Posse Comitatus Act, active-duty military cannot be deployed on US soil. However, these Marine teams were the exception because they worked within law enforcement units of the Marine Corps and specialized in police-like SWAT procedures. If terrorists managed to steal a nuclear weapon from a US naval installation, or kidnap a VIP with top-secret knowledge, the USMC RTT would violently recapture the asset or die trying.

Jake had recently fought beside RTT Marines on a top-secret assignment.

"Yes, General Clemens took control of the POETs," McKay said, referring to the President's Operational Emergency Team. "He felt the group was too powerful to serve at the whim of some possibly unqualified future US president who would be temporarily in charge over a four-year stretch."

"How did President Anderson feel about that?"

Jake had met Daniel Anderson and First Lady Katherine before they were elected, when Daniel was a congressman.

"The president agreed it was a job for RTT Marines, and that a Marine general should be in command of them."

"Smart move to have General Clemens on board," Jake said. "That man is a legend. Every Marine respects him."

"Here's where you come in. The Venezuelan Communist government is freeing prison inmates serving time for murder, assault, rape, and robbery. The communists send these dangerous convicted criminals to the US, where they enter illegally."

Jake cursed. "What's their agenda?"

"They seek to destabilize American communities through the intentional mass distribution of dangerous drugs."

"I heard about Communist cocaine," Jake said.

"Yes, Venezuela's hyperinflation killed their economy and created a cocaine superhighway to the US in a desperate attempt to bring in cash," McKay said. "The country went from a one percent share of the global market to a twenty-five percent share."

"I read that the United States charged Venezuela's president and fourteen of his top government officials with narco-terrorism," Jake said. "It's sad how the good people of Venezuela have to suffer under a rogue regime."

McKay said, "It gets worse. Far worse. Now the regime is using violent criminals to smuggle xylazine into the United States. Homeland has designated the leaders as Tier I drug kingpins and terrorists, pursuant to the Foreign Narcotics Kingpin Designation Act."

"What in the world is xylazine?" Jake said.

"A veterinary drug widely used as a horse tranquilizer. On the street, they call it tranq."

"And people on the street buy and use this animal tranquilizer to get high, knowing it could kill them?"

"Yes, and this gang is mixing xylazine with fentanyl," McKay said. "The combination is extremely dangerous. People are dropping dead from overdoses all across America. The absolute disaster we're seeing is that xylazine isn't an opiate, and it doesn't respond to naloxone."

Jake took a deep breath and let it out. "So, if someone overdoses on xylazine, Narcan isn't going to save their life?"

"No coming back. The victim's heart stops abruptly, and they're listed on the death report as non-responsive."

He thought it over for a moment. "Why would drug dealers want to kill off their paying customers?"

McKay said, "The NSA picked up chatter about a hostile foreign nation paying vast sums to kill US citizens via this animal drug."

Jake paused. "A secret war. How widespread is the problem?"

"The FBI recently seized over one million fentanyl pills in Albuquerque that were laced with xylazine."

"One million? In one city?"

"We believe millions more went to other cities from coast to coast. Xylazine is showing up in one third of all fatal overdoses nationwide right now, and the number is rising. In Philadelphia, ninety percent of opioids tested were tainted with the stuff."

Jake clenched his right fist. "That's astonishing."

Cody leaned in between the front seats and sniffed his handler's shoulder and body chemistry, apparently sensing Jake's emotional intensity.

Jake relaxed his hand, reached out, and patted Cody on the back.

"Xylazine can also cause a horrifying side effect in humans," McKay said. "Deep flesh wounds that fester, get infected, turn gray, and smell rotten."

Jake felt his stomach lurch. "If that becomes widespread, it could overwhelm hospital emergency rooms."

"If the xylazine crime wave and skyrocketing overdoses continue to rise, our major cities might become like war zones with wounded and dead bodies in the streets. Foreign enemies of democracy want it to happen. They're using a drug to undermine the US from within."

"That's unacceptable." Jake punched the SUV's steering wheel with his fist. "Not on my watch. Where can I find the communist drug gang responsible for this attack on Americans? Give me their current location."

McKay nodded at him on his phone display, observing the reaction she'd wanted to see. "I was hoping you'd ask. They're spread out across the nation and difficult to locate. The US government doesn't have access to the Venezuelan criminal databases because we lack effective diplomatic relations with the communist regime."

"And most foreign cartel criminals are undocumented," Jake said.

"Yes, but we have HUMINT that tonight one of the top Tier I narco terrorists is in Key West, not far from you. He has several fake IDs, and is currently using the name Freddy Diaz."

Jake knew HUMINT was an acronym for human intelligence. He looked out the windshield at the beautiful tropical island that now hid a deadly terrorist predator. "Why is Diaz here at the end of the road?"

"He's hiding out and enjoying life before somebody ends it. A rival gang made repeated brutal attempts to kill him in Acapulco, and he fled to the US."

"And now he's Florida's problem," Jake said.

"First, he entered Cancun by boat, posing as a tourist and using a false passport. The Mexican Federal Police captured the man and locked him in prison, but he bribed several guards who let him escape."

"How did he arrive in the Keys?"

"On a boat at night," McKay said. "He can disappear the same way."

"These islands are good places to lie low," Jake said. "Every time I'm in the Keys, I dream of finding a quiet spot to escape from the world."

"Members of his own gang are looking for him, too," she said. "They believe Diaz ripped them off for millions of dollars, and they'll kill him out of pride and the need to command respect—more than over the cash, which is a drop in the bucket compared to their yearly take."

Jake thought about the deadly machismo of narcos who'd served time in prison. Some of them would kill you for looking at them the wrong way. "It sounds like this criminal will die soon, but you want to get the xylazine shut down immediately."

"I want this individual's role ended tonight with vengeance." McKay cursed for emphasis, which was unusual for the stoic agent. "Last weekend, an old friend's nephew died at a party after being talked into snorting one line of cocaine."

"Laced with tranq? That's heartbreaking."

"This is a new kind of terrorism where they murder US citizens using a poison weapon that can't be traced to them. I will not rest until we eradicate tranq terrorism, starting tonight with the trafficker in Key West."

Jake felt her righteous anger affecting him, placing a burden on his shoulders. He thought of the Bible verse from Luke 12:48, spoken by a Marine Corps padre during the bootcamp graduation ceremony at MCRD San Diego.

For unto whom much is given, of him shall be much required.

He took a deep breath and let it out. "If you designate him as a high-value target, I'll troubleshoot the problem for you right now."

CHAPTER 3

"I told General Clemens we could count on you, no matter what," McKay said.

Jake held her gaze for a moment on the screen. "What did Clemens say?"

"He agreed and said you're a Marine's Marine. Semper Fidelis. Always faithful."

Cody barked when he heard the familiar words, Semper Fidelis.

Jake reached back and scratched Cody behind the ears. "After being disavowed from the POETs, am I still a commissioned privateer with full jurisdiction to conduct reprisal operations worldwide?"

"Yes, you're still operating under admiralty and maritime law, giving you broad legal powers on the water. And you're empowered to mete out judgment. Article I of the US Constitution lists issuing letters of marque and reprisal in Section 8 as one of the enumerated powers of Congress. It's essentially a mercenary contract issued by the government that allows privately armed individuals to hunt down our nation's enemies."

"I'll solve this problem on the water or shoreline?"

"Yes, you'll approach an island by boat."

Jake glanced at the SUV's dashboard clock. "When, where, and how?"

McKay said, "After sunset, just outside of town, up close, using a .22 handgun with a silencer attached."

"A CIA assassin's pistol loaded with subsonic hollow-point rounds," Jake said.

"You'll be doing your country a great service, protecting citizens and saving lives."

Jake nodded. "As a privateer for the US government, it's my duty to stop enemy combatants and war criminals from deploying untreatable poison weapons against our civilian population."

"Agreed," McKay said. "With your skills, resources, and privateer status, you're morally obligated to use them for the greater good."

Jake thought about that for a moment. His moral compass aligned with the obligation. "Once the tranq dealer is on his trip to hell, one of my contacts in the media can leak a story that a rival gang made the hit and attribute the tip to a confidential informant." He remembered Linda, a reporter he'd become friends with years before when working as a photojournalist. It was no surprise that former military-trained snipers could become talented photographers.

"I appreciate you doing this favor for General Clemens," McKay said.

Although Jake was no longer active duty, he couldn't say no to the general. Once a Marine, always a Marine. "I'll do it for him, for US citizens, and for you, Shannon."

She paused. They rarely used first names. "Thank you . . . Jake."

"Give me a mission brief."

McKay explained the parameters. He listened carefully and took mental notes, memorizing key details.

"I'd be willing to bet that plan has about a fifty percent chance of success," Jake said. "Good enough."

"I'm assuming you have a pair of black cargo pants and a black long-sleeve T-shirt in your carry-on suitcase?"

"As always. How do I get my hands on the pistol?"

"A woman is about to deliver it to you. She'll drive up and park her car, then give you a white plastic bag that holds three flat clamshell takeout food containers. She'll pretend to be delivering your restaurant order."

Jake watched as a four-door sedan pulled over, and a woman stepped out. He lowered his window, and she handed over a "meal" that weighed a lot more than takeout food, along with a large soda cup that had a straw sticking out the top. Jake tipped her some folding money.

The woman blinked in surprise but didn't miss a beat. "Enjoy your meal, and thanks for using our app." She returned to her car and drove off.

"Eff your app," Jake grumbled. He was mindful of OPSEC—operations security—and avoided installing apps that spied on your phone, accessed your camera, listened to your microphone, scanned your email and text messages, and copied your GPS travel location records.

Some big tech companies created a profile of you that was so detailed they actually called it your voodoo doll. They sold your profile data to anyone with money to spend, including front men for hostile nations that were building files on every individual American.

"I've received the delivery," Jake told McKay.

"Check the contents."

Cody sniffed the bag and growled.

Jake knew Cody smelled the handgun and rounds. He patted Cody on the back. "Leave it."

Jake observed as Cody obeyed the war dog command and relaxed his shoulders, accepting the new addition to Jake's collection of weapons. The scent-trained dog could remember each one as a specific item.

Jake opened the containers and looked inside. The pistol and suppressor came with a modified holster designed to carry the handgun with its silencer attached.

He removed the top from his large soda cup and found thin black gloves and a black nylon balaclava ski mask with holes for his eyes and mouth. He was surprised to see a US Marshals badge, the familiar silver circle-star on a black leather holder, along with fed creds.

"Garcia is returning my badge?" In the past, Jake had been deputized by the US Marshals in California, but Chief Deputy Garcia had taken his badge away for what he'd deemed Jake's reckless actions and insubordination.

"No, he's still convinced you're a loose cannon," McKay said.

Jake shrugged it off. "I'm a work in progress."

"I told him you'd earned a second chance, but he said you'll never again be listed as serving at his office in the San Francisco Federal Building."

"Some good friends of mine work there, including Easton and Greene, but I'm not going to kiss Garcia's foot to remain among them." Jake checked the ID again. "Miami, huh? That's fine with me. If I cause trouble for Chief Garcia, he can blame it on Florida Man."

"Time was of the essence, and a Miami ID is perfect for tonight's mission," McKay said. "It helped that your IED detector dog made a good impression recently by finding explosives in Key West. The Miami chief deputy heard about it and approved."

"Cody makes a good impression everywhere he goes," Jake said. "With me, it's hit or miss."

She gave him a rare smile. "The US Marshals have reinstated you as a deputized civilian K-9 handler who volunteers to assist their fugitive recovery team upon request. That team only."

"My favorite one," Jake said with a nod. "I've missed carrying that Marshals star."

"I pulled some strings for you because you're giving one of Cody and Skye's puppies to my daughter, Aspen," McKay said.

"Thank you." Jake thought of the incredibly smart puppy that Aspen had chosen and named Faith.

"No, thank *you*," McKay said. "The Guide Dogs for the Blind school kept us updated on Faith's training. Now Faith has graduated, and Aspen has never been so excited as when we talk about her dog."

Jake felt his heart swell. He took a breath and let it out, then gazed in the mirror at Cody, whose offspring were going to change lives. His throat felt tight.

The dog pawed at Jake's shoulder as if again feeling there was something going on with his handler.

"Where do I find the kayak?" Jake said.

"Drive out of the dog park, and pull over on Atlantic, behind a pickup on the side of the road with a black kayak in the truck bed."

"Roger." Jake ended the call and followed orders. Once he'd pulled over at his destination, the pickup truck's driver stepped out and beckoned Jake toward him with a hand gesture.

Jake put on nitrile gloves, as did the other man, and

without a word they moved the kayak from the truck bed to Jake's SUV roof rack.

The man handed Jake a double-bladed paddle and some bungee cords, walked away and drove off, never having spoken.

Jake wondered about the man's background. He had the look of a combat veteran. It takes one to know one.

He secured the kayak, tossed the paddle in his SUV's back cargo area, and reported to McKay. "Kayak on board."

"Now, drive north on A1A and stop at the Shark Key Wayside Park Boat Ramp at Mile Marker 11," McKay said.

"Roger." Jake drove to the designated location, pulled over, and sent a text. *I'm at the Mile Marker.*

McKay replied. *Stand by.*

Roger. Standing by.

Jake set his phone on the dashboard. He and Cody sat patiently, the way people in every branch of the military soon learned to hurry up and wait.

Jake was already wearing the black cargo pants. He stepped out, opened the back hatch, and donned his black, long-sleeved shirt. Returning to the driver's seat, he double-checked the .22 pistol, magazine and rounds, then attached the suppressor with practiced hands.

Cody watched his handler intently, smelling the ammo, studying the new weapon, and awaiting orders.

Finally, the text from McKay lit up Jake's phone. *Commence mission.*

Jake replied. *Mission underway.*

CHAPTER 4

Jake drove north past the entrance to Cannon Royal Drive on his left that led to the island of Shark Key, formerly Raccoon Key. He passed by the private community with its gated entry and guard shack and pulled over on the gravel shoulder to his right just before the Shark Key Bridge.

There was an area where you could park your car to pick up and drop off folks who wanted to go for a walk on the Florida Keys Overseas Heritage Trail that ran along the highway and had once been part of Henry Flagler's Overseas Railway.

Jake knew it well. He'd done some bridge fishing there in the past and caught his share of mangrove snapper. Now, the walkway was blocked off and closed due to damage when a sizable chunk of it had collapsed and fallen into the water. Time was taking its toll on the beloved old bridge.

Jake felt the passing of an era. Future generations might never know the joy of bridge fishing at this spot and half a dozen others that needed repairs. He was grateful to have taken advantage of the opportunity when he could.

He sat in the SUV with its engine and AC running, turned to face Cody and looked his dog in the eyes. "Cody, *stay* and *guard*. That's an order, Sergeant."

The retriever whined in protest, and pawed at Jake's shoulder.

Jake knew the former war dog suffered from separation anxiety if his handler went on a mission and left him behind. And that the scary-smart K-9 was aware of Jake's new weapon, could hear his serious tone of voice on the phone, and smelled his elevated level of adrenaline.

Jake guessed Cody's sharp ears had overheard and recognized Agent McKay's voice. The dog knew something was going to happen, and he wanted to be part of it, protecting his handler and doing his duty as a Marine. That was the job they'd trained him for. He was an MWD—military working dog—who wanted to work. He and Jake were partners, joined by the leash between them.

"I'll be right back," Jake said, opening the sunroof and turning off the engine. "It's important that you protect the Humvee for exfiltration. Can I count on you to do your part in the mission? Semper Fi?"

Cody barked once, deep brown intelligent eyes watching his handler as he moved his weight restlessly from one front paw to the other.

Jake put on the black gloves and balaclava face mask, which made Cody growl at him. He waited until there were no car headlights approaching from either direction, and then opened his door with the dome light turned off. Jake stepped out into the moonless night, removed the lightweight black plastic kayak from the roof rack, and set it on the bike path.

He opened the vehicle's back hatch, grabbed the double-bladed paddle, and set it in the kayak. His gaze fell upon a custom-made guitar case that held his twelve-gauge pump shotgun. The weapon's antique stock had been fashioned out of teak wood salvaged from a shipwreck offshore of Key West in years gone by.

The shotgun reminded him of a Marine and close friend who'd been killed. The veteran's parents had given the shotgun to Jake in honor of his loyal friendship to their son who was a "Conch," born and raised in Key West, the Conch Republic.

Anger once again burned in Jake's chest as it often did. He would've loved to use his friend's shotgun to take care of this problem, but he left it there and instead placed the .22 handgun into its modified belt holster.

Before he could reach up and pull down the SUV's hatch, Cody climbed over the back seat, into the cargo area, and leapt out onto the gravel.

"No, Cody. You have your orders. Get back inside." Jake reached for the headstrong dog's collar, but Cody evaded him and hopped into the kayak, where he sat down, giving Jake a challenging look.

Jake let out a breath. "I admire your loyalty, but right now, I need your obedience to my commands."

He grabbed the handle on Cody's vest, lifted him up like a suitcase and set him in the SUV.

Cody whined.

"Are you a Marine or not? Guard the Humvee. Do not honk the horn. Do not open a window." Jake closed the hatch and pointed a finger at his dog. "Sit. Stay."

Cody stared at him for a moment through the back window, then sat down.

Jake let out a breath of relief when his dog obeyed. He never knew when the ornery K-9 might go rogue. Nobody else could control the highly intelligent animal. If Cody rebelled against Jake, it would encourage petty bureaucrats who thought war veteran K-9s should only be allowed to live on military bases and wear muzzles at all times. Jake would *never* let them take his best friend away and do that to him.

He carried the lightweight boat across the road using an attached shoulder strap, stepped over the guardrail, and eased the kayak down a concrete and rock embankment, into the water of Shark Channel in time to avoid being seen by an approaching motorist.

As the car's headlights came closer, he sat in the kayak and paddled it under the bridge, out of sight. He waited there, hoping a chunk of the old railroad wouldn't break loose and fall on his head.

Once the car passed by, Jake put on night vision goggles and quietly made his way along the shoreline of Shark Key. He paddled toward a newly built multi-million-dollar mansion that McKay had told him was currently being rented by a corporate property management firm for a client who wanted total privacy.

McKay had said the wealthy neighbors minded their own business. They weren't easily impressed by rumors of a celebrity living among them and taking an extended vacation. Florida had an overabundance of rich and famous people. Sometimes a limo came and went, but the guards at the gate only saw the hired driver and never the passengers behind tinted windows.

Jake continued moving past several of the palatial homes that cost multiple millions of dollars. He spotted a woman in the backyard of one home, sitting at a patio table while smoking a cigarette and talking on her phone. She faced the water but wasn't staring at him. Not yet.

Jake stopped paddling, bent forward to lessen his profile, and held his breath as he drifted past on momentum. A few houses down, a dog barked as Jake floated by. The dog's owner yelled at it to be quiet.

Soon, Jake had left the complications behind and he paddled to where the HVT—high value target—was hiding out.

In years past, when Jake had served in the Marines with several overseas deployments, he'd killed a number of terrorist leaders. Now that he was a civilian, suffering from PTSD, McKay should let him rest and heal, but evil never stopped rearing its head, which meant Jake could never stop fighting it.

He quietly made his way closer to the targeted mansion and did recon to locate the hot tub. According to McKay, Diaz relaxed there after dinner every night with the Jacuzzi jets bubbling as he smoked an expensive Cuban cigar and drank the finest liquor.

Diaz would often entertain guests, usually aspiring models and actresses he lied to while claiming to be a Hollywood producer on vacation and sourcing new talent in Florida for an upcoming blockbuster movie. If they were cooperative, they could become movie stars and win Academy Awards. They'd marry a world-famous actor, live in Beverly Hills, and be envied by their jealous friends back home.

Jake saw a glossy white go-fast boat tied up at the criminal's dock. Known as a cigarette boat, it was ready and waiting to make a quick getaway if needed.

He paddled his kayak up to a next-door neighbor's dock, where a twenty-foot sailboat blocked their home's view of him. He tied his bowline to one of their dock cleat hitches and eased himself into the water, holding the pistol above his head with one hand.

After doing the sidestroke, he waded up the shore into a

thicket of trees and bushes separating the two luxury home properties.

Jake spotted his mission target, busy entertaining several attractive women in bikinis. Some of the most in-demand people on both coasts were beautiful, half-dressed women who pretended to laugh at rich men's jokes. Jake felt sorry for them and their unfulfilled hopes and dreams of Hollywood fame that would probably never come true.

A bodyguard stood off to the side of the spa, armed with a MAC-10 Ingram 9mm submachine gun with a two-stage suppressor and 32-round magazine. It was not accurate at a distance like the far superior MP-5, but reliably lethal up close. A low-noise, concealable murder weapon favored by cartels. This one had a second 32-round magazine duct taped alongside and opposite the other, giving it a 64-round capacity. The guard ignored his job of keeping watch for threats and instead ogled the alluring ladies who were out of his league.

Jake sent a text message on his encrypted waterproof sat phone he'd set on dark mode to mute its glow. *In position.*

Moments later, he saw police-style lights strobing in front of the house, lighting up palm trees and neighboring homes. He heard a radio squawk with chatter from dispatch. Somebody knocked hard on the home's front door three times, and a deep male voice shouted, "Monroe County sheriffs. Open up. We have a search warrant."

Diaz climbed out of the hot tub and ran to the speedboat, along with his guard, leaving the startled women behind.

The guard set down his submachine gun in the boat and grabbed the wheel and key, starting the engines while the cartel boss hurried to untie the lines.

Jake took aim while the drug lord target was bent over the cleat hitch. He double-tapped Diaz in the head with two subsonic .22 hollow-point rounds. The gun coughed twice, and twin projectiles flew at a velocity below the speed of sound and didn't make a loud crack. And what noise they did make was drowned out by the boat's growling engines.

The rounds expanded inside the criminal's brain and caused maximum damage as they were designed to do, killing him instantly. Diaz collapsed facedown onto the wooden dock, obviously not knowing what hit him.

The guard gaped at his dead boss, stepped away from the wheel, grabbed his submachine gun, and raised it toward Jake's direction.

CHAPTER 5

Jake remained hidden as he quickly aimed his pistol and fired two shots, dead center. The hollow-point rounds made the criminal stagger and drop his MAC-10. Jake double-tapped him again, and the guard stumbled backward over the gunwale and into the water.

Jake thought for a second about how the guard should've pushed the throttles forward against the dash to make the boat roar away, snapping the line and taking him out of range.

The female guests screamed when they saw their host lying prone on the dock and bleeding. Jake felt relieved there had been no civilians harmed.

A handsome Asian man came running out of the house dressed in a Miami Vice style linen suit and carrying an expensive-looking burgundy leather briefcase with gold clasps. He handed each woman two wrapped bundles of bills. "Here's a lot of money to keep your mouths shut. More to come if you don't screw up. Go inside and get dressed. Another boat will pick you up and take you back to the yacht club, then it's off to Hollywood."

Each of the surprised women accepted twenty thousand dollars in cash and dashed into the house.

Jake studied the Asian man, who didn't appear to be armed, then stepped out of the thicket of trees and moved toward the go-fast boat. He finished untying the lines, climbed aboard, and fired a headshot at the guard floating in the water nearby.

Better safe than sorry. Jake didn't need a wounded *sicario* hunting him and seeking revenge. The Marines trained their infantry to do one thing—kill the enemy—and Jake had years of practice.

The Asian man with brightly whitened teeth and movie star hair stood perfectly still and called out to Jake. "Please get me out of here, and I'll pay you a hundred thousand dollars."

Jake played along. "Two hundred thousand, and show me the money first." He added some blistering profane insults.

The criminal grinned. A businessman who understood financial negotiations. Money solved problems, and he had plenty to spend. He opened his briefcase and displayed bundles of hundred-dollar bills stacked in rows.

"I'll give you *all* of this money, over two hundred and fifty grand, if we leave immediately and you deliver me to a safe place. There's plenty more cash if you'd like to work for me. Much more. Every month. You'll be rich beyond your wildest dreams. Plus, hot actresses and fashion models in your bed. A different babe every night of the week."

"Welcome aboard, my new friend," Jake said with a sweep of his hand. "Stash your briefcase under that bench seat. Sit down, hang on, and act innocent." He pointed at a seat cushion.

The man embarked and lifted the seat to reveal a cabinet space. He reached down to place the briefcase inside, and that was when Jake cracked him on the head with the butt of his pistol.

The man dropped facedown on the boat's deck with a thud and lay there unconscious and drooling.

Jake placed the suppressed .22 pistol in the man's right hand, leaned it over the gunwale, and fired a round into the water. He holstered the pistol, grabbed the MAC-10 off the deck, and set it on the dashboard, then motored away from the mansion with lights off and at low speed, so as not to cause a wake or attract any more attention.

Although the suppressor had quieted down the small-caliber pistol, his shots made a noticeable sound when fired. That, along with the sheriff's loud demands, would definitely draw attention from the closest neighbors.

Hopefully, the police lights would make folks stay inside their houses with doors locked, while pulling their window curtains closed and trying to avoid getting involved or having their faces and homes appear in the media.

Jake left the kayak behind as he slowly cruised his stolen speedboat toward the bridge where Cody awaited his return. On arrival, he cut the engines, drifted up to the embankment, and disembarked. He left the keys in the ignition and tied the lines to a rock.

Monroe County sheriffs would find the boat later, or somebody would steal it. Jake didn't care which. He'd love to keep the sleek boat, but it wasn't meant to be.

He put the stunned prisoner over his shoulder in a firefighter's carry, grabbed the briefcase and MAC-10 submachine gun, and hiked up the bank.

Finding the road clear, he crossed to his SUV, opened the back hatch, and dropped the unconscious man inside, along with his briefcase and weapons.

Cody sat in the backseat, snarling at the prisoner and displaying his teeth.

"Easy, Cody. Stand by." Jake put double zip ties on the man's hands and feet and zipped both to a back seat headrest post. He placed the .22 handgun and holster in the custom guitar case and wrapped the MAC-10 in a black towel that blended in with the vehicle's black interior. With that done, he closed the hatch and sat in the driver's seat, where he locked the doors and sent a text. *MA. EX.*

After Jake signaled mission accomplished, and exfiltrating, he received a quick reply. *Copy MA. EX.*

He sent a follow-up text. *One complication. I picked up a stray.*

There was a pause. *What? Bring the stray to my local branch office. I'll have a friend meet you.*

He'd expected that. *On my way.*

The phone went dark.

Jake did a U-turn and drove back the way he'd come, toward Mile Marker 8 and Naval Air Station Key West on Boca Chica Key. Minutes later, he saw the exit, drove down the ramp, and approached the NAS gate.

He noted a familiar sign.

WARNING.
This Property Patrolled By
Military Working Dog Teams.

"And I have the A-Team top dog right here in my rig," Jake said. "It's okay to be jealous."

He stopped where a uniformed Navy officer stood at attention, waiting for him. The officer held out a phone. "Thumbprint."

Jake complied, and the phone screen lit up with a green circle.

"I'll ride with you," the officer said, pocketing his phone. "Command your K-9 to stand down."

"Yes, sir." Jake wondered who this guy was but trusted McKay. "Out, Cody. Be friends."

Cody sniffed the man who opened the door and sat next to Jake. He let out a low growl in warning to the armed stranger but obeyed his handler and remained calm.

The officer gestured at the windshield. "Follow this road, and I'll tell you where to turn."

"Roger." Jake drove in silence, not asking questions or offering explanations.

The prisoner groaned in the back cargo area and mumbled, "You promised to let me go, not kill me like you killed those other men."

The Navy officer turned and looked back, then at Jake.

Jake kept his eyes on the road. "This operation is classified Top Secret."

"I have clearances," the Navy man said.

"Maybe you do, but this intel is on a need-to-know basis," Jake said. "All I can tell you is that prisoner shot two cartel sicarios. He'll try to lie his way out of this. Be sure to check his hands for gunshot residue."

The officer nodded and directed Jake to turn right. Soon they arrived at an aircraft hangar. The door rolled up as they approached. Jake drove inside without being asked, and the door rolled down again.

Four armed Marines in Combat Utility Uniform "cammies" quickly surrounded the vehicle and aimed their rifles at the occupants. They acted deadly serious, all business, willing and able to kill enemies.

Recapture Tactics Teams were made up of Marines who

were handpicked for their physical abilities and marksmanship skills. These four were intimidating, but Jake felt he was one of them.

"Hold your fire," he said through his open window. "I have a Marine war dog on board."

CHAPTER 6

A man with broad shoulders, a flat stomach, and buzz-cut hair came to Jake's door and looked him in the eye.

"Jukebox, you ugly mo-fo. We only let you in here because we wanted to see Cody."

Jake smiled and nodded in recognition of his old buddy, Carl "Hutch" Hutchinson, a fellow combat veteran and trusted friend for life. "Hutch, I still can't believe some fool mistakenly put you in charge of these RTT Devil Dogs. How did that even happen, bro?"

Jake noted how the other three Marines visibly relaxed, lowered their weapons, and grinned at the rude joking between their commanding officer and his unexpected but apparently well-known visitor.

"I heard you were making a delivery. I hope it's pizza and beer," Hutch deadpanned.

"I wish," Jake said. "I found a lost dirtbag from an FTO and brought him in for questioning."

The Navy officer said, "How can you be sure he's with a Foreign Terrorist Organization?"

"That intel is on a need to know basis."

Hutch said, "Take his word for it. Jake served as a Marine war dog handler on multiple deployments overseas. He's no longer enlisted but works with us RTT Marines on occasion as part of the Joint Interagency Task Force South."

"Under what authority?" the Navy officer said. "No offense."

Jake said, "None taken, sir. The US Marshals Service deputized me to work on their fugitive pursuit detail, which gives me worldwide jurisdiction to help protect America from terrorists and criminals, both foreign and domestic." He displayed his Marshals badge and creds.

The Navy officer inspected Jake's cred pack and gave a nod of approval. "Good to know you're squared away and not some CIA hothead who thinks he's Jason Bourne."

"Nothing like that," Jake lied. He held back saying that without CIA agents, your kids might be speaking Russian in school. In CIA headquarters there was a wall featuring stars with no names beneath, and the words, "In honor of those members of the Central Intelligence Agency who gave their lives in the service of their country."

Jake was a killer of killers, fighting a secret war against foreign enemies who wanted to harm American citizens. His life had changed one fateful day years before when he'd taken a road less traveled.

He unlocked the car doors, stepped out and moved to the rear of the vehicle. The Navy officer followed him.

Hutch pulled the back door open, and raised it above his head. "What do we have here? Does anybody else think this guy looks familiar?"

Jake pulled out his phone. "Let's check facial recognition." He took a picture of the prisoner's face and texted it to McKay. *Is he in your database?*

McKay called him a moment later. "Yes, our software found an instant match for a criminal named Chang Quan. The Miami DEA is offering a reward of up to five million dollars for information that helps bring him to justice. It's posted on their website and social media."

Jake received a link to the webpage, and displayed his phone to the Navy officer. "The DEA lists him as a narcoterrorist."

"Good to know," the officer said. "I'll let you men take it from here." He exited through the pedestrian door and closed it behind him.

Jake walked away from the Marines for privacy. "Five mill? Make sure the DEA spells my name correctly on that reward check."

McKay paused a moment. "You're off the books, so I'll make sure the reward goes toward funding . . . crucial activities I'm working on."

Jake shrugged. Easy come, easy go. He wasn't in it for money. "Do I at least get a ten percent finder's fee?"

"I'll call you right back." McKay clicked off.

The money situation reminded him of a famous quote by legendary baseball pitcher Tug McGraw about what he'd do with his high income. "Ninety percent I'll spend on good times, women, and Irish whiskey. The other ten percent I'll probably waste."

Jake might do the same.

He saw Hutch pull a knife and cut zip ties to release the prisoner from the headrest. Hutch dragged the man out of the SUV, sat him in a metal chair, and aimed a pistol at his face.

Cody hopped out of the SUV's open back door, trotted to Hutch, sniffed the prisoner's waist, and barked.

Hutch raised the man's shirt and found a flat stretch belt around five inches wide. He pulled the Velcro apart and removed a smuggler's belt. "Cover him," he said to the other Marines, and unzipped the belt pouch.

Jake observed his friend pulling out a plastic zip-top bag full of small pills. Cody sniffed the bag and sat down to indicate chemicals. Jake held up his phone. "Let me get a picture of that."

Hutch set the bag on an empty chair.

Jake zoomed in, took a close-up photo and sent it to McKay. Each pill was stamped with the capitalized word ASPIRIN, but it was misspelled ASPRIN.

Hutch turned to face the prisoner. "Do you get headaches?"

The man didn't reply.

Jake's phone buzzed, and he patted his thigh. "Cody, heel."

Cody trotted over and stood next to Jake like his shadow.

Jake closed the SUV's hatch and walked away again as he answered the call.

McKay said, "The name of the man you captured, Chang Quan, is a play on the word *changquan*, which means long fist, a style of martial arts."

Jake raised his eyebrows. "Sort of like naming himself Kung Fu?"

"Pretty much, if you speak some Mandarin, but most Westerners don't get the inside joke."

"Is he a greedy drug dealer, or a communist army soldier with a plan to harm US interests?"

"We suspect both," McKay said. "One of China's top diplomats claims the man turned traitor and is now a wanted fugitive, but the CIA says he used to be a high-ranking intelligence operative in the People's Liberation Army."

"The largest army in the world," Jake said.

"Traitor or not, he now earns millions by trafficking illegal drugs into the US," McKay said.

"Are those mislabeled aspirin pills actually tranq?"

"Yes, you guessed it."

"Is Chang Quan the primary source?"

McKay said, "No, but he's one of the biggest dealers and might lead us to the main source, or someone close."

"Maybe Cody could growl at the man's crotch and frighten him into telling me useful intel."

"Thank you two for your service tonight, but you should get on the highway," McKay said. "I need you on the West Coast tomorrow to search a cargo ship. I'm paying Bart a generous sum to stand by. Go on and catch your flight. I'll see you in Napa a day or two later."

"See you." Jake ended the call and was reminded of the reason McKay had plans to visit him in California's wine country. She would finally take possession of a puppy sired by Cody, who'd mated with another highly intelligent dog named Skye. The pick of their litter was a female golden retriever offspring named Faith, who had now completed training at Guide Dogs for the Blind, a non-profit organization founded in 1942 to help veterans who had been blinded in World War II.

Faith had received additional training by Ellen, the same dog breeder who raised and trained Cody before he'd served in the Marines. Faith was one of the smartest and most well-trained service animals in the world. She was also incredibly valuable, almost priceless, but Jake refused to accept any payment from McKay.

He walked back to the SUV with Cody at his heels, opened a passenger door and snapped his fingers. Cody hopped into the back seat, and Jake closed the door.

The Marines had Chang Quan handcuffed by his wrists and ankles to the four arms and legs of the metal chair. Quan muttered about police brutality.

"You really hammered his head," Hutch said. "Did you ever work in construction?"

Jake said, "He'll live. Listen, I have orders to exfil. Semper Fi, brother."

"Semper Fi." Hutch shook hands and then raised the overhead door.

Jake backed out and drove off. A few minutes later, when he passed through the front gate, two armed guards stared at him as if he were some kind of CIA "spook" legend who'd appeared briefly, only to vanish again. Jake gave them a respectful nod in thanks and headed onto the overseas highway, where he traveled north toward Palm Beach International Airport.

Ever cautious of reprisal actions, he checked his mirror often to make sure nobody was following. It wouldn't be the first time. If trouble found him, he'd trouble-shoot the problem. No more trouble. He was armed with a shotgun, his Sig 9mm pistol, the CIA-style .22 with a silencer, and a narco-terrorist's MAC-10 submachine gun.

"Come at me," he said. "Save me the time of hunting you down."

CHAPTER 7

As he drove north, Jake recited a Robert Frost quote to his dog. "I have promises to keep and miles to go before I sleep."

Cody put his front paws on the center console, leaned into the front seat area, and sniffed the gunshot residue on Jake's arm. It was one of the dog's habits. He did it every time his handler fired any weapon.

Jake scratched his faithful dog behind the ears. "It's all good, Cody. Thanks for standing guard. You were essential to the mission. I'm proud of you."

Cody huffed. The dog might not understand every word, but he knew the tone of voice meant approval.

Jake thought about how McKay had briefed him on her clever use of a drone outfitted with lights, a loudspeaker, and a rubber mallet battering ram to impersonate a sheriff car and deputy. He'd watched it fly down from above and move toward the front of the house.

He'd been told in advance it would strobe police-style lights and ram the mallet against the front door three times, followed by the shouted orders to open up.

An attached wireless signal jammer would block cell phones, Wi-Fi, Bluetooth, and security cameras for 100 meters. When McKay received Jake's mission accomplished text message, the drone would go dark and fly away.

Once again, he was highly impressed with Agent Shannon McKay and her resources.

After driving for hours nonstop and listening to trop rock while Cody napped, Jake arrived at the airport in Palm Beach and parked next to a private hangar and nearby Gulfstream jet.

A man stood in the dark, waiting for him. He wore a suit and had a white earbud in one ear. Jake noted the bulge of a handgun under his suit jacket.

"The keys to your car," the Secret Service agent said without greeting. He displayed his badge and ID. "I'll have it sanitized inside and out and return it to the rental company for you."

Jake had been expecting this. He checked the agent's cred pack and handed over the keys. "I'll get the .22 handgun for you."

"My orders are that you're to keep it. Remove everything from the vehicle."

"Roger that." Jake lifted the back hatch, placed the MAC-10 into the custom guitar case, grabbed his carry-on, and then realized the luxurious briefcase full of cash was still sitting there. He'd been so focused on the mission and prisoner, he'd forgotten to say anything about the money to McKay or the RTT Marines.

They'd never believe him. Nobody would.

He thought of all the good he could do with the criminal's ill-gotten gains, and whispered, "Cody, this is going to make the families who rely on Father O'Leary's soup kitchen very happy indeed."

Jake set the briefcase on top of his rolling carry-on and walked to the jet with Cody trotting by his side.

The G-man drove off while Jake set down his gear and carried Cody by his vest handle like a suitcase, climbed up the fold-down steps, and boarded the private jet.

They were greeted by a cheerful blonde flight attendant wearing a blue skirt suit and a name badge that read "Dawn."

She smiled at them. "Welcome aboard, gentlemen. Always a pleasure to have you two on a flight."

"Thank you, Dawn." Jake said. "Cody, sit. Stay. Be friends."

He went down the stairs again and avoided saying a joke. *Thanks for calling me a gentleman. Nobody ever does that except at the gentlemen's club.* Maybe he was maturing a bit? Nah, just being polite to Dawn.

He grabbed his gear, climbed back into the jet, and stowed his luggage in bins over the wings, attempting to distribute the weight equally on either side.

"May I get you two anything to eat or drink?" Dawn said. She glanced at Cody.

"Water for Cody, please."

"How about you, counselor? No needs?"

Jake carefully ignored what might or might not be innuendo meant to test his male reflexes. "Hennessy for me. Thanks for asking."

"Coming right up." Dawn made her way toward the wet bar.

Jake headed to where Bart sat in an office area, reading through a stack of legal documents. He nodded at his multi-millionaire attorney friend. "Thanks for waiting, Bart." He patted his dog on the back. "Be friends, Cody."

Cody hopped onto an empty row of luxurious padded leather seats near Bart, sat down, looked at the man and tilted his head.

Bart smiled at Cody. He wore upscale golf attire, had graying, well-groomed hair, and spoke with a slight Harvard University Law School accent. "Good to see you two. How did it go with the sailboat purchase?"

"Smooth sailing, literally," Jake said.

"Our clients were happy?"

"Couldn't be happier. We looked at two pre-owned boats, and I found hidden damage on one, but the other was in near-perfect condition. They'll get years of enjoyment from that. I told the couple if they didn't love it, I'd buy it from them and pay ten percent more than they paid. A no-risk investment."

Bart nodded in approval. "That was a smart thing to say."

"I meant it. That boat was a steal." Jake showed him a photo on his phone of the happy couple in front of their sailboat.

"A beautiful vessel," Bart said. He studied Jake for a moment, perhaps noticing the weariness in his eyes. "Do I want to know why Agent McKay asked me to delay our flight for several hours?"

"No, you probably don't," Jake said. "But McKay thanks you for your patriotic help with a matter of national security."

"Good lad. Carry on." Bart waved at Dawn, who was approaching them. "We're ready to depart."

"Okay, I'll tell the pilots." Dawn gave Jake three bottled waters and a canvas gift bag imprinted with blue sky, white clouds, and the words "Welcome Aboard."

Jake glanced into the bag and saw a half dozen minibar 50ml bottles of Hennessy cognac. "Do I look like I need six drinks?"

She stared into his eyes with a shrewd awareness, but made light of it. "Some for tonight, and some extras to take home with you."

Before he could reply, she moved to the cockpit and spoke

to the pilots. One of them announced over the PA system, "Prepare for takeoff."

Jake and Cody sat with Bart until they were airborne, and then Bart bid them good night and headed into his private stateroom.

Jake was always impressed at how the aircraft could seat up to nineteen passengers and sleep up to eight in its four cabin zones. It was the same model jet once owned by golf legend Tiger Woods.

He set up a guest bed, climbed in, and stretched out. His dog hopped on the bed, turned around three times, and lay beside him. They were a team—a Marine war dog handler and his beloved IED detector K-9. Joined at the hip, seldom apart. The duo could read each other's thoughts and feelings using an unexplainable energy that ran up and down the leash between them as they worked.

Jake felt Cody's intelligent eyes upon him. He nodded at the special dog. "We're going to see Sarah. You're off duty. Get some sleep, Marine. We'll be wheels down in SFO by sunrise."

The dog's tail thumped on the mattress at hearing the name of his favorite woman. He laid his head down on his front paws, closed his eyes, and let out a sigh.

Jake used his phone to take a picture of Cody and send it to his girlfriend, along with a text. *We're on our way. Night flight. See you tomorrow.*

It was three hours earlier in California. Sarah replied with emojis of smiley faces, hearts, and kisses. *Can't wait.*

Jake tried to relax and fall asleep while ignoring the familiar craving for alcohol. It didn't work. It never did.

He'd killed two terrorists and captured a third tonight. America was a safer place to live now. He deserved a drink to soothe his frayed nerves. *Needed* a drink was more like it. The liquor helped to keep some violent memories from rising to the surface.

Nobody wanted that to happen.

Jake couldn't allow himself to lose his temper. He was painfully aware of what a dangerous animal of prey he'd become and of his responsibility to only use his powers of life and death for the good of innocent civilians.

Sitting up, he drank a shot of Hennessy and felt his shoulders relax in anticipation of the familiar effect.

Cody opened one eye and watched him.

"Mind your own business," Jake said.

He gulped down a second shot like it was water, considered a third, held off and waited, then gave in and drank it. He consoled himself by thinking at least it was only liquor and not powerful opioids.

With three shots under his belt, he lay on his back and let out a sigh, knowing there were three more if needed. *How does Dawn seem to understand my emotional trauma?*

It crossed his mind that technically he was having a sleepover with the smart, capable and attractive flight attendant. Not that he'd noticed.

He ignored those reckless thoughts, and instead of wondering what she wore to sleep in, as many men would, he recalled pleasant memories of visits to Lake Tahoe. The mind trick sometimes worked to help him forget about life for a while.

The tension slowly seeped out of his body as he listened to Cody's breathing and paid mindful attention to his own.

Breathe in, breathe out. Think of the mountain lake. Breathe in, breathe out. Think of the sandy beach. Breathe in, breathe out. Think of boating and fishing.

After several minutes, the two combat veterans dozed off

and slept soundly on their red-eye flight to the West Coast, where more trouble awaited them.

CHAPTER 8

After a long day of hard work at her veterinary clinic, Dr. Sarah Chance bid good evening to her last client.

The man was a highly paid computer nerd guy named Pax, who worked at an online tech company and usually scheduled a health checkup appointment near closing time for his cat named Simon. The tall but shy man was awkward when it came to dating. He'd often asked Sarah to go out for coffee or a drink, and she'd always said no.

"So, uh, what are you up to after work?" Pax said.

"My boyfriend is taking me out on a date," Sarah said.

The man who couldn't take a hint, finally accepted reality. "You're dating someone?"

"Yes, I'm in an exclusive relationship," she said politely, "with a Marine combat veteran who has a law degree and lives on a motor yacht with his adopted war dog." She held up her phone and displayed a photo of herself with Jake, both of them dressed to the nines at a fancy restaurant.

The photo always gave her a feeling of desire. In her opinion, Jake was an honorable rogue with the charming cheekiness of his Irish side and the dark, seductive eyes of his Italian side, along with the killer instinct of both. He could be the right woman's dream and the wrong man's nightmare.

Pax said, "Oh, that's great. I'm happy for both of you."

"Thank you. Have a nice evening." Sarah ushered him out, flipped the "open" sign on the glass door to read "closed," and locked the deadbolt.

"Thanks for working late, Madison," she said to her assistant.

Madison grabbed her purse. "No worries, Dr. Sarah. I can always use the extra pay. Is Jake really coming home? How long has it been? Two weeks?"

"Yes, he promised me, and if he doesn't show up, I'm going to hunt him down and shoot him in the foot," Sarah said with a wink. She thought about the way Jake looked on his recent video calls. He'd picked up an island tan and appeared even more outdoorsy and in prime health. Once Sarah got him alone, she wouldn't be able to keep her hands off him.

Madison laughed. "Did you two make a decision about living together?"

"Not yet." Sarah removed her white lab coat and hung it on a coatrack.

"May I ask why?"

"An incident in the Caribbean made us both realize we should think it over a while longer."

"What kind of incident?"

A car pulled up in the dark, flashed its lights and honked.

Sarah looked out the window. "That's your Uber. See you tomorrow."

"Good night." Madison went outside and hopped into the car.

Sarah followed her out and locked the clinic door. She

placed her crossbody handbag's strap over her head so it rested on the left shoulder and draped across her chest to position the bag near her right hand. She opened the top and reached in to grasp a pistol. Now she was ready to walk in the dark to her car.

If she had to shoot an attacker in self-defense, that would be a shame, but she wouldn't hesitate to protect herself from criminal violence. Anyone who assaulted her would suffer dire consequences and regret their mistake for years to come, if they survived.

Many men had no idea what millions of women put up with in their daily lives, always being on alert to threats of potential danger. Sarah would never become a victim. She'd make the criminal a victim of her wrath.

Test me. You'll fail. I'll win.

She was the proud holder of a hard-to-get California concealed carry permit, and she practiced firing her handgun at the range once a week with her police friend, Homicide Detective Beth Cushman, aka Scooter.

Hurrying to where she'd parked her car on a side street, she didn't see it anywhere. With a sinking feeling in the pit of her stomach, she pulled out her paid parking receipt and checked the note she'd jotted down on the back. *Across the street and five spaces down.*

She found another car parked in that spot. Had she miscounted? Sarah checked each vehicle up and down both sides of the street. She clicked the lock button on her key fob, hoping to set off her car's horn and lights. No luck.

"Someone stole my car?"

As she stood there for a minute in shock, a man wearing filthy jeans and a tattered hoodie walked straight toward her, stumbling on his unwashed bare feet.

"Give me money," he said, slurring his words and

appearing to be under the influence of drugs or alcohol. Maybe both. He held a wooden garden stake in one hand.

Sarah's chest tightened. "I have a gun, and I'll give you a bullet in the stomach if you come any closer. It's a slow, painful way to die." She walked up the sidewalk to the more brightly lit main road, glancing over her shoulder a few times.

The drugged man hesitated a moment and then continued following her like a zombie, glazed eyes unfocused, probably going through withdrawal symptoms.

Not good. What to do? Sarah whipped out a canister of pepper spray and blasted the criminal with a powerful stream of liquid that traveled a long distance. The man screamed in pain and fell to his knees.

Someone watching her from a dark alley retreated and disappeared.

"Yeah, that's right," Sarah said, firing another blast high in that direction.

Now, Sarah could either go back inside her clinic and wait for a taxi or Uber, or else hop on a cable car that traveled past at this time of night. Hearing the famous "ding, ding," of the bell as the antique trolly approached, she jogged for a block and caught a ride. The driver, a Black male senior citizen with short gray curly hair, pulled on the brake lever to slow down and allow her to jump on board as the car rumbled along.

Sarah gave him a grateful smile, relieved to see a friend, and to feel safe. "Thank you, Clarence."

"Always a pleasure to see you, Dr. Sarah."

"How's Gus doing?" she said, referring to his dog.

"He's all better after you gave him that medicine. My wife and I thank you, ma'am." Clarence tipped his baseball cap.

"You're welcome. Everybody loves Gus."

He beamed at her. Sometimes Clarence brought the

Yorkshire terrier with him to work. Dogs were allowed to ride on cable cars, and Gus was a city favorite.

Sarah found one empty spot on an outside bench seat and sat down on the polished wood that was far older than her. She faced the sidewalk and wondered how many people had taken a ride on this car, built before she was born.

The well-preserved piece of history, a moving work of art, chugged past a local pizza restaurant, and Sarah smelled her favorite food.

At the next stop, an older woman with worry lines on her face boarded and looked around for an empty seat. Sarah stood up and offered hers.

"Thank you for your courtesy," the woman said in an Eastern European accent. "There's room for both of us if we squeeze in."

A man next to them took the hint, nodded, and slid over to make more space.

The cable car continued on and stopped near a new rave nightclub. The club's door opened, and the sound of loud dance music cascaded out of loudspeakers, drawing Sarah's attention. She saw a woman come outside dressed in a rave outfit consisting of a black and white zebra-striped skirt, a matching tube top, white fishnet stockings, and black high heels.

A tall man yanked a fabric cover off a car to reveal it was a yellow cab. The light came on, and he called out to her. The woman opened the car door, and Sarah got a good look at her face. She could've been her twin sister who'd died.

Sarah's heart pounded in her chest, gooseflesh ran up her arms, and she called out, "Bianca?"

The woman turned, looked at Sarah, shook her head, and got into the cab, which promptly drove off and turned a corner.

Sarah noticed a flash of light inside the cab a moment before it went out of view. Maybe the passenger's cell phone, or a cigarette lighter? She had a weird feeling about the taxi driver, and she asked the woman next to her, "Did you see that?"

"No, I saw nothing, and I don't want to discuss it."

"I'm wondering why that driver was waiting there with his taxi hidden under a car cover?"

"You should mind your own business," the woman said in her distinct accent. "Never get involved."

"I'm curious."

"Curiosity killed the cat." The woman disembarked at the next stop and walked away shaking her head.

Sarah wondered if that was the woman's regular stop or if she was ditching her.

As the cable car rumbled through the city, Sarah couldn't stop thinking about the dancer who looked like her deceased twin sister, Bianca.

CHAPTER 9

Once Sarah had traveled into her own neighborhood, she exited the cable car and walked to a historic Victorian house where she rented the second-floor master bedroom that had been converted to an apartment.

She climbed the outside stairway to her balcony, opened the front door and stepped inside, then watered two house plants named Thelma and Louise. One was a pothos, the other a snake plant. They cleaned the air in her home.

Moving to the fridge, Sarah looked inside with low expectations and was pleasantly surprised to see a pizza box she'd forgotten about. She flipped it open. *Yes, one large slice left.* She zapped the slice in the microwave, grabbed a cold beer, sat on the couch, and reached for the TV remote.

At that moment, there was one incredibly hard knock on her front door that opened onto the stairway landing and balcony. Startled, she dropped the pizza slice and ran to grab her pistol.

With gun in hand, she looked out the peephole and saw what appeared to be a throwing knife stuck into her wooden door. She could see the red handle and part of the shiny metal blade. There was a folded piece of white paper attached to the handle with a wire twist tie.

She reached for the doorknob and then froze. Another knife could hit her in the face. She ran to the curtains, stood aside, pulled the cord to close them, and called 911.

"What is your emergency?"

"Somebody threw a knife at my apartment, and it's stuck in my door. I'm under attack by a violent predator."

"I'll dispatch an officer. Stay away from any windows."

"Thank you, ma'am. I've closed my curtains." Sarah answered a few more questions and ended the call.

She took a breath and picked up her slice of pizza off the carpet where it had fallen. "Screw it."

A woman in danger needed fuel, right?

Although the slice had landed face-up, the edges caught some carpet fuzz. She picked off the lint, ate the slice, and washed it down with several chugs of beer to calm her nerves. "Life goes on in the big city."

She unloaded and reloaded her pistol in a ritual that had a calming effect. "Lock and load."

A few minutes later, a spotlight illuminated her balcony and window. She peeked out between the curtains and saw a black-and-white police SUV. The emergency lights came on and strobed blue and red upon the buildings along both sides of the street.

A dark-haired woman dressed in a blue uniform stepped out and held a phone to her ear, the other hand on her sidearm. She appeared to be a badass cop who you'd better not mess with or you'd regret it.

Sarah's device buzzed. "Hello. This is Dr. Sarah Chance."

"Police Officer Tammi Martinelli calling. Are you all right?"

"I'm only frightened. The knife stuck in my door has a note attached."

Martinelli looked up at Sarah's balcony. "Don't touch that."

"I haven't. I won't."

"Wait a minute while I search the alley across the street."

"Thank you, Officer."

The call ended. Sarah gazed out the window again and watched Martinelli grab a flashlight out of her rig. She held it in her left hand near the lit end, leaving the handle sticking up like a billy club packed with heavy batteries, and kept her right hand free to grab the pistol on her belt holster.

The cop shone her light down the alley, then walked over and opened the lid of a dumpster. "Stand up. Let me see your hands."

A shirtless, skinny, long-haired white male stood up. He had scribbled blue ink prison tats on his face. In one hand, he held a glass crack pipe, in the other a butane lighter.

Martinelli grimaced and wrinkled her nose. "Oh, the smell. Get out of there. Move along."

The man climbed out, scampered down the alley, and vanished.

Sarah watched Martinelli return across the street, climb the stairs to her balcony, and put on nitrile gloves. Holding a plastic evidence bag in one hand, she used the other to carefully pry loose the knife and drop it in the bag. Then she knocked on the door.

Sarah opened up. "Please come in, Officer."

Martinelli stepped inside, and her eyes swept the room. "You look like a woman I once saw having dinner at Amborgetti's restaurant."

Sarah raised her eyebrows. "I've been there a few times with Jake Wolfe. Did he introduce us?"

Martinelli stared at Sarah's bed for a moment as if imagining Jake in between the sheets. "No, it was that one time there were shots fired on the street out front and dispatch sent me to arrest the perps."

"Oh, I remember now," Sarah said. "Thank you for your service."

"You're welcome, and thank *you* for giving discounts to first responders. We appreciate that."

"You folks earn it. May I offer you some coffee or tea?"

Martinelli glanced at the beer bottle with a thirsty look. "No, I'm good, but thanks for asking." She set the plastic bag on Sarah's small dining table.

Sarah looked at it. "Is that a throwing knife?"

"Yes, a perfectly balanced throwing knife." Martinelli pulled out the weapon and removed the twist tie. She unfolded the paper note carefully as if worried it might have some kind of white powder sprinkled inside.

The note featured three words written in block letters with a felt pen.

ALWAYS
WATCHING
YOU

Sarah felt her skin crawl. "What does it mean? Who could it be from?"

"I'll have it analyzed by our best people. We might get lucky and find DNA or fingerprints."

"That reminds me, when I got off work, my car was missing."

"Rough day," Tammi said. "Go online to the police website and fill out a car theft report. Then call your insurance company."

"Thank you, Officer."

"I'll let myself out. You have my number. Call me if there's any more trouble." Martinelli walked to the door, hesitated, and then said, "By the way, Alicia Hayes thinks you're perfect for Jake. I thought you might want to know."

"Thanks," Sarah said. "Alicia and I have become good friends. She thinks of Jake as a brother-in-law since Terrell donated his blood to save Jake's life overseas."

"Blood brothers for life. Family forever."

"Speaking of families, when I saw you at Amborgetti's, I couldn't help but wonder if you belong to *the* Family," Sarah said, referring to the local Italian Mafia.

"No, the Family would never allow a cop on the inside." Martinelli shook her head. "It could hurt my career if you ever say that to the wrong person. So don't."

"I think the Family would find it incredibly helpful, but if you say that's not happening, I'll take your word for it and never mention it again."

Martinelli's dark eyes stared hard at Sarah. "Ask Jake why you should never talk about me and the Family." She went out the door and closed it with a thud.

Sarah locked her door and wished she hadn't voiced her suspicions about Officer Martinelli.

CHAPTER 10

In the early morning before sunrise, Jake awoke onboard the private jet and took a moment to remember where he'd spent the night.

He turned on a small light to illuminate the sleeping area, blinked his eyes, and gazed around at the jet's plush and luxurious interior. The sounds of the aircraft's engines were changing in tone as the jet descended. A pilot spoke politely over the PA system. "Prepare for landing."

Cody looked at him with wise brown eyes. Jake knew his dog had already sensed changes in the jet's sound and altitude.

He patted Cody on the back. They'd slept well on the night flight. Marines could usually sleep anywhere at any time. It was part of their combat readiness training. They treated their bodies like hot-blooded Thoroughbred war horses that required feeding, watering and rest between missions.

In the past, Jake had always lived that way. However, after his end of active service and return Stateside, he'd often suffered through sleepless nights due to painful old wounds, along with nightmares and lingering PTSD from things he'd done in the Middle East to rescue female hostages who were slated to be beheaded by terrorists for refusing to become sex slaves. He'd saved the women, and had killed many terrorist men, but it was a recurring bad dream he often tried—and failed—to block out.

Jake wondered if he slept well on the private jet because it was airborne and secure like Air Force One. Nobody could sneak inside, the way they might in your house or apartment. It was one of the few places he benefited from a night of deep, untroubled sleep.

He knew his dog needed to pee, but Cody would have to wait a few more minutes. If necessary, Jake could open one of the extra-large absorbent pads stored in the guest bathroom and let his dog relieve himself.

Cody watched Jake, trusting his handler, but perhaps ready to pee on the jet's carpet and raid its galley for breakfast in an emergency situation.

Jake looked out a window at the dark, early morning sky. The city below was lit up with twinkling lights, and the horizon displayed a hint of orange. Soon the street lights would go out and the sun would rise over the water and shine on the bay, painting the sky and water in rich colors. It reminded him of the Journey song "Lights," with Steve Perry on lead vocals.

San Francisco had always been considered one of the most photogenic cities in America. Situated on a peninsula surrounded by sparkling blue water, it had steep hills with breathtaking views, charming cable cars, and historic Victorian houses, along with fantastic seafood restaurants resupplied daily by hardworking people on fishing boats. It was the most visited city by European tourists.

However, in recent years, the charming city had suffered

from a plague of drug addiction, lawlessness, and an invasion of homeless people from other states who arrived seeking free money from the municipality's well-meaning but apparently naive city council.

Jake wasn't sure what to do about the situation. Give up, move away, and abandon the beautiful place, like so many friends had, or stay and try to help bring back the good old days when military personnel deployed to the Pacific would have a good luck drink with their sweethearts at the hotel bar named Top of the Mark.

He hoped the city could heal itself. One positive aspect was that he lived across the Golden Gate Bridge on the other side of the bay in the delightful small harbor town of Sausalito. His home was the *Far Niente*, a sixty-foot motor yacht berthed at Juanita Yacht Harbor, and his address was... Mother Ocean.

Thinking about the *Far Niente* made him appreciate how he would soon take her out onto the water, do some fishing, and enjoy the kind of solitude only available on a boat at sea. He thanked his lucky stars.

Cody trotted to the bathroom door, turned the knob with his teeth, and opened it. He looked up at Jake with those bright eyes.

"Okay, buddy." Jake went inside and set an absorbent pad on the floor. "Pee now, Cody. Pee there."

The war dog had been trained to go on command. As the pilot made a perfect landing and the wheels thudded onto the runway, Cody doused the pad and let out a deep huff in relief.

"So dramatic." Jake smiled and grabbed several large zip-top plastic bags from a cabinet, folded up the pad, and placed it into one bag after another until it was behind three layers. He tossed it into the trash bin and washed his hands.

Handler and K-9 stepped out into the aisle as the jet taxied slowly toward Bart's private hangar.

Dawn approached them and handed Jake a cup of black coffee. "I hope you two will stay on board for breakfast."

Jake took a sip of perfectly brewed java. "Thanks, Dawn. We'd love to, but we have plans."

"All right. Enjoy your day. Hope to see you both again soon." She opened the jet's door and unfolded the stairs.

Jake set down the coffee, then gripped the handle on Cody's vest with his right hand and the stair rail with his left. He carried Cody downstairs to the tarmac, where the dog barked at an Italian man who stood waiting next to Jake's armored black Jeep Grand Cherokee Trackhawk. An off-the-books gift from McKay.

The man had dark hair, jaded eyes, and wore dress slacks and an Armani shirt along with expensive Italian leather shoes and a linen sport coat Jake knew concealed a pistol and holster.

"Out, Cody. Be friends. You remember Beppe," Jake said.

Cody sniffed the man's waist and holstered pistol.

"I bought a new handgun from Wesley, your pararescue veteran friend," Beppe said. "Nothing gets past Cody's nose."

"Tell everyone you know to buy their gear from Wesley," Jake said.

Beppe handed Jake a key ring. "Thanks for letting me live on the *Far Niente* while you were in Florida."

"Thanks for boat sitting. I knew she was safe in your hands. Did you catch any fish?"

"Oh, yeah. Plenty of striped bass and halibut. I gave all of them to Father O'Leary's soup kitchen like you told me to, except for one extra-large halibut that went to Anselmo for the restaurant."

"Good man. I'll grab my bags and give you a ride."

Jake climbed the stairs into the jet and retrieved his custom guitar case, carry-on bag, and the briefcase full of hundred-dollar bill bundles. He felt Dawn's curious eyes on him and saw her in his peripheral vision, but he didn't look in her direction. Had she smelled the gunshot residue on him? Dawn would never peek inside his guitar case, would she?

Returning to the Jeep, he pressed his key fob to open Cody's police-style K-9 door on the driver's side of the SUV. The door swung open on automatic hinges. Cody hopped in and sat down on the back seat with his feet and tail safe from the door. Jake thumbed the remote again and the door slammed shut.

Dawn walked up to the SUV and handed Jake his to-go cup. "You forgot your coffee, counselor. I think you'll need this."

"You're right. Thank you."

They held each other's gaze for a moment.

"Be careful," Dawn said. "I worry about Cody."

Jake nodded. "I do, too. Luckily, he's a genius who warns me when we might be in trouble."

"And were you . . . in trouble?"

"Cody was perfectly safe."

Dawn appeared relieved. "Good. I'm glad to hear that." She headed back to the jet.

Jake made an effort not to watch Dawn walk away, although she was a beautiful sight that any man with a pulse would notice and appreciate. He turned his back on her. It wasn't meant to be. Jake already had a special woman in his life, and Dawn was far too professional to get involved with one of Bart's staff attorneys or clients.

For a moment, he wondered why people wanted more than one lover. Was it plain selfishness or the age-old tendency of humans to seek novelty and brand-new shiny objects? He'd noticed that some people always wanted what they couldn't have, and when they finally had it, they no longer wanted it.

In a memory flashback, he heard the voice of his bootcamp drill instructor shouting at him and the other recruits. "Semper Fidelis means always faithful. You will live by those words. Always. Faithful. Understood? Answer me."

"Understood," Jake said to himself. He looked in the rearview mirror and saw Cody tilt his head and quirk a brow at him in curiosity. The dog had such an inquisitive mind. In his own way, Cody was more intuitive than the average person.

Beppe sat in the front passenger seat and slammed the door.

Jake drove toward the city and felt a premonition about what might be happening there with the animal tranquilizer drug, xylazine. He'd have to ask Sarah, a veterinarian, for more details about the medicine. It might put her in danger, but she was a brave and capable woman who carried a gun and knew Jeet Kune Do.

CHAPTER 11

Driving through town, Jake headed to the city's beloved North Beach area and a neighborhood known as Little Italy.

He stopped at Amborgetti's Italian Restaurant and dropped off Beppe, who sent a text and gained entrance to the kitchen's locked back door.

An armed man let Beppe inside and nodded at Jake.

Jake nodded in reply to his close friend, Vito, and then made his way to Fort Funston Beach. It was one of the best dog parks in America. A gorgeous stretch of sand at the south end of Ocean Beach, where dogs could run free off-leash, play in the surf, and enjoy life to the fullest.

To Jake, it was a rare miracle. After Cody's patient obedience during the mission in Key West, and his best behavior on the flight, the faithful K-9 deserved some well-earned relaxation time.

Jake, too, needed a walk on the beach with his dog. That particular seashore worked wonders to relieve stress.

In the past, many Vietnam veterans had walked on Fort Funston Beach with beloved dogs, where the sand and surf healed their hearts and souls. Now it was also a refuge for veterans of battles in the Middle East.

Upon arrival, Jake pulled into the empty parking area. The sun was rising on the horizon, but the sky was still dark, and there was a blanket of stars overhead. They had the place all to themselves for the moment.

He and Cody left the 200-foot-high clifftop and headed down a long dirt trail with embedded horizontal fence posts for steps. Jake shone an unusually bright keychain flashlight used by Secret Service agents. After a vigorous hike, they arrived at the water's edge, where moonlight sparkled on waves that rumbled onto the sandy seashore.

"Off duty, boy," Jake said.

Cody happily ran and splashed his paws in the surf.

Jake was pleased to see his four-legged best friend enjoying himself. The dog stopped now and then to smell an item that had washed-up on the beach—a sand dollar, a starfish, or a dead crab. Jake knew Cody loved the old familiar area with so many pleasant memories.

Jake's heart swelled as they walked along the shore and breathed in the clean scent of the ocean. He made sure to appreciate the moment, and the freedom he and Cody enjoyed right there, right then. Life could end any day in a heartbeat. He'd lost so many friends.

He picked up a starfish and gently tossed it back into the sea. It reminded him of the old starfish story about a boy who did the same, attempting to rescue dozens of starfish before they dried up in the sun. A man told the boy there were too many starfish for him to make any difference. The boy tossed another starfish into the water and replied, "I made a difference for that one."

The retriever dog ran into the water to play fetch.

Jake said, "Leave it." He threw a tennis ball instead. Cody

fetched the floating hollow ball, dropped it at Jake's feet with a challenging gaze, and shook out his fur, spraying his handler with salty water.

"Good dog," Jake said.

They wandered farther along as waves crashed against the beach. Jake savored breathing in the fresh, clean, salty sea air, and watching the sun glow golden red as it peeked over the horizon and shone on the ocean.

Cody abruptly stopped and held still, raised his nose to sniff a scent, and let out a growl as his hackles bristled.

Jake's pulse quickened. He looked around but didn't see anyone else nearby.

"Boy?"

Cody pawed the wet sand and gazed at a nearby bluff.

Jake gave a hand signal. "Seek."

Cody trotted inland away from the shore, and Jake followed closely on his heels, trusting the highly trained war dog. Jake drew his handgun when Cody stopped near some bushes and driftwood at the base of a cliff and sat down to indicate he'd found something.

Jake's Marine infantry-trained eyes missed nothing as they swept the area until he spotted a woman's body sprawled in an awkward position. At first glance, it appeared the woman might be his girlfriend, Sarah.

His head spun, and he felt as if someone had punched him with a bruising fist to his heart.

CHAPTER 12

While making a closer inspection, Jake kept hoping and praying the woman wasn't Sarah. He hyperventilated while noticing she had a symbol tattooed on the top of her right foot, no blonde highlights in her hair, and she was dressed in what appeared to be a night club outfit. This person couldn't be Sarah unless, while he'd been away, she'd added the tattoo, changed her hair, and started partying at wild clubs without him.

Unlikely.

While his mind argued against the possibility, his stomach dropped, and he clenched his teeth as cold sweat broke out on the back of his neck. He'd seen quite a few dead bodies during his military service, but right then he couldn't believe he was seeing Sarah's face on a possible dead body here at home.

Was he having an episode of PTSD? It *couldn't* be her. It would crush his soul beyond repair.

"Please, God, I'm begging you."

Jake knew he shouldn't touch a potential murder victim at what might be a crime scene, but he pulled a nitrile glove out of his coat pocket, put it on and felt the woman's wrist. No pulse, no warmth. She was a dead ringer for Sarah . . . and actually dead.

Cody whined as Jake removed the glove, tapped on his phone, and sent a text to Sarah.

Hi, we're back in town. Thinking of you.

Sarah didn't reply, and there was no sound from the dead person's phone, if she had one.

Jake then called Sarah on FaceTime. He had to. He stared at the body, hoping a phone wouldn't ring or vibrate anywhere nearby.

After several rings, Sarah finally answered in a sleepy voice. "Good morning, babe. I just saw your text. Thanks for the wake-up call."

Jake almost fell to his knees on the sand. He was a tough-as-nails Marine who'd killed enemy combatants with his bare hands, but this was beyond his ability to compartmentalize.

He took a deep breath and let it out. "Hey. I need to . . . talk."

Her tone changed. "What's wrong?"

"Cody found a dead body. She could be your twin sister."

Sarah was quiet for a moment and then spoke slowly. "I had a twin sister named Bianca who died in a car crash when we were teenagers. I've never told you because it's painful for me to talk about her."

Jake felt stunned. "I'm sorry for your loss," he said with sincerity, and left it at that. He'd spoken the five words so many times.

"Last night, when I was riding a cable car, I could've sworn I saw Bianca get into a yellow cab."

Jake glanced at the deceased woman's unusual outfit. "What was she wearing?"

"A rave dancing outfit," Sarah said. "A zebra-striped skirt and matching tube top."

Jake looked at the body. "The deceased is wearing that same outfit. She has a symbol tattooed on the top of her right foot. The zodiac sign of Capricorn."

Sarah's voice came out as a rough whisper. "Bianca was a Gemini, same as me of course. She was afraid of needles, didn't have any tattoos, and swore she never would."

"Jane Doe can't be Bianca," Jake said.

"My parents held a closed-casket funeral because of Bianca's injuries. I didn't approve of it because I needed to hold her hand one last time and say goodbye."

Jake looked at his phone and saw Sarah's eyes well up in tears.

"That's understandable," Jake said, feeling helpless to console her.

"Over the years, I've sometimes felt that keen awareness twins have of one another. For a while, I thought Bianca might still be alive. Eventually, I realized it must only be similar to feeling a phantom limb after losing an arm or leg." Sarah broke down and sobbed.

"I'm sorry I called you before the police made positive ID," Jake said.

"But you wanted to be sure I was all right?"

"Yes, both Cody and I needed that."

She paused a moment. "How's Cody doing?"

"He didn't go crazy, so I knew deep down it couldn't be you," Jake said. "But Cody is upset about the body and how I'm reacting."

Cody whined when he heard Jake speak his name.

"May I see our boy and reassure him?"

"Good idea." Jake admired her veterinarian skills at

comforting dogs. He held his phone so Cody could see the screen with Sarah on FaceTime.

Sarah talked to Cody in what dog handlers described as the *squeaky* voice. "How's my *boy*? You're *such* a good dog, aren't you, Cody? Yes, you *are*. And I love you *so* much. Yes, I *do*."

Cody woofed at Sarah and wagged his tail.

Jake said, "Sarah, this can't be your sister."

"I can't accept it, either. To lose Bianca and find her again, only to lose her once more. That would be too much for me."

"When Terrell and his fellow officers arrive, I'll drive to your place."

She wiped her eyes. "Thanks, but I'll be going in to work early. I'm treading water to pay the ever-rising rent. Barely hanging on."

"All right. I'll meet you later at your clinic."

"May I see the woman's face?"

"No, I don't think that's a good idea."

"Take a picture. After I know it's not Bianca, I'll risk a look."

"I'll think it over," Jake said.

"See you." Sarah ended the call with tears streaming.

Jake held eye contact with her until the FaceTime went blank.

Cody pawed at Jake's shoe.

Jake sent a text to his best friend, a rough-and-tough Marine veteran, Homicide Detective Terrell Hayes. They'd served together on multiple deployments until Jake took a bullet in the thigh during combat and almost died. Terrell's blood transfusion in a helicopter had saved Jake's life. It was controversial among some people because Terrell was Black and Jake was White. *Hey, I'm back in town. How are you folks doing this morning?*

After a moment, Terrell replied. *What's up, my brother? We're sitting down to breakfast. If you're nearby, come over to the house. Boo Boo dog says hello to Cody.*

Jake felt sorry for interrupting the couple's meal. Terrell and Alicia had the type of marriage that made you believe "happily ever after" was truly possible.

Sorry to spoil your morning, but Cody found a dead woman at the base of a cliff.

There was another pause. Jake could picture Terrell's infamous scowl.

Your location?

Fort Funston beach dog park.

I'm on my way. I'll call it in.

Roger.

Jake patted his dog on the back. "Marine Lieutenant Terrell Hayes is on his way. We'll stand guard until he arrives. Semper Fi?"

His words had the intended effect on Cody. The dog needed something to keep him occupied, a job to do, and he understood the words *Marine, Terrell,* and *stand guard.*

Jake heard a rustling in some bushes near the base of the cliff. He drew his handgun and aimed it in that direction. "Cody, heel."

CHAPTER 13

A seagull flew away, and Jake took a deep breath and let it out as he holstered his pistol.

The only positive aspect of this situation was that he'd found the woman before seabirds began pecking at her face.

Soon, Terrell Hayes came walking down the beach. A tall Black man with an athletic body, dressed in his trademark dark suit, crisp white shirt, plain tie, and perfectly shined black shoes.

Jake waved Terrell over to where he held Cody on a short leash. "I tried to avoid disturbing the scene, but I put on gloves and checked her wrist for a heartbeat because she looks like Sarah and I was freaking out."

Terrell nodded. "I would've done the same if she looked like Alicia. You called Sarah to make sure she's okay, right?"

"Right. She's at home in bed."

"Good. CSI will be here any minute."

Cody barked at his close friend, Terrell, and pressed his head against the man's stomach hard enough to knock an average person down. Terrell took the expected hit without reaction and patted Cody on the head. "Welcome back, devil dog."

Jake glanced up at the clifftop. "Do you think she fell, jumped, or was pushed?"

Terrell squatted, his knees making cracking sounds, and inspected the body. "I think her neck is broken. The question is, did she break it in the fall, or was it already broken before she went over the edge?"

Jake knew Terrell never believed an easy explanation for an unusual death. "That two-hundred-foot drop could do it."

Terrell studied the body with the flat gaze of a man who'd seen too much death in his life. "She's wearing gold earrings and a matching bracelet, so it probably wasn't a robbery. And there are no signs of struggle, and not a single bruise or scratch on her face, arms, or legs that I can see."

"So, why do I have such a bad feeling about this?" Jake said.

Terrell straightened up, turned, and looked at two people jogging toward them—a man and woman, both dressed in sport coats and slacks, carrying gear bags. They stopped near Terrell, gloved up, and put on coveralls, hairnets, and disposable shoe covers.

The woman said, "That hike down here was a workout."

Terrell nodded. "Going back up is worse than leg day at the gym."

Cody growled at the unfamiliar people who wore pistols he'd never smelled before.

"Out, Cody. Be friends." Jake held tight to the leash.

Both CSI cops leaned down and studied the body without apparent emotion. Jake got the impression they'd seen it all, and there weren't many things that could shock them.

Terrell observed them and asked, "COD of the vic?"

"Looks like the victim's cause of death was a broken neck," the man said.

The woman looked up at the clifftop. "We'll let you know when we confirm."

Jake displayed his US Marshals star for the benefit of the CSI people. "Lieutenant Hayes, on your orders, I'll have my K-9 search the clifftop."

"All right," Terrell said. "Don't disturb any evidence."

"I'll be careful." Jake led his dog away, and they climbed up the trail stairs. At the top, he pointed. "Cody, search."

The scent dog began moving along a sandy bluff overlayed by ground-cover plants that held it together and prevented a landslide.

Jake noted a sign.

DANGER

UNSTABLE CLIFF AREA

People and dogs have been injured falling from these cliffs.

STAY BACK FROM THE EDGE

"Cody, heel." Jake snapped his fingers, and the dog trotted over. Jake attached a leash to Cody's collar. "Okay. Search."

The Marine Corps had trained Cody to be an IED detector dog who could find the scent of chemicals used in weapons. He was not a cadaver dog or a police dog. However, the scary-smart animal instinctively found any scent that didn't belong in its surroundings.

Cody wove his way along the bluff, zigzagging and following a scent cone, until he stopped and spent a minute closely studying one patch of scrub and sand. He sat down.

"Good dog. Heel." Jake patted his thigh, and Cody trotted to his side. Jake stayed several feet back to avoid spoiling evidence or collapsing the cliff.

He used his phone's camera to zoom in and take a closer look at Cody's discovery, a silver, heart-shaped photo locket engraved with the words "Always in my heart." Nearby lay a thin silver chain with a broken clasp. Jake took a picture and sent it to Terrell.

The families of whoever's photos might be inside the locket would soon receive heartbreaking news from the police.

Jake wondered if FBI Agent Brenda Reynolds might be in town or nearby. She served on the bureau's Victim Services Response Team (VSRT) and was trained to help families cope with their heart-wrenching, tragic loss.

"Cody, sit. Stay." Jake moved carefully toward the cliff edge and looked to his right, not finding any signs of a struggle—not even footprints.

If someone had stepped too close to the edge, it would've broken away underfoot. He looked down and saw the CSI people directly below where Cody found the locket.

Terrell glanced up at Jake, his situational awareness honed in battle and much more highly tuned than his fellow police investigators.

Jake used the red laser on his keychain flashlight to pinpoint the location of the evidence.

Terrell waved in acknowledgment. The CSI folks didn't even notice while they were absorbed in their work. They'd never known the feeling of snipers always trying to find you so they could put a round in your heart.

Backing away, Jake returned to Cody and wondered how the sand could be undisturbed near the crime scene. There might have been a stiff ocean breeze the previous night, causing wind-blown sand to cover up any footprints and markings. Or else, someone might have swept the sand as they walked backward, covering their tracks.

Closer inspection revealed a single corn fiber bristle from

an old-fashioned broom, and the outline of a footprint way larger than could've been made by the woman below.

Jake guessed that somebody had broken the woman's neck, brought her there and tossed her off the cliff, then attempted to cover his tracks. He or she must have been an individual strong enough to remain several feet back from the edge and throw a body that far.

Most spontaneously violent killers were men. That was a fact proven by statistics. FBI profilers believed testosterone played a role. The powerful hormone could make some people feel aggressive.

Female killers tended to plot and scheme against someone who'd scorned them. They were smarter and more conniving in the execution of their crimes. Some men were "murdered by medicine" when given overdoses that appeared to be routine errors.

FBI profilers didn't publish these findings in any medical articles because it was not politically correct to talk about hormones, even though the chemicals were an incredibly important aspect of human behavior in the criminal justice system.

A female doctor who specialized in bioidentical hormone treatment had once told Jake that her female patients said testosterone made them feel invincible and estrogen made them feel *everything*.

Jake thought of the dead woman, cut down so early in life, and felt a familiar anger ignite in his chest and burn with the urgent need for old-fashioned justice. He had to find the criminal who'd done this and stop him from ever doing it again. Terrell would put the murderer in a cage, or Jake might put him in a grave.

As if sensing his handler's emotions, Cody growled, ready to bite someone who deserved it.

CHAPTER 14

Jake took a few more pictures and sent them to Terrell, along with a text. *I'm getting ready to hit the road.*

He watched as the sun rose and shone on the coast. Mother Ocean's waves sparkled in the early morning light. A man strapped into a hang glider leapt off the bluff and flew over the shoreline, casting a shadow.

Jake received a call from Terrell and answered a few questions about the scene. "Am I dismissed, Lieutenant?"

"Dismissed." Terrell ended the call.

Jake patted his dog on the back. "Let's go. We have someone to see."

He drove to Sarah's veterinary clinic and parked a block away to leave a space free for one of her clients. He walked down the sidewalk with Cody trotting by his side.

At the clinic, Jake held the door for a woman who exited carrying a shih tzu dog in the crook of one arm. She wore a T-shirt printed with the words, "I Shih Tzu not."

Jake led Cody inside and noted the waiting room filled with early morning customers and their pets. He said hello to the attractive receptionist, who was in her mid-twenties. "Hey Maddie. How's it going?"

Madison gave his tall, muscular body a quick glance up and down and blushed when he said her name in his deep voice. "I'm good, Jake. How are you and Cody?"

"Never better, thanks."

Cody stood on his hind legs, placed his paws on the counter, and huffed at Madison while wagging his tail.

Madison ruffled his ears. "I missed you, Cody." She glanced at Jake again and quietly sang the chorus of "The Boys Are Back in Town."

Jake was aware of the obvious attraction and compatibility between Madison and himself but acted as if he had no clue. She seemed ready, willing, and eager to grant his every wish. Most single, straight men would appreciate her offer.

However, it would be totally wrong if he had feelings for his girlfriend's employee. He reminded himself he was a one-woman man, and he made a conscious effort to avoid flirting with Maddie—the tempting treat and potential home-wrecker.

He glanced at the hallway leading back to the treatment rooms. "Is Sarah free to say hello for a minute?"

Madison nodded, appearing resigned. "Yes, I'll let her know you're here." She picked up the handset of her corded desk phone and tapped a button. "Dr. Sarah, Jake and Cody have stopped by to see you."

"Thanks," Jake said.

Madison nodded. "Jake, do you have a younger brother? My dating life is a joke."

"There are plenty of men out there if you lower your standards," he teased.

Madison shook her head. "Come on. I'm serious."

It finally dawned on Jake that Madison didn't have a crush on him in particular. She just wanted a steamy relationship like Sarah had. "No younger brother, but I have a cousin your age who isn't seeing anyone right now. I could introduce you, if you'd like." He showed her his phone and displayed a photo of Beppe and himself on the *Far Niente*. Beppe held up a prize-sized fish he'd caught, and Jake held a beer. Both men were bare-chested, wearing only board shorts and dark sunglasses. It was obvious Beppe stood equally tall as Jake's six feet and was into fitness and weight lifting.

Madison gave him a big smile. "Yes, please."

Moments later, Sarah walked into the reception area, appearing professional in office attire and a white lab coat. She carried a pet crate from which a calico kitten peered out, watching Cody intently.

Cody ignored the cat and pressed his head against Sarah's stomach, wagging his tail.

Sarah placed the crate on Madison's reception counter, patted Cody on the head, and looked at Jake. "I was starting to think you two might never come back from Florida."

At the sight of her, Jake felt the familiar pang in his chest. She had a hold on his heart like no other woman before. That morning, when he'd thought she might be dead, it had felt like the end of the world. "I love visiting the Keys, but it was my work that kept us busy. Looks like you're in the same situation."

Sarah let out a sigh. "Yeah. It's been like this every day since I began advertising discount health checkups for military members and first responders."

"You're helping a lot of good people and their fur babies," Jake said. "It's a noble effort, and I'm proud of you."

She looked up at him as he towered over her. "I'm trying to be mad at you."

"Try harder," he said, leaning in for a kiss.

A young woman dressed in an EMT uniform and holding a puppy on her lap observed them. "Ooh la la. You go, Dr. Sarah."

Several people chuckled at the rare public display of affection from their typically overly-serious and totally professional pet doctor.

Sarah took a deep breath after their intense kiss. "Dinner tonight at my place?"

"Looking forward to it." Jake led Cody out of the clinic and noticed Madison's reflection in the glass door as she gazed at his backside.

He walked down the street and crossed to a sports car with darkened glass. The driver's window buzzed down, and Beppe nodded at him.

Jake said, "Beppe, thanks for keeping an eye on the clinic for me while I was out of town."

"But now you have new plans?" Beppe said.

"I want you to meet Madison, Sarah's assistant. She asked me if I had a younger brother."

Beppe glanced at the clinic with interest. "I couldn't help but notice Madison doesn't seem to have a boyfriend who picks her up after work."

Jake nodded. His instincts had been correct. "I think you'd be good for her. She needs a reliable young man like you in her life."

"You're giving me your blessing?"

"Yes, and responsibility for her safety. She's as pure as Lake Tahoe snow."

"She'll be safe with me, and very happy. I give you my word of honor."

Jake held out his hand, and Beppe shook it with an iron grip.

"Follow me, and I'll introduce you to your new girlfriend." Jake walked back inside the clinic, with Cody and Beppe following along. "Madison, meet my cousin, Beppe Amborgetti. You asked if I had a younger brother. Well, he's the next best thing. A brother from another mother. I'm thinking you two could become good friends."

Madison blinked several times. "You mean Amborgetti, as in the Italian restaurant and . . . Family?"

"The very same," Jake said. "I have standing reservations, so I'm buying dinner for both of you tonight. Order anything you want and a good bottle of wine. It's on my tab."

"Thanks, boss," Beppe said.

"Oh my gosh," Madison said, blushing.

"My work here is done," Jake said with a smile. "Exchange phone numbers, and remember, the dress code is look-your-best, celebrity style."

Jake and Cody left the clinic as Beppe handed Madison his phone so she could type in her number.

CHAPTER 15

Jake headed down the sidewalk with Cody trotting alongside. They passed an attractive gray-haired woman sitting at a card table covered by a red silk sheet. She wore a matching silk scarf around her neck. Her lipstick and fingernail polish were red as well. A deck of Tarot cards sat on the tabletop before her, next to a Bible. A plain sign read, Palm Reading and Tarot Fortune-Telling.

He realized she hadn't been there when they'd first arrived. He would've noticed. The woman had a kind face and seemed to gaze at passersby with empathy, as if knowing they all suffered from troubles and heartaches in their lives and she wanted to help them.

She turned her head, stared directly at Jake, and held eye contact. "Come here, please," she said in English with an Italian accent, waving her hand for him to obey directions.

Jake thought she might be playing him, but he'd heard about a Sicilian palm reader in town who might have some kind of strange gift. He remembered once being told the word *Tarot* was derived from the Italian *Tarocchi*, which were the original cards. Many in his Italian family were superstitious and believed some older, wise women could give you "the evil eye" and put a hex on you.

He walked over to her table. "How are you doing on this fine day, young lady?"

She ignored his flirtatious banter. "Let me see your right hand."

"Sure." He held it out, palm up, figuring she'd blow smoke up his tailpipe and demand he pay a hundred dollars for a generic astrological report she'd found online. He always lied about his zodiac sign to mess with people who thought they had him figured out.

She took his big hand in both of hers and rubbed one thumb over the calloused palm of an outdoorsman and fisherman. "You have an old soul."

Jake agreed. "My soul probably ages in dog years."

Cody stood on his hind legs and sniffed her hands.

"Be friends, Cody," Jake said.

After the woman studied Jake's hand more closely, her face paled. She blinked several times and nodded. "I knew it. I felt it. I saw it in your aura."

"Knew what?"

Taking a deep breath and letting it out slowly, she asked, "How many souls?"

Jake saw understanding in her eyes but pretended he didn't. "How many . . . what?"

She lowered her voice. "How many evil men have you killed and sent to Hell, where they belong?"

Jake stared at her for a moment. "Not enough of them."

She put one hand on the Bible and whispered, "The avenger of blood shall put the murderer to death."

It was Jake's turn to blink. He'd recited that Bible verse

many times. His greatest fear rose up inside him. "Can you see the future? I worry about my dog."

She gazed at Cody. "Your dog will live a good long life thanks to your overprotective nature. Be alert, always."

Jake blew out a breath. "Whew. Thank you."

"However, *your* future will be filled with violence, pain, and sorrow," she said. "You are in grave danger today. Right now."

Jake knew it was the truth. He glanced up and down the street. "I believe you."

"You feel as if you don't fit into this world," she said. "It's because you're here to create a better one."

Jake said nothing.

She studied his palm again and then spread out the Tarot card deck facedown, moving them in a random pattern with her eyes closed. "Pick a card. Any card."

Jake reached down, picked up one card, and turned it over.

She opened her eyes and gasped. "Number thirteen. The death card."

Jake studied the image of a knight wearing a black suit of armor and riding a pale horse while carrying a flag on a pole. The knight's face was a skull. It appeared he was riding into battle. "What does it mean?"

She tapped one red-painted fingernail on the card. "The armor is a symbol of feeling invincible, but the skeleton inside reminds us that death comes for every person. His horse is a much-needed, powerful ally. A boat is sailing towards the sunrise, which is a sign of hope and the beginning of a new journey—perhaps to a new life, or a noble death and the afterlife."

"Why is the knight carrying a battle flag?"

"A black flag reveals he's on an important mission for a

noble cause. A white rose indicates hope. The number five represents change."

"A noble mission to hopefully change a dangerous situation?" Jake asked.

She observed his facial reaction. "You are on such a mission, yes?

Jake didn't know what to make of it but played along. "How do you interpret this card for my near future?"

"Someone will attempt to kill you and stop your mission. You can delay death with help from your powerful ally . . . that dog. He is the horse. And there is a boat involved. I'm not sure where or how."

"We live on a boat."

She nodded. "The boat symbolizes that we can transform our lives by sailing off toward the horizon."

"My boat is a Horizon PC-60."

She looked him in the eyes. "Your dog can save you. Trust him with your life."

"I already do. What kind of death threat am I facing?"

She stared off into the distance for a moment. "The people who want you dead are so evil my heart is blocking me from seeing them."

"It's a long list of people, believe me."

"There are many ways to die," she said, "but you're not afraid, because you've been dead before."

"Yes, I've had a near-death experience when I drowned and came back to life."

She steepled her fingers as if in prayer. "And what did you see when you died?"

"I saw my deceased grandfather, and then my dog rescuing me, and finally, I was looking down from above at my dead body being revived by a woman I'm now in a relationship with."

She looked at Cody. "It was fate. That dog brought you and the woman together."

"Yes, he did." This was freaking Jake out a little.

"His name is Cody, yes?"

Jake raised his eyebrows. "How could you possibly know that?"

She winked at him. "I heard you say it as you made your way up the sidewalk."

"You're good. And honest, too."

"My advice is to be alert for a surprise attack today or tomorrow. Trust Cody's warning if you want to survive."

"That's worked so far."

Cody barked and placed his right paw on the table, copying Jake.

She smiled and held the dog's paw in both of her hands. "You two are joined at the hip and heart. Cody's parents were special, and now he and an equally remarkable dog have brought another litter of special puppies into the world. True?"

"True. Am I being punked on some kind of candid camera TV show?"

She held onto Cody's paw for a moment longer. A tear rolled down one cheek, and she spoke to Jake. "Two of your dogs who crossed over the rainbow bridge are happy together now in the afterlife."

"Duke and Gracie?" Jake felt himself getting choked up. This couldn't be real.

"A Belgian male and a Labrador female, I think. Jake, you're like a guardian angel. Be careful not to become a fallen angel."

Jake held her eyes. "Someone once told me Cody is so loyal, he'd follow me into Hell and fight the devil."

She shook her head. "Know your limits. Entry to Hell as a team would require both of you to die."

Jake gave her a respectful nod. "I'll make sure that doesn't happen."

He noted her fondness for the dog and thought about how when people met Cody it was love at first sight. Everyone was protective of the smart K-9 with bright eyes and a retriever smile.

Cody growled at a man who approached. He pulled his paw free and stood by his handler's side.

The intruder said to Jake, "Enough BS about dogs. Move on. I need to speak with her."

Jake noticed the woman cringed and seemed afraid. He turned to face the threat. "This is my Nonna. Who might you be?"

"I'm her best customer," the man said. "She tells me who might win at sports."

"Do you place bets with Vito Amborgetti?"

The man's face revealed Jake had guessed correctly. "It's none of your business."

Jake said, "Vito is one of my closest friends. We're cousins. What if I tell him you're bothering his Nonna?"

The man lifted his chin in defiance. "You're lying. Get out of here."

Jake pulled out his phone, swiped on the screen, opened FaceTime, and put it on speaker.

"What's going on, Jake?" Vito said. "Why the emergency code?"

Jake turned his phone display toward the man. "Vito, do you know this asshat?"

"Yeah, I know him well. Is he causing any problems for the Family?"

"Good guess. He's bothering one of our honored Nonnas."

The man put both hands over his face and cursed.

In a voice indicating barely controlled anger, Vito said, "Let me talk to him."

CHAPTER 16

Jake continued holding up the phone. "Talk."

"Hey, Vito," the man said in a faked cheerful voice. "No worries. I'll stay far away from your Nonna."

Vito said, "Listen to me and listen carefully. That man you're messing with is authorized by the Family to kill you and drop your body in the ocean with an anchor chained around your waist. No questions asked. *Capisci?*"

The man swallowed hard and took a deep breath. "*Capisco*, Don Vito. Please forgive me, Godfather, for I have sinned, but I meant no harm."

Vito was silent, waiting for Jake. It was his decision.

"You're forgiven this one time," Jake said. "But never show your face around here again or my dog will rip it off, eat it, and leave the digested remains on the sidewalk."

The man glanced at Cody, who was showing his teeth. "I'll leave town."

Jake nodded. "Good plan. Leave now. I'll put the word out to search for you after sundown."

"I'm free to go?"

Jake pulled back his coat and placed a hand on his holstered pistol. "Move, before I change my mind."

The man turned and ran.

Jake watched him and held the phone so Vito could see.

Vito said, "I never liked that guy. He won sports betting too often, using some kind of secret he wouldn't share with me."

"He was getting tips from a fortune-teller lady who is now officially part of our Family," Jake said. He turned the phone so she and Vito could see each other.

"If she can predict winners, I invite her to enjoy a wonderful lunch at our restaurant as a guest of honor today."

Jake raised his eyebrows and told her, "I'd accept. Great food, new friends, and Vito will pay you a thousand dollars a week to give him winning tips."

Vito said, "What? A thousand? Are you kidding me?"

Jake grinned, held up his other hand, and displayed two fingers.

She looked at Jake and said, "Two thousand, Don Vito."

Vito groaned. "Jake told you to say that. We can talk about it over lunch."

She said, "Before I decide, I want Jake to draw a card for you, Vito."

"Pick a good one," Vito said.

Jake aimed his phone camera at the table and randomly flipped over a "cups" card. It had an IX at the top and an illustration of a wealthy man with nine large cups of wine.

"Nine of Cups," the woman said, "which represents achieving what you desire. Experiencing luxury. Savoring a delicious meal. Appreciating the arts. Loving an exceptional woman."

"You accurately described my life," Vito said. "I'm looking forward to our conversation at lunch."

"She's under our protection now," Jake said.

"Yes, understood," Vito said. "I'm downtown in the limo. Where are you?"

"We're a block west of Sarah's veterinary clinic."

"I'll be there in five or ten minutes. Ciao."

"Ciao." Jake pocketed his phone.

The woman scooped up her cards and set them in an ornately carved antique wooden box.

Jake wondered how old the relic might be. "Why don't you place bets yourself?"

She gazed up at the sky. "I've found that if I use the gift for self-glorification, it fades away for a while in what might be punishment."

"Here's an idea," Jake said. "If you help me win money, I'll give it all to your favorite charity."

She looked into Jake's eyes and nodded. "It's worth a try." She reached out to shake hands.

Jake gave her hand a gentle shake. Cody reached out his paw as a reflex, and she shook with him, too.

The woman appeared in need of reassurance. "Tell me more about Vito."

Jake said, "I promise you can trust Vito. He and every person at the restaurant will treat you like *amici di famiglia*. Friends of the Family."

"I trust you, Jake. I've read your heart. And if you trust Vito, that's good enough for me."

"It's more than trust. It's a matter of honor. You are now under the protection of the Family. Vito would never dishonor the *omertà* he's sworn to uphold."

She studied his face. "You have many secrets. You're haunted by memories and carry heavy burdens on your shoulders."

He nodded. "Sorry I acted like a beast when that man posed a threat to your safety."

"You're protective of your pack. Part wolf. It's in your nature. What's your name?"

"Jake Wolfe."

She closed her eyes for a moment. "Appropriate."

"And yours?"

"Beatrice. Named after Saint Beatrice d'Este."

"Beautiful name." Jake noticed she didn't give him a last name. Maybe she only had the one, a mononym, like so many musicians.

"Beatrice, I don't know if you can help me, but I'm looking for a man."

"Of course you are. A terrible person, I'm sure." She glanced at passing cars in concern as if any one of them could be a threat.

"Yes, he imports an animal tranquilizer drug into the country, and it kills many of our citizens."

Her eyes lost focus. She spoke in a different voice and vocabulary, as if reciting something she'd been told. "I know of whom you speak." She reached out. "Your hand."

Jake dutifully held out his right hand, and she took it in both of hers. This time, she didn't look at his palm but placed it against her heart and gazed off into the distance toward the ocean.

"He's not who you suspect. Laughing at you. From some distant land with no relation to your search. A broker of the lethal powder not meant for human consumption. He murders anyone who gets in his way. You're on his kill list."

"It's an undeclared war against the United States," Jake said.

Beatrice let out an exhausted breath. "Carry my table." She stood up and gathered her belongings.

Jake folded the table's legs and carried it as they walked toward an arriving black limo that pulled over and stopped, blocking traffic. There were times when Jake did whatever a special woman might ask of him. This was one of those times. One of those women.

He noted how Cody trotted beside his handler's new friend. He knew the dog would protect Beatrice, because Jake protected her. She belonged to their pack now, and pack was everything to Cody.

The dog's loyalty reminded Jake of a favorite line by Rudyard Kipling. "For the strength of the Pack is the Wolf, and the strength of the Wolf is the Pack."

He opened a limo door and helped Beatrice into the back seat. "Vito, meet Beatrice."

"Pleased to meet you," Vito said.

"Pop the trunk," Jake said.

Vito did so, and Jake placed the folding table inside.

Jake returned to Beatrice and gave her a business card that listed his cell phone. "You can call me anytime, day or night."

She held his gaze. "Please remember that Gandhi believed an eye for an eye could make the whole world blind."

"Most of the world is safe from that," Jake said. "The average person only wants to live in peace."

"But you can't."

Jake said nothing.

Cody barked at Vito, who turned to him. "Good dog."

"Cody is Beatrice's agent, so he gets ten percent of the *three* thousand a week," Jake said.

Vito laughed. "Sure thing. I'll pay Red Rover with Italian meatballs." He drove away smiling, back to his usual semi-amused self.

Jake waved at Beatrice and watched them go around a corner. "Cody, you just never know who you might meet in this unusual city. There's no other place in the world quite like it."

The handler and dog walked to their Jeep and drove across the Golden Gate Bridge, to where the *Far Niente* awaited them in Juanita Yacht Harbor.

Jake checked his mirror to see if they were being followed.

CHAPTER 17

Jake exited the Golden Gate Bridge and drove into the lush green Marin Headlands, taking a right turnoff that led down a long hillside road to Sausalito. The aromas of eucalyptus trees and salty ocean air wafted on the breeze.

Cody stood up, put his head out the open window, and wagged his tail while sniffing the familiar scents of his neighborhood.

Jake observed his dog in the mirror. He knew the seaside air was far more pleasant than when on patrols in scorching hot desert villages overseas where there were no toilets—only open ditches you could smell from a mile away. Jake had never realized what a modern luxury indoor plumbing was until he'd visited impoverished towns that didn't have any.

He drove through the harbor town and felt grateful to call it home. Sausalito had mild weather, clear blue skies, a sparkling bay, sun-kissed marinas filled with boats, and rolling hills dotted with mature trees and charming older homes.

Jake enjoyed seeing his favorite parks, coffee shops, and

restaurants again. He turned into the parking lot of Juanita Yacht Harbor and found an empty space.

When he and Cody walked toward the docks, Jake looked up at a nearby light pole and saw a surveillance camera aimed at his boat.

He sent a text to Beppe. *I thought you dealt with the spy cam.*

Beppe sent a reply text. *We blacked out the lens. An under-eighteen Italian youth shot it with a paintball gun and got a ticket for graffiti.*

Jake sent another text. *I'll pay the ticket.*

Cody ran down the floating docks to his familiar gate, stood on his back legs, and pawed at the lock.

Jake said, "If you had thumbs, you'd open that with your own key, huh, boy?"

Once Jake had unlocked the security gate, Cody trotted to the *Far Niente* and went aboard. Jake caught up and found his dog lying on the sun pad at the bow.

"You look right at home." Jake moved aft to the stern deck, which was like a backyard patio complete with outdoor furniture. He opened the bulletproof glass sliding door and stepped into the galley and salon area of the catamaran.

A fancy bottle of Italian grappa sat on the bar top, along with a simple handwritten note signed by Beppe and featuring the words *Molte Grazie*, which in Italian meant "Many thanks."

Jake recognized the grappa as one from Anselmo "Big Mo" Amborgetti's private stash made out of wine grapes left over from the pressed harvest and then distilled into liquor and poured into hand-blown antique replica glass, similar to historical bottles from the old country.

Beppe couldn't afford a princely sum for the rare treasure. Big Mo must have given it to him for rendering a highly valued service to the Family.

Either way, the bottle was a collector's item, rarely for sale at any price. The fact that Beppe had given it to Jake spoke volumes regarding their friendship.

Jake sent Beppe an obligatory text. *Thank you for the priceless gift. You are Family to me.*

Beppe replied. *Family is forever, my uncle.*

Forever meant death. Beppe would fight to the death for Jake. His loyalty was absolute. There was only one acceptable reply and Jake sent it. *Yes, we are Family forever, you and I, my nephew.*

Jake now had confirmation Beppe was at his command, anytime, day or night. The reliable young man would always take Jake's call and spring into action at his orders. If Cody was in trouble, Beppe would rescue him or die trying. If Sarah needed help, Beppe would protect her. If Police Lieutenant Terrell Hayes and his wife Alicia were threatened, Beppe would fight for them. The young man had come a long way from when he'd been a parking valet at the Amborgetti's restaurant.

Cody trotted inside to a water dispenser with an inverted jug on top, pressed one paw on the blue lever to pour spring water down a clear tube into his bowl, and drank noisily.

Jake filled a bowl with kibble for his dog, locked the sliding door, and walked to his stateroom and ensuite head. Ten minutes later, he'd quickly showered, shaved, and dressed in clean clothes.

He returned to the galley and went out onto the stern deck. Gazing at Richardson Bay and breathing in the sea air, he felt the need to spend time on the water.

A quote came to mind. "To live with ghosts requires solitude."

It reminded him he needed solitude on Mother Ocean after taking down that high-value target in Key West.

He threw off the dock lines and prepared for departure. Climbing to the pilothouse, he started the twin engines, lightly bumped the throttles, and slowly idled away from his slip, pointing the *Far Niente*'s bow toward the marina entrance while respecting the no-wake zone.

Several people on nearby boats waved at him and Cody, happy to see them again. Jake returned their waves, and Cody barked in reply, making them smile.

Jake often fixed problems on neighboring sailboats and motor yachts, sometimes diving underwater to find the inevitable wear and tear. He knew what to look for. Grateful friends baked him pies and casseroles and gave Cody dog treats.

A few neighbors asked if they could introduce Jake to their friends and relatives who were single females wanting to date an eligible bachelor. Jake politely let it be known he was no longer eligible. He was currently in a committed relationship without a marriage license, similar to actors Ryan Gosling and Eva Mendez.

After Jake had cruised into open water, he brought the motor yacht up on plane and piloted her out onto Richardson Bay, where he saw something that took his breath away.

CHAPTER 18

He gazed in wonder at the breathtaking, stunning vista that included a vast stretch of luminous blue water, the Golden Gate Bridge, Angel Island, Belvedere, and Tiburon. It reminded him of what Scottish novelist Alistair MacLean once wrote. "There can be few more beautiful and spectacular views in the world than that from Sausalito."

Jake played Little River Band's song, "Cool Change," a tribute to being alone on the ocean. An oldie but goodie from before he was born, and a guilty pleasure for a war-weary veteran with PTSD who loved saltwater and solitude.

Cody stood up on the bow sun pad to let the fresh ocean breeze ruffle his fur and to feel the salty spray on his face, totally enjoying life.

Jake wanted to spend some time fishing, catch a few halibut and give them to Big Mo for the restaurant's Friday night seafood dinners. Many older Italian Catholics still ate fish on Fridays. Years ago, the church said it was no longer necessary, but some people wouldn't break the tradition. Jake understood.

His phone buzzed with a call from Agent McKay. That put an end to his rare moment of peace.

He answered the call. "Guido's Pizza. Will this be dine-in, takeout, or delivery?"

"I need you and Cody at the Oakland docks in one hour to help search a container ship," McKay said.

"Sure, I was heading to Oakland in my boat," he lied.

"Doubtful," she said.

"We're only taking a much-needed rest between your stressful missions."

"Make it quick."

Jake shouted to Cody, "No rest for the wicked, and that means you, buddy."

The dog stared at him with one eyebrow quirked, as if trying to understand.

"It means you're the best dog in the world and you put up with me."

McKay said, "You talk to your dog as if he's a person."

"He *is* a person. And that's how you should talk to your new, highly trained and overly intelligent dog," Jake said. "Trust me. If Faith had thumbs, she'd take your car keys and drive to Petco."

"I do trust and respect your advice about K-9s," McKay said.

Jake turned the wheel to come about, cruised in a wide half circle, and headed back toward the harbor. "Sitrep on Oakland?"

McKay gave him a situation report about another one of the gang members designated as a Tier I drug kingpin. "We have intel that suggests he's expecting a shipping container full of xylazine smuggled through the Port of Oakland. It's a busy port, among the nation's top ten."

She texted him a chart of stats. Jake saw there were over 17 million shipping containers in use around the world. Most were 20-foot equivalent units (TEUs). Cargo ships could hold approximately 15,000 TEU containers, and larger vessels up to 24,000. Dockworkers unloaded millions of containers per year at that one port alone. There was no way to search all of them, not even with hundreds of K-9s working around the clock.

Jake said, "If we found their one-in-a-million container, what would we be looking for? How are they hiding the tranq?"

"We don't know."

"I think Pablo Escobar once hid cocaine inside hollow plastic bananas with real ones piled on top."

McKay said, "I'm hoping with Cody's nose, we might get lucky."

"That would make him a target."

"You can always say no."

Jake shook his head. There was no way he could refuse the mission when innocent Americans were being targeted for death by foreign terrorists. She knew that. "Of course we'll be there."

"I never doubted it. I'm only keeping you on schedule." McKay ended the call.

Jake rocketed across the water to Juanita, docked the boat, and tied up. "Cody, let's roll."

They disembarked and headed to the parking lot.

Using a key fob, he opened the automatic K-9 door to the Jeep's back seat so Cody could hop inside.

Taking the driver's seat, Jake looked in the mirror to make sure Cody was safely away from the door, and then used the fob to close it with a thud. He'd missed that K-9 door while driving rental cars in Florida.

They raced across the Golden Gate Bridge, with the Jeep's

hidden police lights flashing under the front grill and back window. Once in the city, they traveled toward the Bay Bridge that led to Oakland.

Jake thought about something Terrell had told him recently. His best friend and former commanding officer in the Marines had said Jake belonged in law enforcement. He could be a good cop if only he didn't have such a rebellious nature, smart mouth, and a talent for annoying the brass.

Jake shrugged. He couldn't help it. He was born this way. Sometimes his methods were creatively unorthodox, but they'd resulted in a winning track record of putting criminals and terrorists out of business.

The brass thought he was "broken."

Jake refused to believe he and Cody were broken. They were survivors.

"If it's not broken, don't fix it," he said.

Cody growled.

Jake drove across the Bay Bridge and kept his police lights on to help him move in and out of traffic.

An SFPD patrol car fell in behind his wake and followed. Jake looked in the rearview mirror and saw his friend Officer Wilson, who reached out the window and gave Jake a thumbs-up.

Jake returned the gesture, took an Oakland exit, and headed for the shipping docks and rail yards.

If intel was correct, one of the container ships in port was carrying enough xylazine to kill the city's entire population.

CHAPTER 19

Upon arrival at the designated location, Jake spotted a tangle of tall cranes next to massive ships loaded with colorful containers stacked sky high. Every container was the size of a railway car, and there were more of them than he could count. It was a surreal place like no other.

He found Secret Service Agent Yvonne Greene sitting in the driver's seat of a black Suburban with her window down. Agent Easton, a serious man of few words, sat next to her in the passenger seat.

Jake had a history with both of them. They'd worked together several times, and he trusted them with his life.

Yvonne Greene meant more than that to him. One time, they'd almost gone to bed together, but Jake had stopped at the last minute and remained true to Sarah. He felt Greene was standing by in case Sarah didn't work out.

Greene held his gaze now with sea blue eyes and gave him a challenging look as she ran one hand through her auburn hair.

Jake made an effort to ignore their undeniable chemistry.

How did he meet so many lovable women? Maybe because he appreciated them so much? He didn't believe in *finding* the one who could magically fulfill his life. He believed in *choosing* the one with whom they could both work at building a life together.

He exited the vehicle, placed the Marshals star on his belt, clipped a leash on his dog's collar, and walked toward the federal agents.

Cody barked at Greene and wagged his tail.

She stepped out of her rig. "Hello, you golden fur ball from hell."

"Cody, be friends," Jake said.

Greene patted Cody on the head. "Is he still a handful?"

"Cody defines handful."

Greene opened a back passenger door of her Suburban with the practiced moves of a Secret Service agent. Her eyes flicked to doorways, rooftops, and ships, searching for threats.

Jake had once seen her kill a man in order to save his life.

McKay exited the vehicle, and the typically stone-cold serious agent smiled in approval at the dog who'd sired a puppy for her daughter.

Jake stood ramrod straight out of respect for her. "Jake and Cody at your service, ma'am."

"I brought an old friend bearing gifts." McKay turned and spoke to someone inside the SUV.

A door opened and closed on the other side, and a self-assured man walked around the back.

Jake recognized Chief Deputy US Marshal Garcia, who worked in the local federal building. The same Marshal, who in the past, had allowed Jake to be deputized, but then had taken away his badge due to what he'd deemed insubordination and reckless conduct. Garcia was an authoritarian, and Jake admired him, but now that Jake had the badge again, Garcia was the last person he wanted to see.

"Chief Deputy Garcia, sir," Jake said politely. When his dog growled, he added, "Out, Cody. Be friends."

Garcia had broad shoulders, a flat stomach, and short black hair salted with gray. His Mexican-American blended face was ruggedly good-looking, which helped offset his ever-grouchy personality. He had intense eyes that drilled into people and were now doing so to Jake. Garcia shook Jake's hand in an iron vise grip, asserting dominance and control.

Jake could kill Garcia with one Jeet Kune Do punch to the throat, but he pretended to be subdued by the man.

Garcia said, "This goes against my better judgment, but Agent McKay talked me into letting you assist us today. You'll be acting as a deputized citizen K-9 handler on the joint task force."

"Thank you, sir. It's an honor to be of service."

"Yes, it is. One you don't deserve." Garcia pointed a finger at Jake's belt. "Treat that badge with respect, or I'll take it away again and you'll never get another chance."

"I give you my word I'll respect the badge and your orders, sir." Jake felt tempted to say his new creds were from Florida, not California, and Garcia couldn't take them away, but he held his tongue for once.

Garcia stared at him, appeared to make a reluctant decision, and opened the back hatch. He handed over two bulletproof vests—one for Jake and the other for Cody. Both were adorned with printed lettering.

POLICE

US MARSHALS

Jake put the dog vest on Cody first and then his own.

Garcia glanced at Jake's Sig handgun. "Marshals carry Glocks. All of our magazines and rounds can reload any other handgun in the service."

"Yes, sir, I understand," Jake said. "Glocks are excellent pistols. I'm carrying a Sig because the SFPD issues them to every cop in the city. My pistol mags fit detective Terrell Hayes's handgun, and vice versa."

Garcia nodded. "Fair enough. The majority of personnel on this task force today are police officers from Oakland and San Francisco."

He reached into the SUV again and handed Jake a black ball cap and a navy-blue windbreaker jacket that were both emblazoned with the word "POLICE."

Jake put on the ball cap and changed jackets.

Garcia hesitated, let out a breath, and gave Jake a federal parking permit. "This is for today only."

"Thank you." Jake opened his SUV and tossed the permit on his vehicle's dashboard.

Garcia said. "Just remember . . . you're not qualified to be a real US Marshal."

"That's right, I'm not," Jake said. "I haven't gone through the US Marshals Academy."

Thanks to McKay, Jake knew Garcia had completed five months of basic at the academy in the Federal Law Enforcement Training Center, in Georgia. Years before, Garcia had served in the Special Operations Group (SOG), which was the USMS equivalent of SWAT. Jake admired him for that.

"You are only authorized to conduct K-9 duties on this one task force and nothing more," Garcia said.

"That's the job we're trained for, and Cody has the best nose in the business. Good thing, too, because this vessel holds twenty-thousand TEU containers, and we only have six K-9s available to search right now. That's three thousand, three hundred and thirty-three locked containers per dog, which is an impossible task."

Garcia squinted at the ship. "We're short on dogs?"

Jake almost laughed. The man knew nothing about search dogs. Did he comprehend the math? It was a hopeless situation, and they needed a miracle.

Another dog barked nearby, and Jake spotted a uniformed SFPD officer named Ryan, and his police dog, Hank. Ryan had sandy hair and the lean body of a runner. Hank, a Belgian Malinois, growled at Cody.

Cody raised his hackles and growled in reply.

"Easy, Cody. You remember Ryan and Hank," Jake said.

Ryan gave orders to his Malinois and then called out to Jake. "Thanks for the assist, but Hank's gonna show Cody how it's done, and then you'll owe me a six-pack of Coors Light."

Jake took the familiar ribbing with a smile. "Good luck, my friend. When you hit the store later to buy my winnings, remember that I drink Modelo Especial."

Agent Easton stepped out of the Suburban. He was a stalwart and formal man with squared shoulders and earnest, all-seeing eyes. He moved to the cargo area and opened a black plastic fishing tackle box. Stepping back, he pointed at Jake and then the box.

Cody raised his nose, growled in warning, and stepped in between Jake and Easton.

CHAPTER 20

Jake patted his thigh and led Cody to the rear bumper, but held him back a moment. "What do we have here?"

Agent McKay said, "This box contains a zip-top bag of xylazine pills like the ones Cody smelled at Naval Air Station Key West."

Jake looked into the box and saw pills imprinted with the misspelled word "ASPRIN." "If I took one of these, how long would it take to knock me on my butt?"

"You'd be on it now," Greene said, taking a sideways glance at the topic of conversation.

Jake noticed her but feigned ignorance. "Good idea to have Cody get reacquainted with the scent." He pointed at the box and asked his dog, "What is it?"

The scent-detector dog raised his nose and profiled the entire vehicle interior first, as was his habit, then moved closer to the box. After giving it a thorough close-up olfactory inspection, he let out a growl and turned his nose toward the docks, nostrils flaring, tail down.

Jake patted him on the back. "Is there more? *Where*? Seek, Cody. Seek. Seek. Seek."

Cody walked toward a docked cargo ship stacked with containers, while Ryan ordered Hank to sniff the box and repeat Cody's inspection.

Jake gave Cody his head and let him pull on the leash. They moved quickly and came to the particular ship where a tall, muscular security guard held up a hand to signal stop.

Jake shouted, "Law enforcement task force coming aboard for an inspection."

The guard shook his head.

Terrell and several uniformed police officers followed closely on Jake's heels.

"Police," Terrell said, displaying his badge and creds.

Another man said, "CBP. Customs and Border Patrol."

Jake tapped on the silver circle star clipped to his belt on the right between the buckle and the pistol holster. "US Marshals K-9 search team. The Coast Guard will be here soon. I advise you to cooperate."

The guard frowned, but relented and swept his hand toward the ship in a go-ahead gesture, as if this problem was above his pay grade. His steel gaze and body language struck Jake in a threatening way.

Cody sniffed and growled. The man was armed.

Jake held the leash in his left hand and drew his sidearm in his right. He and Terrell had profiled threatening men overseas who tried to enter their FOB—forward operating base.

"Hands above your head, right now," Jake said.

SFPD Officer Wilson appeared next to Jake, aiming a shotgun at the guard's crotch. "You heard the man."

Cody sniffed at Wilson, a man he knew and trusted, and then turned toward the threat again.

The big guard raised his hands and gave them a flat gaze as a red laser dot painted his chest from an elevated location.

"Stand perfectly still," a police officer shouted over a loudspeaker.

Terrell stood next to Jake and Wilson, raised his handgun, and aimed at the guard. "Team. Weapons down."

Everyone near Terrell lowered their weapons, and the red laser dot vanished.

"Lie on the deck with your hands behind your head," Terrell commanded.

The guard placed his hands where instructed and went down onto his knees, facing away from the group. When he fell forward, he quickly rolled onto his back, drawing a gun and raising it at Terrell.

CHAPTER 21

Jake, Terrell, and Wilson all shot the guard at the same time. A protective vest and crotch guard saved his life, but he groaned in pain and let go of the handgun.

"Roll over, face-down," Terrell said. "One threatening move, and I'll blow your brains out in self-defense."

The guard slowly rolled over and placed his hands behind his neck.

Terrell put metal cuffs on him. "Looks like you have experience at being handcuffed."

A Coast Guard helicopter arrived and hovered, and a deep voice spoke over the PA system. "Crew of the *Empress Odyssey*, surrender to law enforcement officials. Stand in place with your hands above your heads. Your vessel is being detained by the US Coast Guard."

Jake pointed a finger at the wounded criminal. "Cody, search."

Cody searched the cuffed man and pawed at his left ankle on the inner side.

Terrell gloved up and found a small zip-top plastic bag holding a dozen of the tranq ASPRIN pills.

Jake cursed. "I hope that small quantity wasn't what brought Cody to this ship."

Cody whined and pawed at the man again.

Terrell discovered a folding knife crusted with dried blood. "CSI will run DNA tests on this."

The joint task force swarmed onto the enormous ship and began handcuffing crew members. Several police K-9 teams searched the endless number of containers and didn't find any tranq in the lower ones.

Jake stood there, observing.

Chief Deputy Garcia approached him. "What is this? Get your lazy butt to work."

"I'm thinking," was all Jake said.

"C'mon, that's a working dog. Why isn't it working?" Garcia pointed at Cody, who watched his finger as if deciding whether he'd have to bite it off or not.

"Shhh," Jake said to Garcia.

Garcia let out a breath. "I knew you'd screw up."

Jake looked at Terrell, who was watching and waiting for the surprise from his intuitive dog handler friend.

"Grinds, it's impossible to search all of these containers stacked sky high while they're being unloaded. Can we line up the crew? I want Cody to smell every one of these sons of beaches."

Terrell nodded wisely. "Yeah, I get it." He shouted orders, and several uniformed cops rounded up the crew, making them stand side by side in a lineup.

Jake whispered, "Cody, intimidate." He walked his dog in front of the crew, and Cody growled at each one, sniffing their crotches and baring his teeth.

The crew members faced straight ahead and stood

perfectly still. Most appeared afraid, but none of them gave any sign they might know something.

At the end of the row, Jake turned and moved slowly behind them. "Cody, *search*."

The dog took his time on every person, smelling their shoes, hands, and clothes. At the twenty-third person, he sat down to signal he'd found a problem.

Jake pressed the end of his gun barrel against the back of the man's head. "Don't move, or I'll order my dog to bite off your parts."

The man wet his pants. "They'll kill me."

"Who will?"

"I can't tell you." He took off running and leapt over the rail with his hands zip-tied behind his back.

"Don't shoot him," Jake shouted. "He knows something."

But it was too late. The sniper popped him in midair as he fell into the water.

The Coast Guard helicopter flew low and hovered, and a rescue swimmer jumped out and splashed down. Soon, the Coasties lifted a stretcher into their helo.

Minutes later, Jake's phone buzzed. He answered, "Wolfe."

Agent McKay said, "The man who jumped ship is alive, shot by a rubber bullet, but that's on a need-to-know basis. We'll let the rest of the crew think he's bleeding to death."

Jake gazed up at the helo. "Ask him which container we're looking for."

"Working on it. He's babbling about tranq and how the crime gang threatened his life. If we get lucky, this shouldn't take too long. If not, it's all up to Cody."

The call ended.

Jake had Cody continue searching crew members. The talented dog found various guns, knives, and drugs, and last but not least, a shrunken head with a bone through its nose. It was the size of an orange, and caused quite a commotion.

The shrunken head was found in the fanny pack of a Pacific Islander who worked on the ship, but only knew a few words of English. He was an enormous man, similar to a big Hawaiian or a Samoan, yet his words sounded like a person from Tonga.

When Jake had been stationed at K-Bay Marine base on Oahu, he'd once deployed to the island of Tonga for joint training with Tongan Marines. He believed the Tongans were good-hearted people, and he felt a fondness for the archipelago of islands and their inhabitants. Sometimes, when life in the US was stressful, he secretly dreamed of going back to Tonga and marrying a brown-skinned island girl with a kind smile and cheerful personality.

Jake checked his phone and quickly learned about the cultural phenomenon of shrunken heads among Pacific Islanders. Shrunken heads were mostly attributed to South America, but the practice was also exhibited in the Pacific by the Māori people who migrated from Tahiti to New Zealand on canoe voyages.

Jake wondered if this man was from Tahiti or New Zealand, and if he might understand some of the Tongan words Jake had picked up during his time there.

Jake said hello in Tongan. "Mālō e lelei."

The man appeared shocked, but said hello in reply.

Jake was onto something. He said, "Ko Jake au." I'm Jake.

The man tapped his chest and told Jake his name was Vaiura. "Ko Vaiura au."

"Vaiura," Jake said. He held up his phone and showed Vaiura a photo of his broad-shouldered Hawaiian friend, Mano Makua. "Talk story?"

The man nodded. "Talk."

Jake sent a picture of Vaiura and the shrunken head to Mano and then called him and tried to speak in Hawaiian pidgin. "Braddah, you evah seen da kine li' dat?"

Mano laughed at Jake's "mainlander" attempt at island talk. "Yeah, I have a buddy who married a pretty Tahitian babe and now lives at the beach."

"Where did we go wrong in life?"

"I often wonder."

"It would help Terrell if you could talk to the Polynesian merchant marine," Jake said. "My new friend is Tongan. Do you speak the language, or maybe some Tahitian? We could get your lucky buddy's wife on the phone. This is a matter of life and death for thousands of people."

CHAPTER 22

Jake felt relieved when Mano said, "I know a lot of Tongan words and a little Tahitian. Let me try talking to him."

"I've put you on speaker," Jake said. "Please reassure him you and I are trusted friends."

Mano spoke to the islander in Tongan first, and it worked well. They had a fast back-and-forth conversation.

Jake listened but only knew a smattering of what they were saying.

Mano said to Jake in English, "Do you have a laser pointer?"

"Yeah, there's one I carry around that can attach to my pistol," Jake said.

"Give it to the big guy. The laser, not your pistol," Mano said. "He can point out the container for you."

"You're good." Jake turned on the laser pointer, swept it along some containers, stopped on one, and held it there. He raised his eyebrows.

The man nodded. He held out a large hand and accepted the item, then aimed it high at a different stack. Copying

Jake's moves, he brought the red beam to rest on a specific container and held it there.

Jake gazed through a monocular. He saw another red beam appear from the police sniper and paint a dot on the container.

The man looked at Jake with a question in his eyes.

Jake said, "Thank you."

The man nodded in reply. He knew those two words.

Jake asked Mano, "Can you tell him he helped the police and is now under their protection?"

Mano did so, and then said to Jake, "He wants me to visit the docks and help make sure he stays out of jail. Not that he doesn't trust you mainlander people."

"Fair request from one Pacific Islander to another," Jake said. "You can charge your hourly limo rate to the city."

"Which one?"

"Both. I'll have Bart's law firm send separate invoices to Oakland and San Francisco."

"Cool. Try to bill state and federal agencies while you're at it."

Jake texted a picture of his Marshals badge and ID creds. "Show that to anybody at the docks who tries to stop you from entering. Ask them to call Terrell for confirmation."

"I've been driving across the Bay Bridge while we were talking," Mano said. "Give me the exit and address."

Jake recited it, and a few minutes later, Mano walked up to him, being escorted by Detective Beth Cushman.

Mano spoke in Tongan to the big Polynesian man, who gave him a bear hug and jabbered in the same language.

Mano listened closely. "He said the container is third from the top of that huge stack in the corner, where he shone the laser."

"Right," Jake said. "Where no K-9 can smell it."

Mano continued. "As one of the first unloaded, it would be misdirected onto a waiting truck-bed before workers get into a rhythm."

The man pointed at Cody. "Kumi kulii."

Jake remembered one of the words meant *dog*."

Mano said, "He knows Cody is a search dog."

The curious K-9 watched them with bright eyes after hearing his name.

Vaiura pointed up at the specific container. "Faito'o monumanu. Ngaahi laumālie koví."

"He's talking about animal medicine and evil spirits," Mano said.

Jake said, "Tell him that with his help, my dog will find the animal medicine and stop the evil spirits."

Mano translated Jake's words.

A tear rolled down the islander's face. He said, "*Malo*," and then something about "*fāmilí*."

"He says thanks and asks that you protect his family from the criminal gang," Mano said.

"Tell him the Marshals can offer witness protection or pay for a flight home to Tonga." Jake held out his hand and shook with the big Polynesian, whose crushing grip felt like it could crack a coconut.

A uniformed woman approached them, leading a German shepherd on a leash. "Berkeley Police K-9 Officer Heinz and my search dog, Zelda. At your service."

Cody growled at Zelda while Jake sized up Heinz.

"Is your nickname Fifty-Seven?" Jake asked.

"Of course," Heinz said, with a smile.

"The city of Berkeley hasn't always been kind to Marines," Jake said.

"My apologies," Heinz said. "I'm here on my day off, if that might help to soothe your butt-hurt."

Jake grinned. "It does indeed. My butt appreciates it. You and I are going to get along fine."

"Why would you ever go to Berkeley, anyway?" she asked.

"To spend my money at Kermit Lynch Wine Merchant, enjoy some amazing restaurants, and visit an old friend at UC Berkeley," Jake said.

Heinz said, "I've heard stories about you and that dog, Cody."

"He gets all the glory," Jake said. "I'm his chauffeur."

"Riiight," Heinz said.

Jake looked at the shepherd. "Hey, Zelda. You're a good dog. I like you."

Zelda wagged her tail, then looked at her handler for permission. Heinz patted her dog on the back. "Zelda, these are cops, like us."

Cody growled at Zelda again, and the shepherd growled back.

Heinz considered Cody. "I've never seen a golden retriever scent dog try to intimidate a German shepherd."

Jake nodded. "He isn't neutered. No war dogs are fixed. We need them to be natural and unaltered for their jobs."

"And now that he's home?" Heinz asked with a skeptical look.

"It's too late," Jake said.

"Hmmm," Heinz said.

Jake raised his eyebrows. "Please don't talk about removing my dog's *cojones*. He's a sensitive guy."

She smiled. "Sorry, Cody. I apologize."

"Apology accepted." Jake held out a treat to Cody, who snatched it from his hand. He then held one out to Zelda, who did the same. "Poor discipline, Heinz. More training needed."

Heinz's face turned red. "That was a trick."

"No, it was a test. A training exercise we use in the

Marines. Your spayed dog failed my test, so don't judge my un-neutered war dog who risked his life overseas."

Heinz looked at Cody. "Thank you for your service, Cody."

Cody barked at her and wagged his tail when she said his name.

"I'm afraid my dog wants to hump Zelda right now, so we'll have to keep them apart," Jake said.

"Why did he pick Zelda out of the other K-9s?"

"He has good taste. Zelda is a very special dog."

"She's not neutered," Heinz said. "You were wrong, big shot."

"I apologize."

"Apology accepted."

"I'm wrong many times per day," Jake said.

Heinz raised her eyebrows. "Often wrong, but never in doubt?"

"Is Zelda a former war dog?"

"Yes. Army. She has a touch of PTSD."

"Cody and I do, too." Jake looked at Heinz in curiosity.

"I didn't serve in any branch of the military," she said. "I served in the blue uniform at home."

"It's a tough job, but a proud and noble profession."

Her gaze softened. "My dad was a cop for ten years. He got injured in the line of duty and was unemployed for a long time. The IRS took our house and..."

"I'm sorry," Jake said. "My dad was a firefighter who saved a child from a burning building, was injured, and had to retire."

"We have things in common," she said.

"Be friends, Cody," Jake said.

Cody pressed his head against Heinz's stomach, and she patted him on the back.

A crane operator started up the engine on a nearby rig and

began removing the top containers, one by one, and stacking them on a loading dock.

Terrell pointed at the crane. "We'll allow the operator to place that one container on the suspect's 18-wheeler."

Jake nodded. "And then follow that truck."

Terrell said, "Everybody get in position and stand by."

CHAPTER 23

Jake sat in his rig and watched surveillance video, split into thirds, on his dashboard display. Roxanne Poole had launched two drones that provided overhead views. The third section featured a map.

When the targeted semi-truck pulled into position, the crane operator lowered a container directly onto the truck's flatbed trailer. The driver hopped out and secured the container to the flatbed, then drove to the exit gate.

A uniformed female security guard came out of the booth, leaving the red-and-white-striped boom arm in the horizontal position and blocking the road. She spoke to the truck driver for a moment, while a male guard did a walk-around inspection and used a mirror on a stick to look under the truck. As the guard passed around the back of the container, he pressed a magnet-mounted bumper beeper onto one of the two metal doors.

After completing his rounds, he gestured with one thumb up. The other guard raised the boom arm, and the tractor trailer drove away.

Jake saw the map light up with a blip that tracked the container's progress. In another section of video, he saw a live view from one drone's camera as it landed on top of the shipping container and held fast. The other drone rose into the sky and followed the truck from above.

When Roxanne drove off, Jake followed her from a distance. The truck took an on-ramp onto Interstate 880 South and increased speed. Minutes later, Jake was on I-880 and wondering how the drone held onto the container while it moved so fast. Electromagnetic landing gear?

After traveling several miles, the truck took an exit into an area of warehouses. It drove several blocks, stopped at a light, and then the bumper beeper veered off to the left and onto another street. The drone camera on top of the container swiveled and displayed live video of a man on a motorcycle speeding away.

Roxanne's voice came over the radio. "All units. Tracker one is now a decoy. Stay with tracker two."

The truck drove back onto I-880, and after a dozen miles, pulled off once again and made its way to an industrial area.

Jake glanced at the live video and noted the warehouses were grittier. He saw gang symbols spray-painted on concrete walls. Faded tents and broken-down cars in empty lots provided shelter to camps of homeless people.

The truck arrived at an old warehouse in need of paint and passed through a six-foot-tall chain-link fence cantilever sliding gate that rolled aside. The warehouse featured a long dock with several overhead doors. The driver backed up and parked. As the nearby door rumbled upward, he jumped out of the truck cab and climbed a short flight of concrete steps to the walk-in access door, then knocked and waited.

The drone camera on top of the container zoomed in on him. When the door opened and he went inside, a SWAT police sniper outside the gate fired a stun grenade into the building. It flashed and banged, and the door swung closed on automatic hinges.

Jake watched on video as cops in riot gear surrounded the building. Several ran inside with rifles up and ready to fire. The SWAT armored vehicle drove into the loading zone and blocked the container truck from escaping.

One of the overhead doors rolled up, and a man jumped off the dock to the asphalt. He fired a pistol as he ran toward the fence, but a SWAT cop gunned him down in self-defense.

Terrell Hayes drove up and parked. He walked up the stairs, then paused at the top and looked around as if searching for someone in particular.

Jake arrived at the fenced-in warehouse, following Rox's van. He called his best friend on the phone. "Anybody in this hood need a search dog?"

"We're ready for you two," Terrell said. "Roll in with your lights flashing."

"Roger." Jake flipped on the lights behind his front grill and lowered Cody's window as he drove to the gated entry. The well-armed group of police officers noted the lights, a K-9 in a police vest barking at them, and Jake holding out his badge. They waved him through.

Jake parked next to Terrell's SUV and led Cody up the stairs, where Terrell held the door open for them. Cody pressed his head against Terrell's stomach.

"Good dog," Terrell said, patting Cody on the head.

Jake sniffed the air. "Cody needs every overhead door open to dissipate the smell of that flash-bang."

Terrell shouted orders, and cops opened every door. Fresh air off the nearby ocean swept through the building.

Jake saw the container's two doors open wide and cops

removing an ever-growing mountain of plastic bags filled with pills. "Tranq?"

Terrell said, "Yeah, field test results are positive for xylazine."

"How many doses?"

"Many hundreds of thousands so far. I'm guessing several million in total."

Jake felt a weight on his heart and a task of enormous responsibility on his shoulders. He'd now found this same drug on both coasts and had agreed to stop the criminals from importing and distributing it. These millions of pills taken off the street were a good start, but Jake's mission target was the top man on the supply chain.

Terrell gestured at a group of men lying facedown on the floor with their hands cuffed behind their backs. "They've been patted-down and disarmed. Hank sniffed them. Now I want Cody to double-check."

"Roger that." Jake led his dog to the first criminal in the row. "Cody, search."

Cody's nostrils flared as he inhaled aromas and scents of each person, one-by-one. At the end of the row, he found a woman with shoulder-length brunette hair tied back in a ponytail. Cody sniffed her left ear and sat down to show Jake he'd found something.

Roxanne stood watching Cody. "Did he find a tranq pill in her ear?" She approached the handcuffed woman. "Jake, call your dog away."

"Cody, to me. Heel."

Cody trotted to his handler's side.

Roxanne gloved up, took a knee, and removed the woman's clip-on earring, holding it up to the light for a closer look. "It appears to be a tiny antenna." Roxanne tagged and bagged the item. "Maybe to boost a cell phone signal." She stepped back and gestured for Jake to resume. "I'd forgotten how Cody can find electronic items."

Jake pointed at the row of people. "Cody, search."

Cody growled at the woman's left ear again and sat down.

Roxanne squinted and drew her pistol. She took a knee and placed the barrel of her gun against the woman's head. "I'm nervous. My hands are shaking. You'll get a headshot if you move one muscle."

"I won't move," the woman said in accented English as she closed her eyes.

"What am I seeing in your ear?" Roxanne said. "Tell me or I'll try to dig it out with a knife."

"An embedded earbud and mic."

"Clever," Roxanne said. "Can your accomplice hear what I'm saying?"

The woman didn't answer.

"Terrell, keep your gun trained on her," Roxanne said.

Terrell only put his hand on the holstered gun. "Will do."

Roxanne lay down and shone a penlight into the woman's ear. "Interesting." She reached into a pocket of her navy-blue uniform cargo pants for a multi-tool with needle-nose pliers. "This won't hurt a bit."

Jake watched as Rox pulled something from the woman's inner ear. It looked like a tiny hearing aid.

The woman cursed in another language, feeling pain or anger—maybe both.

Roxanne held the item up for inspection. She pushed her tortoise-shell-style glasses up the bridge of her nose with one finger and stared at the thing in curiosity. "This is new, and weird, and unknown to me. So, I don't like it."

Jake squinted at the odd device. "Who might invent that kind of tech?"

"Could be a foreign government spy agency," Rox said.

"Any guesses?"

"Not yet, but give me time, and I'll figure it out."

Jake said, "Grinds, I have to make a phone call in private. You know who, and you know why."

Terrell nodded in understanding. "Yeah."

Jake gestured at what Roxanne held in her gloved hand. "Can you take a picture of that and text it to me?"

Roxanne did so. "Tell her I said hello."

"Will do." Jake walked away, and Cody followed without being told.

They returned to the Jeep, and he called Agent McKay, who was currently working at the Secret Service office in the local federal building.

CHAPTER 24

McKay answered the FaceTime call. "You found the container of xylazine."

"Yes, and Roxanne also found a strange new type of earbud communication device," Jake said. "High tech from Russia's SVR or similar."

"Have Roxanne send the earbud to Washington."

"May I suggest having her examine it on a video conference first and then send it? Faster intel."

"Good idea," McKay said.

"I'll let Rox know."

"Jake."

"Yes."

"You and Cody deserve a medal for finding those millions of xylazine pills."

"Thanks, but we were only doing our duty."

"You saved countless innocent lives."

"We all did. It was a team effort, with you in charge, ma'am."

McKay held his eyes. "Talk soon."

Jake walked back into the warehouse, and Cody led him over to a newly arrested prisoner he hadn't smelled yet.

Terrell said, "That guy was hiding in the office."

Cody sniffed the man's ear and sat down.

Roxanne told the man, "Don't move while I look in your ear, or this dog will attack you."

The man's eyes went wide, and he nodded in fear. Jake stood in front of him, hand on pistol.

Roxanne shone the penlight. "Found another device."

"Isolate the two perps who wore earbuds," Terrell said. "Cuff their ankles. Shackle them to this iron pole that's holding up the roof beam."

Jake said, "McKay is at the fed building and wants a conference call with us in Rox Star's van."

Terrell asked some SWAT cops, "You have this?"

"We might survive without you," one joked.

"I worry," Terrell said. "Can I bum a smoke?"

The cop shook his head. "Sorry, Lieutenant. Alicia would slap me silly."

"I'll cross you off my Christmas bourbon gift list." Terrell walked out along with Jake, Cody, and Roxanne.

Jake heard the cop say, "That is just wrong, man."

Outside, Jake studied Terrell's face. He knew that look. His friend needed coffee, nicotine, and ibuprofen. The man was trying to quit smoking, but a small cigar would be okay because he wouldn't inhale.

Jake reached into his Jeep and withdrew two pop-top cans of coffee and a white metal tin holder of Ashton Esquire cigarillos. Terrell gratefully accepted a coffee, tossed several ibuprofen tablets into his mouth, and washed them down, then plucked a cigar from the open tin and lit up.

Roxanne sat in her driver's seat and stared at them. "Um, the meeting?"

Jake said, "Could you give us a minute, please?"

Roxanne observed Terrell in pain and nodded in sympathy. She and all their fellow officers knew Terrell was a veteran with old war wounds. After Terrell had healed from brain surgery, he still had painful moments when tensions were high on the job.

"Rox, why don't you talk to McKay about the high-tech devices?" Jake said. "It's all Greek to us anyway."

"Of course." Roxanne brought McKay up to speed.

When Terrell finished his coffee, Jake gave him the unopened can he'd been holding in reserve.

"Thanks." Terrell drank half of it in one long pull.

Jake observed his best friend. He would kill for that man and had done so in the past, far away on the other side of the world.

Roxanne snapped her fingers. "McKay says maybe you could join the conference now."

"So demanding." Jake got into the van along with Cody.

Terrell put out his cigarillo on the dock and sat in the front passenger seat.

Roxanne pinched her nose. "My God, the stench of that cigar on your clothes."

Terrell said, "The aroma grows on you."

Roxanne shook her head. "Nope."

McKay displayed a video on the van's dashboard display. "Based upon your drug seizure, authorities swarmed the Port of Los Angeles and searched three ships owned by the same shell corporation. Each ship was loaded with one container that held millions of xylazine pills."

Jake pointed at the display. "Look at that, Cody. You did good."

Cody stared at the screen in curiosity and quirked a brow.

McKay continued. "Every port in America is being scoured

by US Marshals Joint Taskforce teams, as we speak. What you did in Oakland gave us the breakthrough we needed."

"Now I see why you want to give Cody a medal," Jake said. "Or you could buy him a double cheeseburger. It's all the same to a K-9 hero."

McKay smiled. "Call it a day and go home. The Oakland Police, SFPD drug squad, and the DEA will take it from here." She ended the call.

Roxanne said, "Out of the van, boys. I'm late for a date."

"Wesley?" Jake said.

She looked at him. "How could you possibly know that?"

"I was buying some ammo at his shop when he called you for the umpteenth time and you finally said yes."

"Did you encourage him to try again until I ran out of excuses?"

"I told him you two would make a cute couple."

She laughed. "There's no way you said those exact words."

Jake and Cody exited her van. "I told Wesley he'd better be good to you or I'd kick his ass."

"Now, that I believe," she said. "He's taking me to North Beach Restaurant, which is being good to me."

"Very good." Jake closed the van door, and Roxanne drove away with a smile on her face.

Jake followed Terrell to where they'd parked. "Give my best to Alicia."

Terrell sat in his police interceptor. "She was singing your praises last night when we opened a good bottle of wine you gave us."

"How's her wine rack looking these days?" Jake said. "Time for a refill?"

"She always appreciates it when you send a case from the wine shop locker, but I don't want you giving away all of that expensive grape juice."

"There's more in Dylan's collection than I could drink in a lifetime," Jake said. "You and Alicia have to drink some or else my liver might explode."

Terrell chuckled. "All right, brother. Send her whatever you choose. And we both thank you." He started the SUV and drove off.

Jake texted a photo to Sarah that he'd taken of Cody standing in front of the container full of tranq. *Cody was a hero, and now we're on our way to your place.*

She didn't reply. Maybe working late or at the gym? He worried that her stalker could return at any time.

CHAPTER 25

It was nearly six o'clock when Jake drove back across the Bay Bridge. There were plenty of commuters on the road. He resisted the temptation to use his police lights because that might cause a traffic jam behind him for people on their way home from a long day of work.

He arrived at Sarah's place, found a parking spot nearby, and continued wearing the police vest and ball cap as he made his way down the sidewalk with Cody heeling by his side.

Jake took his time. He wanted people in the neighborhood to see a law enforcement officer and his K-9 dressed in bulletproof vests printed with the word "POLICE."

As expected, the duo attracted plenty of attention on their walk, mostly positive. Jake said hello to folks he knew. Several people used their phones to take pictures and video.

Soon, gossip on the street would include news about a badass police dog and his handler spending time in the neighborhood and inside the Victorian house. People would talk about how the K-9 could probably sniff for illegal drugs as he walked past you. And if you carried a gun, you'd better have a permit.

The news would reassure law-abiding folks who appreciated the police and would put fear into any criminals who might be prowling in the area.

Jake had seen on the news that in a recent sweep, the San Francisco police found most drug addicts arrested were people from other states. Only three out of forty-five people listed San Francisco as their address. That meant ninety-five percent were coming from elsewhere for the purpose of using recreational drugs on the overly-friendly city's streets, and that was not okay.

He climbed the stairs and knocked three times. Sarah answered the door wearing a short white pleated tennis skirt, a sleeveless white V-neck top, and matching tennis shoes.

Jake let out a low whistle at the sight of her toned legs.

Sarah gave him a warm smile. "Do you like my outfit, handsome stranger?"

Jake returned her smile while removing his hat, vest, and gun belt. "Yes, you look like a fashion model for a sports clothing catalog."

Cody barked for attention.

Sarah patted him on the head. "Hello, lovable doggie. Haven't I seen you around here before? It's been a while." She scratched him behind the ears and removed his K-9 vest.

Cody wagged his tail and headed to the water bowl for a noisy drink.

Sarah put her arms around Jake and held on tight. "I've missed you so much."

"Same," Jake said, returning her embrace. He felt the need to say more, but his male mind went blank as he inhaled her perfume and felt her breasts pressing against him.

After a long kiss, Sarah's chest heaved as she took deep

breaths. "May I offer you a beer? A police officer named Ryan delivered a six-pack of Modelo Especial with a note that said Congratulations from Hank." She opened the fridge and bent over to reach for the lowest shelf, inadvertently giving him an eyeful when her short skirt rose up and partly revealed the white bikini briefs hugging her curvy bottom underneath.

Jake's mouth fell open as he was entranced by the beautiful view he'd missed for far too long. He turned away and spoke to his dog. "Off duty, Cody. You want your Kong?" He pushed two dog treats into the center of the Kong chew toy.

Cody understood the words, smelled the treats, and pawed the floor in anticipation.

Jake handed over the Kong, let his dog out onto the balcony, and set down a fresh bowl of water. "Stay, Cody."

The dog plopped down prone and began chewing on his favorite toy.

Jake closed the door, locked the deadbolt, and turned to face Sarah.

She handed him a bottle of beer, took a drink of her own, and then her eyes sparkled when she said, "You wanted to talk in private?"

"Yes, I've been looking forward to a long conversation with you."

She kicked off her shoes. "These beers can wait. I need some lawyer-loving right now, counselor."

"I concur." Jake reached out for Sarah's hand and guided her to the bed.

Some time later, the lovers took a shower together and then

ordered food delivered. They sipped beers and used chopsticks to eat Chinese food out of white paper cartons.

Jake savored a bite of Mongolian beef, glanced at the takeout menu, and read part of it out loud. "There are more Chinese food restaurants in the US than all the McDonald's, Taco Bells, Pizza Huts, KFCs, and Wendy's in America combined. Thank you for choosing ours. Please enjoy your meal and come back many times."

Sarah dipped her chopsticks into the carton of walnut shrimp. "That's amazing, and so is this food."

"We'll have to thank Wan for recommending that place."

"It was a sure bet," Sarah said. "A Chinese restaurant, located in Chinatown, recommended by our Chinese Jeet Kune Do instructor."

"Can't go wrong." Jake bit into a potsticker.

"Madison and I saw our boy on the clinic television," Sarah said between bites.

Jake took a sip of beer. "Cody did good today."

"You did good, too. At work, and at home." She gave him a wink.

He smiled. "Thanks. I try my best."

"Are we still going to Napa this weekend to give McKay one of Cody and Skye's puppies?"

"Yes, and McKay said Aspen is so excited to adopt Faith." Jake swiped on his phone and displayed a photo of the dog.

Sarah took his phone in her hand for a closer look. "Faith is such a beautiful blend of Cody and Skye." She accidentally swiped the screen and brought up a photo of an attractive woman in a bikini, who'd captioned it, "Hi Jake, let's have a "who's-better-in-bed-contest. I'm hoping to be a sore loser. Love, Venus."

Jake glanced at the photo and groaned. "That woman is stalking me."

Sarah frowned. "How did the stalker get your number?"

"She got it by lying to Bart's secretary at the law firm. She pretended to be shopping for a motor yacht. As you know, Bart often has me work as a boat broker."

"Seems like a lot of effort by Venus for a roll between the sheets when she could go to any bar in the financial district and pick up a broker in five minutes."

Jake said, "Moon Hee thinks Venus wants to seduce and marry a man who owns a million-dollar yacht, and then take it away from him in a brutal divorce. She was planning on using me to meet wealthy boat owners. I guess when she found out I live on a sixty-foot power catamaran, she added me to her list of potential targets."

Sarah raised her eyebrows. "And who is Moon Hee?"

"Bart's secretary, who gave Venus my number." Jake held out his hand. "I'll delete that photo and block the number. Or, you're welcome to do it, and feel free to look through the rest of my photos while you're at it."

"Hmm. Don't mind if I do." Sarah opened his photos app and only found Jake's nature photography along with pictures of Cody enjoying life. There were also many of Jake and herself on dates, which provided a photo history of two people who were growing closer, day by day, in a happy, long-term relationship. Her eyes softened, and she handed him the phone. "Sorry I acted jealous."

"It was a perfectly normal reaction," he said. "Hey, I'm jealous of that nerdy guy Pax who constantly asks you out on dates."

Sarah laughed. "I finally got Pax to accept that I'm in an exclusive relationship with you. He seemed to take it well."

CHAPTER 26

In the morning, Jake, Sarah, and Cody went out to breakfast at the nearby bakery.

They walked in and were greeted by a woman in a white apron who had a dusting of flour on her arms.

Vicky held out her open palm and gave Cody a pat of butter. "Hello, sweetie. I've missed you."

"Did you miss me, too?" Jake asked.

"Yes, but not near as much as Cody."

Jake laughed at how the woman always teased him. "Oh, sure. I see how it is."

Sarah said, "Hi, Vicky. We'll have the usual."

"Coming right up, neighbor." Vicky gave Jake a kind smile, a wink, and a pat on the back as she walked away.

Jake and Sarah grabbed cups of self-serve coffee and found a table. Minutes later, a waitress set down plates of the menu's Egg Scramble #3, along with toasted slices of sourdough baguette, orange juice, and refills of their coffee. For Cody, a doggie egg scramble with cheese.

After a leisurely meal, they took a long walk, did some

window-shopping, stopped at a dog park, and caught up on various topics of conversation.

Returning to Sarah's place at noon, they were surprised to find the apartment empty. Someone had taken everything except the bed.

Sarah gasped. "I've been robbed."

Jake drew his pistol and checked the bathroom and closet for an intruder.

Sarah let out a long breath. "Oh my god. Be careful, Jake."

Jake completed his search. "Clear!" He moved toward the door. "I'll sweep your apartment for hidden cameras. Be right back." He went downstairs to his Jeep and returned with a black handheld device similar to a monocular.

"This can find spy cams." He held it up to his right eye and looked around the room. When he aimed it at the smoke detector above his head, a ring of tiny IR LED lights blinked fast. "Found one." He checked the bathroom next. "Found another in the overhead fan."

Returning to the main room, he dragged the bed into position, stood on it, and removed the smoke detector's cover to reveal a tiny wireless camera. "There it is. Anyone can buy these online."

Sarah wrapped her arms around herself. "Someone's been watching me?"

"And probably recording videos," Jake said.

"Who could it be? My landlord? Or a maintenance person with a master key?"

Jake thought it over. "No, this kind of camera only transmits about as far as you can throw it. The perp must be someone in this house, or one next door."

He went into the bathroom, stood on the bathtub rim, and removed a camera from the overhead fan. Holding out his gloved hand so Cody could sniff the two tiny cameras, he said, "Do you smell the man?"

Cody sniffed the devices several times, then went to the balcony door and smelled the handle. Jake opened the door, but Cody went out and came back in. The dog searched Sarah's master bedroom studio apartment and ended up at the door leading into the Victorian home's hallway.

Jake turned the deadbolt lock and opened the door. Cody trotted into the hallway off leash and followed a scent cone as Jake and Sarah kept up with him. He went down the stairs, searched the large home, and then stopped in front of a bedroom door and sat down.

Jake knocked on the door. "Fire department."

He heard a man reply. "What do you want?"

"Routine safety inspection," Jake said. "We sent everyone a notice."

The man opened his door a few inches. It was held in place by a chain lock. A thirty-something white male peeked out. "I never received any notice. Now isn't a good time."

"Can't be helped." Jake looked through the open space and saw what looked like Sarah's small square dining table with her decorative fruit plate sitting on top.

"I'll need to see a firefighter's ID," the man said.

Jake flashed his Marshals badge and held his thumb over the word Marshal. He put his shoe in the doorway's open space. "Sarah, look, he has your stolen property."

Sarah gazed past Jake's shoulder. "Yeah, that looks familiar. He added price tags to everything. Having a sale?"

When the man saw Sarah, he gaped in recognition and tried to push the door closed just as Cody stuck his head into the apartment and growled.

Jake's foot in the gap saved Cody from harm. With the threat to his dog, Jake's anger flared. He slammed his shoulder into the door and flung it open, tearing the chain from the doorjamb.

The man stumbled back and fell down, but leapt to his feet and held out a knife. Jake kicked him using Jeet Kune Do. His legs were longer than the assailant's arm, and his shoe crashed into the opponent's stomach, knocking the wind out of him. The man dropped to his knees, and Jake kicked him when he was down. Unfair but effective.

While the man lay on the floor, groaning in pain, Jake grabbed zip-ties from his coat pocket and cuffed his detainee's wrists behind his back. Cody picked up the knife by its handle, carried it to the other side of the bedroom, and dropped it.

"Good dog," Jake said.

Sarah came inside and pointed at the man's laptop computer playing a video of her doing yoga, dressed in booty shorts and a sports bra top. "I can't believe this creep."

Jake sent text messages to some friends, including Terrell and Officer Wilson. "He's going to jail."

Cody sniffed at a closet door and sat down.

Jake opened the door. "What is it, Cody?"

The scent dog inhaled through his nose and pawed at a puffy jacket.

Jake gloved up, dug in the pockets, and found a prescription bottle containing small pills stamped with the misspelled word "ASPRIN." He turned to the suspect. "Who sold you the tranq? I want a name."

The man shook his head. "I don't know what you're talking about."

Jake held out the item. "You put the tranq in a medicine bottle with your name on it, dumbass."

Someone buzzed the home's main front door, and Sarah used her phone to check the entry camera. She held the phone so Jake could see a gray-haired uniformed cop with the name

"Wilson" on his uniform shirt above the pocket. He lifted his cap in a jaunty greeting. Sarah remotely opened the lock, and Wilson jogged down the hallway like a man half his age.

He shook hands with Jake. "Welcome back, you troublemaker. And it's always great to see you, Cody."

Cody barked and wagged his tail at Wilson, one of his favorite people.

"But I'm happiest to see you, Sarah," Wilson said. "You saved my cat's life, and that means you're a hero to me."

Sarah shrugged modestly. "You're one of my heroes, too, Officer Wilson."

"You are too kind," Wilson said. "Now, what do we have going on here?"

Sarah pointed out all of her various items that had been stolen.

Jake showed Wilson a spy camera video on the laptop, but one with Sarah fully dressed, carrying in a bag of groceries, taking off her coat, and putting the food away. "He spied on Sarah, tried to hurt Cody, and then came at me with a knife." Jake displayed the prescription bottle. "And he's in possession of xylazine."

Wilson scowled at the zip-tied suspect. "You're under arrest for burglary, violation of the wiretap act, assault with a deadly weapon, attempted animal cruelty, and possession of a controlled substance."

The man cursed. "Possession of that drug is not illegal."

Jake said, "Dispensing it without a veterinarian license is against state and federal law."

"I've never dispensed tranq," the man said. "Only bought it from someone."

"You just confessed to conspiring with the person dispensing tranq," Jake said.

Sarah glanced at the video again. "And somebody threw a

knife at my balcony door, with a note attached that said 'Always watching you.'"

"The cameras and videos are proof this guy was always watching you," Wilson said.

Jake pointed at the knife where Cody had placed it on the floor. "And he likes knives."

Wilson scowled. "Jake, I need to take the computer with me as evidence, but first, delete most of the spy cam videos except that one I saw and a few similar where my veterinarian friend is fully dressed."

Jake, who'd once earned a living as a freelance photographer, made quick work of the files.

Sarah looked over his shoulder as he sat at the table and fast-forwarded through a collection of brief video clips. They showed her doing yoga, pole dancing, getting dressed and undressed, walking around the apartment in her underwear, and having intimate conversations on FaceTime with Jake when he was away in Florida.

Jake turned and glanced at her as he joked. "Um, Sarah? Can I keep a copy of this collection, for . . . posterity?"

She smiled and lightly punched him on the shoulder. "No, but you're invited to spend the night in my bed."

"Even better. I will RSVP, ASAP." Jake deleted nearly all the files, then erased them permanently using a free computer cleaner software he downloaded using the man's internet.

"There you go, Wilson."

Wilson put on gloves, closed the laptop, and set it in a large zip-top plastic bag, along with the wireless cameras, knife, and prescription bottle. "Thanks for the assist. You're making me look good to grouchy Chief Pierce today." Wilson perp-walked the suspect down the hall and outside.

Jake said, "I'm relieved your stalker is on his way to jail."

"Yeah, me too." Sarah looked around at her stolen

possessions. "Remind me to call a locksmith and upgrade my apartment's door locks."

She began inspecting the man's place, slowly gathering her stolen items. Not long after, a large Hawaiian-Samoan man knocked politely on the doorjamb. He looked like Dwayne "The Rock" Johnson, but younger and dressed in a tuxedo. "Somebody call for a limo?"

Jake shook hands. "Sarah, you remember my friend Mano Makua."

"Yes, of course. How are you, Mano?"

"I'm good. Jake asked me to help move your stuff back home." The big man placed his suit jacket on a chair and carried heavy items up the stairs, single-handedly, as if they weighed nothing.

Terrell walked in. "I need to borrow Jake and talk with him outside for a minute."

Cody barked at Terrell and wagged his tail.

Sarah said, "McKay gave me top-secret clearances, if that helps."

"Duly noted," Terrell said. "This is different. On a need-to-know basis."

"Be right back," Jake said. "Cody, stay. Protect Sarah." He followed Terrell out onto the sidewalk.

Terrell said, "I have bad news about the Fort Funston beach vic's COD."

CHAPTER 27

Standing on the sidewalk, Jake asked, "What was the victim's cause of death?"

"The woman you found at the beach died from a tranq overdose," Terrell said.

"Partying too hard at the rave club?"

"No. CSI found she'd been shocked by a Taser, given an injection of tranq, and then taken advantage of while stoned out of her mind."

Jake cursed. "Sarah told me when the taxi drove away she saw a flash of light inside. She thought it might be a phone or cigarette lighter."

"Probably the Taser. There were no traces of smoked substances in the vic."

"Have the police noticed a pattern, or is it the only case of this type?"

Terrell said, "The one and only, thank God. Tranq could be an extreme date-rape drug, where the victims die afterward. No witness."

"It's appalling, and I won't stand for it." Jake gazed out at the city. "I have to find the killer before he harms Sarah, or another woman."

"That's the plan," Terrell said. "Agent McKay called me. She invoked my top-secret clearances and briefed me about your one-man war on tranq terrorists."

"I told McKay I needed your help to cut the head off a snake," Jake said.

"*Always* ask for my help, boot."

"Roger."

"McKay said it's on a need-to-know basis, and Sarah doesn't need to know." Terrell held a small cigar in one hand. He cut a slice off the cap with a sharp knife and then used a butane lighter to torch the foot at the other end.

Jake observed the sure sign of stress in his friend. "How's the not-inhaling idea working out?"

"Doing fine, and Alicia is on board." Terrell puffed a cloud of smoke. "Thanks for these Macanudo Gold Ascots, by the way. My favorite so far."

Jake nodded. Dylan's humidor on the *Far Niente* contained hundreds of cigars. "Sarah needs to protect herself. I can give her enough intel that she takes the threat seriously."

"There's more," Terrell said. "Last night near Alamo Square Park, a woman called 911 to report an attempted breaking and entering." He held up his phone to display a photo. "Look at the size of that footprint outside her bedroom window."

Jake stared at the photo. "Looks like that one Cody found on the clifftop."

"Here's the worst part." Terrell swiped on his phone screen. "This is the woman who called it in."

Jake saw the image of someone who appeared closely

related to Sarah. The eyes, nose, mouth, chin, and hair all had an eerie resemblance. "Son of a . . ."

"Yep." Terrell reached inside his suit coat, pulled out a metal flask, and took a gulp.

Jake squinted at his friend. "Drinking on the job? I must be seeing things."

"It's cold coffee, fool." Terrell took another drink and put the flask away.

"You might want to put a big green Starbucks sticker on both sides of that flask before a citizen journalist posts a video of you online."

Mano Makua walked out of the building and shook hands with Jake. "Got it done, braddah."

Jake tried to give him some cash, but the big man refused. "Thanks, Mano. Have you been practicing your ukulele for our next jam session on the boat?"

Mano smiled. "You stock up on Pipeline Porter, and I'll bring the Maui Wauwie ganja." He nodded in respect to Terrell, slid behind the wheel of his limousine, and drove away.

Terrell watched the limo for a moment. "Is Mano still driving high-class escorts to their dates?"

Jake pretended to act surprised. "What? He drives personal assistants to . . . assist . . . celebrities, pro athletes, and business people. A good portion of the clients are wealthy women who don't have time for dating idiots. They simply want a handsome, charming and swoon-worthy man for one night of fun without commitment."

Sarah opened the door and walked out, leading Cody on a leash. "Are you talking about my doppelganger Cody found dead on the beach?"

Jake looked at Terrell, who gave him a blank stare.

Sarah watched them. "I guessed it. Was there some bad news?"

"Yeah, it would be upsetting," Jake said.

"Upset me," Sarah said. "I need to know. I have a right to know."

"I agree with you." Jake looked her in the eye. "McKay is keeping the intel on a need-to-know basis. The three of us have to maintain OPSEC."

Cody barked at him.

"Along with our faithful K-9 who won't breathe a word to anyone."

"Was I right about the taxi?" Sarah said.

"Yes, the flash you saw was a Taser," Jake said.

Terrell spoke up. "The taxicab had been stolen. We found the victim's prints in the back seat, but none for the perp who was driving."

Sarah looked out at the bay. "What are you not telling me?"

Jake let out a breath. "The woman was killed by an overdose of tranq, the animal tranquilizer."

"Xylazine?" Sarah asked.

"Right, and McKay has me tracking down whoever is importing the drug into America in mass quantities," Jake said.

"Now I get it," Sarah whispered. "He's a dead man walking. Your mission is to kill him. You stop murderers by becoming one yourself."

Jake looked her in the eye. "I'm an infantry Marine, fighting America's enemies. It's my job to kill them."

Terrell appeared to make a decision and held out his phone to Sarah. "And there was an attempted crime on another person who looks like you."

Sarah gazed at Terrell's phone display, and the image made her shiver. She rocked back on her heels. "That's frightening."

Jake put one arm around her shoulders. "McKay didn't want you to be terrified by this."

Sarah shook her head. "Thank her for me, but I need to know the truth, no matter how awful."

"We think it's the same guy in every crime." Terrell displayed the footprint photo. "A tall man with large feet."

Sarah closed her eyes for a moment. "I just realized, the burglar who hid spy cameras in my studio didn't have big feet. That means the person stalking women who look like me is still out there."

Jake said, "You're staying on the *Far Niente* tonight."

"I'll grab my overnight bag." She handed him Cody's leash and went back inside.

Jake led his dog to a small patch of landscaping. "Cody, pee now. Pee there."

He observed as Cody sniffed the familiar place where hundreds of dogs, including him, had gone before. He marked his territory once again.

Terrell said, "McKay hasn't told Roxanne or Tammi what we're up to yet."

Jake thought about the two female cops who had top-secret clearances. "Rox is invaluable, but Tammi has a tendency to go rogue and cause trouble."

"She reminds me of you." Terrell's phone buzzed, and he checked the display. "Gotta run." He headed to his SUV and drove off.

Sarah came outside, pulling a small black carryon suitcase on wheels. "Ready to go."

"That was fast." Jake wondered if she kept a bag packed in

case he invited her to spend the night. The look on her face told him he'd guessed correctly.

Cody sniffed the suitcase, and Jake observed how the K-9 knew she'd packed extra rounds. He thought about the palm reader's warning and touched the pistol holstered on his right side to remind himself he would kill to protect his pack.

CHAPTER 28

As Jake drove through the city, he came upon a road construction detour that sent him down the Embarcadero, where he passed by Folsom Street and the beautiful brick building complex that housed offices of Google and Firefox.

An attractive woman stood under one of the many palm trees that lined the center divider. She wore new blue jeans and a short-sleeved button-down shirt with several top buttons undone. It appeared she was panhandling by using a basset hound and an empty red plastic gas can as props. Her clean cardboard sign said she was stranded and needed money for gas to leave town and drive to her mother's house.

Jake smiled as he recognized Bree, the former prostitute he'd once talked to in Haight Ashbury while he'd been hunting a killer. Today, her hair was platinum blonde. The first time they'd met, it had been bright pink.

He pulled over and lowered his window. "Hey, Bree. I thought Vito helped you get a job at Google." He waved one hand at the brick building.

"Jake, whatcha doing?" Bree said in a Midwestern accent. "Vito helped me, but I messed it up."

"What happened?"

Bree leaned down toward Jake's window and exposed ample cleavage, then gave him a smile that showed off her dimples. "I went to a company event and recognized a top management guy as one of my former tricks. He was with his wife, so I avoided them like a good hooker should."

"Thoughtful of you," Jake said. Out of the corner of his eye, he noticed Sarah sit up straighter in the seat next to him.

"The next Monday at work, I got laid off."

"He wanted you outta there?"

"Yep, but I demanded a moment with HR and told them I'd get a lawyer who would sue sue sue forever," Bree said.

"Did you hire an attorney?"

"No. I hired a private investigator who gave me the man's cell phone number, and his wife's, too. He'd always used a burner phone to call me and schedule a date."

Jake chuckled. "How did your calls to them go over?"

"He freaked out when I texted him and let him know I'd contact his wife if he caused me any more trouble. The company suddenly improved my severance package by a mile, but I'd rather have kept my job. I was good at sales and marketing."

Jake smiled. "I'll bet you were. Did you choose this spot to annoy your former boss?"

Bree laughed. "Duh."

Jake looked at the basset hound. "If you have money in the bank, what are you doing here running a scam on tourists?"

"This gig isn't bad. It pays the bills, and I don't have to spend my savings or spread my legs."

"You're a savvy entrepreneur."

"Are you going to introduce me to Mrs. Wolfe?"

"Bree, this is Sarah, my girlfriend. And Sarah, this is Bree, who dated Vito for a while."

Sarah waved at the stunningly attractive woman. "How's it going, Bree?"

Bree said, "One time I saw Jake in Haight Ashbury and tried to get him into a hotel bed, but he said no way it's going to happen because he was dating someone very special. I guess that's you."

Sarah looked at Jake.

He met her gaze. "What?"

She leaned over and kissed him.

Bree said, "What's that like, kissing Jake? I'll never know."

"That's right you'll never know, and I'll never have to kill you," Sarah said, with a wink.

Jake changed the subject. "Bree, I'm looking for the person who's bringing tranq into the city. Working my way up to the top of the food chain."

Bree's face paled. "Leave me out of it. I stay far away from drugs."

Jake studied her. "Good idea. Forget I asked."

Cody barked at Jake.

"My dog says it's time to roll," Jake said. "Good luck, Bree."

Bree waved. "Bye, Cody."

Jake glanced in the mirror as he drove away and saw Bree stick her tongue out at him in a seductive tease. Always the temptress. Bree had a big appetite, but Jake wasn't on her menu. He felt Sarah's eyes on him again and kept a neutral look on his face. "Bree was an informant who helped the police. When she solicited me, I said no but donated some money toward her rent in exchange for information."

"She certainly has pneumatic boobs," Sarah said.

Jake chuckled at the word *pneumatic*. "Yes, she's a busty

one. Plastic surgery, no doubt. I prefer natural." He turned and gave her a wink.

"So, you and Bree never . . . ?"

"Never, ever."

"Thanks for being faithful."

"Semper Fi means always faithful. My pleasure, Ms. Chance."

She put her hand on his thigh. "I guess I owe you a reward tonight . . . to encourage your loyal behavior."

"I'm liking the sound of that. Frequent faithful miles points. Let's trademark it."

Jake drove across the Golden Gate Bridge and into peaceful Sausalito, hoping they'd left their troubles behind in the big city.

CHAPTER 29

Upon arrival at Juanita Yacht Harbor, they boarded the *Far Niente*, and Jake grilled steak fajitas while Sarah tossed a mixed greens salad. Cody breathed in the aroma of seared beef as he watched Jake's every move. Jake cooked a separate small batch without seasoning to mix in with Cody's dry kibble.

Minutes later, they sat down to a delicious meal, and Jake poured two glasses of an earthy Napa Valley Cabernet Sauvignon from an absurdly high-priced and well-aged bottle he'd found in the onboard collection. He swirled and tasted, and let out a sigh. "Oh, yeah. That's delicious."

Sarah savored a bite of steak and then took a sip of wine. "This cab is amazing. I think I taste dark cherry and blackberry, some vanilla, and is that an oaky hint of freshly baked bread on the finish?"

Jake smiled. "I agree. The taste reminds me of blackberry pie à la mode."

She took another sip. "It's definitely a velvety smooth, easy-drinking, sexy wine."

He didn't tell her a bottle of the perfectly aged juice would cost twelve hundred dollars if you could find one for sale. Dylan was a savvy investor, and his wine investments had skyrocketed in value. "Dylan gave up drinking and said to enjoy his wine collection but made me promise I wouldn't sell any."

"I'm enjoying every sip of these treasures," she said. "Tell Dylan thank you for me."

"Will do." Jake was pleased at how she appreciated the rare bottled poetry. He spoke to Cody. "How's that steak, devil dog?"

Cody let out a burp and wagged his tail.

During a pause in the conversation, Sarah said, "I was embarrassed when your friends saw my dance pole and high heels among the stolen property."

Jake smiled kindly. "Don't worry. Those guys think it's glamorous, and I'm a lucky man. They're jealous."

"Mano carried my stuff upstairs," Sarah said. "I blushed, but he acted cool. I trust him because you said he's the protective chauffeur of those incredibly beautiful escorts."

"Yeah, Mano is a trusted friend to many actresses and models in this city," Jake said. "Some of them change clothes in the back of his limo while he continues driving and politely keeping his eyes on the road. If you called him at three in the morning and asked for help, he'd drive to your location and pick you up for a rescue ride home. No questions asked."

"He sounds a lot like you, but I wouldn't need his help as long as you're in town and not off in Florida on some wild adventure Agent McKay put you up to." She gazed at him over the rim of her wineglass as she took a sip.

There was an awkward silence until Jake attempted to lighten the mood by grabbing the wine bottle and topping off her glass while raising his eyebrows in dramatic fashion.

Sarah laughed and broke the tension.

Jake stuffed a bite of fajita steak into his mouth and mumbled, "Can't talk with my mouth full. Wouldn't be polite."

Sarah shook her head in amusement. "You can always make me laugh."

After dinner, Jake said to his dog, "Hop on the couch, boy."

Cody leapt onto the salon's sofa and stretched out for a nap with a full tummy. He knew the drill.

Jake took Sarah's hand and led her to the stateroom. She hung on tight, buzzed from wine and knowing what her boyfriend was up to.

"Cody, stay," Jake said before going inside. He locked the door behind him because Cody was quite capable of opening any unlocked door.

Sarah leaned into Jake for a passionate kiss, and they both began removing each other's clothes as they moved toward the bed.

Afterward, Jake lay on his back under a sheet. Sarah curled up to his muscled and battle-scarred body with an arm and leg across him. He held her close in the crook of his left arm and smelled the familiar tropical flower-scented shampoo in her hair.

They lay in comfortable silence for a while until Sarah dozed off, the evening's wine and physical exertion having made her drowsy.

A fresh ocean breeze came in from an open porthole and cooled their heated bodies, and Jake felt the vessel rock gently on the water in its boat slip. He listened as small waves lapped at the hull, the lines creaked, and two passing seagulls cried out to each other.

Jake fit the proverbial description of having saltwater in his veins. When he heard Mother Ocean whispering and calling him to her bosom, he fell under her spell. She was a jealous lover, demanding his loyalty and devotion. He thought of an old saying: The cure for anything is salt water—sweat, tears, or the sea.

His dog pawed at the other side of the stateroom's door, apparently feeling the same.

Jake eased himself free of Sarah's embrace. She moaned in her sleep and hugged his pillow to her breasts. Jake felt jealous of the pillow.

He found his discarded clothes on the floor and pulled them on, opened the door, and patted Cody on the back.

"Who wants to go for a sunset cruise?"

Cody huffed and wagged his tail. Jake knew Cody loved the ocean as much as his handler did. Maybe even more.

Jake walked aft through the salon and galley with Cody following. He turned off the alarm, unlocked the sliding glass door, and went out onto the stern deck, where he disconnected the water and power, and cast off the lines.

Cody stood still, his nostrils flaring as he faced the marina. The dog let out a fierce growl and sat down.

A jolt of adrenaline surged through Jake. He followed Cody's gaze to the parking area where he saw a dark figure holding what looked like a pistol and hurrying to hide behind another boat.

"Cody, to me, now!" Jake led his dog inside the galley and closed the sliding door a split second before a bullet hit and ricocheted off the thick polycarbonate glass with a loud pop.

Jake locked the door, hurried up to the enclosed fly bridge, started the engines, and bumped the throttles forward. The *Far Niente* glided across the marina fast enough to violate the five mile an hour no-wake zone, but not enough to rock all the other boats so hard their lines might tear loose. Jake would apologize later to his live-aboard neighbors for rocking their world.

Cody stood by his handler's side, waiting for orders.

Jake said, "Lie down."

Cody dropped to his belly.

Sarah entered the bridge wearing a T-shirt and leggings. "What's going on?"

"Grab the M-4," Jake said.

Sarah's eyes went wide. "Roger that." She opened a cabinet and pulled out one of the same rifles Marines carried in combat. She'd been firing one like it at the gun range with her police friend, Beth. Sarah held the weapon tight and kept it aimed upward with the safety on and her trigger finger straight. "Where's the target?"

Jake reached for the rifle. "First Mate, take the helm."

She handed him the rifle and moved to the wheel. "Aye, Captain. I have the helm."

"You have the helm."

Jake loaded a round into the chamber of his rifle and opened a bridge porthole. He aimed at the dock.

It was no good. He couldn't find the target. No other boat followed the *Far Niente*, and no more shots rang out. They were in the clear. Jake closed the porthole and returned his weapon to its cabinet.

At the helm, Sarah glanced over her shoulder. "What happened?"

He gestured aft toward the docks behind them. "Somebody fired a pistol at us and hit the sliding glass door one second after Cody and I went inside."

"I heard a loud pop but thought maybe you'd dropped a fishing weight on the deck," she said. "Thank goodness for bulletproof glass."

"Yeah, and thanks to Howard 'Levi' Strauss for insisting his team install it," Jake said, speaking of his friend who'd served in the CIA and now owned the Executive Security Services company.

Cody sniffed Jake's hands, smelling traces of the familiar weapon.

"We're good, Cody," Jake said. "Sarah piloted us out of there like a boss. Saved me from wasting a bullet on a dirtbag."

Sarah gave a one-shoulder shrug but appeared pleased at his compliment.

Jake said, "Cody smelled the attacker's weapon and alerted me in the nick of time."

Sarah patted Cody on the back. "Good dog."

Cody leapt into the second seat and reached out one paw toward the wheel.

"Careful there, copilot," Sarah said.

Jake observed them. His people. His pack. On this beautiful boat he called home. Cruising Mother Ocean on a perfect evening with clear skies. Life would be good if somebody hadn't tried to kill him tonight. Beatrice the palm reader had been right in her prediction. Cody had saved Jake's life.

He used binoculars to look at every boat within range and wondered how many more attacks there might be in the days and nights ahead.

CHAPTER 30

Jake set down the binoculars and thought of how the dock's police camera might have caught the perp on video if he hadn't told Beppe to blind the thing.

"I have to call someone," he said.

Sarah said, "I have the wheel."

Jake tapped a contact on his phone. A gruff voice answered after one ring. "Detective Flynn."

"Flynn, it's Wolfe."

"Wolfe who? Wolf Man?"

"Jake Wolfe, at Juanita Yacht Harbor."

"Oh, I thought you were in the Florida Keys, hiding from bill collectors and smuggling weed."

Jake could hear the smile in Flynn's voice. He'd always liked the Sausalito Police detective. "Speaking of bills, I'm back in town, and I want to pay the bill to clean paint off your security camera at my harbor."

"You broke it, you bought it."

"Agreed, and I can buy a few more if you fine folks need

them in various places. Same with vests for any K-9s who aren't equipped yet."

Flynn paused a moment. "Are you trying to bribe an officer of the law so you can avoid arrest for tampering with police property?"

"Nah, only paying a debt I owe." Jake used his phone to take a picture of his US Marshals badge and creds and text it to Flynn.

"I thought US Marshals were smart, but if they let you volunteer, I might have to rethink that," Flynn joked.

"Everybody makes an honest mistake now and then. They need Cody, so I get a pass."

"I accept your offer to pay for the camera," Flynn said. "Also, we have a new K-9, and she needs a vest. Not next week, or next month. Right now."

"Stop by Sarah Chance's pet clinic to have your dog try on a few vests. You can sign for one and put it on my tab."

"I take back a few of the many bad things I've been saying about you," Flynn said. "And I might even send you surveillance video of who shot at your boat tonight."

"You have another camera at my harbor?"

"Several more, but good guess." Flynn couldn't hide the smug amusement in his voice.

Jake flattered the detective. "My mind is no match for yours—a crime-fighting computer, always two steps ahead."

"Three steps, but who's counting?"

"When are you going fishing with us again?" Jake said.

"Discovered any new secret fishing holes?"

"Yeah, one that's so secret, dolphins can't find it. Are you free this weekend? Bring your wife and that snickerdoodle dog."

"It's a labradoodle," Flynn said. "This weekend is my

meeting at the Anti-Social Social Club. Next weekend after this works."

"Dungeness crab is in season," Jake said. "Drop a trap, have a beer, then use the electric winch to bring it up full of Dungeness."

"No casting and reeling?" Flynn said. "Sounds like the lazy man's way of catching seafood. Now you're talking."

Jake smiled. "Let's do it. Mark your calendar."

"My crime-fighting computer mind will remember," Flynn said. "Be careful out there . . . US Deputy Marshall dog handler."

"You too, Detective Badass." Jake ended the call.

Once they'd motored out of the marina, Sarah pushed the throttles further and brought the motor yacht up on plane. She piloted the *Far Niente* across Richardson Bay and then onto San Francisco Bay the way she'd practiced many times. "I'm taking her for a walk," she said, quoting Jake.

Jake smiled as he resisted the urge to take the wheel for himself and instead allowed Sarah to gain more experience. "She responds to your touch. You feel the *Far Niente*'s soul, and you have a way with her."

Sarah beamed with pride. That was her stated goal, and she'd worked for it. "Thank you, Jake. That means a lot to me. One time, when I broke up with a guy I'd been dating, he told me I was nothing more than a nice pair of boobs he'd been renting."

Jake raised his eyebrows. "The fool said that to a highly respected doctor of veterinary medicine?"

"Yep."

Jake changed the subject. "Let's cruise past the Golden Gate and onto the open ocean."

"Aye, Captain Wolfe," Sarah said, giving him a saucy salute.

"I'm liking that salute a lot," Jake said. "I'm not gonna lie."

Sarah cruised for a while and approached the bridge. "The water looks choppy directly underneath the Golden Gate."

"Good observation. Strong currents and deeper water through there, but you can handle this. Proceed."

Sarah stood up straighter and kept a sure hand on the wheel as they hit some chop and she powered through a bumpy cruise to the other side.

Soon they were on the Pacific Ocean, and Sarah let out a breath in relief of the stress she'd felt.

Jake was glad she'd passed that test and gained more confidence. "Nice piloting. This is a good spot to drop our lines."

Sarah throttled back to idle, dropping off plane and bringing the *Far Niente* to a slower drift forward via momentum only. "Captain, take the helm."

"I have the helm."

"You have the helm."

Jake gently reversed engines and brought the yacht to a standstill. He then dropped anchor, and its chain rattled noisily as it passed over the rollers.

Looking around, he spotted plenty of other sunset cruisers on sailboats and motor yachts off in the distance in all directions. Hopefully, none of them were transporting the person who'd shot at him earlier.

One yacht stood out among the rest. A real beauty, maybe 40 to 45 feet long. Ever curious about boats, Jake gazed at it through binoculars and noticed there wasn't anybody at the helm. As the boat cruised along slowly on autopilot, a well-dressed older couple enjoyed a meal at their dining table on the stern deck. Jake lowered the binos and glanced at the chart plotter. The Automatic Identification System ID'd the boat as *Tiburon*, named after the beautiful local city and island.

He handed the binos to Sarah. "This couple knows how to live."

She gazed at the *Tiburon*. "I love how they dressed up for dinner on their boat. Let's do that one day soon."

"It's a date," Jake said.

He suddenly felt an eerie premonition of danger. His sixth sense of impending violence had been proven correct many times in the past. Right then, he had a strange feeling the *Tiburon* might be a doomed ship headed for trouble, but it wasn't a threat to Jake, Sarah, and Cody.

What should he do? He couldn't simply hail them on the radio. What would he say? They'd think he was crazy.

CHAPTER 31

Wealthy lobbyist Gerald Oliver sat at an outdoor table on the stern deck of his luxurious forty-foot motor yacht, the *Tiburon*, as the vessel slowly cruised west on autopilot toward the setting sun.

The chart plotter and radar helped the *Tiburon* follow a predetermined course on the bay and avoid other boats.

Tiburon meant shark in Spanish, and the boat was aptly named because Gerald was well known as a human shark.

The lobbyist and his successful realtor wife, Rachel, sipped champagne and chatted while gazing at the setting sun reflecting on the water. It was a warm evening, and two patio heaters helped keep the temperature in their comfort zone. On hot summer days, Gerald replaced the heaters with portable evaporative coolers that sprayed a refreshing mist of bottled Fiji water.

The couple were on a romantic date, enjoying a private dinner cruise, while trying to reconcile after recently talking about divorce. Rachel was making an effort that night, but

Gerald had a secret. He'd given up on Rachel and had met somebody else.

Brandi was an amateur social media fashion model celebrity who'd risen to fame in a similar way as the Kardashians. She wasn't a gold digger after Gerald's money. She'd designed a bestselling line of skimpy swimwear that provided her with plenty of tabloid publicity and a generous income. Brandi was simply a high society home-wrecker who didn't care about wedding vows. She had lofty goals and might be using Gerald for his many connections. That was fine with him.

The two adulterers had a spark of chemistry together and were good in bed. Brandi was, as the saying goes, a lady in the streets and a freak in the sheets. Perfect for Gerald's midlife crisis that included a red sports car, a personal trainer, and an endless supply of Viagra.

Gerald felt Brandi offered him a lucky second chance at having an exciting new life. He wanted more than an illicit affair. He wanted Brandi living in his house, sleeping in his bed, and taking her daily bikini selfies on his yacht.

It was a shame Rachel stood in the way. If he divorced his wife, she'd hire a ruthless law firm and use California laws to demand the house, half of Gerald's savings, and large monthly alimony payments for years to come. It would be a financial disaster.

The law cut both ways, and many female celebrities were paying a fortune in monthly alimony to their former boy-toy husbands.

Gerald needed more income, not less, especially after spending a fortune over the past year on extravagant luxury hotel suites for trysts with Brandi. Thankfully, he'd found a secret side hustle that brought in a flood of untaxed money via the *Tiburon*.

He noticed Rachel had gone all out for their date night. She'd dressed up in a stylish new evening gown that flattered her figure, visited the beauty shop to have her hair styled, tried an enticing new perfume, and wore a sexy new color of lipstick that made her mouth appear irresistibly kissable. She'd done it all for him, and he felt a terrible pang of guilt for what he was about to do in return.

Gerald hadn't made any similar efforts on his own appearance. He'd dressed in the same old yachting attire of khaki pants, boat shoes, a white button-down shirt, and a royal blue blazer with gold buttons. When he entertained guests, he would also wear his officer's hat. He believed the outfit made him look like the captain of a Royal Caribbean cruise ship.

While music played in the background, the couple enjoyed a casual dinner of takeout from a favorite deli, including rotisserie chicken, fettuccine Alfredo pasta, and a chopped salad.

Once the sun had set and a waning crescent moon left the night sky darker than usual, Gerald took a deep breath and tried to remain calm as he held up his flute of champagne. "I want to propose a toast."

Rachel raised her glass and teased him. "Are you trying to get me drunk and into your bed, handsome stranger?"

He paused for effect. "Yes, beautiful lady, but I also wanted to suggest we drink a toast to renewing our wedding vows. Maybe even going on a second honeymoon."

Her eyes softened as she clinked her glass to his and took a sip. "After all these years, you can still say the right thing and make my heart beat faster."

He stood up, moved to the boat's sound system controls, and played her favorite slow song. "May I have this dance?"

She stood up and used both perfectly manicured hands to

smooth her dress down each thigh. The bright polish on her nails attracted his gaze.

"Why, yes, kind sir, I've had my eye on you all evening at this party. I thought you'd never ask."

They embraced and slow danced. Rachel whispered in his ear about how loved, sexy, and free he was making her feel. He eased them closer to the swim platform, glanced over her shoulder at the churning water behind, and made a final decision. It was now or never. Letting go of Rachel, he stood back and said, "Let me look at my gorgeous wife."

She surprised him by raising the hem of her dress to reveal a garter belt and stockings, along with panties decorated on the front with the words "FUN WIFE." In the past, Rachel had worn the flirty lingerie once a week to give Gerald a clear sign it was his lucky night. It had been at least a year since the most recent appearance.

"Make love to me babe," she said. "I want you. Right here, right now."

Gerald felt tempted. Fun Wife was back? What a surprise. This was her offer to start over. At close to fifty years of age, Rachel still had it going on. A pretty face, toned body, playful personality, and an intelligent mind. She was as vivacious as she'd been in her thirties. It was only her one major personality flaw that had changed for the worse.

He'd once loved her so much, but in recent years, her daily fault-finding and criticism had worn him down. Why did she have to treat him with so much disrespect and be his harshest, most merciless critic?

Her positive qualities were a powerful draw, and he'd once considered himself a lucky man who should be thankful. That was before she began putting him down and ridiculing him in front of their friends.

Because of their fights and lack of intimate activities, he'd felt abandoned, had fallen out of love, pulled away, and now saw her as an old friend with benefits, but one who'd turned off those benefits.

"Yes, please, Fun Wife," he said with fake sincerity. "Let me grab a cushion." He opened a storage footlocker next to them and pulled out a six-foot-long pad meant for sunbathing on chaise lounge patio furniture. When they'd done this in the past, he would turn up the heaters and dim the lights.

Instead of laying the cushion down on the deck, he stepped closer and deliberately bumped into Rachel. She screamed in fear as he used the cushion to push her stumbling backwards over the stern gunwale and into the bay.

The foam-filled lounge pad prevented him from leaving any bruises on her skin as he might have by grabbing her biceps or pushing on her shoulders.

Rachel sank under the bubbling and churning water behind the twin engines, resurfaced, coughed up saltwater, and began dog-paddling. She shouted in panic, "Gerald, help me!"

CHAPTER 32

Gerald stood and watched as the motor yacht continued slowly chugging along on autopilot, leaving his wife behind in the unforgiving ocean.

Rachel cried out, "Throw me a life preserver, and stop the engines." She coughed up more salt water.

He held eye contact and hoped she might think about all the emasculating words she'd said to him in front of their friends over the past year. He turned up the music system's volume, and the singer of her favorite song drowned out her cries for help. Soon, Rachel would drown as well.

Gerald knew that although it was a warm evening, the bay water remained cold and would soon induce shock. More people drowned from cold shock than hypothermia. He'd read about it online. Submersion in cold water could paralyze your muscles and make you hyperventilate so uncontrollably that you might inhale water and choke in only a few minutes.

Following his premeditated plan, Gerald checked the time and allowed the yacht to cruise on autopilot while he went inside and visited the head. He didn't actually need to use the toilet, so he sat on the closed lid for five minutes.

Once he returned to the stern deck, he switched off the music player and acted out his concocted alibi to imprint it on his memory. "Rachel? Where are you?"

When he didn't hear any reply, he headed back inside and went through the motions of quickly checking the galley, salon, main stateroom, and its en suite head.

Not finding his missing wife anywhere, Gerald rushed to the pilothouse, turned the *Tiburon* around, and headed back. He marked a waypoint on the chart plotter and followed the dotted lines tracking his journey.

Once he had the yacht cruising on a reverse course, he aimed a spotlight forward and grabbed the VHF radio mic.

"Hailing the US Coast Guard. This is *Tiburon*. I have a woman overboard and can't find her. Please help. *Tiburon* over."

The Coast Guard radio operator told Gerald to switch channels. She asked him questions and said, "One of our cutters is on the way, but a police boat is closer and can arrive sooner. I'll hail them and relay your situation. Coast Guard over and out."

"Thank you, Coast Guard," Gerald said. "*Tiburon* out."

Moments later, he saw red and blue police lights strobing. A powerful spotlight swept back and forth on the water.

His radio crackled and a deep, gravelly voice said, "*Tiburon*, this is police boat *Marine One*. I'm Captain Leeds. When and where did your passenger fall overboard? Did you drop a pin on your chart plotter to mark the location?"

Gerald went into his practiced spiel. "I was using the head and didn't see my wife fall overboard, sir. When I returned to the stern deck, she wasn't there. I thought she must be inside getting ready for bed, so I went to our stateroom but didn't find her. When I called her name and didn't hear any reply, I marked the location, turned the boat around, and headed back on a search and rescue course."

"When did you last see her?" Captain Leeds said.

"About ten minutes ago," Gerald said. "We were having dinner out on the deck and watching the sunset, just like we've done many times in the past."

"Ten minutes cruising at what speed?" Leeds said.

"Idling along at five miles per hour."

Leeds asked, "Had your wife been drinking alcohol?"

"Yes. We both enjoyed several glasses of champagne," Gerald said.

"Was she wearing a life jacket?"

"No, sir. I'm afraid not. Neither of us were."

Captain Leeds raised his voice. "Put yours on right now."

"Yes, sir." Gerald donned an inflatable vest.

"Share your chart plotter with me, and we'll retrace your route," Captain Leeds said.

Gerald complied. "Yes, here it is."

"Come to a full stop. Turn off your engines, drop anchor, and wait for further instructions. *Marine One* over and out."

"Yes, sir. Over and out." Gerald pulled back on both throttles and stopped forward thrust, then reversed engines and came to a stop. He used the windlass to lower the anchor.

His heart pounded as he observed the police boat continue searching with a spotlight, while three cops launched a Zodiac and piloted the inflatable boat to the *Tiburon*.

One of them shouted, "We're coming aboard to search for your wife."

"Yes, please do." Gerald broke down and sobbed in front of the police. The tears were real. He now felt like the most selfish, horrible, narcissistic person in the world after murdering a special woman who'd loved him.

What have I done?

All three officers boarded the *Tiburon*, and while two male cops conducted a thorough search from stem to stern, the female asked Gerald to walk her through the evening's events again.

Gerald knew she would use the body-worn camera on her shirt to record every word. After he'd carefully recited his fake alibi, he noticed a look of doubt in her eyes.

CHAPTER 33

Jake and Sarah sat in comfy deck chairs on the "backyard patio," as Sarah referred to the stern deck. They enjoyed watching the sunset that created a beautiful display of vivid colors in the sky and ocean.

After nature's light show, Jake turned on the Furuno fish finder and reached for two of his custom rods and reels. "Striped bass and California halibut are in season all year long."

"Fresh-caught halibut is the *only* halibut," Sarah said. "After being frozen, it's not as succulent."

"Speaking of succulent seafood," Jake said, "Dungeness crab is in season now. Instead of doing hook-and-line fishing, we can lie at anchor here and drop a few crab pots, then kick back and wait a while to pull them up and see if we got lucky."

"I love Dungeness crab," Sarah said. "Let's do it."

"The Dungeness daily bag limit is ten crab per fishing license," Jake said.

"I have my license with me in my purse," Sarah said.

"We can't take any crabs from the bay, but we're in the

ocean here." Jake flipped on some lights and opened a locker. He dragged out two circular, heavy-duty crab pots, each attached to their own two-hundred-foot shot of non-lead sinking line. The crabbing line with a heavy core would sink any excess and keep it away from boat props. He added frozen squid to a pair of bait boxes and secured one to the bottom of each pot. "Good things come to those who bait."

"To those who bait and *wait*," Sarah said with a smile.

"We're going to be crabbing at about one fifty to one eighty feet deep," Jake said. "That should help us find some larger crabs that most folks can't reach with their standard one-hundred-foot-line crab pots."

He noticed Sarah watching the way he handled the fishing gear like a pro. People often told him he could earn a living as a charter boat captain, but he shrugged off the compliments. That would be a proud profession, but he only had time to do it for fun, not for a living.

After Jake dropped both crab pots into the bay, he and Sarah sat on the deck chairs again, watching the moon and stars reflecting on the ocean. Cody stretched out on the deck and placed his head on his front paws.

Jake kept a Remington 700 sniper rifle nearby in case a boat came too close and someone took a shot at the *Far Niente*.

One hour and two beers later, Jake raised a crab pot using an electric line trap and pot puller. "An electric winch is nice when using heavy pots or crabbing in deeper water, and we're doing both."

The wire crab cage splashed to the surface, full of large Dungeness crabs.

"Wow, nice pull," Jake said. "I don't think I've ever seen one with this many crabs. We found a honey hole."

"We'll have to mark the spot," Sarah said.

Jake had the Navionics app on his phone. He tapped it and dropped a pin to save the location.

He then handed Sarah a seven-inch plastic crab gauge to measure the sizes they could keep or throw back. "The minimum size is five-and-three-quarter inches, but plenty of these look like six to seven inches."

She held up an extra-large crab. "The gauge can't even measure this one."

Jake was impressed. "That thing must weigh two, or maybe even three pounds."

Sarah continued measuring and sorting. When she tossed several crabs over the side, Cody barked at her as if she were crazy to throw away seafood.

"I'm thinking these evening pull crabs are bigger than a morning pull," Jake said.

"This is a pregnant female." Sarah pointed out the mass of tiny bright orange eggs clustered on the crab's abdomen, then she gently released mama crab into the water.

"Veterinarians know so many things," Jake said.

Sarah met his eyes. "Surprised?"

"Not at all."

Soon they had ten nice-sized crabs, all over six inches wide, for Jake's limit, and ten more of the same for Sarah's. The rest went back into the ocean.

"We'll have to do this again soon," Jake said. "The moment any humpbacks show up in these waters, state regulators will close Dungeness season early to protect the whales from getting entangled in ropes."

He and Sarah placed the twenty keepers in an insulated hold filled with cold salt water to keep them fresh and alive.

"Crab feast for dinner tomorrow," Sarah said.

"And leftovers for salads and sandwiches the next day," Jake said.

"Have a favorite crab boil recipe?"

Jake said, "Boil crabs. Melt butter. Enjoy."

She smiled. "Good plan. Keep it simple."

In the distance, red and blue lights strobed, and a police boat roared across the water at high speed. Someone onboard used a spotlight to sweep the water's surface in the dark.

"I wonder what that's all about," Sarah said.

Cody stood up and watched the unusual activity.

Jake stood up too. He'd lowered the sound volume of the VHF security band, in order to enjoy some peace and quiet. He turned it up now, opened a locker and grabbed his thermal night vision binoculars with a built-in laser rangefinder. He spotted the familiar sight of a police boat painted with the designation of *SF Marine 1*. The vessel slowed to a stop and bumped boats with the *Tiburon*. The man who Jake had seen earlier now stood near the swim platform and spoke with a uniformed female police officer who was coming aboard.

Jake didn't see the man's female companion anywhere, and he felt a stab of dread that she might have fallen off the boat. He picked up the VHF radio mic. "*Far Niente* hailing police boat *Marine One*. Over."

The reply came immediately. "*Far Niente*, this is Captain Leeds. Over."

"Captain Leeds, sir, this is your friend, Captain Jake Wolfe. I'm doing some crabbing to the west of you, on the other side of the bridge. It looks like you're conducting a search. May I be of assistance to the police? Over." Jake turned on a spotlight and searched the water around his vessel.

"Yes, Captain Wolfe. We have a woman overboard. Please

continue searching west of our position. Thank you, my friend. Over."

"Roger that. Out."

"Over and out," Leeds said.

Jake moved the spotlight back and forth, high and low, near and far.

Sarah stood next to him. "That woman we saw fell overboard?"

"I think so. We didn't notice anyone else on board, and I don't see her there now."

Cody stood near the swim platform, gazing out at the water with bright eyes, his nose up and nostrils flaring.

"Cody, *stay*," Jake said. His independent dog would dive off the boat when it suited him.

Jake spotted a police Quadski, a four-wheeled ATV that could drive down a beach into the ocean and convert to a Jet Ski type of watercraft. The officer began a circular search pattern with an expanding perimeter.

Moments later, Cody barked excitedly. Jake saw what appeared to be a human body with bare legs, long blonde hair, and wearing a blue-and-white-striped dress. The person was floating and drifting toward the *Far Niente*, probably being slowly pulled out to sea by the deeper water current under the bridge.

Jake grabbed the thermal night vision binoculars once again. "Sarah, please turn off the spotlight for a minute."

Sarah flipped the switch, and the light went dark.

Jake aimed his thermal binos at the floating body. Yes, the person had a heat signature and might be alive.

He set down the binos. "Okay, turn the spotlight back on."

Sarah did so and adjusted the aim a little to compensate for the floating person's movement.

Jake spoke into the radio mic. "*Marine One*, this is *Far*

Niente. Captain Leeds, we've spotted a body in the water. Approximately midway under the bridge. Over."

"Good work," Captain Leeds said. "Stand by while we deploy our Zodiac and rescue swimmer. Over."

"Roger that. Over and out."

Sarah kept the spotlight in position as Jake observed an officer piloting the Zodiac boat under the bridge. Another cop in the boat wore a dry suit and held a stretcher with flotation tubes on either side. The Zodiac raced to the body lit up by the *Far Niente's* spotlight.

The rescue swimmer eased into the choppy water, swam to the woman, placed her on the stretcher, and kicked water, pushing toward the Zodiac.

The Zodiac returned to *Marine One*, and Sarah turned off the spotlight.

"Up to the bridge," Jake said, heading in that direction, followed by Sarah and Cody.

CHAPTER 34

Jake raised anchor and started the engines, then slowly motored under the bridge and headed toward the police boat.

He spoke on the radio. "Captain Wolfe on the *Far Niente* requesting permission to approach *Marine One*. Over."

"Permission granted by Captain Leeds. Over and out."

When Jake came closer, he used the binos to watch two police officers raise the stretcher onboard. He confirmed that the rescued person appeared to be a White woman with long blonde hair, wearing a soaking wet cocktail dress that clung to her body. The cops shouted to each other and took swift action.

An officer tried to resuscitate her using a defibrillator. He pressed the paddles against the woman's chest and shouted, "Clear," then gave her a powerful shock. The woman's body bucked upwards off the deck from the jolt. The cop repeated the procedure again and again.

But it was too late.

The officer hung his head in defeat and placed a blanket over the woman's body, covering her face.

Jake's radio crackled, and he heard Captain Leeds say, "Captain Wolfe, thank you for assisting the Marine Police tonight. I'm sorry to report the woman did not survive. Over."

Jake appreciated the captain's professional courtesy. He replied in a low voice, "Terribly sorry to hear that, Captain Leeds. Your fine officers did their best. Over and out."

He turned to look at the brightly lit stern deck of the *Tiburon* and the man onboard who now appeared to be crying. Jake felt sorry for him but also knew the police would follow procedure and look for any possible evidence of foul play.

He thought about how it would be Terrell's job as a homicide detective to investigate the *Tiburon* and its captain. He took a short video with his phone and sent it to his best friend.

A minute later, Jake's phone buzzed with a text from Terrell. *I asked Captain Leeds to have Cody search the Tiburon.*

Jake sent a reply. *Roger.*

The radio crackled. "*Marine One* hailing the *Far Niente*. This is Captain Leeds. Over."

"This is *Far Niente*. Captain Wolfe speaking. Go ahead, Captain Leeds. Over."

"Jake, I heard from Detective Terrell Hayes that you're carrying your Marshals badge once again. Is that right, son? Over."

"Yes, sir, Captain. At your service. Over."

"I am officially requesting you and your K-9 to assist us by searching the *Tiburon*. Over."

"Yes, sir. We're on our way. Over and out." Jake put on the badge, grabbed some nitrile gloves, and moved aft.

Sarah said, "I'm coming with you as part of the K-9 team."

Jake held her gaze and shook his head. "You'd have to ask permission from Captain Leeds. He likes you, but he'll say no because it's a crime scene."

She took a breath. "I get it. Okay, I'll stay and protect the *Far Niente*."

"Thank you, Sarah. There are always good people who have to stay behind and hold down the fort. It's vital to every mission." Jake unstrapped the inflatable dinghy, eased the small boat onto the swim platform, and snapped his fingers. "Cody, hop in the boat."

The smart dog had been watching Jake and was already standing by for action. He climbed aboard with well-practiced moves and sat in the bow.

Jake sat on the dinghy's aft bench and pushed off, turned on the quiet electric motor, and zoomed over to the *Tiburon*.

When he arrived, a uniformed policewoman stood waiting at the stern. The cop stared at Jake's silver star for a moment to confirm and then nodded and held out one hand. Jake tossed her the painter, and she tied the line to a cleat.

Jake saw the *Tiburon's* captain up close now. He recognized Gerald Oliver from when they'd met during a black-tie charity gala hosted at his friend Lauren Stephens's mansion.

"Gerald Oliver?" Jake said after he came aboard.

"Yes. Have we met?" Oliver said, eyes red, tears on his face.

Jake nodded. "I'm Jake Wolfe. Lauren Stephens introduced us at an auction fundraiser for children with cancer."

"Oh, that's right," Gerald said. "Sorry, I'm in total shock right now."

"I understand," Jake said. "Was that your wife Rachel who fell overboard?"

"Yes, I'm afraid so." Gerald wept and put his hands over his face.

"I'm sorry for your loss." Jake once again said the polite military reply automatically from too many experiences with death and pain.

Cody let out a low growl and sniffed the swim platform.

Jake observed his dog. "What is it, boy?"

Cody moved to a footlocker and pawed at it.

Jake gloved up and opened the top, finding two long cushions for chase lounges.

Cody sniffed the top cushion near the middle and then returned to sniff the swim platform again. He looked out at the water and barked.

Jake pondered this activity by his highly intelligent dog and tried to figure out what Cody was trying to tell him. He pointed at an area of the cushion and spoke to the cop. "Can you shine a flashlight right there?"

She shone a waterproof flotation style light on the cushion.

Jake saw a wet spot in the middle area where Cody had sniffed, and he examined the other matching cushion. It was totally dry. Then he did something that often freaked out average people who were not dog handlers. He leaned in close to take a sniff of the wet area, the way Cody had, and recognized a familiar aroma.

"Cody, smell this again."

His dog obeyed.

He pointed at the swim platform. "Now, smell that."

Cody followed orders.

Jake held eye contact with his dog and asked, "Same . . . smell?"

Every IED detection dog understood the word *smell*. And Cody had learned the word *same* from Jake. The dog barked once.

"Genius dog," Jake said. "Find more? Seek, Cody."

Cody raised his head high and then held it low. His nostrils flared. He walked slowly, sniffing a scent cone only a trained scent dog could find. When he stopped in front of

Gerald, sniffed the man's hands and sat down, Jake knew his hunch had been correct.

The cop watched them with a fascinated look on her face. "What did your K-9 find?"

Jake stood in front of Gerald, who stared at Cody in dread. "Gerald, I believe you used that cushion to push Rachel off the stern deck and into the water. She was so terrified, she lost control of her bladder and peed herself."

Gerald gaped at him. "What? That's an outrageous lie."

"CSI will confirm Rachel's urine is on the cushion, the swim platform, and your hands from when you put the cushion back in the locker," Jake said. "How do you explain that?"

Cody growled at the man and showed his teeth.

The policewoman's eyes darkened. She drew her handcuffs. "Turn around and put your hands behind your back."

CHAPTER 35

Jake stood by as the policewoman locked Gerald in handcuffs and placed him under arrest. She escorted him aboard the nearby police boat and into custody.

Gerald said, "Please listen to me. You're making a mistake."

Captain Leeds boarded the *Tiburon*, shook hands with Jake, and spoke in his trademark gravelly voice. "Excellent work. You two want a job with the department?"

Jake smiled at the salty older captain who'd gone fishing on the *Far Niente* a time or two. "Thank you, Captain, but Chief Pierce says I'm a bull in a china shop. But we'll continue searching the *Tiburon* for you."

"I appreciate that," Captain Leeds said. "Carry on, son."

Cody sniffed the Marine Police captain's hand when Jake shook it.

"Be friends, Cody," Jake said. "You remember Captain Leeds."

Cody sniffed the man's shoes and wagged his tail.

"We'll start by walking the perimeter." Jake patted his thigh, and Cody followed him.

The *Tiburon* had full walk-around decks. Jake stepped onto the narrow walkway next to the gunwale, and held out his pistol for Cody to sniff the rounds filled with gunpowder. The scent dog needed an object to seek, but could find other things along the way. "Cody, search."

Jake followed behind Cody as the dog slowly walked in a circular route from the stern. He moved forward along the starboard side, passed around the bow, and then headed aft down the port side.

When they'd returned to the stern deck, Jake opened a door and led his dog inside. Cody searched the salon, galley, head, and main stateroom, then pawed at the door to a guest stateroom. Jake went in and noted a typical layout of two single berths that could combine into a double.

Cody headed straight to a closet that smelled like cedar. Jake let him in and noted the walls were indeed lined with cedar wood paneling to repel insects, reduce humidity, and prevent mold. Jake wondered if Cody was only smelling the fragrant wood aroma, but the dog stood near a dresser, intent on something. Cody studied every inch of the dresser, zeroed in on the bottom drawer, and pawed at it.

Jake pulled out the drawer and found various items of folded clothing in vacuum-sealed plastic bags. He removed each bag and spread them out on a berth. Cody studied them but returned to the empty drawer.

Jake said, "Okay, you got it." He removed the drawer, turned it over to look at the bottom, and then set it aside.

Cody sniffed the empty drawer space, growled, and sat down to signal he'd found something.

Jake dropped prone on his belly and looked into the cavity.

Six vacuum-sealed plastic bags were hidden in the very back, but these didn't contain clothing.

Jake used his phone to take pictures. One inside the opening, another of a bag he pulled out with a gloved hand to get a closeup, and a third of Cody in front of the dresser sniffing the smuggled contraband.

The bag was full of small pills marked with the misspelled word "ASPRIN."

"I have to find the snake who's flooding America with xylazine, and cut the head off that snake." He sent the pictures to Terrell and Captain Leeds with a text. *Cody found these tranq pills onboard the Tiburon.*

He then texted Agent McKay the same photos and a longer message with details.

McKay texted in reply. *I'm calling you.*

Jake's phone buzzed, and he answered with, "Cody says you're welcome."

It was three hours ahead in Washington, and Jake could hear the fatigue in McKay's voice when she said, "Introduce me to Captain Leeds."

"Roger that," Jake said. "Stand by."

He carried the bags of tranq pills to the deck and showed them to Captain Leeds. "I believe Gerald Oliver has been using his yacht to meet drug-runner boats out on the ocean and transport their xylazine the final distance into our city."

Captain Leeds frowned. "That tranq drug is the worst of the worst."

Jake held up his phone. "I have Secret Service Agent Shannon McKay on a video call. She's working late at the White House and wants a quick word."

Captain Leeds raised his eyebrows when Jake mentioned the White House. "A pleasure to meet you, Agent McKay."

"Likewise, Captain Leeds," McKay said. "I want to ask you a favor, and then I owe you one."

"I'm all ears, ma'am."

"I'd like Detective Terrell Hayes to be the one who interrogates Gerald Oliver. He has top-secret clearances, and I can tell him things that are on a need-to-know basis."

"I'm sure that can be arranged," Captain Leeds said. "It's often Hayes and Cushman who interrogate murder suspects. They have the best homicide clearance rate in the department."

McKay said, Captain, will you allow Jake to go onboard Marine One for a minute?"

Captain Leeds gestured at his boat. "Yes, but what for?"

"I want him to put some real aspirin pills in a zip-top bag, and press it into Gerald Olivers cuffed hands to make him think Jake is adding his prints and DNA to the evidence."

"That wouldn't be admissible as evidence in court," Captain Leeds said.

"It's not evidence at all," Jake said. "McKay are you hoping Oliver freaks out and tries to cut a deal?"

"Yes, maybe he'll admit to the drug running and avoid life in prison for murder," McKay said.

"I'll check the *Tiburon* for pills and a plastic bag." Jake went inside and found the items, then returned to the stern deck and held it up for McKay to see on the video call.

Jake said, "Captain, I'm requesting permission to board *Marine One* for a minute while you remain on the *Tiburon* and talk with Agent McKay."

Captain Leeds waved his hand at the police boat. "Permission granted. But I had nothing to do with this entrapment scheme."

"Don't observe me, and you won't be involved." Jake boarded *Marine One*. Cody followed on his heels.

He approached Gerald Oliver, who was handcuffed to a metal ring on the gunwale. Two uniformed cops looked at Jake's badge and watched Cody.

Jake held up the plastic bag full of pills. "This will only take a second."

When the cops shrugged, Jake grabbed Gerald Oliver's right hand and shoved the bag into his grasp, marking it with the man's fingerprints and DNA.

Gerald said, "What's this about? Let go of me."

Jake waved the bag of pills so Gerald could see it. "Enjoy prison."

"I've never seen that before in my life."

Jake leaned in close to Gerald's face, and Cody growled at the prisoner's crotch.

"That was for Rachel," Jake said. "I want you to think about your murdered wife every day while you're behind bars."

Jake shoved the bag into his coat pocket, returned to the *Tiburon* and spoke to Captain Leeds. "Your officers saw the bag, and it's on your boat video, too. It's obviously not the tranq. We can only hope Oliver was so upset he might have fallen for it."

Leeds returned Jake's phone to him, with McKay's face still on the display.

"Jake, can you meet up with Terrell?" McKay said.

"Captain, with your permission, I'll cruise the *Far Niente* to the police dock, meet with Detective Hayes, and give him this bag of aspirin."

Captain Leeds said, "See you there."

Jake moved toward the dinghy and snapped his fingers for Cody to hop in. Once his dog took a seat, Jake untied, climbed in, fired up the motor, and cruised over to his yacht.

When they arrived at the *Far Niente*, Jake tossed the

painter to Sarah, who tied up and then assisted Cody onto the swim platform.

Jake dragged the inflatable craft onboard, tied it down, and told Sarah what Cody had found.

Sarah watched the police boat cruise away toward shore. "I wonder if the man's wife discovered his drug running and he murdered her to hide the secret."

They all headed up to the bridge, where Jake activated the windlass and raised the anchor. He then cruised the motor yacht across the cobalt blue water to a city police dock.

Jake raised his night vision binoculars and saw an unmarked black Ford Explorer police interceptor parked there. A man and woman stood nearby, waiting for the *Far Niente* to arrive.

He recognized Detectives Terrell Hayes and Beth Cushman, working overtime, probably at the request of Agent McKay.

Jake eased back on the throttles and slowly motored to the government boat slips, where a uniformed cop waved him in.

Jake bumped the dock and tied up. "Cody, stay on board with Sarah."

"I have him," Sarah said, placing a leash onto the dog's collar and hanging on tight.

Cody barked at the two familiar police detectives.

Jake disembarked and met with Terrell and Beth.

Terrell frowned at him. "You really messed up this time, Jukebox. I can't believe you'd be so irresponsible. Police Chief Pierce is on the warpath."

CHAPTER 36

Jake met Terrell's eyes. In the Marine Corps, Terrell had yelled at him every day. "What did I mess up this time, Lieutenant?"

"We need to talk in private, boot." Terrell got into the vehicle, not waiting for Jake to agree.

Jake dutifully obeyed his best friend and former commanding officer. He almost opened a backseat door for Cody out of habit before he realized the dog was with Sarah. He sat down in the front seat, closed the door, and noticed Beth walking over to the *Far Niente*. "Is this about Rachel Oliver or the tranq?"

Terrell put his phone on speaker and played a podcast for background noise. "I had Roxanne access the cameras onboard *Marine One*, and she has video of you tampering with evidence."

"That wasn't evidence," Jake said. "McKay had me play a trick on Gerald Oliver."

"You said Cody found bags of xylazine on board the *Tiburon*," Terrells said.

"He did, but that bag you see me with on the boat video is

filled with plain old aspirin," Jake said. "McKay asked permission from Captain Leeds to let me try making Oliver panic and cut a deal."

"Okay, I get it. I'll tell grouchy Chief Pierce he doesn't have to chew your head off."

"Good luck with that."

Terrell said, "Meanwhile, Oliver isn't panicking. He told the Marine Police you must have planted the drugs on his boat," Terrell said. "Do you have another cop as a witness to your discovery?"

Jake exhaled loudly. "No. It was only Cody and me."

"Not very smart," Terrell said. "It's your word against the suspect. Next time you conduct a search, wear a body camera, and have a cop follow along."

"Will do," Jake said. "Good advice. Thanks."

"I chewed out Captain Leeds, too," Terrell said.

"It's my fault, not the captain's," Jake said. "I forgot body cam protocol because I was angry that Oliver murdered his wife, and he's smuggling tranq that kills people."

"Maybe you're too emotional to work in law enforcement," Terrell said.

Jake displayed his phone screen. "The good news is, I took phone video when Cody searched the *Tiburon* and found the drugs."

"Send it to me and Rox and Captain Leeds."

"Sent," Jake said, tapping on his phone. "Oliver could still claim I planted the drugs, but the police boat had its cameras recording the *Tiburon* when I arrived, and I wasn't wearing any bulky clothing that could hide six bags full of pills."

Terrell said, "I'll let Rox know to enhance that video and run it through her tech. It can profile your body like an X-ray and create a topographical map."

"I hope she's impressed with my manly mountain on the map," Jake said.

Terrell gazed out his windshield at the seized *Tiburon* being piloted into dock by one of the Marine Police. "Let's hope we find prints and DNA on the actual evidence."

Jake reached into his coat pocket and took out the bag of aspirin. "Here's evidence that my bag was not really evidence, if that makes sense."

"I'm not gloved up. Toss it in the back seat."

Jake tossed the bag, and then removed his gloves. "Let Roxanne know that video shows me with aspirin not tranq. She can zoom in and get an image to compare with the drugs."

"That works," Terrell said. "I'm so relieved you didn't really tamper with physical evidence. I was going to yell at you about how that worthless internet law school didn't teach you about the penalties for tampering with evidence."

"Hey, I learned from the same textbooks they use at brick-and-mortar law schools." Jake used his phone to access the state website and then recited the law. "California Penal Code PEN 141 states that a peace officer who knowingly, willfully, intentionally, and wrongfully alters, modifies, plants, places, manufactures, conceals, or moves any physical matter, digital image, or video recording, with specific intent that the action will result in a person being charged with a crime or with the specific intent that the physical matter, digital image, or video recording will be concealed or destroyed, or fraudulently represented as the original evidence upon a trial, proceeding, or inquiry, is guilty of a felony punishable by two, three, or five years in the state prison."

Terrell held a small cigar under his nose and inhaled the aroma but didn't light it. "That's enough. You were acting as a peace officer under color of law. I'm glad you're not going to spend several years in prison."

"Same here. So, we're all good now?"

"Yeah, the SNAFU is now SN but not totally AFU."

Jake said, "Courts allow police to lie to anyone, suspect or citizen, if it helps in crime prevention, so the police often do." He took a breath and continued. "I lied to Oliver and said his DNA on the bag would send him to prison. I hoped he'd confess in order to cut a deal."

Terrell let out a breath. "Did Agent McKay tell you to do that?"

"I'm sworn to secrecy regarding anything McKay says or does."

"She told me some of what you're up against, and I support your mission to stop the tranq supplier."

"I want to find and *nuke* the tranq laboratory. Scorched earth." Jake pounded his fist on the dashboard.

Terrell said, "You're angry about the past, and taking it out on any dirtbag you can find who deserves to be punished."

Jake looked out the window. "You know me too well."

"Some folks go into law enforcement because they want to control other people. Is that what you want?"

"I'm fighting to save the lives of innocent Americans," Jake said. "And I make no apology for doing it."

Terrell started the engine. "Come with me to the station and observe Oliver being questioned. I want to do it while he's still buzzed on champagne."

"I guess the *Far Niente* is safe for Sarah and Cody here at the police boat dock," Jake said with a jaded smile. He sent a text to Sarah letting her know he'd be at police HQ for a while. Sarah replied that she and Cody would wait for him on the *Far Niente*. Jake appreciated her teamwork.

Terrell drove away from the docks and toward the new main police station.

Upon arrival, Jake had to walk through the security

checkpoint. A curious female cop behind the bulletproof glass watched him remove all kinds of hidden weapons from his clothing, along with the US Marshals silver star badge.

"I think we've met before," she said.

Jake nodded. "Good memory."

CHAPTER 37

Jake walked inside the new police HQ, along with Terrell. He missed having Cody by his side, but Chief Pierce considered the war dog an "unstable military weapon." Pierce thought much the same about Jake.

Tech Officer Roxanne Poole stood waiting for them. She gazed at Jake with her typical frank appraisal, used one finger to push her glasses up the bridge of her nose, turned around, and walked ahead of them without a word.

They entered an observation area with a one-way mirror view of the interrogation room.

Detective Beth Cushman was already there. She had fiery red hair and a fiery Scottish personality to go with it. Beth gestured at the mirror that revealed Gerald Oliver sitting in a chair with his hands cuffed to an iron ring on a metal table.

Beth removed a set of headphones. "He told the arresting officer he's in shock and needs a doctor but hasn't asked for his lawyer yet."

Terrell frowned. "He's playing us. The man knows enough to demand his lawyer. Why doesn't he say so already?"

Roxanne looked through the one-way window. "What's his agenda?"

Beth said, "Maybe to look honest and innocent, in shock and sympathetic, but never admit anything before he finally remembers to ask for his attorney."

Jake said, "He freaked out when Cody found the chase lounge pad. You could frighten him more by saying the scary K-9 is going to search his house."

Beth nodded. "And I'll add that Rox is looking at his internet browsing history."

Jake asked Roxanne, "Are you able to play a video for him in there?"

"Yes, we can wheel in a TV on a stand," Roxanne said. "What did you have in mind?"

"I thought you could show him the footage of Cody searching inside the *Tiburon* and finding the xylazine. And then Terrell can say the dog is going to his house next."

"I like it," Terrell said. "Rox, I sent the video to you."

Roxanne checked her phone and watched Cody at work. "I'll get this ready."

Beth stood up and looked at Terrell. "My turn to be bad cop?"

"I've lost track," Terrell said. "Go for it."

Beth took several deep breaths, opened the interrogation room's door, and stomped inside. She sat across the table from Oliver and began listing all the charges against him.

Terrell waited behind, giving Beth some time alone with the suspect before he joined her. "I wish Chief Pierce would allow Cody into the station. We could have Beth as bad cop and Cody as bad dog."

Jake grinned. "Cody would like that, but the video of him finding tranq on the *Tiburon* will have to do."

Roxanne tapped on her phone screen. "I'm including the

police boat footage of Cody finding urine on the swim deck, lounge pad, and Gerald's hands."

"I wish we had a video of Cody at the perp's house," Jake said.

"Can you fake that, Rox?" Terrell asked.

"I can use AI to create a quick photo of Cody standing on the home's front lawn. Only take a minute."

Jake swiped on his phone. "If you need a picture of Cody for that, I have tons of them."

Roxanne said, "I keep any and all photos and video of Cody. It's quite the collection."

Jake raised his eyebrows. "Because?"

"We have a bond," she said. "He likes me. You said so yourself."

"That's true."

In his view of the interrogation room, Jake saw Beth yell at the suspect and slam her palm onto the table.

"That's my cue," Terrell said. "Send the picture of Cody to Beth's phone."

Roxanne put on headphones and sat down in her chair. She handed a set to Jake, who put them on and took a seat next to her.

While Roxanne worked on the faked photo, Terrell entered the interrogation room and closed the door. Jake heard him say, "Detective Cushman, I specifically asked you to wait for me."

Beth raised her chin at Terrell. "I got tired of waiting. Maybe try being on time for once."

Jake smiled as he observed and listened to the talented team of Beth and Terrell doing their act of good cop, bad cop.

Terrell said, "Mr. Oliver, can I get you anything? A cup of coffee or water?"

Oliver looked at him in apparent surprise. "Why, yes. I could use a drink of water."

Terrell pretended to talk on his phone in a friendly manner. "Please bring a cup of water to the murder suspect in room three."

Oliver closed his eyes for a moment at hearing the words.

Roxanne removed her headphones, grabbed a bottled water and poured some into a paper cup. "Do I look angry?"

Jake assisted her by saying, "Cody busted that dirtbag for murdering Rachel, and now Oliver hates our mutual dog friend and wishes he were dead."

Roxanne became genuinely upset and it showed on her face. She burst into the room, set down Oliver's cup of water, and glared at him for a moment before leaving as fast as she'd come in.

She patted Jake on the back as she passed by to take her seat. "You're good at making women mad."

"It's a gift," Jake said. He didn't add the usual joke about how it was all worth it for the makeup sex, but Rox gave him a knowing look. He shrugged and pointed at the window. "Scooter is letting him have it."

They observed Beth Cushman delivering a blistering verbal attack on Gerald Oliver. She ended her tirade with, "How could you?"

Oliver looked at Terrell for help.

Terrell shrugged. "Sorry, Gerald, but you have to admit that when hearing only one side of the story, you seem guilty. Why not give us your side of what really happened?"

Gerald remained silent.

Beth lied and said, "The same K-9 who found tranq on the *Tiburon* is now searching your house." She showed Oliver the photo Roxanne had sent. "The dog will find additional evidence to put you away for life in prison."

It reminded Jake once again how courts allow police to lie, and the police often do. Why wouldn't they? It was justified as doing something dishonest for the greater good. Jake assuaged his conscience by telling himself that's what he'd done to Oliver.

A uniformed cop walked past Jake and Roxanne, opened the door to the interrogation room, and wheeled the TV on a stand inside.

After the cop left the room, Beth plugged in the TV and played a video of Cody searching the *Tiburon* and finding bags full of xylazine.

Oliver appeared to be in shock as he stared at the screen. "Someone must've planted that on my boat."

Beth said, "I'm sure CSI will find your fingerprints and DNA on at least one of those plastic bags."

"Jake Wolfe pressed a bag into my cuffed hands," Oliver said. "Two police officers witnessed it. Check their body cameras."

"Speaking of your hands . . ." Beth played the arresting officers body camera video of Jake and Cody visiting the *Tiburon*, and Cody finding the seat cushion and then sniffing Oliver's hands.

Beth froze the image. "CSI took swabs of your hands. Will they find traces of your deceased wife's urine?"

Terrell said, "Gerald, I'd advise you to walk us through the chain of events and state your case so you can clear this up and go home."

Oliver's face paled as he appeared to think it over for a moment, then he swallowed hard. "I want my lawyer here to advise me."

Terrell stood up. "That's it. He's requested a lawyer. We can't ask him any more questions."

"He's guilty." Beth stormed out and slammed the door

behind her. She joined Roxanne and Jake. "Now we'll see if he voluntarily keeps talking."

"I'm innocent," Oliver shouted after her.

Terrell nodded. "Every person who stands accused is presumed innocent until proven guilty in a court of law. We'll give you a phone call so your lawyer can get here as soon as possible." He walked to the door and hesitated for a moment. "I can't ask you any questions, but I'm curious if you might have a question for me."

Oliver teared up and began to sob. "I want to know if Rachel fell overboard, or if she jumped and committed suicide."

"CSI will figure out exactly what happened. They're good. Keep in mind, if the murder charge sticks, a judge might sentence you to life in prison. But if you plead guilty to possession of xylazine with intent to distribute, you could do five years or maybe get out in three for good behavior." Terrell left the room.

In the observation area, everyone watched Oliver crying for the cameras.

Jake said, "He's a good actor."

Beth shook her head. "Not good enough. He's going down for murder one."

"Let's go, Jake," Terrell said. "I'll give you a ride back to the police dock and the *Far Niente*."

"Roger that." Jake walked with Terrell, collected his weapons, left the station, and took a seat in the police SUV.

On the drive, Jake said, "Somebody shot at the *Far Niente*. One round ricocheted off the bulletproof glass door."

Terrell raised his eyebrows. "When and where did it happen?"

"This evening, after dinner, at Juanita Yacht Harbor."

Terrell pulled up to the police dock and parked. "Any idea who it might have been?"

"No, but Detective Flynn of the Sausalito PD is going to send me a video from one of their surveillance cameras. I'll forward a copy to you."

"Did your boat's security system get any video?"

"Nothing useful. The perp was in the shadows."

"All right," Terrell said. "Watch your six."

"Will do. I'm going out of town tomorrow. Hopefully this violence won't follow me." Jake exited the vehicle, sent Sarah a text, and boarded the *Far Niente*.

CHAPTER 38

In the morning, Jake drove with Sarah and Cody to the Napa-Sonoma Wine Country to visit the winery where Cody was born and raised. The breeder, Ellen, was now raising his offspring.

Sarah said, "I can't wait to see Cody's puppies again. They've grown and learned so much."

Cody barked once from the back seat at hearing his name and the new word he'd learned. *Puppies.*

"He's a proud papa," Jake said. "Those dogs will change lives."

In the past, Cody had been raised by a dog breeder named Ellen. Her dog kennels were located at a vineyard and winery in Napa that she and her husband owned.

Jake drove through the gorgeous Wine Country with rolling hills covered by well-tended grapevines. After enjoying the scenic drive, he turned onto the property's long driveway that divided two vineyards of cabernet. Arriving at the winery and a beautiful home, Jake parked next to a black Suburban with Agent Yvonne Greene standing next to it.

Jake, Sarah, and Cody exited the Jeep and approached Greene, who wore a dark pantsuit, as usual.

"Are you and Easton on guard duty?" Jake asked.

Greene said, "Easton is on foot patrol, securing the other side of the home." She looked at Cody. "I heard my favorite golden fur ball from hell went and sired a whole litter of fur ball from hell puppies. Look out, world."

Sarah said, "Hello, Agent Greene. Good to see you."

Sarah and Greene had a history. It would please Sarah if the woman transferred to another city far away from Jake.

"Hello, Doctor Sarah. Good to see you as well." Greene tossed her auburn hair as she fixed Sarah in the calm gaze of her sea-blue eyes.

Jake intervened. "Let's go see Faith again and meet McKay's daughter."

He knocked on the door and was greeted by Ellen.

She was in her late forties, got plenty of outdoor exercise raising dogs and tending vines, and had tanned, beautifully calloused hands.

"Come in, come in," Ellen said. "Well, if it isn't Cody Pooh Bear paying a visit. He's a celebrity around here."

Cody woofed at the woman who'd raised him, and sat at her feet, wagging his tail as she made a fuss and scratched him behind the ears.

Ellen led them into her living room, where Agent Shannon McKay sat on a couch with a middle-school-age girl who held a dog across her lap. The girl smiled happily as tears of joy rolled down her cheeks from behind dark sunglasses. The dog licked her face.

Jake knew she had to be Aspen McKay, Shannon's blind daughter. They'd flown all the way from DC to California so Aspen could bond with the K-9 and then bring her home on an Air Force jet.

Agent McKay said, "Jake, thanks again. Aspen loves her dog. Both of them couldn't be happier."

"That's wonderful." Jake was glad he could help the McKay family. Shannon worked long hours in a high-stress job protecting Americans from threats and received no public thanks or recognition. On top of all that, she was raising a blind child. The dog would be an immense help to both mother and daughter.

Ellen said, "Aspen, I'd like you to meet Jake and his golden retriever mix, Cody."

"Hello, Jake and Cody," Aspen said. Faith woofed at Cody, and they both wagged their tails.

"Be friends, Cody," Jake said. "Comfort."

Cody gently nuzzled Faith and then Aspen's hand as she touched his face.

"There's a family resemblance," Aspen said. "Jake, will you sit next to me for a moment?"

"Sure. I'd be happy to." Jake sat down on the couch.

McKay said, "Jake, is it okay with you if Aspen touches your face?"

"Be my guest."

Aspen reached out with one hand. "Can you guide me?"

Jake took her hand in his and guided it to his forehead.

Aspen traced the contours of his face and smiled. "Nice to meet you, Jake. Thanks for giving me one of Cody's puppies. Faith means the world to me."

"I was happy to do it." Jake felt himself getting choked up. "Allow me to introduce Sarah, Cody's veterinarian. I'll move so she can sit here." Jake stood up and gave Sarah his spot on the couch.

Aspen felt Sarah's face in the same manner as she did with Jake. "Wow, you're an animal doctor? That's so cool."

Sarah smiled. Aspen felt it and smiled, too.

Ellen said, "Jake, could I talk to you outside about Dove?"

"Your chestnut mare? Yes, sure." Jake followed Ellen out, and Cody trotted after Jake.

Ellen led them to the corral. "We'll need Cody on a leash because Dove is upset." She clipped a leash to the dog's collar and held on.

Jake approached a beautiful chestnut mare that whinnied and clopped away from him.

"What's wrong with Hell Bitch?"

Ellen sighed in exasperation. "I've told you not to call her that. Her name is Lonesome Dove."

He held out both hands, palms up. "Yeah, but she always bites me like that horse in the book. It's perfectly natural for me to give her the same nickname."

"We had Dove saddled up so Aspen could ride a horse for the first time in her life. A coyote ran through the property, bouncing over fences like a kangaroo, then landed in the corral for a moment and spooked Dove."

"Want me to talk with her?" Jake said.

"Would you please? She loves you."

"I love her, too." He strolled to the corral fence, climbed over, and leaned his back against it.

The mare held eye contact but didn't approach as she usually would have.

"You remember me, Dove. And you know I'd never hurt you."

She whinnied at him, tossed her mane, and stomped one front hoof.

"May I come closer?" He moved cautiously into the center of the corral.

Dove reacted, standing on her hind legs and pawing the air with her front hooves.

Jake froze. He knew those hooves could kill him. "Easy, Dove. Will you meet me halfway?"

He waited, hoping his patient body language would let Dove know he'd stand there all day.

Dove went to the trough for a drink of water, ignoring him.

Jake smiled. She was trouble, but so was he. They were soulmates. "I'm sorry about what you went through, sweetheart."

She looked at him and snorted, water dripping from her mouth.

"Very sorry," he added.

She walked toward him warily and stopped within arm's reach.

Jake didn't grab her reins or saddle horn. He stood there and whispered sweet words about how she was a special horse and how he'd missed her so much since his last visit.

Finally, Dove nickered and pushed her nose against his chest. Jake kissed her on the forehead and patted her neck. "Love you more."

She nodded against him and then gently bit his shoulder.

"Some things never change," he said with a chuckle.

Dove whinnied again and tossed her head.

"Oh, you think you're so funny, huh?" He patted her saddle. "Okay if I ride you, your majesty?"

The horse stood still for him, knowing the pat on leather was a message of intent.

Jake put his left foot in the stirrup, watched for any sign of a fight, and then swung his right leg over and sat in the saddle.

Dove immediately took off at a slow trot, circling the corral.

"Somebody has pent-up energy," Jake said. He noticed Sarah had come out to the corral and stood watching him.

Ellen opened the gate. "Have a nice ride."

"Off we go." Jake nudged the mare, and they headed along a well-worn trail he'd ridden before on the property.

After a few minutes, they came to a brook, where Dove stopped to take a drink. Jake sat in the saddle listening to the babbling brook, birds chirping, and tree leaves rustling in the breeze. He enjoyed the peaceful moment until it was shattered by the sound of gunfire back at the winery.

"Yah!" Jake snapped the reins, and Dove raced up the trail. Upon arrival, he found a black Mercedes-Benz Sprinter Cargo Van with bullet holes in the windshield.

Jake had left his sidearm in the Jeep. He cursed and rode Dove into the barn and quickly put her in a stall. Seeing a pitchfork near a pile of hay, he grabbed it and ran toward Agent Greene's Suburban.

She was underneath the vehicle and fired off two rounds at someone Jake couldn't see.

"Agent G. It's the dog handler. Where's your target?"

"Behind that van," Greene said.

Jake took off running full out with the pitchfork held in both hands. In his mind, he heard a bootcamp drill instructor shouting, *Marines always run toward the fighting.*

CHAPTER 39

Racing past the van, Jake found a gunman with his pistol aimed toward Agent Greene.

Jake charged forward and shoved the pitchfork's four steel tines into the gunman's ribcage from the left side, trying to stab a kidney. The man cried out in pain and turned to shoot his attacker. Jake shoved hard again, using the pitchfork to knock the enemy off his feet. The man stumbled and fell on his right side. Jake kicked the man's gun hand, knocking the pistol out of reach. He then pulled out the pitchfork tines and used the wooden handle to club his opponent on the head.

Reeling from the blow, the stunned man rolled onto his back and groaned. Jake put his entire body weight into stabbing the pitchfork into his enemy's abdomen, going for both kidneys this time. The man screamed, grabbed the tines, and tried to pull them out of his body. Jake held onto the handle, jumped upward, and brought both of his boots down on each side of the fork's top, driving the tines through vital organs and into the ground.

Pinned down by a giant fork, the man writhed in agony. "Get it out of me."

Jake picked up the man's handgun and aimed it at him. "You'll die soon if I don't call an ambulance. Save yourself. Tell me who you are and what you want."

The man coughed up blood, his face paled, and he shivered while going into shock. "The dogs are worth a fortune. I was only following orders."

"Whose orders?"

A rattling wheeze came out of the dying man's mouth, his head dropped to the side, and his eyes lost focus.

Jake shot the man in the head, to make sure he died, and to put him out of his misery. He called out to Greene. "Target down. He said they're here for the dogs."

She replied, "There are five bogies, counting that one."

"Cover me." Jake opened the driver's door of the van and checked for keys. They weren't in the ignition or above the visor. He popped the hood, opened the fuse box, quickly checked a diagram inside, and yanked out the fuse for the fuel pump.

A bullet hit the underside of the open hood and ricocheted down into the engine. Jake dropped and rolled, then commando-crawled behind the van. He stood up, peeked through the windows, and saw a man running toward him. He called out to Greene. "Bogey at your nine o'clock in three, two, one."

Greene waited as the running man passed her Suburban, then she leaned out and shot him in the back.

Jake watched the man fall. He dropped prone, took aim, and fired a headshot that permanently removed another enemy combatant from the fight. "Two down, three to go."

A scream came from inside the house, and it sounded like a young person ... Aspen. Two dogs barked in distress, and he knew one was Cody. He could recognize his K-9's bark anywhere.

Jake's anger flared up, and he saw red before his eyes. "If these criminals are threatening to kill a blind girl and her guide dog, there'll be hell to pay, and I'll deliver the hell, so help me God."

Hurrying to the Jeep, he lifted the back hatch and pulled out the MAC-10 submachine gun he'd taken from a narcoterrorist in Key West. He ran past the Suburban. "I'm going in."

Greene rolled out from under the SUV. "Right behind you."

Jake fired one round upward into a kitchen window and into the ceiling, shattering the glass to cause a panic.

McKay gave the order, "Get down."

Exactly what he wanted. He stepped inside the kitchen and pressed a button to make the garage door rumble upward.

Greene appeared beside him, and he leaned close and whispered, "Go around back. The garage door will create a diversion."

"Roger." She sprinted away with her pistol held up in front of her.

Gunfire broke out, and Sarah shouted profanity in pain or fear or anger. He couldn't tell which. His heart pounded as rage took hold of him.

Moving through the kitchen and closer to the living room, Jake spotted Sarah aiming her handgun at a door.

An armed man kicked the door open and swung his AK-47 rifle in Sarah's direction. She double-tapped him in the chest, causing the man to cry out and drop to his knees.

Jake blasted him with a dozen 9mm rounds and put him down permanently.

The Marine Corps had taught Jake that when you take an enemy down, your team is counting on you to make sure he stays down. Lives were at stake. Do your job, and do it right.

Jake called out to Sarah. "First Mate, your Captain is on the bridge."

"Take the helm," Sarah said.

"I have the helm." Jake rushed into the living room just as the broken door opened again. He unleashed a stream of rounds at an armed man who fell dead. Jake finished him with one shot in the head.

Another man came in, firing a pistol at Jake as he ran. Jake dropped to one knee, fired rounds at center mass, and walked the rounds upward to the assailant's head. He ejected the empty magazine, flipped it around, and inserted the loaded one that was duct-taped to its side. He had thirty-two more rounds available.

Everything went quiet, and nobody moved.

Jake gave Sarah a quick one-armed hug. "Thank you for protecting the McKays and the dogs."

She took a deep, calming breath. "I didn't think. I just reacted."

"Cody, report," Jake said.

His dog barked from behind a high-backed couch near a wall but didn't come out. Jake assumed Cody was protecting Aspen and Faith, and he felt proud of his dog for doing it.

Greene announced herself and entered. "The back is clear. How many down?"

"All five are down," Jake said.

Greene reported to Agent Easton on her shirtsleeve radio mic. "All clear." She then called out to her boss. "Agent McKay, this is Agent Greene. Do you recognize my voice, ma'am? Protocol seven."

McKay replied from behind the couch. "Yes. Give me the code word so I know you're not under duress."

"Nantucket," Greene said, alluding to the island where McKay had dreams of retiring one day.

"Roger that," McKay said with exhaustion in her voice.

Jake set down his weapon and moved to the couch. It was the kind with a high back due to built-in recliner chairs on each end. Agent McKay sat on the floor holding Aspen on her lap, while Aspen held onto Faith. Cody stood guarding them, and Ellen held onto Cody's collar.

"You're all safe now," Jake said. "Good job, Cody."

Agent Shannon McKay stood up, nodded at everyone gratefully, and helped Aspen to her feet. "You were very brave, Aspen."

Aspen let go of her dog, hugged her mother tight, then held out her hand. "To me, Faith." The well-trained guide dog immediately put her head under Aspen's hand.

Jake noticed Faith was alert but poised and calm, totally focused on Aspen and doing her job. She reminded him of a famous guide dog named Roselle who calmly led a blind man named Michael to safety after a hijacked plane flew into the World Trade Center's North Tower and its jet fuel exploded.

"Ellen, may I offer you a hand?" Jake said.

"Yes, please." With help from Jake and Cody, Ellen rose to her feet. "I'm too old for this crapola."

Jake gave her a warm smile. "Well said. Luckily, we're all still alive and kicking, and the Secret Service will pay to repair your house."

"Speaking of kicking, please find out how Dove reacted to the gunfire."

"I'll go check on her right now." Jake clipped a leash onto Cody's collar.

Agent Greene said, "Jake, the police are on their way. Maybe put that submachine gun in your rig and trade it for your sidearm."

"Good advice. Thanks." Jake picked up the weapon on his way out, placed it in the Jeep, strapped on his gun belt, and moved toward the barn. Cody led the way, somehow knowing what his handler had in mind.

In the barn, Jake's heart sank when he saw that Dove had busted out of her stall. "Cody, do you smell Dove?" He led his dog into the stall. Cody sniffed the walls, flooring, hay, and a saddle blanket on top of one stall divider.

"Find Dove, Cody. Seek. Seek. Seek."

Cody set off, following an invisible scent cone. He raised his nose high, and then low, as he trotted down the trail Jake had taken earlier.

It made sense Dove would run away from the gunfire using a familiar route. Jake hoped she hadn't been injured.

At the stream, Cody stopped and tilted his head, then growled. Jake heard it next—the clop-clop-clop of a horse's hooves. Cody pulled at the leash, but Jake held tight. "Cody, wait."

Dove emerged from the trees, ridden by a Mexican-American man dressed in blue jeans and a long-sleeved checkered shirt. He smiled and waved. "*Hola,* Jake."

Jake waved in reply. "Santiago, thank God you found Dove."

"She ran right up to us in the vineyard, all excited," Santiago said. "Took me a while to calm her down. Was that gunfire I heard?"

"Yes, some men tried to steal the dogs, but we're all okay and the police have arrived."

Santiago was the talented viticulturist of Ellen's vineyards and in charge of a crew that tended the vines. Whenever he came up to the house, he always said hello to Dove and gave her a sugar cube or a carrot. Jake had met him several times and admired the gifted man's talent for producing excellent grapes year after year.

Cody barked at Santiago and Dove.

"*Buen perro*, Cody," Santiago said, telling Cody he was a good dog. "Jake, can you ride Dove home? I have to get back to work."

"Stay in the saddle for one second." Jake took a picture and texted it to Ellen. "Okay, I'll take Dove from here."

Santiago dismounted and handed Jake the reins. His phone chimed and he fished it out of his pocket. "Hello . . . Yes, Ellen? . . . Oh, *Señorita* Dove? She came and found me . . . No, I'm not a hero . . . Well, thanks . . . Okay. Talk to you later."

Jake grinned. "I told her you were the hero who brought Dove home safe."

Santiago shrugged. "All in an honest day's work, *hermano*."

"When can you and the family go on another cruise to Angel Island for a picnic?"

"Gotta check with the boss and let you know." Santiago gave a sigh. "Every weekend we have fútbol games, baseball games, swimming, gymnastics, cross-country . . . whatever is in season."

Jake knew the man and his wife had many children. "Give my best to Paloma."

"I will," Santiago said. "She asked me if you'd married Sarah yet. Paloma expects you to have lots of kids and bring them to visit us often."

Jake laughed. "How could I be married if you didn't get an invitation?"

The look on Santiago's face told Jake he appreciated being on the invite list, if a wedding ever happened, which he doubted. "Tell Sarah I said hello."

"All right, *hermano*," Jake said. "See you again soon."

"See you." Santiago took off at a brisk jog, heading back to the grapevines, his passion in life.

Jake mounted Dove and patted her neck. "Let's go home."

As they came closer to the house, he heard a police radio squawk. Jake took out his phone and called McKay. "Please tell the police I'm a volunteer K-9 handler for the US Marshals. I'm wearing a badge and a gun, and I'm approaching on horseback with my dog trotting beside me."

"Roger that," McKay said. "They're expecting you."

CHAPTER 40

Napa police officials spent hours at the winery, and Jake had to answer a lot of questions. A cleaning and repair service shampooed the carpets, fixed the broken door, and replaced the shattered window.

Jake found Sarah, McKay, and Aspen sitting at an outdoor dining area. He told McKay, "I promised Ellen the Secret Service will pay for the repairs to her house."

McKay raised her eyebrows. "You caused most of the damages."

He shrugged. "While I was working for you."

"Not officially."

"Pay for it using the reward you're collecting for the kung fu guy in Key West."

"Changquan," she corrected him. "Okay, that works."

"How did Aspen take all of this? She appears unfazed."

"She's a trooper," McKay said. "And Faith never left her side."

"Ellen raises some amazing dogs," Jake said. "Faith might be the best one ever."

Aspen, sitting at one of the nearby tables with Faith, spoke up. "I certainly think so."

Jake said, "Aspen, is it politically correct to ask if blind people have better hearing?"

"It's fine with me," Aspen said. "And yes, my hearing is better developed than the average person who never listens."

"Out of the mouths of babes," Jake said.

Ellen approached them. "I hope you're all still planning to spend the night in our guesthouse. I'll have my chef serve a dinner made from our own homegrown chickens, garden vegetables, and fine wines. It would help everyone readjust after what we've been through."

McKay said, "Yes, the Secret Service will deploy a protection team here, if that's all right with you."

"Anything you need," Ellen said.

"We'll stick around, too," Jake said. "I'm here for the wine, to be honest."

Ellen smiled. "A man of good taste." She gave Sarah a wink.

Jake went out to the barn and stables, where he repaired the door on Lonesome Dove's stall. She bit his right biceps in thanks.

"Love you, too, Hell Bitch."

McKay entered the barn to have a moment in private with Jake. "None of the men who attacked us were carrying ID. We put the prints into AFIS, the automated fingerprint identification system, and one set matched a wanted terrorist."

Jake frowned. "They weren't here to steal priceless K-9s?"

"That was a cover story," McKay said. "I believe they were assassins . . . sent here to kill us."

"Who sent them? The xylazine drug kingpin I'm hunting down?"

"We believe he may have put a contract out on whoever has been sabotaging his network."

Jake held her gaze. "You and me."

McKay looked out the open barn door. "I'm letting the local cops handle things for now. Ellen doesn't need to know this intel."

"May I inform Terrell Hayes?" Jake took out his phone.

"Yes, keep him in the loop." McKay headed back to the house.

Jake sent Terrell a terse situation report and ended with, *I'll debrief you tomorrow.*

Sarah wandered into the barn, appearing lost and vulnerable. Jake hugged her for a long time without a word, and she clung to him and cried.

Finally, she let go and wiped her eyes. "I killed a man. Now that my adrenaline has worn off, I think I'm in shock."

Jake shook his head. "No, you shot a terrorist in self-defense. And you saved lives. Keep that in mind."

"I feel like going to bed, pulling the covers over my head, and sleeping in the fetal position for hours."

"If that's how you feel, that's what we'll do," Jake said. "Let's go to the guesthouse." He sent a text to McKay, letting her know.

He led Sarah to their room. In bed, she curled up to Jake, and he put one arm around her shoulders. Cody leapt up and lay at their feet.

"You wounded him, but I killed him," Jake said. "This is on my shoulders, not yours."

Rubbing Sarah's back until she fell asleep, he held her and thought about Lake Tahoe as he listened to the soft breathing of his sleeping girlfriend and dog.

Later that evening, when things quieted down, the group

enjoyed a simple but delicious dinner, along with well-aged collectible bottles of wine from the cellar.

After the meal, everybody headed off to their bedrooms while a team of armed Secret Service agents roamed the property. A sniper stood guard on the roof, and one of the Suburbans sat parked near the road, blocking the long driveway.

Jake slept well knowing some of the world's best elite armed professionals were protecting him and his loved ones.

In the morning, Ellen's chef served a buffet breakfast. Jake put together plates of food and delivered them to Secret Service agents standing guard outside. Sarah handed out to-go cups of coffee.

After the meal, everyone said their goodbyes, and Jake drove home to the Bay Area. Sarah and Cody both fell asleep as Jake sipped coffee and kept driving until he arrived at Sarah's apartment.

A locksmith's van sat parked in front, painted with a logo of a key and words offering a variety of services, twenty-four hours a day. A cheerful, middle-aged couple stepped out, met with Jake, and handed him a set of keys.

"Thank you so much," Jake said. "Sarah, these are the same locksmiths who fixed the door to your clinic when FBI Agent Reynolds busted it down. Beth Cushman gave me their number."

The husband-and-wife team shook hands with Jake and Sarah and drove off in their van.

Sarah accepted the keys from Jake. "Thanks. How did you do this without permission from my landlord?"

"Oh, I had permission. A polite phone call from Bart

saying there's no need for a lawsuit against the landlord worked wonders."

"Thank Bart for me." Sarah checked her mailbox, tore open an envelope, and showed Jake a check for thousands of dollars. "Insurance payout. They said the Fresno Police found my car in a chop shop, stripped for parts."

"We can do some online car shopping."

"What are your plans for today?"

"To hang out until you're ready, and then drive you to work."

Sarah kissed him and headed up the stairs.

Jake and Cody followed, and Jake thought maybe, with luck, they'd have an ordinary, peaceful day for once.

CHAPTER 41

At eight o'clock a.m., Police officer Tammi Martinelli positioned herself diagonally across 7th Street from the front doors of County Jail #2. She waited in the city's vehicle impound parking lot, hidden behind a tall chain-link fence covered with a canvas privacy screen that kept the cars out of sight.

Tammi had her body camera turned off as she lay in the bed of a pickup truck that was backed up to the fence and parked under the highway overpass. The only way anybody could see her would be if they entered the secure lot, walked right up next to the pickup, and looked into the truck bed. With the tailgate down, she used a monocular to gaze through a circular hole she'd cut in the fence and cover.

Gerald Oliver's lawyer had convinced a judge his client wasn't a flight risk. In a few minutes, the jail would release Oliver on bail.

Dressed in her dark blue police uniform, Tammi hadn't drawn any attention to herself when appearing in the lot with a sheet of paper in her hand. And what better disguise to wear when you flee a murder? Although she preferred to think of it as capital punishment.

Waiting with the patience of a big-game hunter, she looked across the street and observed a reporter facing a camera while holding a microphone and talking in an overly-dramatic voice.

Tammi couldn't hear her but knew the story well. Gerald Oliver, the wealthy pillar of society, had been charged with murdering his wife, Rachel, in order to collect her life insurance and avoid a costly divorce.

His online browsing history revealed how he'd checked her policy's terms, looked up California divorce laws, and read all about the risks of drowning in cold water.

An anonymous tip to the police revealed Gerald had been cheating on Rachel with an internet fashion influencer named Brandi, and she'd dumped him the moment he'd come under scrutiny. Brandi fled to Mexico and began dating a famous Latin musician. She appeared in entertainment news stories with headlines such as, "Brandi turns heads in a daring red bikini on vacation in Cozumel."

The district attorney held a press conference and promised Gerald Oliver would stand trial for murder and possession of xylazine with intent to distribute.

Oliver was a wealthy man who could afford to pay the four-million-dollar bail and his high-priced team of lawyers. The well-connected millionaire may have also pulled some political strings.

His dead wife, Rachel, had been one of Tammi's old friends from years before. They hadn't kept in touch very often, having gone down different paths in life, but remaining on good terms.

When Tammi saw Gerald on the news being perp-walked into jail, she'd studied his body language and facial expression, and felt in her heart that he was guilty of murder. It was an Italian woman's intuition. Men could doubt that power at their own risk. She'd wanted to punch Gerald's smug, Botoxed face repeatedly until he confessed.

Thinking of Rachel's murder reminded Tammi that someone had thrown a knife at the door of Sarah Chance's apartment. Who had done it, and why? Were they after Sarah because she was a woman? Or, because she was the girlfriend of Jake Wolfe, a man with enemies?

Jake was one of the few people who knew that in addition to being a cop, Tammi had taken the oath of *omertà*, the Family's pledge of loyalty and secrecy. Tammi had earned the nickname Razor when she'd allegedly killed an evil man by posing as a barber and slitting his throat with a straight razor while giving him a shave.

Too bad she couldn't get Gerald Oliver into a barber's chair.

Aiming her monocular to the right, Tammi observed the crowd of reporters and camera operators growing restless. They stood near the building that housed both Jail #2 and the Intake and Release Center, which shared a common lobby.

As reporters shouted questions, she spotted her target emerging from the door. Oliver was flanked by a beefy sheriff deputy and a slender woman in an expensive suit, whom she recognized from TV news segments as a celebrity lawyer.

Gerald wore sunglasses, and they all had stern expressions on their faces. Upon reaching the sidewalk, the sheriff escort withdrew, headed back inside, and closed the door.

Reporters continued shouting questions at Oliver and his lawyer. Tammi frowned at seeing Oliver's pompous smile. It was go time. She grasped a hunting crossbow in her gloved hands and aimed it through the fence hole at her target. It was one of the only reliably deadly weapons that could kill from a distance but didn't give off gunshot residue to taint your clothing with evidence.

One reporter shouted louder than the rest. "How in the world did you make bail?"

As Oliver was about to slip into a waiting limo, he turned, looked at the news cameras, and answered the question in an overly sincere voice. "Truth and justice prevailed for . . ."

Tammi fired the crossbow, and its big-game hunting arrow struck Oliver in the heart, one split second after he spoke his favorite and final word: ". . . me."

A roar erupted from the shocked crowd of reporters as news camera operators broadcast the man's untimely demise to their viewers.

The door to the building opened, and several uniformed sheriff deputies ran outside. Tammi was shocked to see one of them who looked like a former police coworker. That wasn't possible because the woman currently resided in a rehab facility.

Dropping the crossbow, Tammi slipped out of the truck bed and ran with her head down. She moved along the inside of the fence, behind a row of parked cars, and quickly reached a corner near a large eucalyptus tree. She climbed over a section of fence where she'd previously placed a weighted blanket to cover the razor wire and dropped to the sidewalk of Harrison Street. Her police cruiser was illegally parked next to the fence, ready for a quick getaway up the onramp to Interstate 80.

As Tammi moved toward her car, a woman ran around the corner. She looked like a former police officer named Corrine Denton. Tammi was shocked to see the emotionally unstable person wearing a sheriff's uniform with its seven-pointed gold badge pinned above her left breast pocket.

Denton's eyes were cold and calculating when they fixated upon Tammi as if measuring her body for a coffin. Denton drew her pistol and shouted, "Sheriff. Hands above your head."

Tammi raised her hands. "Police officer. Hold your fire, Denton."

Denton looked at Tammi's gloved hands and jumped to conclusions. "You killed Gerald Oliver. You're under arrest for murder."

"No, I saw that blanket and pulled over to investigate." Tammi risked lowering her left hand to her shoulder microphone and pressing the button. "Officer needs assistance. Outside jail number two."

Denton shouted, "Drop the gun." She pulled the trigger on her pistol three times, apparently going for the classic two in the chest and one in the head.

Tammi took one misaimed round in the stomach that knocked her back on her heels, making her stumble and turn to the side. The second round hit her police car, and the third zipped past her ear with a high-pitched whine.

Clutching her painful stomach, Tammi crumpled to the ground, holding onto her shoulder mic for dear life. "Officer down. I've been shot by Corrine Denton. Attempted one eight seven. Repeat. Officer down, shot by Corrine Denton."

Police sirens immediately approached from all directions as Denton stood over Tammi and looked down with a cruel smile on her face.

"You're under arrest for murder," Denton said. "You'll get life in prison for this, and your new friends will abuse you every night."

Two police cars screeched to a halt, and uniformed cops stepped out.

Police Officer Wilson shouted, "Denton, stand back from Martinelli. Let me see your hands."

Holding a pair of metal handcuffs in her right hand, Denton spun toward Wilson.

Wilson drew his sidearm.

CHAPTER 42

At Sarah's apartment, Jake waited until she'd changed into work clothes, then gave her a ride to the pet clinic. She went inside, and Jake talked for a moment with Beppe, who stood protectively out in front.

Beppe said, "Don't worry. I've got this."

"Thanks, but I don't think the assassins were after Sarah. They were sent to stop the tranq hunters—me, my dog, and my fed boss."

"Well, if any more show up here, that'll be the last thing they do," Beppe said.

Jake drove off and wondered if Terrell had time to meet for a situation report about Napa.

He pulled over and sent a text. *Sitrep with coffee and pie?*

Terrell replied. *Affirmative. When and where?*

Jake typed. *Anytime. You know where.*

Terrell confirmed. *See you in 15 minutes at Billie's.*

Jake drove to the restaurant and found a parking spot down the street. He led Cody on a leash to an old-fashioned diner that had the best pie in town.

Terrell pulled up in his police SUV, stopped in a no-parking zone, and tossed a city permit on the dashboard. He grabbed the radio mic. "Ten-seven, for coffee at Billie's Diner." He recited the address, stepped out of the car, and asked Jake, "Why not use your fed parking permit?"

"I'm being careful not to draw any attention from Chief Deputy Garcia," Jake said. "Meanwhile, I'm going to make an exact copy with my new three-D printer."

"The printer that can make ghost guns? Firearms without serial numbers?"

Jake reached for the door. "Yep. I bought it online."

"Signs of the apocalypse."

Cody woofed at his good friend Terrell.

"Hello, fuzzy butt." Terrell patted Cody on the back.

They all went inside, and Billie greeted them like family. Wearing a blue apron, the attractive grandmother exuded the Southern hospitality of her native Nashville. "Well, now. You three come in and set a spell. It's about time my favorite boys stopped by to see little old Billie. I was getting worried about y'all."

"We've been away in the Florida Keys," Terrell said.

"Ah, one of my favorite places in the world."

Jake said, "But Cody missed you so much we had to hurry back."

Billie smiled at him. "You do carry on." Looking down at Cody, she added, "I missed you, too."

Cody woofed and pawed at the floor.

"Be friends, Cody," Jake said, letting his dog off leash.

Cody trotted straight to Billie and pressed his head against her stomach, wagging his tail.

She ruffled his ears. "What a good boy you are."

Terrell sat down in a window booth, and Billie was quick

to pour him a cup of coffee. "Brain fuel for the smartest detective."

"You're too good to me, Billie."

Jake sat across from Terrell, and Cody automatically sat on the floor next to his handler.

"I'll be right back with some pie," Billie told them after pouring coffee for Jake.

Jake raised his eyebrows at Terrell. "Did you order pie?"

"No, I guess Billie ordered for us," Terrell said with a smile.

A waitress hurried past, carrying a tray of breakfast orders to another table. She glanced at Jake as she passed and made eye contact for one second.

Terrell said, "What is it with you?"

"Do I look like I'm an easy lay?"

"And a big spender?"

"It's my awesome dog," Jake said. "Chicks dig it."

Billie returned and set down two plates with slices of apple pie à la mode. "Baked this morning and still warm."

Jake took a bite of heaven. Melt-in-your-mouth apples and buttery crust, topped with cool vanilla ice cream. "This is the breakfast of champions. I want to eat this every morning for the rest of my life."

Terrell's phone buzzed with a call. "Hayes." He listened for a moment and then cursed.

Billie looked at him in surprise. "Do you talk to your mother with that mouth?"

"Sorry, Billie. I have to go. Officer down. Attempted code one eight seven."

"Tell me it isn't Scooter," Jake said, referring to Terrell's homicide detective partner, Beth Cushman.

"No." Terrell said. "Martinelli."

Now it was Jake's turn to curse. He and Tammi Martinelli

were friends with a rocky history but were bound to each other by the Italian oath of *omertà*.

Billie handed each of them cardboard cups for their coffee, and to-go containers for their pie. Cody stood up, sniffed Jake's pie and ice cream, and wolfed it down.

Jake let out a long breath. "I won't be needing a to-go container."

Cody licked his snout and quirked a brow, giving Jake an innocent look.

As the three of them headed out the door, Billie called out, "Please be careful, boys."

Terrell took a seat in his police SUV and lowered the window. "Tammi is alive and in an ambulance on her way to the hospital. I'm heading there now. You want to ride with me?"

"No, I'll meet you there," Jake said. "I have to call Anselmo Amborgetti, and you can't be privy to our conversation."

"Understood." Terrell drove away with lights flashing and siren wailing, making other cars pull over to let him pass.

Jake made a phone call as he drove to the hospital.

"Little Buddy," the extra-large man answered.

"Big Mo, someone shot Razor," Jake said. "Attempted murder. She's in an ambulance heading to the ER."

Anselmo was silent for a moment and then spoke in a menacing voice. "Who shot Tammi? I want a name. He'll be dead by sundown."

"I don't know yet, but Razor obviously needs the Family to protect her."

"I'll send our people to the hospital," Anselmo said. "Including Vito."

"Tell Vito I'll meet him there."

"I knew the Family could always count on Giacobbe il

Coltello," Anselmo said, using the nickname "Jake the Knife," bestowed upon Jake by his Italian relatives.

"Always," Jake said. "I'll call you again when I know more." He clicked off and pocketed his phone.

"This is bad, Cody."

Jake broke the speed limit, driving like a bank robber, and forgetting to use the Jeep's installed police lights. No cops in the city would write him a speeding ticket because he was the de facto lawyer of every officer on the force, including Chief Pierce.

When he arrived at the hospital, his friend Vito stood waiting. The man always wore the finest Italian suits and shoes and a semi-amused look on his face. Right then, he didn't appear amused at all.

"How is she?" Jake asked.

"She was gut-shot up close, but a bulletproof vest saved her life."

"That's gotta hurt bad, though," Jake said.

"She's being evaluated for possible blunt-force trauma to internal organs. Nuns are praying for her." Vito cursed loudly and waved his hands, sending people scattering.

"Easy, brother," Jake said, leading his emotional friend inside before a citizen journalist recorded and posted a video on social media.

As they walked along the hospital hallways, Jake noted there were uniformed police officers out in force.

Vito checked his phone and looked at Jake. "I found out who shot Razor."

"Who is he? Mo wants his name."

"He is a she. Corrine Denton."

Jake stopped walking. "I thought that angry nut job was in a rehab center far away from here."

"Now she's back, rehabilitated, and working as a

detention deputy at jail number two on Seventh Street," Vito said.

"What in the literal f—" Jake was interrupted by the vibration of his phone. He thumbed the answer icon. "This is Jake."

A woman's voice he recognized said, "I'm coming for you . . . and your dog." The call dropped.

"That was Denton," Jake said. "She called on a burner phone to gloat and threaten Cody."

"We won't let her near Cody."

Jake said, "Police Chief Pierce will have to call the new chief deputy sheriff and let her know their HR department made a terrible mistake by hiring Denton."

"Denton needs to be in an unsolved hit-and-run accident," Vito muttered under his breath.

"Not an option." Jake had always tried to avoid causing harm to women. He was an old-fashioned knight in rusty armor. But even though he was a caveman relic, Denton had shot a policewoman and threatened his volunteer US Marshals K-9. That made her a criminal who belonged in prison.

Terrell walked up to them, and Jake asked, "Why would the sheriff's office hire Denton?"

Terrell frowned. "I just heard the bad news. Most US cities are experiencing a shortage of qualified candidates for law enforcement jobs. Staffing is as low as it's ever been, and so is LEO morale nationwide. This is a rough time to be a cop with all of this crazy talk about defunding the police."

"Wasn't Denton taking anti-psychotic meds to treat delirium or whatever?" Jake said.

"Psychosis, but she completed rehabilitation," Terrell said. "Many law enforcement agencies have had to lower their hiring standards lately."

"They should pay more," Jake said. "Raise the starting salary for recruits, and increase it even more for veteran officers."

"Denton was cop-hopping. That's where a troubled officer resigns to avoid getting fired and losing their certification, then hops to another agency."

"I thought Chief Pierce fired her."

"Nope. Denton resigned for medical issues," Terrell said. "When she applied to the sheriff's department, her résumé listed plenty of past training and experience. The chief deputy sheriff gave her a chance."

"And Denton shot a uniformed police officer," Jake said. "She needs to be decertified by the state commission on Peace Officer Standards and Training."

"Denton would simply move to another state and cop-hop again," Terrell said.

"At least we'd be rid of her."

"When Gerald Oliver took an arrow in the chest, Denton was one of the jail deputies who were sent outside to find and arrest the shooter. She claims to have witnessed Martinelli drop a crossbow and climb over a fence while wearing nitrile gloves."

"She's lying," Jake said. "I've been to that jail. The impound lot across the street is hidden by a fence with a privacy screen. I'll subpoena her body camera video."

Terrell didn't comment on the time Jake had been locked up in that jail after being arrested by Denton's former partner, Ray Kirby.

They rode the elevator up, and a uniformed cop allowed Jake and Terrell access, but not Vito, who scowled and said a few choice words in Italian.

CHAPTER 43

Jake walked down a hospital hallway with Terrell and Cody by his side. He'd changed the Velcro patch on Cody's vest for one that said "Therapy K-9."

Terrell stopped for a word with a fellow cop. "Jake, I'll catch up with you in a minute."

Jake continued on, and a uniformed male police officer he didn't know stepped forward, eyes on the duo.

Jake held out the US Marshals star and creds. "Friend of Officer Tammi Martinelli. We worked together on a task force." He displayed a picture on his phone of Tammi standing next to him and his dog, all of them wearing bulletproof vests.

The guard swept his hand. "Go ahead."

"Thank you." Jake arrived at a room with a large window closed off by vertical blinds that were open an inch and allowed him to peek in.

Two cops stood outside the door. One of them was Jake's friend, Officer Wilson. "Jake, I knew you'd show up quickly."

"Not as quick as you, Wilson." Jake shook hands. "What happened?"

"Somebody shot Gerald Oliver with an arrow. Denton claimed it was Martinelli."

Jake was one of the few people who knew that might be possible. "That's absurd. Does Denton have body-cam video to back up her crazy accusation?"

"I guess we'll find out," Wilson said. "When I told Denton to show me her hands, she was holding a pair of handcuffs. It looked like a gun, so I drew my sidearm and almost shot her."

Jake smiled at the man. "Did that lower Denton's enthusiasm a little?"

"Oh yeah," Wilson said. "Now I'm in trouble with the chief."

Jake glanced at Tammi's door. "What kind of damage are we looking at?"

"Blunt-force trauma gut punch from one round to the bulletproof vest. It missed the liver above and the pancreas below."

Jake blew out a breath. "Whew. No penetration?"

"No. Only the equivalent of a hammer to the stomach and intestines. The vest saved her life." Wilson held his hand out to Cody, who was watching his every move. "How ya doing, buddy?"

"Be friends, Cody," Jake said.

Cody sniffed Wilson's hand and let out a whine as the familiar cop ruffled his ears.

"He's upset," Jake said.

"Can he smell Martinelli inside the room?"

"Yeah, he can smell her adrenaline and body chemistry. If she was bleeding, he'd run in there when the door opens."

"Internal bleeding only, but it's going to be okay."

"How are you so well informed?"

"I'm dating a nurse."

Jake raised his eyebrows at the man who was near retirement age. "Good for you."

An attractive female senior citizen dressed in nurse scrubs stopped by and looked at Jake with a wary eye.

Wilson said, "You can trust my good friend, Jake."

She hugged Wilson and then spoke to Jake. "The doctors said Tammi won't need surgery."

"That's good to hear."

"Are you related?" the nurse asked, glancing at his dark hair and eyes.

"No, I'm her lawyer, Jake Wolfe."

"Oh, she said Jake would come."

While the nurse continued talking, a woman slipped past behind Jake into Tammi's room.

Cody barked and tugged at the leash.

"What is it, boy?" Jake said.

Cody pawed at the window, knocking the vertical blinds aside.

Jake spotted Sheriff Denton in plain clothes, wearing her badge and gun and a ball cap. She held up her phone and recorded a video as she leaned over Tammi and appeared to be asking questions and demanding answers.

"Oh, hell no." Jake moved toward the door, displayed his Marshals star to the cop, and went inside, taking video with his phone.

Tammi, high on pain meds, spoke in a weak, groggy voice. "I want my lawyer. I take the Fifth Amendment right to remain silent and not testify against myself."

Denton scowled. "That means you're guilty."

Jake spoke in a low, threatening voice. "Get away from her."

Denton put one hand on the holstered pistol at her side.

"Do you think you can outgun a Marine?" Jake said, staring her down.

She hesitated, looking death in the face.

He gestured at an upper corner of the room. "There are cameras in here. Draw your weapon. Give me a reason to defend myself."

Denton swallowed hard. "I'm on the job."

"Not for long. You shot a uniformed police officer. Your career is over."

"No, you and Martinelli will leave town. I'll own this city."

"Do you want to walk out of the hospital under your own power, or wearing handcuffs and perp-walked on your tiptoes by two police officers in front of TV cameras?"

She glared at him. "They wouldn't dare."

"How about if my friends in the media ruin your life? You'd wake up in the morning to news vans parked in front of your home, reporters shouting questions and shoving microphones in your face, and voicemails from your boss saying not to come in to work."

"This isn't over yet."

"We agree on something."

"You'll be sorry."

"Speak for yourself." Jake stood next to Tammi's bed, ready to protect her with his own life. He'd sworn the omertà and would honor his oath to the Family.

Before Denton walked out, never taking her hand off the sidearm, she said, "This criminal murdered Gerald Oliver, and she's going to be arrested tomorrow."

Jake kept his eyes on her as she left. "If anyone gets arrested, it'll be you."

Denton slammed the door.

Tammi let out a long breath and allowed her heavy eyelids

to close. "Thank you, Jake . . ." Her voice trailed off, and her breathing slowed.

"You're welcome. You'd do the same for me."

She tried to reach out for him.

Jake held her hand as she fell asleep. "Rest easy, Tammi. We'll be right here."

There was a knock on the door, and Terrell entered. "I told the new cop that Denton may not come near Martinelli."

"I couldn't believe he let her in here."

"He's new, from out of town. Never seen Denton before. She badged him and claimed to be Tammi's friend."

"Denton's face will be on every news program within the hour," Jake said. "A uniformed sheriff deputy shoots a uniformed police officer? That's never happened before."

Terrell looked at Tammi with concern. "Wilson told me she's going to be okay. She took a brutal hit in the stomach but didn't suffer a hernia."

"Not yet, anyway," Jake said. "Wilson's nurse friend said Tammi needs to rest in bed and not do anything that would put a strain on her abdomen and belly button."

Terrell studied Jake's face. "Vito is pacing back and forth in the lobby like a caged animal. If he crosses paths with Denton . . ."

"I'll ask Wilson's nurse friend to list Vito as family—a cousin—then he can visit Tammi."

"Good plan. I'm going to make sure Denton leaves the building." Terrell walked to the door.

"Send Wilson in here," Jake said.

Terrell exited, and Wilson came inside. "Sorry I didn't catch Denton slinking past behind you. I was focused on my girlfriend, and didn't notice someone with a badge and gun passing by."

"Listen, one of Tammi's cousins wants to see her. Could

your nurse friend list Vito Amborgetti as family so he can visit?"

"Hmm, I may have heard of that Family," Wilson said with a wink.

"They would owe you a favor," Jake said. "A limo ride to their five-star restaurant any night except Friday or Saturday, where you and your lady will enjoy fine dining at no charge."

"You talked me into it." Wilson pulled out his phone and sent a text message. He read the reply. "Wait five minutes, and tell Vito he's on the list."

"Thanks. Now that I think of it, add Beppe Amborgetti on there, too."

"Does that earn me another winner-winner chicken dinner?"

Jake squinted at him. "No, but I'll add a free bottle of fine wine to your meal."

Wilson grinned, sent another text, and left the room.

Vito arrived and took a picture of Tammi asleep with Jake standing guard, wearing a badge and gun. "I sent that to Anselmo."

Jake understood. Big Mo always wanted proof that his orders were being carried out. "Tell him I'll be the one to stay by her side."

Vito looked at Jake's US Marshals star. "No one else can be here after visiting hours unless they're wearing a badge."

"I'll protect her with my life," Jake said.

"The Family thanks you." Vito invoked the code words that meant Jake was doing an enormous favor and the Family owed him one in return. He gave Jake a nod and walked out.

Jake took out his phone to let Sarah know what was going on. This would require some finesse. He couldn't say, "I'll have to miss our dinner date because I'm going to spend the evening in Tammi's room."

He composed a text. *Sarah, our mutual friend Officer Tammi Martinelli has been shot, but a bulletproof vest saved her life. She's sedated and asleep. I'm at the hospital with Cody, Terrell, Wilson, and Vito. We'll be here a while. You're invited to join us when you get off work.*

Sarah didn't reply.

CHAPTER 44

In the morning, sheriff deputies swarmed into the hospital room and claimed Tammi was under arrest for the murder of Gerald Oliver.

Jake argued with them, using every legal reason he could come up with. The sheriffs far outnumbered the police because many cops who'd been there in the evening were gone.

One sheriff handed Jake some papers. "We have a warrant for her arrest. It's all legal and proper. If you fight us, we'll have to arrest you for aiding and abetting the suspect in resisting arrest."

Jake glanced at the warrant. "Calm down. I'm a friend of Chief Deputy Sheriff Ritter."

The sheriff rolled his eyes. "Yeah, sure you are. Gerald Oliver was killed by an arrow. Denton witnessed Martinelli dropping a crossbow into a pickup truck bed, running along the fence, and climbing over an area covered by a thick blanket. We have the crossbow in evidence."

"Denton is an unreliable witness," Jake said. "How could she see behind a privacy screen? Does she have X-ray vision?"

"This is your last chance to step aside, or go to jail along with the murder suspect."

Jake stood aside while they took Tammi away on a stretcher in handcuffs, transporting her to jail. "Stay strong, Tammi. I'll work on getting you bailed out ASAP."

Tammi held his eyes, silently pleading for help as a sheriff wheeled her out.

Jake saw Denton standing by the elevators. She sneered at him as another deputy pushed Tammi's gurney into an empty elevator and she joined them.

A Black female sheriff stayed behind when the others left. She said to Jake, "Alicia Hayes is my daughter's third grade teacher."

"You're lucky," Jake said. "Alicia is the best teacher ever."

"As a sheriff, I wanted to let you know that many of us are sorry we had to arrest a cop. We can't even believe it."

"It's not your fault. You were following orders. Just be careful around Corrine Denton. I think she may be criminally insane."

"That would explain this mess," she said.

Jake gave her his lawyer business card, left the hospital, and took Cody for a walk. He then sat in the Jeep, sent a text to Anselmo Amborgetti, and drove to the law offices of Gregory "Bart" Bartholomew so he could prepare for his jail visitation with Tammi.

He entered and said hello to the receptionist, a South Korean woman named Moon Hee. She had long, perfectly straight, silky black hair and was well-dressed in professional office attire with a feminine touch. Her slender, knee-length gray pencil skirt, ivory silk blouse, and shiny black pumps accentuated her figure but weren't overtly provocative. In her spare time, she sang in a local K-pop group of four Korean women.

Jake always kept a suit and tie and a pair of dress shoes in the conference room at the firm. He went there to get dressed in his "disguise," as he called it. He took off his street clothes and pulled on a pair of black suit pants. As he reached for a white Oxford shirt with a button-down collar, the door opened and Moon Hee entered the room carrying a stack of file folders.

She set them on the conference table and then spotted Jake. "Oh, I'm so sorry." She blushed upon seeing him shirtless.

Jake pulled on his shirt. "No worries. If you've seen one man's bare chest, you've seen them all."

She stared at him. "Not one with that many scars. How are you not dead?"

Jake buttoned up his shirt, tucked it in, and zipped his pants. "Dumb luck, I guess."

"That angry red scar by your left collar bone must be the recent one I heard about."

Jake still had a round entry wound scar the size of a silver dollar on his upper chest. "I'm lucky the bullet went clean through like an arrow. I have a matching red scar on my back from the exit wound."

He tied his classic plain tie without using a mirror, stepped into his shiny black leather dress shoes, put on the black suit jacket, and moved toward the door.

"Wait a minute." Moon reached out and straightened his tie.

It was an innocent, helpful gesture by a friend with a perfectionist streak, but it felt surprisingly intimate to Jake, like a wife and husband routine. They both noticed it in an awkward moment, but neither spoke.

The door opened, and Bart entered. He saw Moon's hands on the tie, and Jake's discarded clothing on a chair. "Excuse me. Is this a bad time?"

Moon withdrew her hands as if Jake's tie was red hot. "No, I was only..."

Bart said, "You both know I prohibit relationships among my staff."

"Moon dropped off those files and noticed I couldn't get my tie right without a mirror. It was crooked, and she fixed it like you would have. That's all. I give you my word, Bart."

Bart paused for a moment. "I did ask her to deliver those files here, and I'll take your word of honor any day of the week. Besides, Sarah would shoot you."

"You're right, as usual."

Moon Hee stood there like a deer in the headlights.

Bart said kindly, "You may go back to work, Ms. Hee. No harm, no foul."

Moon rushed down the hallway to the front desk.

Jake said, "I'm headed to the jail."

"It will seem familiar, eh?"

Jake ignored Bart's friendly dig about past indiscretions. "We can't leave Tammi in there. Her life is at risk."

"Agreed. Do your best to get her out. Call me if you need my help. I'm friends with the mayor and other people who can intervene."

"Thanks. I'm sure I'll be calling you."

"Get going, and take your laundry with you." Bart opened several of the file jackets and flipped through papers, dismissing Jake.

Jake grabbed his clothes he'd almost left behind, and as he was leaving the building, he smiled kindly at Moon, who covered her face with her hands.

"I'm sorry, Moon. I should have locked the door." He went outside, took a seat in his rig and drove off.

Cody leaned in between the front seats, sniffed at Jake's tie, and huffed.

"It's not what you think," Jake said.

He arrived at County Jail #2, found a parking spot in the shade on 7th Street, and opened the sunroof to let in fresh air for his dog. "Cody, stay in the Humvee. That's an order, Marine."

Cody growled at him, but obeyed.

Jake walked to the jail entrance and presented his ID at the window. "Jake Wolfe, attorney at law. Here to see Police Officer Tammi Martinelli."

The uniformed female sheriff checked her appointment list and buzzed the door open.

Jake emptied his pockets and went through the metal detector and imaging machine. The attendants appeared surprised to see his US Marshals badge.

"It's a long story," Jake said, handing out lawyer business cards with handwritten notes on the back that read, "No-charge legal consultations for LEOs."

Once inside the jail, a female detention deputy guided Jake down hallways toward an attorney-client booth. The name tag on her shirt read "MOORE."

"It breaks my heart to see a fellow cop in jail," Moore said as they walked along. "How is she even in here? I have a lot of questions."

"Thank you for your courtesy. May I offer a small token of my appreciation? Dinner is on me tonight." He held out a small gift-card-sized envelope.

"We can't accept bribes," Moore said, eyeing him.

"I missed your birthday. That's all. My business card is in there, too. I'm your attorney now. No charge."

Moore accepted his envelope and peeked inside at the birthday card and a one-hundred-dollar bill. "Thanks. You're all right for a lawyer."

Jake flashed his US Marshals badge and creds as he continued walking down the hall. "I'm also deputized to assist on a task force as a K-9 handler when needed." He held up his phone and displayed a photo of himself and Cody wearing police vests and standing with Captain Leeds of the police boat *Marine 1*.

"I'd love to join the sheriff's marine unit and spend all day on the water." Moore turned a corner and pointed at some doors up ahead. "This jail duty is wearing thin. With our long hours, guards like me spend more time with inmates than we do at home with our families. We're doing time, too."

"That's rough," Jake said. "You hardworking deputies deserve shorter hours and a pay raise."

She shook her head. "Good luck with that. I'm trying to get transferred."

"May I ask you one favor, Deputy Moore?" Jake often used reciprocity, knowing if you gave somebody a gift or did them a favor, you might influence them with a desire to reciprocate.

Moore shot him a doubtful look as they arrived at a steel door. "Maybe. What is it?"

"I hope the guards will please keep in mind how Officer Martinelli could not and would not draw her gun and shoot a uniformed deputy sheriff. Not even in self-defense. She's a friend of all sheriffs and will always give backup to you fine people out there on the street."

Moore nodded thoughtfully, opened the door, and gestured with one hand.

Jake stepped inside, and the steel door banged shut behind him.

CHAPTER 45

Inside the attorney-client booth, Jake found Tammi sitting and waiting for him behind a thick polycarbonate glass window. She wore orange prisoner scrubs, her dark hair was pulled back in a ponytail, and she had a fresh bruise on the cheek below her left eye.

Tammi stared at his tailored Italian suit, but didn't comment that he cleaned up well, the way some people did.

He took a seat across from her, looking at the bruise with concern. "How are you doing in here?"

Tammi shrugged. "This is nothing. I can do it blindfolded."

Jake didn't believe it was nothing. "I heard they put you into the general population. Any trouble with inmates who don't like cops?"

"Yes, but I made an immediate and violent example of one in self-defense. Now the rest are afraid of me."

Jake wasn't surprised. Tammi was not someone to be trifled with. "As a law enforcement officer with potential enemies in lockup, you should've qualified for keep-away status in a private cell instead of being tossed into the gen-pop quarters."

"I'm sure Denton is behind it," Tammi said. She gripped both hands into fists. "The sadist wants me in prison, alive and suffering daily abuse for decades."

Jake noted the controlled anger. "The sheriff's department never should've arrested you."

"And yet, here I am."

"I put in a good word for you with a deputy named Moore."

Tammi touched her bruise. "Moore stopped the fight before everybody else could gang up on me."

"She said it breaks her heart to see a fellow cop in jail," Jake said.

"Have they set my bail?"

"The prosecution is recommending two million dollars in bail for the first-degree murder of Gerald Oliver. We'll try to cut that in half."

"Oh, good," Tammi said. "I can cover one million with the cash in my mattress, but two mil would be a real challenge."

"Anselmo will put up the collateral for your ten percent bond."

She raised her eyebrows. "Tell him I said thank you very much."

"Here's the plan until then. You'll tell the prosecutor you're going to defend yourself pro se."

"If I represent myself, doesn't that mean I have a fool for a client?"

Jake shook his head. "I'll serve as your co-counsel and backup stand-in attorney until the time comes for Bart to defend you at trial."

"How much is Bart going to charge me?"

"Anselmo will pay Bart's fees."

She stared at Jake. "Big Mo is a man of honor."

"Pro se affords you some perks. You're treated more like an attorney than a helpless prisoner. On days you appear in court, you'll be allowed meetings with me in a private courtside holding cell."

"Meetings before court would be helpful." She took a deep breath and let it out.

"We'll file a motion asking the judge to let you dress in work clothes instead of jail scrubs. I'd like you to wear your police uniform, but we'd settle for you in a business suit. I don't want the media taking pictures of you looking like a convict. Tons of potential jurors will see the news photos."

She gazed at him with a glimmer of hope. "I'll admit I was worried about internet tabloid trash. It lives on forever."

"Once you're approved to wear a suit, we might test adding your badge on a lanyard to see if the prosecution objects. They probably will, but even if they do, the press will have seen it."

"You might actually know a thing or two," Tammi said.

Jake showed her a video on his phone of a short media sound bite where he wore a suit and spoke to a crowd of reporters. "I want every person in this city to know that it's never okay for anyone to shoot at a cop. Never!"

The fierce look on his face as he shouted the last word wasn't lost on Tammi.

"I'll push hard and get you bailed out of here," Jake said. "You have my word."

"Your word is one of the few things in life I know I can count on."

Jake almost said, "We're Family," referring to how they both belonged to the Amborgetti Italian Mafia Family. He hesitated because their words were probably being illegally recorded, despite attorney-client confidentiality.

He put his right palm on the glass, and from the other side, she put her palm onto his.

Jake made a fist with his other hand and put it over his heart. She did the same.

"You'll be free soon. Stay strong." Jake stood up.

As Jake stood, Tammi did too, her eyes glistening. She started to say something, bit her bottom lip, then walked away without another word.

Once Tammi was gone, he headed outside. He felt a weight on his heart. Jake had never seen her so vulnerable and would fight hard to gain her release.

Returning to fresh air and freedom, Jake thought of Deputy Moore, who'd said she was serving time along with the prisoners. That was a tough job and one he couldn't handle. Just the thought of spending every day inside the jail made him want to cruise the *Far Niente* to Tahiti and get away from it all.

Cody popped his head out of the Jeep's sunroof and barked at Jake as he approached.

Jake smiled. It was one of Cody's favorite tricks, and the clever dog had taught it to himself.

He took a seat in the vehicle, did an illegal U-turn, and drove back toward Bart's law office. It was time to confer with the best lawyer in town about Tammi's bail hearing.

CHAPTER 46

The next morning, Jake drove to court for the bail hearing. He waited for Tammi to arrive on a prison bus with other inmates. When the prisoners were escorted to detention, a sheriff led Tammi to meet with Jake in a private courtside holding cell.

Jake stood up when Tammi entered. He noted she appeared grateful to be in the small, empty room, away from the inmates she'd been riding with on the bus.

"Where's my change of clothes?"

"They should arrive any minute now," Jake said. "Had to go through inspection and approval."

Soon, a courtroom deputy stopped by, delivered a hanging garment bag, punched Jake on the shoulder, and left again.

Tammi looked at Jake. "Friend of yours?"

"I helped his sister stop a legal hassle. He owed me a favor, and now we're even."

She opened the bag and found two wardrobe items. One was her blue police uniform and cop shoes, the other a charcoal gray pantsuit, white blouse, and pair of low-heel dress shoes.

"Why both?" Tammi said.

"I didn't know if they'd allow your uniform through. The pantsuit was backup." Jake felt thankful Bart had made a call to someone.

"So, I'm wearing the uniform?"

"Yes, and I'll go wait outside the door."

"Don't bother. Just turn your back." She quickly stripped off her orange scrubs and changed clothes. A couple minutes later, she said, "Ready to go."

Jake didn't say what he was thinking. Now the deputy and anybody else in court who'd been watching might know she'd changed clothes with Jake in the room.

"I have your badge, but let's wait for you to wear it, in case the deputy objects. And that way he can't be blamed."

"All right. It's never felt so good to wear my blues."

"You look good in uniform," Jake said. "Keep a neutral expression on your face, and act like a police officer who's here to testify in a routine case. Totally professional."

She tenderly touched her face. "I wish I had some makeup to cover this bruise."

"No, I want the media to see it. When we enter, slowly turn your head left and right as if looking for friends and family in the gallery. Let news cameras record the bruise and your calm demeanor."

"Got it," she said.

"A lot of court procedure is simply acting for the judge and jury."

"Sure. Next stop, Hollywood."

He called out to the same deputy who allowed them entry through the steel door and directly into the courtroom.

When the deputy walked away, Jake handed Tammi her

badge. She pinned it to her shirt, and they walked toward the defense table as everyone stared. Jake felt like a deer in the headlights, but faked being calm and told himself he'd already won an early victory over the prosecution.

A row of reporters took pictures and video. Jake heard a low murmur among the crowd when people saw a uniformed female police officer with a serious bruise on her face.

He recognized two prosecutors, a man and a woman from the Major Crimes Unit, sitting at the opposing table. Tough opponents who fought to win, they both frowned at seeing Tammi in her blues and wearing the badge.

Jake and Tammi were about to sit down when a bailiff said, "All rise."

Everyone stood up as a door behind the clerk's station opened and Judge Emerson stepped into the room and took the bench.

"You may be seated." Emerson consulted his written notes. "Our first order of business is . . . the defense filed a motion to reduce bail." He began going through step-by-step procedures.

When Emerson called upon the prosecutors, the male attorney named Bennett stood up. "Objection, Your Honor. When a defendant is acting pro se, their clothing may include attorney-type work clothes, but not previous daily job attire. A scuba diving instructor would wear a business suit, not a wetsuit."

Jake feigned surprise as he leapt to his feet. "Your Honor, that's not a fair comparison. We aren't underwater here."

This brought out quiet chuckles from the crowd.

The judge squinted at Jake over his reading glasses, making it clear he knew Jake was a trickster. They had a history. "At the next meeting, Police Officer Martinelli must wear a business suit."

"Yes, Your Honor," Jake said, pleased the judge had referred to Tammi by her job title. "I promise that Police Officer Martinelli will wear a business suit."

The judge noticed Tammi's bruised face and scowled. "Officer Martinelli, how are your injuries healing up?"

Tammi had testified before Judge Emerson many times in past cases against criminals she'd arrested, but never as a defendant.

Tammi glanced at Jake, and he whispered, "Stand up next to me and tell all. Take your time."

Tammi rose to her feet. "Deputy Sheriff Corrine Denton shot me in the vest when I had my hands up, causing blunt force injuries that required a visit to the hospital ER. The bruise on my face is from being attacked by an inmate in jail." She sat down.

Jake said, "Your Honor, the jailers put Police Officer Martinelli in general population lockup with criminals who hate cops. Her life is in danger every hour of every day."

Bennett let out a long breath. "Your Honor, we can request to have the murder suspect placed in keep-away status in a private cell."

Jake said, "Your honor, Police Officer Martinelli would still be in danger at meal times. For example, the bruise injury on the police officer's face occurred when an inmate attacked her in the cafeteria. Next time, Officer Martinelli could lose an eye ... or her life."

For the following ten minutes, Jake gave reasoned arguments for lowering bail, and Bennett, the prosecutor, argued in opposition.

Jake finally said, "The prosecutor's two-million-dollar bail request is unconstitutional and amounts to cruel and unusual punishment."

Reporters scribbled notes. Jake knew most people had no

idea what constitutional law said, or didn't say, or what it might mean in this case.

Bennett said, "Your Honor, we're talking about first-degree murder charges. The bail fits the crime."

Jake argued, "The Eighth Amendment protects people from having bail or fines set at an amount so high that it would be impossible for all but the richest defendants to pay."

"The defendant can take out an equity loan," Bennett said.

Jake shook his head. "This is outrageous. Police Officer Martinelli did not draw her weapon. Not even when Deputy Sheriff Corrine Denton shot her without legal justification."

"Objection," Bennett said. "At this time, there is nothing to indicate the deputy did not have justification."

"Sustained. Defense shall limit remarks to the currently known facts." Judge Emerson raised an eyebrow at Jake.

"Yes, Your Honor," Jake said. "We currently know for a fact that Officer Martinelli did not fire or even draw her weapon. We know she was fired upon by Ms. Denton and would have died if she had not been wearing a bulletproof vest. She's lucky to be alive."

Bennett stood up. "Your Honor, this line of argument is preposterous. The defense knows the murder charge is for firing an arrow that killed Gerald Oliver."

"Objection," Jake said. "There is absolutely no evidence tying my client to the arrow in question. The charge is contrived, unsubstantiated, and frankly, ridiculous."

"Sustained, but save it for the trial," Judge Emerson said. "Give me your reasons to lower bail."

"Your Honor, Officer Martinelli is not considered a flight risk."

"Every murder suspect is a flight risk," Bennett said.

Jake held up his hand. "This is Officer Martinelli's home town. She owns a condo here, has plenty of family and friends, loves her job at the police department and is looking forward to a court victory that clears her name."

"Irrelevant when charged with murder," Bennett said.

"Two million dollars is an oppressive amount for someone on a police officer's salary," Jake said. "If it may please the court, bail of two hundred thousand would be more than sufficient."

Bennett started to argue, but Judge Emerson interrupted him. "I'm setting the bail at half a million."

"Thank you, Your Honor," Jake said, bowing his head in respect and to hide his smile.

He and Tammi exited the courtroom and waited in the private courtside holding cell until Anselmo made bail and Tammi was released on a five hundred thousand dollar secured bond.

At 11:20 a.m., Jake walked out of court with Tammi by his side. Deputy Moore carried the garment bag with Tammi's business suit, obviously glad to see her getting out. Tammi wore her blue uniform, dark sunglasses, and a blank expression. They paused outside on the steps, and the media went wild. Cameras flashed and reporters yelled questions.

Jake announced, "My police officer client is looking forward to a fair trial where she's found not guilty and vindicated. Then she can get back to work protecting this community the way she always has before being shot without just cause by an alleged sociopath."

They both took their seats in the Jeep, and Cody woofed at Tammi as Jake drove away.

Tammi said, "Thank you, Jake. Now, I could use a good meal and a strong drink, away from prying eyes."

"I know just the place."

CHAPTER 47

Walking into Clancy's Pub, Jake said in the Irish way, "God bless all here." He led Cody and Tammi to the bar.

The regulars raised their pints, waved, and smiled at Jake and his lovable dog, Cody.

Clancy had bulging muscles in his short-sleeved emerald green polo shirt. He used a clean white hand towel to wipe the beautiful antique redwood bar top. "Look what the cat dragged in."

Jake smiled at the familiar banter. "I want that bar top to shine when you're done, Paddy."

Clancy laughed, pulled a pint of Guinness, and set it on the bar before an empty stool.

Jake said, "Officer Tammi Martinelli is a good Italian Catholic girl, here trusting the Irish scoundrels not to take her angelic virginity."

"You came to the wrong place with the wrong man," Clancy joked. "What can I pour for you, Officer?"

Tammi looked at the wall of bottles behind the bar.

Jake answered for her. "A shot of Irish whiskey."

"Redbreast, as usual?"

"Of course, are ye daft, lad?"

Clancy poured a generous amount of whiskey into a tumbler and placed it next to the pint of Guinness. "Nice try with the Irish accent, but you need a lot more practice."

Tammi stood in a daze, appearing relieved to be free of incarceration and safe among people she could trust.

Jake put a gentle hand on her shoulder, guiding her to the stool. "Have a seat. Drink with friends. This is a historic bar that survived the nineteen oh six earthquake. In the old days, long before we were born, most of the cops in town were Irish men, and they all drank here after their shifts. Now, an Italian female cop will brighten up the place."

Tammi sat down and took a sip of her whiskey, followed by a gulp of Guinness.

Clancy watched her with concern. "How did you get that bruise, young lady? I want the name and address of whoever did it."

"You should see the other person," Tammi said.

Clancy glanced at Jake, who pointed at a menu featuring the soup of the day.

"I'll be right back." Clancy headed into the kitchen.

Jake went behind the bar, as Clancy allowed him to, and grabbed a bowl he filled with water for Cody.

Tammi continued sipping whiskey and Guinness, and the color started returning to her cheeks. "The jail fed us sandwiches made from one slice of bologna on the cheapest white bread. I'm starving for a good meal."

Clancy returned and set a large white porcelain plate in front of her. It held a round, hollowed-out loaf of crusty sourdough bread filled with steaming hot clam chowder. Next to that was a row of cold prawns and a dish of red cocktail sauce for dipping. A lemon wedge and a soup spoon completed the presentation.

"Thank you, Clancy," Tammi said.

Jake observed Tammi closing her eyes for a moment in silent prayer, saying grace. She made the sign of the cross and then dug into the food.

Cody sniffed the air and watched the bartender with his bright brown eyes.

"What are you looking at, Fido?" Clancy smiled at the dog and set down a bowl of beef, carrots, and potatoes he'd scooped from a pot of Irish stew and rinsed off with cold water.

Cody attacked the food, his dog tags clinking against the bowl as he chowed down.

Clancy set a glass of Guinness in front of Jake.

"Oh fine," Jake said. "I see how it is. I'm buying meals, but all I get is a pint?"

Clancy reached over to a half-empty bowl of pretzels and slid it across the bar. "Don't say I never did anything for you."

Jake laughed. "What's your special of the day?"

"Reuben tacos. Quick and easy, and surprisingly tasty."

"You talked me into it. Reuben tacos might be the only kind I haven't tried yet."

Clancy called out the order to his cook and then told Jake, "Coming right up. Are you taking good care of my favorite dog?"

"Cody keeps asking me when you're going out on the bay with us again. Dungeness crab is in season right now."

The pub door opened, letting a shaft of bright sunlight inside, and a man stood silhouetted there.

Jake put a hand on his pistol and gazed in the mirror over the bar. Recognizing his friend Vito Amborgetti, he turned and said in his best Irish accent, "Close the door or I'll hit ya with a shillelagh."

Vito walked inside, and stood next to Tammi. "I'm here to pick up Officer Martinelli and deliver her to Anselmo's office."

Jake shook his head. "No, you're here to have a drink with us, enjoy some of the best pub grub in the city, and *then* give my client a ride to see her benefactor, Big Mo."

Vito sat down next to Tammi. "You okay?"

She continued eating hungrily and spoke with her mouth full. "It was a picnic."

Clancy set down two plates with bread bowls full of chowder and Reuben tacos on the side. "That chowder has some halibut your friend Beppe caught."

"A good one?" Jake said.

"Folks raved about it."

Jake tried the chowder and grunted in approval.

Reaching for Jake's plate, Tammi took one of his tacos and devoured it, then grabbed one from Vito's plate.

Jake took one of her prawns, removed the tail and tossed it to Cody, who caught it in mid-air.

Cody sat on his haunches, one eyebrow quirking up and down as he watched every bite the trio ate.

After Jake had eaten most of the chowder and it had cooled off, he set his plate on the floor so Cody could enjoy leftovers.

Tammi finished off her meal and sipped Guinness. "If I drink any more of that whiskey, I'll need a nap. In jail, I slept with one eye open."

"A nap might be just what the doctor ordered," Vito said. "After your meeting with Anselmo, you can go home and sleep. Wake up around seven o'clock tonight and come to the restaurant for a celebratory dinner."

Tammi cleared her throat. "Speaking of dinner. Um, Jake . .

. One night this week I plan on cooking my world-famous spaghetti and meatballs with vodka sauce. I know how Cody loves meatballs. You two are invited if you don't already have other plans."

Jake gave her a warm smile. She was testing him. Women were always testing him. "That's one of my favorite dinners in the world, and you're one of my favorite people. I'd love to join you, but I'm dating a jealous woman who knows martial arts and carries a handgun in her purse."

"Sarah is a good shot," Tammi said, slightly buzzed. "I saw her practicing at the gun range with Beth Cushman."

He said, "And because you're such a catch, Sarah would never believe it was a platonic dinner. She'd open a can of whoop-ass on both of us."

Tammi had a wistful look in her eyes, apparently pleased by the compliment, but not happy about the situation. "We can't have that, can we? The dinner invitation is always open, but I wish you two all the best in your relationship."

Jake received the message. *If it doesn't work out, you have my number.*

Vito said, "Time to go."

They all stood up, and Tammi tossed her last prawn to Cody.

Jake paid the tab and included a 100% tip, then followed them out. "Vito, I need a word with you."

Vito gestured to the limo. "Hop in. Talk."

Jake opened a backseat door for Tammi and ordered Cody to join her. He sat next to Vito in the front seat. "I need to do some money laundering. Around two hundred thousand dollars I seized from a narco terrorist in Key West."

Vito nodded, unfazed. "Big Mo can take care of it. Where do you want the clean funds deposited?"

"Write a check and donate it to Father O'Leary's soup kitchen and food bank."

Vito raised his eyebrows. "That's quite a donation. What does Anselmo get out of it?"

"He gets a large tax deduction for making a generous donation to a non-profit organization."

"You've thought this through."

"Big Mo can charge me a fee, too," Jake said, referring to the vigorish, the vig, the cut, the margin. "Whatever it takes to help the Padre." Marines called every church leader Padre.

"You're a good man, Jake. I'll personally walk it through the process. There will be no fee, no vig."

"Thank you, brother. I'll deliver the funds to you soon."

Jake exited the limo and opened the door to let his dog out. He looked at Tammi and said, "My advice as your lawyer is that you don't seek revenge on Denton. Let it go. She'll screw up soon enough, lose her job, and move away."

Tammi didn't reply, but the look on her face told Jake she wouldn't be following his advice.

CHAPTER 48

Jake drove home to Juanita Yacht Harbor, and took Cody for a walk. He bought a coffee to go, then strolled along a tree-lined sidewalk as he sipped his beverage and felt the sun on his face.

When they returned to the harbor parking lot, Cody headed to the Jeep and pawed at the back hatch.

Jake smiled, knowing if Cody pawed his K-9 door, he wanted to go for a drive. If he pawed the back hatch, he wanted one of the doggie treats Jake kept there.

"You want a treat?" Jake unlocked and opened the hatch.

Cody stood on his hind legs, and nuzzled the plastic container, his tail wagging.

Jake picked up the jar, twisted the lid off, and fed a chewy treat to Cody. It occurred to him that Cody the genius dog had trained his handler to perform this trick.

As they stood there, a white Toyota sedan pulled up and stopped. The driver's door opened, and a man stepped out. He had a long beard, and wore a turban and sandals.

Jake didn't want to be biased against the man's religious

beliefs or dress code, but his appearance triggered memories of overseas battles he wanted to forget.

The man smiled cheerfully as he opened a back passenger door for a college-age woman in a head cover, who joined him outside the car. She wore blue jeans and a plain blouse, but not a jacket that might hide a concealed weapon.

Having seen Toyota cars explode several times on deployments in the Middle East, Jake felt paranoid and feared this one might contain a suicide bomb.

It wasn't the Toyota company's fault that terrorists favored their vehicles for reliability in harsh desert conditions.

He was sorry to act prejudiced but couldn't help it as he reached for the Taser shotgun McKay had given him in the past. He kept it stashed inside a long cardboard box with a picture of a leaf blower on the outside. When Agent Greene had delivered it, she'd told him the Taser X12 pump shotgun had a range of one hundred feet and held five rounds the size of D batteries with tiny hooks that would stick to skin or clothes. Each round delivered five hundred volts to stun a target for at least twenty seconds.

He removed the shotgun from its box and set it within easy reach as he called out, "How may I help you?"

The young lady walked toward him with a purposeful stride.

Jake displayed his Marshals star. "Police. Stop right there. Hands where I can see them."

She looked at him with sad eyes, as if seeing the pain he carried. "I mean no harm."

"Hold still while I deal with your friend." Jake turned to the man, raised his shotgun, and recited words from overseas deployments. "Lay facedown on the ground and don't move. Your life depends on obeying my commands. Nod if you understand."

The man blinked in surprise, but nodded and did as requested. He said in perfect English, "Yes, sir, Officer. I understand your words, but not your strange behavior."

Cody pulled on the leash and sniffed the air, but didn't alert his handler to any guns or explosive devices.

The young woman said, "I'm only here to say thank you."

Jake lowered his shotgun, but watched her carefully. "Go ahead and say it."

"Thank you for saving my life. Years ago, my mother and I were taken captive by rapist-terrorists, along with many other women. Those of us who refused to be slaves were scheduled for beheading the next day. The killers dug shallow graves and told us our deaths would be recorded on phone video and uploaded to the internet as a warning to others."

Jake studied the woman's face, but couldn't remember if he'd seen her before. "And?"

"You came alone in the middle of the night to kill our tormenters and rescue us."

She appeared sincere and knew details about his top secret mission, but Jake didn't trust her. He rarely trusted anyone after all he'd been through. "I'm glad you survived."

"Ever since then, my mother and I have been living in Europe under new names."

Jake wondered if she was pretending to be one of the rescued hostages, but actually a terrorist bent on revenge for one of the men he'd killed. "How do I know you're telling me the truth?"

A tear rolled down her cheek as she held out a small Beanie Baby stuffed animal dog that fit in the palm of her hand. "You gave this to me when I was having a panic attack. You said it was your good luck charm. It quieted me down so we wouldn't get caught and killed." She started to cry.

"What's your name?"

"Leena," she said.

"I remember giving my good luck charm to a girl with that name who understood English."

"Yes, I'm Leena. Many years older now. You do remember me."

Jake gestured at the car. "Try to see this from my perspective, Leena. Imagine if that car was packed with a bomb that might kill my war dog."

She wiped her eyes. "I'm sorry. I know you have to be careful the rest of your life."

"Leena, it's good to see you're doing okay." He spoke to the driver. "Sir, you may stand up now. I apologize for having an episode of PTSD."

The man stood up, shrugged and smiled. "No worries. This is a roundtrip, so I'll be hanging out until she's ready for a ride back to the city. If that's okay with you." He lit a cigarette and stood there smoking and looking out at the beautiful yacht harbor and boats.

Leena asked, "May I approach you, Jake?"

"Yes, but first, please let Cody sniff you for a gun. I'm sorry to act so paranoid, but you know why." Jake let Cody off-leash.

"I understand." She waited for the dog.

"Cody, search." Jake pointed at Leena.

CHAPTER 49

Cody trotted to Leena and circled around her, sniffing both ankles and the back waistband of her blue jeans for a concealed weapon. Faithfully protecting his handler. The same thing he'd done overseas for a handler who'd died. Cody had never gotten over it.

Leena stood there patiently, giving the dog a chance to do its job.

Jake thought she obviously had experience with or knowledge about how K-9s searched people on the war-torn streets during her childhood.

Once Cody was satisfied, Jake set down the Taser shotgun, moved to Leena, and held out his hand to shake.

They met halfway, and she threw her arms around him in a platonic hug, crying tears of joy. "Thank you. Thank you. Thank you."

After the hug, Jake didn't know what to say. He'd rarely been thanked for his top secret work. That was fine, he knew it was a thankless job. He said, "You're very welcome, Leena. How's your mother?"

"She sends you her love and gratitude. Agent McKay told me to meet you here. I thought you knew."

Jake's phone buzzed. He pulled it out and saw a call from McKay. "Speak of the devil."

Leena stared at him with curiosity, obviously not understanding the reference.

Jake answered, "You rang, boss?"

"You'll be getting a visit from a young Muslim woman. She was one of those you rescued on that semi-authorized mission you went on without Brinkter's permission when you were supposed to be recuperating in the hospital."

"She's already here, and I nearly shot her male friend driving the car," Jake said. "Next time, maybe call in advance?"

"She arrived early? I'm so sorry. I'm working on only a few hours of sleep."

"Please get more sleep. Take care of yourself."

McKay let out a breath. "Good advice, but I'm totally focused on working my way up the tranq chain of distribution."

"Let me know if there's anything I can do to help you."

"Did I cause you to suffer PTSD?"

"Leena showed up with a bearded guy wearing a turban and sandals," Jake said. "Yes, that triggered me. I apologize for acting biased."

McKay said, "It's understandable with your history of overseas combat."

"It's good to see Leena. Thanks for making this happen."

"You're welcome." McKay ended the call.

Jake asked Leena, "Can you tell me anything about your life, or is it top secret?"

"We lived in London for years. My mom went to nursing school and got a job at a hospital."

"Good for her," Jake said. "What brings you here?"

"The MI-Five agent who protected us found out a terrorist had come to London seeking revenge. We had to move, and I asked to disappear in America, in a city near an ocean or lake."

"It seems too coincidental for me to think it was random you'd end up here."

Leena looked him in the eye. "Agent McKay thought my mother and I would be safer with you nearby." She hung her head. "I'm sorry if that makes your life more complicated."

Now Jake understood. He'd gone through hell to rescue Leena and her mother, and absolutely would not let anybody harm one hair on their heads. "McKay is always thinking. She's the brains of the operation. I'm her blunt instrument."

"McKay told us you have nightmares about the rescue mission. She thought maybe seeing us leading happy lives might create new memories and help ease your post-traumatic stress."

"It does help," Jake admitted. He handed her a business card. "I'm your attorney now. No charge."

"That's very generous of you." She pocketed his card. "Can we be friends?"

"Yes, of course." He turned to his dog. "Be friends, Cody."

Cody pressed his head against Leena's stomach while wagging his tail.

"May I pet Cody?"

"Oh yeah, he'd like that."

Leena patted Cody on the back and scratched him behind the ears.

Jake asked her, "Is this man you're with a relative or friend?"

"No, I used Uber, and he seemed nice and polite," Leena said.

Jake felt a cold tingle at the back of his neck. He moved to the Jeep, grabbed the Taser shotgun, and slapped his thigh. "Cody, heel."

The dog stood next to his handler's left thigh, and when Jake moved toward the man, he trotted alongside.

Jake displayed his Marshals star again. He aimed the shotgun at the ground. "US Marshal. Please show me some ID."

"Sure, no problem." The man reached into a pocket, pulled out a knife, and lunged at Cody in a surprise attack.

It happened so fast, Jake was almost caught off guard, although he knew some terrorists and criminals would attempt to kill the K-9 first and level the playing field.

He didn't want to risk Tasering Cody, so he leapt into the air and kicked his attacker in the face, knocking him backward to the ground.

The man jumped to his feet, wiped his bloody nose on his sleeve, and charged again.

Jake sidestepped and tripped him with the shotgun barrel, causing him to face plant onto the pavement. "Stay down. Drop the knife. You're under arrest."

The attacker rose to his feet once more and ran straight at Jake, Cody, and Leena with his knife up and threatening.

Jake fired the Taser shotgun and sent a round at the attacker's chest, where it knocked him off his feet and delivered five hundred volts.

The man landed on his back, hit his head, and lay there convulsing, writhing, and gasping.

Jake waited a few seconds until the shocks ended, then grabbed some zip ties out of his rig and cuffed the man's wrists and ankles.

He put on leather driving gloves, removed his Taser round from the criminal's shirt and returned to the Jeep. "Are you all right, Leena?"

She'd clasped one hand over her mouth, eyes wide, body shaking.

Jake hugged her to him, and she cried on his shoulder.

She sobbed. "When will they finally leave us alone?"

"Hopefully, that man is the threat from London, and he'll spend the rest of his life in prison."

Leena took a step back. "Now I'm having my own PTSD flashback. I remember seeing you shoot men who wanted to hurt me. Here we are again."

Jake pointed at the criminal. "The difference is, he's not dead, only stunned."

"Still, it's too much for me."

"Cody will sit in the Jeep with you and help you feel safe. Go ahead and hop in."

She took a seat, still gripping the Beanie Baby tightly in her hand. It triggered Jake's memory of that fateful night. "Cody, comfort."

Cody leapt into the back seat and nuzzled Leena's hand.

"Leena, you can pet Cody again. He likes you."

Leena patted Cody on the back. She put her stuffed dog away and hugged a real dog for emotional support.

Cody stretched out across her lap, wagged his tail, and shook his head to make his ears flop.

Jake saw once again how Cody's unconditional love could work a miracle to ease someone's PTSD. "Leena, is your mother at home right now?"

"No, she's interviewing for nursing jobs."

"Okay, I'm going to close the door, but I'll be standing right here."

"Thank you, Jake." Leena began gently scratching Cody behind the ears again. The dog nodded his head with his tongue hanging out, acting silly to comfort his new friend.

Jake sent a text to Agent McKay. *Leena's Uber driver tried to kill us. He knows where they live. Please find the mother and take her into protective custody.*

McKay replied. *Roger that. I'll track her phone and send Easton and Greene.*

Jake let out a breath and called Detective Flynn. "Hello, it's me, your favorite person, Jake Wolfe."

"Wolf Man, talk to me," Flynn said.

"Well, I Tasered a perp in self-defense at the parking lot in front of Juanita Yacht Harbor. I displayed my Marshals badge, identified myself, and asked him to drop his knife."

"I'm guessing he didn't cooperate?"

"No, he attacked me and my dog, and a young woman who was visiting us."

Flynn sighed. "On my way."

"Tell your cops not to shoot me."

"Sheesh, you're so detail oriented." Flynn ended the call.

Jake held up his badge to the gathering crowd of gawkers. "US Marshal. This is a crime scene. Please stay back or you might be arrested for interfering with a federal investigation."

At hearing the word "arrested," many of the people moved on. Some took video for their social media feeds. Jake was glad Leena and Cody were out of view.

An unmarked black SUV drove up. Detective Flynn stepped out wearing his usual gray slacks, blue shirt, and navy sport coat. With a cynical look on his face, Flynn held up his gold badge for all to see. "Sausalito Police."

CHAPTER 50

While Jake talked with Detective Flynn, a Sausalito police car arrived and a female uniformed officer put the terrorist in her car's backseat behind a partition cage.

Later, a black Suburban arrived. Agent Greene lowered the driver's window and gave Jake a nod.

Jake pressed his key fob to open the Jeep's K-9 door, stood next to it and spoke to Leena. "McKay sent her trusted agents to give you a ride. Your mom is already in their SUV, waiting for you."

Leena exited the Jeep with Cody by her side. "A ride where?"

"To the federal building. That driver picked you up at home, right?"

Leena held his gaze. "Yes. Why didn't he attack me there?"

"He wanted both of us," Jake said. "He could then stake out your home and wait for your mother to return. You'll both need new phones, and McKay will help you move to a new address."

"What about you?" Leena said. "He might have given away your location to another terrorist."

"Detective Flynn will look through his phone," Jake said. "If he gave someone my address, I'll act as your lightning rod and keep the danger away from you."

Leena put one hand to her forehead and groaned. "We shouldn't have moved to your city. It was a mistake."

"No, it all worked out. Flynn told me the man had a stamp on his passport from Heathrow Airport. He's the assassin who searched for you in London. You drew him here, and now he'll go to prison."

"You saved my life again," Leena said.

"Just doing my job. Let's not keep your mother waiting. We'll meet again, Leena. My girlfriend and I will take you and your mom for a whale-watching cruise on my boat."

Leena's eyes lit up. "Really? I can't wait."

Jake led her to the Suburban. Leena got in, and hugged her mother tight. "Jake protected me."

Her mother looked at Jake. "We're in your debt and can never repay you."

Jake shook his head. "You already paid me back when you earned a nursing degree and made it your career to save lives." He closed the door and Agent Greene drove off toward the Golden Gate Bridge. Jake waved goodbye in case Leena was looking back at him and Cody from behind the darkened windows.

Flynn asked him, "Why would a terrorist use a knife instead of a gun?"

"Some assassins prefer knives because they're quiet, and don't leave any ballistic evidence."

"This guy is an assassin?"

Jake nodded, and his phone buzzed with a call from McKay.

"Thank you for protecting Leena," she said.

"Agent Greene is bringing her to your office as we speak."

"I'm calling because there are rumors about a drug dealer at Ocean Beach offering tranq to the surfing community. He's probably a small-time loser, but might give us a lead. I want you and Cody to investigate."

"Roger that. We'll head over there now."

Jake said goodbye to Flynn, returned to the *Far Niente* and dressed in board shorts and a T-shirt. He carried his surfboard to the Jeep and strapped it onto the roof rack, tossed a gear bag into the back cargo area, sat in the vehicle along with Cody, and drove to Ocean Beach.

Referred to by locals as OB, it was known as the spot where surfing legend Kelly Slater won his historic 11th world title in a Rip Curl Pro contest. Jake liked how there were no high-rise buildings nearby, and the Parks Service allowed visitors to build a bonfire in one of the designated firepits.

He pulled over and parked, then sat for a moment to observe dozens of surfers paddling their boards out onto the water to catch a wave and ride it back. The beach-friendly weather made it a good day for surfing, with warm sunshine, calm sea breezes, and no fog.

Jake used a DSLR camera and telephoto lens to take close-up views of people on the beach. He didn't notice any suspicious activity. An osprey fish hawk with a five-foot wingspan flew slowly over the coastline. Jake took pictures as the raptor dove to the water, grabbed a small leopard shark in its talons, and flew away.

"One less shark to bite a surfer," Jake said.

Taking nature photos made him reminisce about when he'd worked as a freelance photographer for a living after he'd EAS'd, completing his End of Active Service in the Marines. Nature photography had done wonders to heal his PTSD, and at times like these, he missed the stress-free, low-paying career when he'd slept in his car and subsisted on Subway sandwiches.

He opened the back hatch and hid the camera under a black towel, along with his phone, pistol, and key fob. After placing an old-fashioned Jeep key and the US Marshals star into an airtight flat holder that fit into a zippered pocket on his board shorts, he said, "Cody, are you ready to go surfing?"

The dog barked once and wagged his tail as if he'd already figured out what was going on.

Jake dressed himself in a wetsuit made up of a long-sleeved top and leggings, and put a K-9 wetsuit vest on Cody that would also help the dog float. This area of water could be hazardous if strong rip currents pulled a swimmer southward down the coast.

He unstrapped his surfboard and walked along a path between sand dunes to the dog-friendly, off-leash stretch of beach, where he put his board into the water.

"Cody, hop on the surfboard."

Familiar with the routine, the dog stepped onboard and sat down in the front. Jake had situational awareness, and he ignored surf groupie ladies watching him and his dog as he lay on the surfboard behind Cody and paddled out into the water. The duo crested several incoming waves until going far enough past the breakers to turn around and face the shore.

Jake waited patiently for the right wave to come along. While appreciating the chance to surf in cold water, he couldn't help thinking of good times in Oahu, Hawaii, when he'd been stationed at K-Bay Marine Base and enjoyed surfing in the beautiful warm waters of the North Shore.

Jake caught a wave and rode it toward the beach as Cody wagged his tail the entire time, making Jake smile.

Jake caught up with a female senior citizen surfing with her French bulldog.

A young male punk on her other side surfed too close and bumped her board, sending the woman and dog into the water. The guy followed her board to the beach, grabbed it, and held up the stolen item in victory while laughing and preening for his buddies.

Jake couldn't stop his trajectory or he'd wipeout and send Cody flying into the air.

Not an option.

When he reached the shoreline, Jake ran up the beach and punched the thief in the stomach, hitting him hard enough to knock the air out of him but not do any damage that would require immediate medical attention.

The man fell to the sand and groaned.

"Bullies are cowards," Jake said. "I don't want to see your face around here again."

Cody growled while showing his teeth.

"Get your dog away from me," the bully said, gasping for breath.

"He's trained to surgically remove your pathetic junk if he thinks you're a threat. And he has that crazy look in his eyes right now."

The young man's face paled and he quickly backed away, never taking his eyes off of the dog.

"We'll be looking for you every time we come to Ocean Beach," Jake said. "Find another place to be an idiot."

A uniformed policeman rode up on horseback. "Do we have a problem here?"

The group of buddies scurried away.

Jake displayed his Marshals badge and ID. "I'm on the job, sir. Those punks assaulted a female senior citizen in the water. I have to go help her avoid a riptide."

The cop glanced at the woman and dog swimming toward shore. "Go on. I'll arrest the perps." He galloped his horse in pursuit of the young men.

Jake ran toward the woman and her dog. If he didn't rescue them, they might be "on their way to Monterey," as surfers at this beach described the experience most of them would suffer through at one time or another.

"Don't fight the current," Jake shouted. "It's like a river. Go with the flow."

He waved at her to float in the direction he was carrying her board.

She managed to avoid panic and ride the current as her bulldog paddled alongside.

Jake set her surfboard on the water. "Cody, rescue."

Cody hopped onto the board, and Jake pushed it toward the woman and her bulldog, wading into the water behind and then swimming fast and kicking hard.

They crossed paths with the duo, and Cody leapt into the water and swam to the woman.

"His vest floats," Jake said. "Hold on to him like you would a life preserver." Jake grabbed her little twenty-five-pound French bulldog by the nape of its neck and lifted it onto the board.

The exhausted woman gratefully placed one arm over Cody's back, and the retriever paddled to Jake with her in tow.

Jake straddled the board and helped her climb on and sit in front of him, along with her dog. Once she was seated with the dog on her lap, Jake politely removed his arms from around her waist, slid into the water, and pushed the board to shore as Cody swam with him.

Jake kept an eye on his dog with concern, but Cody was having a good time. Retrievers were water dogs, especially

Cody, who somehow read the currents here and avoided trouble.

When they arrived at the beach after Cody led the way, both dogs made friends. They sniffed each other, play bowed, ran in circles, and raced up and down the water's edge, splashing and barking.

Jake held out his left elbow like a gentleman from the old school. The woman smiled in appreciation of his manners and held on to his biceps with both hands. Once she was standing a few yards up the beach, he stepped away and pulled her board up beside her.

CHAPTER 51

The woman gave him a shy smile. "Hello."

"I'm Jake," he said. "A pleasure to meet you."

"Peggy." She shook his hand. "Named after Peggy Lipton. My mom was a fan."

Jake almost said it was a pretty name for a pretty lady but went with, "Nice board. She's a beauty."

"Thanks," Peggy said. "I bought it from a big Hawaiian guy who drives a limo."

Jake noted the decal for Pipeline Porter Hawaiian beer. "Mano Makua?"

She stared at him in amazement. "Yes, do you know him?"

"He's a good friend of mine. We surf here together now and then. That board looks familiar, and Mano told me he sold one of his boards to a beautiful lady."

She blushed. "You two are a lot alike—charming rogues with an air of danger about you."

"Nah, that's just a rumor." Jake gave her a wink.

"I saw you punch that young man who stole my board."

"He deserved worse, and I needed the exercise."

"You rescued us like it was your job," she said.

"Last week, the Coast Guard spotted a dozen great white sharks offshore of here. We couldn't stand by and let you get taken away by a riptide."

"Did you serve in a branch of the military?"

"Yes, my dog and I are Marine Corps veterans. Why do you ask?"

Peggy nodded as if that explained it all.

They stood gazing at each other for a moment.

He gestured at a nearby ocean view cafe. "Join me for coffee?"

"We're too far apart in age to go on a coffee date, and you know it," Peggy said, appearing amused but also pleased.

"As I'll explain to my long-suffering girlfriend, it isn't a date, only two newly met platonic friends having a coffee to discuss how we're going to win the dog surfing contest."

She raised her eyebrows. "You mean how *I'm* going to win."

"Right. That's what I meant." He gave her his best smile.

"You talked me into it. I want to win and prove something about women of a certain age."

"I'm all for it."

Peggy toweled off her wet hair and pulled on a loose T-shirt coverup imprinted with the words "Happiness Comes in Waves."

Jake patted his thigh twice. "Cody, heel."

Cody immediately trotted to his handler's side and looked up at him, awaiting further orders.

Peggy called her dog three times until it finally returned.

"How did you train Cody to obey you like that?"

"I can't take credit. He's a former war dog, trained by Marines. And later on, after he became a civilian, he received further training as a service dog. Cody is one of the smartest dogs in the world. No kidding."

"I believe it," Peggy said. "He appears to be scary smart. Does he ever cause you any problems being so intelligent?"

Jake laughed. "Oh yeah. Tons of problems. You have no idea."

Cody woofed and gave her a big retriever grin.

At the cafe that welcomed dogs, Jake paid for their coffee drinks, and they sat near a sunny window.

After Peggy took a sip of coffee, she said, "I saw you hold up a badge to that police officer on horseback."

Jake displayed the Marshals star. "Yes, sometimes Cody and I volunteer to help the US Marshals on a task force when they need an extra search dog."

"That sounds exciting, but is your dog ever in danger?"

Jake glanced out the window. "Cody is smarter than any criminal. They're the ones in danger, not him."

Cody lay on his side next to Jake, tired from the rescue swimming. Upon hearing his name, he wagged his tail and made it thump on the hardwood floor while Peggy's French bulldog curled up and fell asleep.

"What are you searching for at the beach?" Peggy said.

"We're trying to find out who's selling a drug called tranq."

Peggy followed Jake's gaze out the window for a moment. "I've seen a few drug buys up close. Younger people don't even notice me. It's like I'm not there. Invisible."

"I'm sorry. Cody and I noticed you and your cool dog and badass board."

She smiled. "You're a smooth talker. You aren't trying a con game on a grandmother, are you?"

"I'm actually an upstanding citizen who bends the law once in a while," Jake said with a smile. "For example, my friends in law enforcement don't write me speeding tickets because I'm their no-cost attorney."

"You're a lawyer? That's the last thing I would've guessed."

"Should I be flattered or insulted?"

"Neither. If I had to guess, I'd have said . . . let me think. Firefighter or race car driver."

"My father served as a fireman, and I often drive a car like I stole it. But, please tell me more about these drug deals you've seen going down."

She took another sip of coffee. "It's always the same guy selling. I've noticed him three times."

"Could you describe him to a police sketch artist?"

She frowned. "I don't want to get too involved. No trip to the police station. None of that."

"I understand. What if SFPD Senior Tech Officer Roxanne Poole came here and had coffee with us for a few minutes?"

"How would that help?"

"Her sketch artist is an AI computer program similar to ChatGPT. She's a genius who created the program herself."

"Yes, I'd like to meet this smart woman," Peggy said, appearing intrigued.

Jake tapped on his phone and made a call. "Rox, could I interest you in testing your AI sketch artist program to assist in a federal case?"

"Maybe," Roxanne said.

"You'd do it at Ocean Beach while talking to the woman who's favored to win the upcoming dog surfing contest, and you'd be sipping a triple mocha latte with two pumps of vanilla, foam topping and candy sprinkles."

Roxanne chuckled. "That was quite a sales pitch. You know the way to a tech officer's heart. Where at Ocean Beach?"

Jake gave her the address. "See you soon?"

"Yep, I'll use my lights." Roxanne ended the call.

"She's on her way," Jake said.

Peggy said, "May I ask you a legal question and have it remain confidential?"

"Yes, sign my retainer and you'll be protected by attorney-client privilege." She recited her number and Jake sent the form to her for a digital signature.

She looked at her phone. "Your retainer is one dollar?"

"Yeah, but I'm seriously thinking of doubling my fees."

She smiled at him. "You're the nicest lawyer I've ever met."

"Don't tell anyone. You'll ruin my scary lawyer image."

Peggy took a deep breath and blurted out her story. "I've been married nearly fifty years to the love of my life, but we plan to get a divorce, so my health issues will qualify for more assistance."

Jake felt a weight on his heart. "I've heard of other people who felt compelled to do that."

A tear rolled down her cheek. "And my husband won't be stuck with crushing medical bills if and when I finally pass away from cancer."

Jake listened with a familiar sadness of death and loss he knew only too well. "I suggest you don't tell anybody. Not one soul. Quietly get the divorce, but keep wearing your rings and living together as if nothing has changed."

"Could you secretly handle the paperwork?"

"I have a friend who is a divorce mediator," Jake said. "She has the forms in her computer that spell out how there is no alimony, etcetera."

"I want my husband to get the house, of course." More tears rolled down her face.

Jake handed her a paper napkin. "You're the boss.

"Whatever you want. It's none of my business, but if I may ask, how are your treatments going?"

"Pretty well," Peggy said. "I've been lucky, but my insurance isn't the best."

He let out a breath. "Some are better than others."

"My doctor is an angel, though."

"I know people at the hospital. Cody is a favorite visitor to the children's oncology unit. Let us go with you next time."

She wiped her tears. "Love to."

"Okay, you have my number Give me a call and we'll meet you there." Jake spotted a uniformed woman enter the cafe, walk to the counter and gaze at the chalkboard coffee menu.

He called out, "The officer will have a number eleven. On my tab, please."

A cheerful young barista said, "Coming right up." She gestured at the bottom of the list for Roxanne's benefit.

Jake saw Rox look at number eleven, which was named Rox Star. He'd tipped the barista to add the officer's favorite drink to their daily top ten.

Roxanne turned to glance at Jake and used one finger to push her glasses higher on her nose. "This place has class."

They exchanged a smile. "It was Cody's idea."

Cody trotted over to Roxanne.

"Be friends, Cody," Jake said.

She patted him on the back.

"Good dog."

Roxanne carried her coffee to Jake's table, with Cody escorting her.

Jake stood up and pulled out a chair for Rox. "Officer Poole, this is my new friend, Peggy."

Peggy shook hands. "Pleased to meet you, Officer Poole."

"Call me Roxanne."

They all sat down, and Roxanne swiped on her phone.

"Please describe the person of interest, and my AI bot will try to draw his face."

After Peggy gave her best description, Roxanne asked questions about the resulting image. Peggy offered corrections to the hair, nose and chin. Several minutes later, she appeared amazed at the result. "Yes, that looks like him."

Jake studied the face on Roxanne's phone. "Send that to me, please. I'm going to show it to a cop on horseback."

CHAPTER 52

Roxanne texted the image to Jake's phone.

He thanked her, said goodbye to Peggy, then walked Cody along the beach and spotted the cop. Jake waved at the police officer and approached his horse slowly and politely. "Cody, be friends. Sit. Stay."

Cody obeyed. He raised his nose and sniffed, but sat still and didn't frighten the horse.

The cop said, "I arrested those young men, and they got a free ride in a police car."

Jake smiled at the old joke. "Good work. Did one of them look like this sketch?" He held up his phone.

The cop reached out his leather gloved hand to take the device and study its display screen. "That guy was carrying tranq."

"Powder or pills?" Jake said. "I'm looking for a dealer."

"He had the pills that look like aspirin, but the word is misspelled."

"Quantity to distribute?"

"Yeah, and his pockets were stuffed with cash."

"You did me a huge favor, and now I owe you one." Jake handed over his business card. "I'm assisting a federal task force investigating tranq supply lines in the city and state."

"Have you learned anything we can use here in the city?"

Jake nodded. "Yes, and the guy you busted will tell us more."

"Glad I could help the task force today." The cop tipped his hat and rode off.

Jake drove through the city to the Golden Gate Bridge. Crossing the span, he gazed out at the blue water on both sides. It was an amazing sight he never grew tired of. He noticed how Cody always stuck his head out the window, sniffed the breeze and looked at the water, too. It was as if the smart dog was trying to understand how they could be on a road in the sky.

On the other side, he took the exit to Sausalito, headed downhill and arrived at Juanita Yacht Harbor.

As they walked through the parking lot, Cody sniffed the breeze and barked at Jake.

Jake could smell the grilled chicken. "You hungry after that swim, buddy?"

Cody trotted to a nearby food truck and drank water from a large bowl.

"Cody wait." Jake chased after his ornery dog.

An attractive Japanese woman looked out the window. "Hi Jake, where have you guys been?"

"Hi Yumi, we were in the Florida Keys, helping two clients buy their dream boat." He pronounced her name as you-mee.

"You want your usual?" Yumi asked. "One order of teriyaki chicken, and one of plain grilled chicken?"

"Yes, please. We'll take it to go."

"Coming right up."

Jake sat down at one of the picnic tables. "Don't ever run away from me off-leash. Do you hear me, Cody?"

Cody hung his head, with a guilty hangdog expression that Jake had seen many times.

Jake scratched Cody behind his ears. "You're still a good doggie."

Cody immediately perked up and wagged his tail.

A few minutes later, Yumi set the take-out order on her window tray, and rang a desk bell.

Jake tipped her a ridiculous amount, and led Cody to their marina.

They boarded the *Far Niente* and Jake sat down to eat. Cody gobbled up his grilled chicken as if Jake had been starving him for days.

Jake received a call from an unknown number, the kind most people wouldn't answer. "Hello?"

A Russian-accented voice said, "Jake. It's Dmitry. Remember me?" The man coughed and sounded like he was having trouble breathing.

"How are you, my friend?" Jake said with concern for the older man who had health issues. They'd once almost killed each other but now were friends.

"Listen to me. You kicked a hornet's nest."

"What else is new?"

"This is on another level," Dmitry said. "You could lose your boat, your dog, your girlfriend, your Marshals badge, and your license to practice law, if you live through it."

"What are you talking about?"

"There's a way out if you hurry."

Jake took a deep breath. "I'm listening."

"Sheriff Deputy Corrine Denton planted tranq on your boat. She's going to bust you for possession with intent to distribute and then confiscate the yacht via forfeiture laws."

"She's a sociopath."

"Also a devious, cunning and obsessive malignant narcissist with borderline personality disorder."

Jake let out a breath. "Borderline? She's crossed that line by now."

"Don't underestimate her. After you're arrested, Denton will plant more tranq at Sarah's pet clinic, along with paperwork that shows Sarah bought it in batches from various online companies."

"Nobody in their right mind would believe that about Sarah."

"Reality doesn't matter. People in law enforcement will follow orders. Once you and Sarah are incarcerated, Cody will go live with Terrell and Alicia."

"And?"

Dmitry coughed again. "Denton will plant tranq at their house, too."

"Leaving Cody alone and vulnerable."

"Exactly."

"How do you know all of this?"

"I have my sources," Dmitry said. "Listen, your only hope is to take the *Far Niente* out on the ocean and dump the tranq overboard with fishing weights attached."

Jake looked out at the water. "Tossing that drug into the ocean could kill tons of sea life."

"It's in an airtight container."

"How much time do I have?"

"None. Denton is on her way to Juanita Yacht Harbor as we speak. Get your boat out of there. Go right now." Dmitry hacked violently and let out a wet cough.

"Hang on." Jake untied the lines, hurried up to the bridge, and motored toward the bay. "We're leaving the harbor now."

He glanced back and saw a sheriff's car arrive. A

uniformed deputy stepped out. Corrine Denton. She raised her pistol and aimed at the departing motor yacht.

"Cody, take cover." Jake and Cody dropped prone.

Jake heard Denton fire all seventeen rounds from her sheriff department-issued Glock 17 pistol, and several bullets hit the *Far Niente*.

Jake heard the impact and wondered where they'd landed. If he grabbed his rifle and quickly returned fire while Denton reloaded, she'd be a sitting duck for an infantry Marine. But he would never fire a weapon at a law enforcement officer.

"Stay down Cody." He stood up and flattened the throttles against the dash, causing the boat to rise up on plane and rocket across the water.

Setting his phone on speaker, Jake said, "Denton shot at us without warning or probable cause."

Dmitry said, "Go under the bridge and onto the ocean. Cruise to international waters as fast as you can."

Jake turned the wheel to avoid hitting a sailboat at full throttle. "California's jurisdiction of the coast is three nautical miles. I'll be there soon."

Dmitry hacked and cleared phlegm from his throat. "Harbor security cameras recorded Denton. Your friend Detective Flynn of the Sausalito PD can forward a copy to the Chief Deputy Sheriff."

"How do you know more about what's going on at my harbor than I do?"

Dmitry chuckled. "Jake, my old friend, if I tell you a secret, can you keep it to yourself?"

"Yes, you have my word." Jake raced under the Golden Gate. He patted his thigh. Cody leapt to his feet and stood close.

"I'm sure you remember Elena Savina," Dmitry said. "She

once hacked into a SFPD police car laptop computer and then all of the city's security cameras."

"How could I forget the Russian mafia's crime queen of California?"

"After she went to prison, I gained entry to her network and now have access to cameras and laptops all over the Bay Area."

Jake's phone buzzed as he received a video of Denton firing her pistol at the *Far Niente*. "I see what you mean."

"Send that to Detective Flynn."

"I'm doing it now," Jake said.

"Here's another video from early this morning when she planted the evidence."

Jake watched the video as he cruised past the Golden Gate and onto the ocean. He saw Denton tie a heavy-duty fishing line to the *Far Niente*'s anchor at the bow. She then attached a large clear orange juice bottle with a handle and screw cap. The bottle was full of pills and Denton lowered it down below the water's surface, out of sight.

Unknown to Jake, he'd been towing the contraband under the *Far Niente*'s bow between the catamaran's twin hulls as he headed for international waters.

"Now I understand why Cody didn't smell the drugs and alert me."

"I'll let you go so you can sink that tranq," Dmitry said.

"Thank you, my friend." Jake ended the call.

He reached the three nautical mile destination, entered international waters, and then brought the *Far Niente* to a full stop and let her drift. He gloved up, moved to the bow, reeled in the fishing line, and grabbed the plastic jug full of pills. Cutting it free near the handle, he left the fishing line attached to his anchor and tossed it back into the water.

Jake brought out a crab pot and put the plastic jug inside,

then lowered the pot deep and left it there with a red-and-white float attached to the rope at the surface. He opened the Navionics app on his phone and dropped a pin to save the location.

Once the drug stash was no longer on board, he motored away fast, leaving the anonymous crab pot behind. Most boaters stayed in the bay and wouldn't pass near the float. If anyone did, they'd steer clear to avoid having a rope wind around their propellor. Theft from crab pots happened sometimes, but it wasn't common.

As Jake cruised miles away from the drug stash, he called Terrell, who answered with, "Coffee break?"

"I wish." Jake gave Terrell a brief situation report and sent him the two videos starring Denton.

Terrell whistled. "What a mess for the chief deputy sheriff to clean up. I feel sorry for her."

"Yeah, she'll have to ask for Denton's resignation," Jake said.

"I'd bet the sheriff's marine unit is receiving an anonymous tip right now about the *Far Niente*."

"I've talked to those fine folks on many occasions," Jake said. "We get along well."

"That won't stop them from arresting you if you're in possession with intent to distribute," Terrell said.

"Thank goodness I'm not in possession."

"You confirm you're on the *Far Niente* and there are no drugs on board?"

"Confirmed," Jake said. "Denton attached the tranq to my anchor, but now there's only a length of fishing line hanging off."

"Smart move," Terrell said. "The sheriffs will think the line broke and the planted evidence floated away or sank to the bottom."

"I'm in international waters right now."

"Out of jurisdiction, but happy to cooperate with your friends in maritime law enforcement," Terrell said.

Jake thought about the quantity of pills. "Where would Denton get her hands on that much xylazine? A value-size bottle of aspirin holds five hundred pills. You could pour ten bottles worth into that big juice jug. That's five thousand doses."

"She might have stolen it from the sheriff's evidence storage warehouse," Terrell said. "But most times those pills are found in vacuum-sealed, airtight plastic bags. Why transfer them to an orange juice jug?"

"Maybe to make sure it looks different from the evidence locker stuff."

"I'll dispatch Captain Leeds and *Marine One* to your location at high speed. They can inspect your anchor before the sheriff's boat arrives." Terrell ended the call.

Soon, Jake spotted *Marine One* roaring across the water toward him.

CHAPTER 53

The *Far Niente's* VHF radio crackled and Jake heard the familiar deep, gravelly voice of Captain Leeds. "This is police boat *Marine One*, hailing the *Far Niente*. Over."

"Aye sir. This is Captain Wolfe of the *Far Niente*. How may I be of service to the marine police today? Over."

"I'm asking permission to come aboard. Over."

"Permission granted, Captain. You are always welcome aboard. Over."

"Thank you," Captain Leeds said. "Stand by while we deploy our Zodiac. Over and out."

Marine One slowed, came to a stop, and the police launched their rigid inflatable boat. Captain Leeds came aboard the *Far Niente* and shook hands with Jake.

"Welcome aboard, Captain," Jake said. "Be friends, Cody."

Cody sniffed the familiar hand of Captain Leeds and wagged his tail.

"I saw the surveillance video of my former coworker planting evidence on your boat anchor and then firing a pistol at you," Captain Leeds said.

"Denton had a busy day." Jake noticed the Zodiac pilot idling over to the bow where the anchor was located.

Captain Leeds's phone pinged, and he studied the screen. "You have fishing line attached to your anchor, but no contraband." He held the display so Jake could see it.

"I was cruising pretty fast," Jake said. "The *Far Niente*'s twin engines provide over seven hundred horsepower each."

"Did you hear anything bump against the hull?"

"Sometimes we'll hit a small piece of driftwood that thumps and bumps."

Captain Leeds gazed out at the ocean. "If we could find that big bottle of tranq pills, it would be evidence against Denton."

Jake nodded. "But since you didn't, the SFPD won't have to get involved. You can let the chief deputy sheriff handle it internally."

Captain Leeds raised his chin toward an arriving sheriff boat.

Jake observed the brand new M2-37 twin-engine aluminum Moose Boat racing toward them with lights flashing. The water-jet-propelled diesel outboard catamaran was fast, probably cruising at a speed of 25 to 30 knots. It was a popular boat among law enforcement agencies and fire departments from coast to coast.

A sheriff hailed them on the radio. "Ahoy *Far Niente*. This is Deputy Sheriff Captain Yoshida of sheriff boat *Patrol One*. Over."

Captain Leeds said to Jake, "May I?"

Jake handed him the radio mic. "Be my guest."

"Captain Yoshida, this is Police Captain Leeds of *Marine One*. By any chance did you receive an anonymous tip there was a quantity of xylazine attached to the *Far Niente*'s anchor? Over."

There was a pause and then Captain Yoshida replied, "Yes, but we can see there's nothing attached, Captain. Over."

"Agreed, Captain. Someone played a prank on us. *Marine One* will move on now. There's nothing to see here. Over and out." Captain Leeds tipped his hat at the sheriff's boat, which turned and sped back toward the bay. He waved at the Zodiac pilot to come pick him up.

"Thanks for handling that," Jake said.

Captain Leeds nodded. "I didn't want Yoshida to get involved in Denton's mess by no fault of his own. Like you said, let the chief deputy sheriff handle it." He took a seat in the Zodiac, and the pilot returned to *Marine One*.

As the police boat cruised away, Jake checked the *Far Niente* for bullet holes. He followed the starboard walkway of the boat's full walk-around decks, went around the bow, and came down the port side. The damage wasn't too bad. It could have been worse. He'd get it repaired right away, keeping his promise to Dylan that he'd take good care of the motor yacht. Dylan had given Agent McKay his blessing for Jake to use the *Far Niente* in privateer actions.

Thinking of Dylan, Jake was reminded of his friend's other boat slip at Pier 39. He could cruise over there, have dinner with Sarah, and invite her to spend the night on board. The next morning he'd take Cody for a walk along Beach Street to visit the Marina Green.

While cruising toward the pier, Jake stopped by the fuel dock and topped off his boat's tank with marine diesel.

With that done, he idled toward the marina entrance. His phone buzzed with a call from Terrell, who asked, "Where are you?"

"On the boat, arriving at Pier Thirty-Nine," Jake said. "Why? What's up?"

"Chief Deputy Sheriff Leslie Ritter wants a private word with you on board the *Far Niente*."

Jake wasn't sure what to make of that. "Roger. I'll wait for her at the boat slip."

"Good to go."

Soon Jake motored into the pier marina and then idled through a no-wake zone toward the east side full-time tenant docking. He saw a familiar sign advising all vessels entering the marina to contact the harbormaster. Jake called Kevin and put the phone on speaker as he berthed the *Far Niente* at Dylan's boat slip and tied the lines.

Kevin said, "Hi Jake. Chief Deputy Sheriff Leslie Ritter is waiting here to see you."

Jake placed the US Marshals star on his belt. "Please send her to my dock. I'll unlock the gate."

"She's on her way." Kevin ended the call.

Jake was pleased to see Leslie Ritter. "Chief Ritter, it's always a pleasure." He opened the gate and held it for her.

"Thank you, Jake." Chief Ritter walked onto his dock.

"Yes, ma'am. What can I do for you?"

"Let's talk on your boat."

"Okay, please allow my dog to smell your pistol first. He's a war dog veteran who can't help it. Be friends, Cody. The chief is a Marine."

Cody sniffed the woman's pistol and looked up at her with bright eyes.

"Are we friends now that I've somehow become an honorary Marine?"

Jake smiled. "Friends forever." He led her down the dock past assorted sailboats and motor yachts to the *Far Niente*, and they boarded. "Please have a seat in my office."

They both sat down at the patio table.

"Can I get you anything?" Jake said. "Coffee, tea, water, a soda?"

Chief Ritter shook her head. "No, I'm good."

Jake clasped his hands. "What can I do for you?"

"First of all, thank you for helping me with that insurance claim a while back."

"My pleasure. Most insurance companies do good work, but a few require motivation."

"I see you're wearing a US Marshals badge."

"Yes, ma'am. Sometimes Cody and I volunteer when a task force needs an extra K-9 and handler."

She looked at the Bay Bridge that led to Oakland. "Your dog found that shipping container full of xylazine."

Jake only nodded.

They sat in silence for a moment as she gazed at passing boats on the water. "I need that orange juice bottle full of tranq. I'll use it to make Denton resign."

Jake looked her in the eye. "How would that work?"

"I'll have it sitting on my desk when I call her into my office for a discussion about her career options."

Jake nodded. "Some people in law enforcement fire their weapons and justify it in a report."

"Right, but Denton's possession of that much xylazine, along with a video of her in possession..."

"That would be a career-ending event for Denton, but also an embarrassing moment for the new chief deputy," Jake said.

"That's why I want to handle it personally and privately. I'll take the deadly contraband off your hands and use it to make Denton quit the sheriff's department."

"Two birds, one stone. You're good. All right, let's do this." Jake stood up. "You're finally taking a spin on the yacht like I've invited you to, but not for a fun reason."

Ritter stood. "I'll still enjoy the experience."

"Please join me at the wheel and sit in the second seat." Jake untied the lines.

When they passed the sliding glass door, Chief Ritter noticed the star-shaped marking. "Looks like the result of a round hitting bulletproof glass."

"Denton shot at me and my dog."

He led Chief Ritter up to the bridge, and they took seats in the black leather and chrome chairs before motoring out of the harbor and onto the bay. He showed the chief his phone and where he'd dropped a pin on his Navionics app.

They passed under the bridge and cruised on the ocean for a while until Jake arrived at the location and spotted the red-and-white float. "There it is."

He came to a stop, dropped anchor and set up the electric winch. Minutes later, he pulled the crab pot up to the surface and set it on the stern deck. Jake gloved up, opened the pot, and removed its contents. He placed the juice jug into a dark green trash bag and tied the top in a knot.

"There you go. It's all yours, Chief."

"Clever hiding place. I owe you a favor."

Jake looked her in the eye. "I have one in mind."

"Let's hear it."

"I made friends with a detention deputy named Moore at jail number two," Jake said. "She did me some favors when Police Officer Martinelli had been locked up in the general population quarters. The deputy can't stand working in jail and wants a transfer to patrol, or else she might quit."

"I'll see what I can do," Chief Ritter said. "I'm short on deputies and can't lose her."

"Since I'm asking, I'll add that she'd love to be on the water with Captain Yoshida of *Patrol One*. I saw the new boat and noticed there weren't any female deputies on board."

Chief Ritter squinted at him. "Really? The last thing I need right now is a gender discrimination lawsuit."

"Moore could help you prevent that."

"Thanks for the idea." Chief Ritter swept her hand toward the shoreline. "Now let's head back."

Jake returned the way they'd come and soon pulled the *Far Niente* into its boat slip and tied the lines. They all disembarked and walked up the dock.

Chief Ritter put the trash bag in the back cargo area of her sheriff's department SUV. "Remember to keep this between us."

Jake nodded. "Will do. Attorney-client privilege. And remember, you're welcome on board the *Far Niente* anytime."

"I can't believe I have to make one of my deputies resign." She shook her head. "After I gave her a fair chance to redeem herself."

"It's a shame, but you're doing the right thing to ensure public safety. You don't have any other choice."

Chief Ritter gave him a grateful smile and drove away.

Jake hoped Denton wouldn't become violently angry when Chief Ritter forced her to turn in her badge and gun.

CHAPTER 54

After Chief Ritter left, Jake and Cody took a cab to Bart's law office where Jake spent several hours going over strategy to help Tammi. McKay had given Tammi top-secret clearances so she could assist Jake when necessary. She wanted Tammi back on the job at the police department.

Later that day, he returned to the *Far Niente* and invited Sarah to have dinner with him and spend the night.

After work, Sarah rode a cable car to Fisherman's Wharf. Jake and Cody met her, and they all walked a short distance to the pier.

They ordered takeout food, dined on the stern deck patio, and Jake told Sarah about his day.

Sarah shook her head. "Good grief. You had a more interesting day than I did."

"I don't think Denton knows about this other boat slip, so hopefully we're out of sight and out of mind."

"It's so convenient for both of us at this marina," Sarah said.

Jake changed the subject. Sarah enjoyed the busy city life,

while he preferred the peace and quiet of small-town Sausalito. Maybe they could compromise. Some nights here, and some there. Jake found he could enjoy the pier on weekdays, but not on Friday, Saturday, and Sunday when tourists mobbed Fisherman's Wharf.

The next morning, Jake and Cody accompanied Sarah to the cable car stop and saw her off. Once she was on her way to the clinic, Jake walked Cody along beautiful Beach Street to the Marina Green, where they enjoyed the 74 acres of grass next to the bay. People were flying kites, enjoying picnics, tossing Frisbees, walking dogs, riding bikes, sunbathing, jogging, rollerblading, and enjoying the views.

"Off duty, Cody," Jake said.

They strolled on lush green grass along sparkling blue water. After a while Jake led Cody across to the sidewalk along Marina Boulevard where a food truck sold ice cream cones. He bought a scoop of vanilla in a paper bowl and set it down on the grass for Cody to enjoy.

While his dog tried to set a world record for devouring ice cream as fast as possible, Jake admired the beautiful homes across the street. One was for sale, and a quick check online using his phone revealed the bargain price of "only $15 million."

As he stood there, a junker car drove past going slow. Too slow.

Cody alerted, barking at a perceived threat to his handler.

Jake felt a chill as he saw the masked driver aiming a small handgun out the window. "Cody, take cover." He flipped a wooden picnic table on its side, and they both ducked behind it as the drive-by shooter fired.

A single bullet hit Jake on the left side of his upper chest. The wound felt like he'd been pierced with a red-hot drill that twisted into him. As blood gushed out of his body and stained his shirt, time slowed down. He became dizzy from shock and loss of blood. This had happened before on a deployment, and he knew the familiar process.

He sat on the grass bleeding and called 911, which wasn't a luxury available overseas. Cody howled and sniffed the wound that could kill his handler.

"Easy boy. We're both still alive, so far," Jake said.

"Nine-one-one, what is your emergency?"

Jake had to make an effort to speak slowly and clearly, despite the flood of adrenaline in his bloodstream. "There was a drive-by shooting. I've been hit by one bullet. I'm bleeding from a gunshot wound and need an ambulance at the Marina Green, across the street from the following address." He glanced at his phone and recited the address of the home for sale.

"Ambulance en route. Apply pressure to the wound."

"Yes, ma'am. Thank you."

Next, he called Beppe and told him the news. "Can you come here and take Cody to stay with Sarah?"

Beppe cursed in Italian. "On my way."

A crowd gathered, and Cody barked at them.

A short, slender Asian woman stepped forward and displayed a professional looking first aid kit. "I'm a doctor. Tell your dog to stand down, and let me help you."

Jake held his right hand against the flowing wound, applying direct pressure and trying to staunch the blood loss. "Open the first aid kit so I can see you don't have a gun in there."

She blinked at him and unzipped the red soft case with a white cross, to expose the contents. "All good?"

"Be friends, Cody," Jake said. "This woman is a Navy corpsman."

Cody understood the words Navy corpsman, and he allowed her to get close, but he sniffed her for any hidden weapons.

She kneeled by Jake and applied a QuikClot gauze dressing to the bullet wound.

Jake had seen it many times. A hemostatic wound dressing that promoted rapid blood clotting. Navy corpsmen called it combat gauze.

After the doctor stopped the bleeding and applied a bandage on top, she used white medical tape to hold it in place.

Jake said, "Thank you, doc."

"Keep the pressure on like you did before," she said. "I've seen a lot of gunshot wounds in my career. I'd say the bullet was from a small-caliber round. Maybe a twenty-two short. Let me see your back."

Jake nodded. "The handgun looked and sounded like a pocket pistol. A Saturday night special." He let her pull his jacket up and inspect his body.

"The bullet went clear through," the doctor said. She placed another QuikClot gauze to the wound on his upper back. "Can you feel your left arm?"

"It's going numb." Jake pressed his right hand harder onto the bandaged wound on his chest, and the doctor put hers on his back.

He groaned in pain as a patrol car screeched to a stop and a uniformed police officer stepped out. He recognized the Black woman named Gabriella. She'd been with him that time Beth Cushman's son Kyle had hacked dozens of drones and taken control of them.

Gabriella said, "Jake, you'd better survive this, or I'll be mad as hell at you. Did you see the shooter?"

Jake gave a pained smile in reply to his friend's attempt at cop humor. "Anonymous person driving past in an older car wearing a Guy Fawkes mask."

"Like in that movie, V for Vendetta?" Gabriella said.

"Yeah."

"No way to ID the perp," Gabriella said. "What about the car?"

"Probably stolen." Jake was angry that after all he'd been through and survived, a cheap little gun and tiny bullet might be what finally killed him.

Sirens pierced the air as an ambulance approached and pulled over. Two EMTs jumped out and put Jake on a stretcher.

Cody barked at them, but Beppe ran up and said, "Out, Cody. To me, buddy."

Jake told his dog, "Cody, stay with Beppe. That's an order, Marine."

Cody pawed the sidewalk and whined.

Jake said, "Beppe, grab the Jeep keys out of my coat pocket."

Beppe did so, and Cody sniffed his hand. The dog had seen Jake's friend drive the SUV before and pilot the *Far Niente*.

Beppe used the fob to open the Jeep's automatic K-9 door.

Jake said, "Cody, get in the Humvee."

Cody gave one last bark and then obeyed orders.

As soon as the dog was safe inside, Beppe closed the K-9 door, slid behind the wheel, and nodded at Jake.

The two EMTs loaded Jake into their ambulance. He waved at Gabriella as she spoke into her shoulder mic, and he told the doctor, "Thank you."

The doors closed, and the female EMT drove while the man hooked Jake up with an IV of fluids.

Jake wondered who had shot him and why. It seemed like the dirtbag had been aiming for Cody. He would find that person and teach them a lesson.

The male EMT now held a syringe in his hand.

Jake fought to stay focused. "Local pain meds only. Do not give me addictive drugs."

The man paid no attention to Jake, aiming the syringe at the IV drip bag.

Jake reached out to grab the EMT's wrist, but the man dodged Jake's hand and injected something into the bag.

Jake's body and mind became fuzzy and numb. He cursed the man and mumbled profanity as he began slipping into a fog.

The EMT grinned at him and whispered, "This is for the best. It's a painless death for you and huge money for me. I can finally settle my payday loans. Die quietly now. Go to sleep."

Jake felt weak, losing consciousness. He decided that if he was going to die, he'd go out with a bang, using one last move he'd practiced a thousand times—one his body would reflexively perform in almost any situation.

He exercised sheer willpower to force his bloody right hand to draw his sidearm in one smooth motion and shoot the grinning man at point-blank range.

With the last of his strength, Jake tore the IV needle out of his arm, desperately hoping to avoid an overdose.

His mind reeled from the kind of drug he hated with a passion. The kind that had killed so many friends. He struggled to keep his eyes open and take deep breaths as his vision blurred and his pulse slowed down while his strong heart thudded heavily in his wounded chest as it labored against the chemical's debilitating effects.

CHAPTER 55

As the ambulance arrived at the hospital ER, Jake continued fighting to remain conscious. He heard a roaring in his ears.

The female EMT driver jumped out and placed him on a gurney. She ran inside and handed him off to a nurse who immediately took charge and rolled the gurney along a hallway while shouting at people to get out of her way.

Jake's world came in and out of focus as he lay on his back, looking up at bright fluorescent ceiling lights flashing past, one after another.

The nurse said, "Hang on. Stay with me."

Jake tried to talk, slurring his words. "I'm on some kind of drug."

"One EMT gave you an overdose of morphine," she said. "You shot him with a gun. The other EMT pulled over and gave you Narcan."

"God bless her."

"The man you shot is barely alive. He's going into surgery, like you. The ambulance driver told police you acted in self-defense."

"Two people have tried to kill me within the past hour," Jake said. "Good and bad things often come in threes."

"I'll try to avoid being a third." The nurse rolled Jake into a surgery room where a man in scrubs stood waiting.

"Hello Mr. Wolfe. Do you remember when you threatened me and said I'd better save Detective Terrell Hayes's life, or else?"

Jake blinked at the man as a memory came back to his addled mind. "Sorry about that, doc." He wondered if this guy would be the third person who might try to kill him.

The doctor smiled. "Oh, good. You do remember. Well, no hard feelings. I happened to be here today and volunteered to do surgery on you. Aren't you the lucky one?"

Jake said, "Wait a minute. You're a brain surgeon."

The doctor held a hissing plastic mask over Jake's nose and mouth. "Everybody says you should have your head examined."

Jake tried not to breathe the gas, but fell unconscious as he reached for his missing pistol he'd let go of in order to grab the IV and yank it out. The holster was empty. Everything went dark.

Sarah walked along the hospital's antiseptic hallways toward Jake's room. She wore her doctor lab coat and dress clothes from work in order to fit in and gain the cooperation of staff. Cody trotted by her side wearing a vest featuring the words "Therapy K-9." The dog's nails made a *click-click-click* on the linoleum as the duo approached a young uniformed police officer who stood guard outside of Jake's door. Sarah presented her ID. The man checked a list on his phone, nodded, and stood aside.

Entering the room, Sarah found Jake in bed, sound asleep, with Secret Service Agent Yvonne Greene standing beside him and holding one of his hands in both of hers.

Greene turned to look at the door when it opened. She let go of Jake's hand and stepped back. "McKay told me to check on him, but I was just leaving. I took his pulse and it's strong. The nurse said he's been asking for you, Sarah. I'm glad you're here."

Cody woofed at Greene, and she patted him on the head as she hurried out.

Sarah said nothing. She was aware of the woman's interest in Jake as more than a friendly colleague. But that was too bad. Agent Greene would have to find somebody else. Sarah would stay close to Jake while he took time to heal.

Jake slowly awakened from the dark fog of anesthesia. He felt someone holding his hand.

"Come back to me, Jake," a woman's voice implored him.

Opening his eyes, he found himself in a hospital bed with an IV tube connected to his inner elbow by a shunt. Glowing monitors kept track of his vitals.

An attractive woman stood by his side, holding his hand tightly in both of hers.

"Sarah," Jake whispered, his mouth and throat dry.

"Hey, sleepyhead." Sarah appeared to be fighting back tears and downplaying her anxiety about his gunshot wound. She reached for a cup of ice chips and fed some to him.

"Thank you," Jake said, licking his dry lips.

Sarah leaned in and kissed him. "You had us worried, but I told Cody you're too ornery to get into Heaven, and the devil is afraid if he lets you into Hell you'd kick his butt, so you'll probably be sticking around here on Earth for a while."

Cody stood on his hind legs and licked Jake's face.

"Ugh, dog slobber," Jake said with a smile and ruffled his dog's ears.

Jake felt high on meds and a bit confused. Did he smell a slight aroma of two different perfumes lingering in the air? Sarah's usual favorite, and another that seemed familiar.

Sarah might have been reading his mind when she said, "I bumped into Agent Greene when she stopped by to check on you. She said McKay told her to visit."

"McKay cares about her people," Jake said innocently.

The look on Sarah's face told Jake she wasn't buying it but hoped this too shall pass. "Hmm," she said.

"I feel so tired."

"You're getting pain meds in your drip."

"My left arm feels limp."

"You'll need months of PT to rebuild muscle strength."

"Is there a bandage on my head?"

"No, why would there be?"

Jake shrugged. "A brain surgeon gave me a hard time."

"I don't understand."

"No worries. I hope the bullet wound doesn't leave a scar on my chest." Jake smiled at his own attempt at humor.

Sarah smiled, too. "A fresh scar on each side added to your collection."

"Scar tissue is what holds me together."

Sarah picked up a get-well card from a bedside table, glanced inside and handed it to Jake. "It's from Father O'Leary."

Jake read the hand-written note out loud. "No weapon forged against you will prevail. Isaiah Fifty-four Seventeen. NIV Bible."

"I wonder if he gave you the last rites when he stopped by." Sarah closed her eyes for a moment and wrung her hands.

Jake paid close attention to her emotional state and changed the subject. "Maybe you and I could fit in this bed together. There's a hospital bed shortage, you know. We'd be doing our part to help."

Sarah climbed in on his right side and gently curled up to him, and Cody leapt up and lay at their feet.

The door opened, and Beppe entered, followed by Madison.

"Is this a bad time?" Madison asked, her face turning pink.

Jake smiled at them. "No, it's perfect timing because Cody needs a drink of bottled water."

"Coming right up." Beppe went out the door.

Madison said, "How are you doing, Jake? Please tell me you're going to be okay."

"It hurts like a . . . but doc says I'll heal up like new in no time."

"Oh, thank God. I was so worried."

"Thank you, Maddie."

"And thank *you* for introducing me to Beppe. He's the best thing that has ever happened to me."

"And you're the best thing that has ever happened to him. It was meant to be. Take good care of each other."

Beppe came back inside and poured water into Jake's cup of ice chips for Cody to drink.

Jake said, "Oh sure. Give my ice to Cody. I see how it is."

The dog gave Jake a retriever grin with ice water dripping off his mouth.

Sarah said, "I can get you another one."

"Thanks, but I'm good," Jake said. "I just had to give Beppe some grief."

Beppe placed both hands on his heart in an over-dramatic gesture.

Madison smiled. "You two are sooo Italian. I see it now."

"Joking aside, did they find out who shot me?" Jake said.

"Family and friends are on the lookout and we have one lead," Beppe said.

"I want his name and how he knew where to find me."

Beppe held his phone close to Jake so only he could see the photo of a face on its display. "Anselmo orders you to let the Family handle it."

Jake felt his dormant anger flare up when he recognized Denton's face. As a law enforcement official, she could log into a website and track his phone. He hoped Chief Deputy Sheriff Ritter would make Denton resign ASAP. Maybe she already had and Denton was breaking the law by using the website without legal authority. If so, she could continue stalking Jake until the chief revoked her log-in and password.

CHAPTER 56

A female doctor entered Jake's room, dressed in a white lab coat and carrying a clipboard. "Jake, I'm Dr. Rousseau. We need to talk."

"Any relation to the late great philosopher Jean-Jacques Rousseau?"

"I'm not sure, but I'd like to think so," she said. "Why is there a woman in your bed?"

"I paid extra for the deluxe suite."

Sarah chuckled, and Cody barked at the doctor.

"Out, Cody." Jake added the magic words, "Navy corpsman."

Dr. Rousseau squinted at Jake. "This is highly unusual."

"Not for me, it isn't." Jake glanced at the clipboard and papers. "In my experience, if a woman says we need to talk, it's rarely good news." He gave her a playful wink.

She narrowed her eyes. "You were lucky as far as gunshot wounds go."

"I eat Lucky Charms cereal for breakfast."

"I'm a hepatologist who specializes in liver health. After reviewing your bloodwork, I had some concerns."

Beppe and Madison left the room to give Jake privacy.

"I don't have hepatitis, do I?" Jake glanced at Sarah, who raised her eyebrows in alarm.

"No, you don't," Dr. Rousseau assured him.

"Whew. Then what's the bad news?"

"I ordered a CT scan and MRI to check your liver for scar damage." Dr. Rousseau consulted one of the papers on her clipboard.

Sarah asked her, "Scars from cirrhosis?"

Dr. Rousseau nodded. "Yes. The damage slowly grows over many years of alcohol abuse. Scar tissue replaces healthy liver tissue."

Jake wasn't surprised. "What percent is still healthy?"

The doctor consulted her notes again. "Over ninety percent healthy. And lucky for you, the liver is the one and only organ that can regenerate and grow new tissue to replace injured areas."

"So, I don't need a transplant?"

Dr. Rousseau set her clipboard down on the bedside table. "Not if you give up alcohol."

Jake paused a moment as the idea sunk in that he'd been harming his healthy body with alcohol. "I'd imagine there must be a long waiting list for a donated liver, and I might not qualify."

"Approximately twelve thousand people around the world go on the list every year," she said. "But you'll never be added because you can only qualify for a liver transplant if you're not considered at risk of future alcohol abuse."

It sounded to Jake like a well-rehearsed speech the doctor had recited many times. "I don't think of my drinking as alcohol abuse. I'm simply an enthusiastic imbiber of tasty adult beverages."

Dr. Rousseau shook her head. "You're in denial. What do you drink? Beer, wine, liquor? How much, and how often?"

Jake shrugged one shoulder. "All three. Every day. More than my fair share."

Sarah closed her eyes for a moment and nodded in agreement. She knew.

Dr. Rousseau observed Sarah. "My official medical advice is that you give it up."

"Which one?" Jake said.

"Stop drinking alcoholic beverages of any kind for ninety days."

"I want a second opinion." Jake smiled at seeing her facial reaction. Sometimes he tried to overcome his fears by using humor. "Besides quitting cold turkey, is there another option?"

"If you continue drinking, one day in the future we may have to surgically remove half of your liver."

"Then what? Drink half as much?"

The doctor stared at him, not amused. "You'd need to abstain from alcohol until your half liver grew back to full size and full health."

"Option three?"

"If the damage becomes too serious, as a last resort, we might remove your entire liver and replace it with the transplanted half of a donor's healthy liver. Each divided liver grows back to full size in both your body and the living donor's body. Providing that you avoid alcohol, of course."

Jake gazed at the doctor in curiosity. "Where do you find a donor willing to give up half of their healthy liver?"

"Sometimes a friend or family member will volunteer. Then we test them to see if they're a match."

Jake thought it over. "I feel like that would be far too much for me to ask."

"In a rare coincidence, one person already offered to be your donor if, and when, you might need one, but if you stop drinking right now, they won't have to take the risk." Dr. Rousseau glanced at Sarah.

Jake said, "Sarah and I don't have the same blood type. Who offered, and how did they know before I did?"

"I'm not allowed to divulge the potential donor's name at this time. A nurse was treating someone for a minor issue and they mentioned you."

"I don't understand," Jake said.

"This person asked about your recovery and said you're such a good guy they'd donate a kidney for you. They said it in jest as a figure of speech, but I was in the room, so I talked to the person about donating half of their liver if needed someday."

"That sounds like my best friend, Terrell Hayes," Jake said. "He once donated his blood to me in a battlefield transfusion."

Dr. Rousseau ignored the question. "Jake, with every single option we've discussed, you'd have to give up alcohol. Why not cowboy up and quit right now?"

Jake put one hand on his abdomen. "Sounds like the liver is a miracle organ and I've been taking mine for granted."

"Yes. It's your body's largest internal organ, and the only one that can regrow and repair itself."

"All I have to do is stay sober for a while and give it a chance?"

Dr. Rousseau nodded. "The scars on your liver tell a story."

"A story of Irish whiskey and fine wine, Hennessy cognac, cold beers on warm days, frozen concoctions, boat drinks and ... damn."

"Now I'm required to ask you something," she said. "Do

you have suicidal thoughts? Are you drinking yourself to death on purpose?"

Sarah shook her head at Dr. Rousseau.

Jake said, "No. I drink to numb my violent memories of combat."

"You don't want to die?"

"Just the opposite. It's important that I stay alive." Jake patted Cody on the head. "People are counting on me."

"If you really mean that, do it for them," she said. "Become a temporary teetotaler."

Jake looked at Sarah instead of the doctor as he said, "Okay, I'll do it. I promise."

Sarah reached out to put one hand on his cheek.

A nurse in scrubs rushed into the room. "Doctor, I need a consult."

As they huddled for a moment to discuss symptoms and treatments, Jake picked up Dr. Rousseau's clipboard, flipped through some pages and found the potential donor's name.

It was Leena, the girl he'd rescued from terrorists and given a Beanie Baby.

He felt a weight on his shoulders. After everything Leena had survived, she was willing to risk an operation to surgically amputate half of her liver for Jake, all because his memories of rescuing her drove him to drink.

No way. He couldn't allow that. He'd take better care of his liver from then on, for Sarah, Cody, Leena, and all of his family and friends who relied on him to remain healthy.

The nurse hurried out, and Dr. Rousseau turned to see Jake setting her clipboard on the table. She gave him a stern look of disapproval. "Any questions?"

"My liver is a potential match for Leena's?"

"You violated her privacy."

"Yes, I did. I'm sorry, and I apologize."

"We'd have to do a lot more testing to find out if you and Leena might be a match," Dr. Rousseau said. "Even if you did match, it would be better if a donor's body and liver were similar in size to yours."

"But beggars can't be choosers?"

"Correct. I collect donors like you collect liver scars."

"I would never put Leena through that. She's suffered enough."

"She told me what you did for her overseas. Were you brave or crazy?"

"Maybe both," Jake admitted.

"How many men in the terrorist camp did you kill that night?"

He looked her in the eye. "All of them."

"And you drink to numb that memory?"

"Yes, and several more that haunt me at night when I try to sleep."

She looked at him with compassion. "I could prescribe sleeping pills."

"No thanks," he said. "I'll just take the allergy medicine that causes drowsiness for man or beast. Benadryl or whatever."

"That repurposed medicine is safe and non-habit-forming."

Someone knocked on the door.

"Come in," Jake said.

Leena opened up and looked at him shyly. "Is it visiting hours?"

Dr. Rousseau smiled at her. "Yes, come in."

As Leena walked inside, she said, "How are you feeling, Jake?"

"Much better. The bullet wound is going to heal up fine.

And Dr. Rousseau said my liver has cirrhosis, but it will magically repair itself if I stop drinking."

Dr. Rousseau patted Jake's hand. "Jake is going to give up alcohol for the sake of everyone who cares about him."

"Only for three months, to rest and rejuvenate."

Leena gave him a big smile. "That's wonderful news. Good for you, Jake. My mom and I care about you very much."

Jake wanted to thank her for offering to be a donor, but he only said, "I know you'd do the same for me."

"You saved my life, and I want to pay you back in some way."

"Send me a daily text message and encourage me to avoid alcohol for ninety days," Jake said. "You'll have paid me back in full."

Leena held out her hand. "Deal. Let's do this."

Jake shook hands. "I have no chance of backing out now. This is one determined young woman." He handed over his phone, and Leena typed in her number.

"My work here is done," Dr. Rousseau said. "Thank you, Leena, for helping me practice medicine."

Leena said, "If my mom gets hired here, she could help you every day."

"Yes, we're all rooting for her and keeping our fingers crossed." Dr. Rousseau opened the door.

Leena waved at Jake. "Get well soon. I'll be checking in."

Jake sighed. "I like to drink a cold beer while watching SportsCenter."

"You can drink a cold, non-alcoholic beer," Leena said.

"Okay, fine. My accountability partner has spoken."

Leena laughed happily and left the room, following Dr. Rousseau.

Sarah said, "Leena is one of the people you saved on that mission you dream about?"

"Yes. And her mother."

"Maybe this will give you closure. With your connections, could you help Leena's mother get the job she applied for here at the hospital?"

"That's a great idea." Jake grabbed his phone and sent a text message to Agent McKay.

CHAPTER 57

Several weeks passed while Jake's bullet wound healed.

In the meantime, someone attacked another woman who looked like Sarah. She'd gone to the gym for an hour of exercise, and when she arrived home to her apartment complex, a tall man lay in wait. Somehow knowing where she lived and what kind of car she drove, he came at her with a red-handled throwing knife, but the neighbor's Doberman pinscher bit his wrist and chased him away.

Jake saw Terrell on a news report where he interviewed the woman and held a brief press conference. "If your condo or apartment building asks you to display a parking permit in your car when you're home, do not hang it on your rearview mirror while you're out running errands."

He displayed a police educational video that showed a car pull up and park in front of a gym. A sexy woman got out wearing painted-on booty shorts and a sports bra top. She sashayed inside, enjoying life the way she should be able to in a civilized society. Moments later, a man in a hoodie went to her car and took a picture of the parking permit that listed her apartment complex's name and address. Then he took pictures of her car and license plate.

Terrell said, "Safety tip. Never display the parking permit unless your car is in the parking lot at home. You might say life shouldn't be this way, and you're right, it shouldn't, but it is what it is."

Jake realized the former tenant of Sarah's building was in jail and couldn't be the stalker who wielded throwing knives. He felt torn, on a mission to eradicate the xylazine threat, but also wanting to act as Sarah's bodyguard. On top of everything, he had Tammi Martinelli's murder trial coming up and was duty-bound to her by his oath of omertà.

When the trial date arrived, Jake sat in court at the defense table with Tammi on his right. Bart Bartholomew sat on the other side of her in support but allowed his rookie attorney to defend their client.

After a long exhausting day of testimony from various witnesses, in the late afternoon it was finally time for Denton to testify.

Judge Emerson said, "Prosecutor, call your witness."

Prosecutor Bennett stood. "Your Honor, the people call former Sheriff Deputy Corrine Denton."

Jake stood up. "Objection, Your Honor. The title is *former* Sheriff Deputy."

"That's what I said," Bennett argued.

"I request that the court reporter read it back to me," Jake said.

Judge Emerson scowled at him. "I'll allow it."

The court reporter read back Bennett's words. "Former Sheriff Deputy Corrine Denton."

"Former sheriff deputy," Jake repeated.

The attorneys went back and forth with arguments until every person in the courtroom was sure Denton was a former sheriff deputy and not currently on the job.

Bennett stared at Jake as if realizing this new guy could fight like an animal.

After Denton was sworn in, she sat down in the witness box and glared with hatred at Jake and Tammi.

Jake noticed the row of reporters paying close attention.

Bennett took his time walking Denton through her law enforcement career, what had happened the day of Gerald Oliver's murder, and how she'd reluctantly had no choice but to shoot the suspect who was now on trial for murder.

He established that Denton wasn't required to wear a body camera as a jail detention deputy. And Denton testified that Tammi Martinelli had been wearing a body camera that day, but claimed in a deposition she'd turned it off when using the bathroom, as allowed, and had forgotten to turn it back on.

Jake stood when it was his turn. He consulted a file folder as if it contained truth, answers, and secrets. "Ms. Denton, why did you leave your job at the police department?"

Denton stiffened. "It was time for a career change."

"How long were you in rehab before returning to work in law enforcement?" Jake asked.

"It's a private matter."

Jake looked at Judge Emerson and raised his eyebrows. "Your Honor, I'm asking about the amount of time unemployed between jobs."

Emerson said, "Ms. Denton, you will answer the question as it relates to your work history timeline."

Denton recited dates and said, "As a war veteran and a

police officer, I suffered from temporary PTSD and needed time off to heal."

Jake nodded wisely in understanding. He read notes on a legal pad. "Since you brought it up, did time off and powerful anti-psychotic meds help treat your delirium, acute psychosis, bipolar disorder, and schizophrenia?"

Bennett, the prosecuting attorney, leapt to his feet. "Objection. The defense is violating Ms. Denton's protected health information under HIPAA privacy rules."

"Sustained." Judge Emerson slammed down his gavel and glared at Jake. "You know better. Don't test my patience."

Jake said, "I apologize, Your Honor. No excuse, but this is my very first trial. I'm also healing up from being shot while acting as a volunteer dog handler for the US Marshals Service. My dog Cody found that shipping container full of xylazine at the Oakland docks."

There was a murmur among the crowd. The drug bust had been big news.

Emerson squinted at him. "Where were you hit?"

Jake pointed at his upper chest. "The bullet went clear through and missed any bones or arteries." He glanced at Denton, who had a smug smile on her face.

Emerson looked at Denton as well and then stroked his chin. "You may continue."

Jake consulted his folder again for the benefit of the jury, who were men and women of varied ages and races. Bart Bartholomew had handled the jury selection. Jake was reminded of an old quote. "A jury consists of twelve persons chosen to decide who has the better lawyer."

He stared at Denton, the deranged woman who wanted to kill his dog, Cody. "Ms. Denton, isn't it true that after you lost your job at the police department and joined the sheriffs, you soon lost that job, too?"

"I didn't lose either job," Denton said. "I voluntarily resigned."

"Why did you resign from your position as a jail detention deputy?"

"It's none of your business." The depth of Denton's hatred for Jake was apparent to every person in the room.

Jake held out both hands, palms up. "None of my personal business, I agree, but you're sitting on the witness stand in a court of law and must answer my questions."

Denton angrily reached for her glass of water and accidentally knocked it off the stand. It crashed to the floor and shattered. "You're an evil scumbag, and your dog is worse."

CHAPTER 58

Jake let out a long breath for the jury. "I'm sorry you hate my dog."

"Hate isn't a strong enough word."

"Your Honor, may I show the news video evidence at this time?" Jake cited an exhibit number.

"Yes, go ahead."

Jake walked to a TV monitor on a stand and used the remote to play a one-minute segment.

A bleached-blonde news anchor gave an emotional report. "A sheriff's spokesperson said the department typically does not comment on ongoing investigations or personnel matters. After Sheriff Denton's use of her weapon against a police officer in uniform, the department put her on administrative leave and condemned the alleged acts."

The video cut to a uniformed female sheriff who read a statement. "The behavior described in the allegations against Ms. Denton falls well below the standard of conduct we and the public expect of peace officers. It is not reflective of the hard work and dedication of the fine men and women of the San Francisco Sheriff's Department."

Jake appeared on TV for a moment, dressed in a suit and tie, with a reporter holding a microphone in his face. "I'm Jake Wolfe, attorney for Police Officer Tammi Martinelli. We both agree with the sheriff's statement, and believe our city is lucky to employ some of the finest deputy sheriffs in America. If there was one bad apple, it does not reflect upon the other excellent officers whom we admire, respect, and appreciate."

Jake turned off the TV and walked back to the defense table. The courtroom was silent, all eyes upon him.

Denton said, "I'm surprised you didn't kiss your own face on the television."

Jake ignored her jab. "The sheriff's department representative said you were on administrative leave. Why did you resign?"

"Personal reasons."

Jake changed tactics. "When you were hired by the two law enforcement agencies, did you take an oath swearing to uphold the US Constitution?"

Denton sat up straighter. "Yes, I was proud to take the oath."

"Could you tell us what the Constitution says, that you've twice sworn to uphold?"

Denton blinked at him like a deer in the headlights. "I've read it and understood it but haven't memorized it."

"Do you recall any of the first lines or paragraphs?"

"We hold these truths to be self-evident. All men are created equal, and . . . uh . . . have rights to life, liberty, and the pursuit of happiness."

"No. You're wrong. Those words are from the Declaration of Independence," Jake said. "Please tell us something, anything, from the Constitution that you've sworn to uphold."

Denton recited, "You have the right to remain silent. Anything you say can and will be used against you in a court of law. You have the right to speak to an attorney, and to have an attorney present during any questioning."

Jake shook his head. "No. That's the Miranda warning. Let me help refresh your memory of the Constitution you've sworn to uphold. We the People of the United States. . ."

Denton raised her voice. "We the People of the United States, in order to form a more perfect Union and establish Justice, do ordain this Constitution."

Jake nodded. "That's a partial excerpt from one paragraph, at least. Tell us about the amendments you've sworn to uphold."

Her eyes lit up. "I uphold the Second Amendment that protects our rights to keep and bear arms."

"Good. Now we're getting somewhere." Jake consulted his notes. "You skipped the First Amendment that you've sworn to uphold. Can you tell us what exactly you're upholding there?"

Denton took a calming breath. "Freedom of speech."

"And?" Jake continued staring at his notes.

"Freedom of the press."

"And?"

"That's it."

Jake shook his head once more and read from a printout. "The First Amendment is considered one of the safeguards of liberty. It prohibits Congress from obstructing the exercise of certain individual freedoms, including freedom of religion, freedom of speech, freedom of the press, freedom of assembly, and the right to petition. The amendment guarantees an individual's right to express and to be exposed to a wide range of opinions and views. It was intended to ensure a free exchange of ideas, even unpopular ones."

Denton said, "And your point is?"

"You've sworn an oath to uphold these safeguards of liberty, but you don't even know what they are."

Denton raised her voice. "I upheld the Constitution every day on the job."

Bennett stood. "Objection. The defense is badgering the witness."

"Overruled," Emerson said. "But the defense will get to the point."

"Yes, Your Honor." Jake turned to Denton. "Please tell us what the third amendment is about."

"I don't remember specifically."

"Ballpark guess?"

She shook her head.

Emerson said, "The witness will answer verbally for the record."

"No, I don't have a ballpark guess."

"Fourth Amendment?" Jake said.

Denton nodded. "The Fourth Amendment protects citizens against unreasonable searches and seizures."

"Very good." Jake was mocking her, but she preened for the crowd. "Fifth Amendment?"

"The right to clam up and refuse to talk." Denton glared at Tammi again.

Jake paused a moment so the jury could see Denton's reaction, then moved on. "Sixth Amendment?"

"The right to an attorney?"

"You're asking me?"

She didn't reply.

"Seventh, Eighth, Ninth and Tenth amendments?"

Denton let out a long breath. "I don't recall."

Jake had her now. He slowly closed his folder and set it on the table.

"Ms. Denton, besides the few we've discussed that I could count on one hand, can you name *any* more of the Constitution's twenty-seven amendments you've sworn to uphold and claimed here on the witness stand under oath to have upheld every day on the job?"

Everyone in the courtroom could've heard a pin drop as they watched Denton, awaiting her reply with bated breath.

CHAPTER 59

Denton said, "I can't recite the amendment names, but I protect them in spirit with my gut instinct for honesty and fair play."

Jake barked a laugh and then covered his mouth. Seeing Judge Emerson pick up his gavel, he removed his hand and said, "I'm sorry, Your Honor."

The judge slammed down his gavel. "Don't do that again in my courtroom, or you'll never set foot in here again."

"I apologize, Your Honor. Rookie mistake." Jake looked at Denton but spoke for the jury and audience. "Isn't it true that you swore an oath to protect the Constitution, but you've demonstrated here today you know nothing about what the Constitution says?"

"Asked and answered," Denton said.

"Do you realize your sworn oath was a falsehood and you should be decertified by POST—the Commission on Peace Officer Standards and Training?"

"You're an idiot," Denton said.

"Can you understand that when you shot a uniformed

police officer, you acted without authority because your sworn oath was false, therefore you do not have qualified immunity?"

Bennett shot to his feet. "Objection. Sheriff Denton is not the person on trial here."

Jake argued, "Your Honor, I'm establishing the fact that when Ms. Denton shot a police officer, she was not functioning at the professional level required of law enforcement officials in the state of California."

Judge Emerson said, "You've made your point. Move on."

"Yes, Your Honor." Jake picked up his folder, took out a single page and read from it as if this was the moment of truth. "Ms. Denton, did you or did you not ask questions of Police Officer Tammi Martinelli at the hospital while she was in excruciating pain and under the influence of powerful meds? We have video if you'd like to see yourself in the act."

Denton squirmed in her seat. "I did my job and questioned the murder suspect."

Jake frowned. "Your Honor, the defense asks to play a hospital video of Ms. Denton questioning Police Officer Martinelli. We admitted it into evidence and provided a copy to the prosecuting attorneys."

"Yes, proceed," Judge Emerson said.

Bennett shouted, "Objection. The defense has already stated that anything the suspect said at that time is inadmissible."

Judge Emerson said, "Overruled. The defense wants to show alleged misconduct by Ms. Denton."

The crowd murmured as Jake moved to the TV on a stand and played a hospital security video of Denton sneaking into Tammi's room and bullying her with profanity.

Tammi, injured and high on pain meds, slurred her words.

"I want my lawyer. I take the Fifth Amendment right to remain silent and not testify against myself."

On the video, Denton scowled. "That means you're guilty."

Jake turned off the hospital video. He clenched his jaw and walked slowly back to the table. "Your Honor, the defense moves to strike anything my police officer client might have said while incoherent and fighting to survive being shot by Ms. Denton."

Emerson nodded. "Agreed. Nothing Officer Martinelli said while wounded and sedated is admissible."

Denton shouted at Judge Emerson, "Martinelli is guilty. It became obvious in the hospital when she took the Fifth Amendment as I asked her questions."

Jake slammed his folder down on the table, along with his powerful hand. "Objection, Your Honor! The witness has *disparaged* the defendant's Fifth Amendment right to remain silent and not testify against herself. This is prosecutorial misconduct, in that the prosecutor must have failed to instruct the witness she can never comment on a defendant's right to remain silent."

Judge Emerson glared at Bennett. "Both of you counselors approach the bench."

They stood before him.

Bennett said, "Your Honor, I made it clear to the witness she could never mention the Fifth, and—"

Emerson interrupted and gave him a withering stare. "You obviously didn't make it clear enough. It's your job to be certain the witness understands court procedures and adheres to them."

Bennett sputtered excuses.

Jake said, "Your Honor, I demand remedy for this egregious abuse of my client's constitutional rights."

"Are you moving for a mistrial?" Emerson said, almost appearing relieved it could be over.

Jake nodded. "Yes. I hereby move for a mistrial, and I request that the state dismiss this case with prejudice due to prosecutorial misconduct."

"Duly noted," Emerson said. "Write the motion and get it in."

Bennett said, "Your Honor, this was an error, not misconduct."

"Don't lecture me on the law. The defense could add a motion for sanctions, too, you know."

Bennett let out a breath.

Jake reached into his suit jacket, removed an envelope from his inside left pocket, and politely handed it to the judge. "Here's the motion, Your Honor. I had a feeling Denton might do this."

Judge Emerson gave Jake an appraising look, as if realizing the hotshot newbie lawyer had been hoping for it, deliberately provoking it, and was well prepared for it. He opened the law firm envelope and read the one-page sheet of printer paper. "Your motion is granted. Both of you return to your places. I'll instruct the jury."

Bennett walked to his table and gave Denton a look of resigned exasperation.

Jake sat next to Tammi, who whispered, "What just happened?"

"The judge will explain it," he whispered back.

Judge Emerson spoke to the witness. "You may step down, Ms. Denton."

"But I have more testimony to give," she argued.

"Your testimony is concluded, and you will either step down as I've asked, or I'll have you removed."

Denton stood. "This isn't over yet."

Emerson hammered down his gavel. "Say one more word, and I'll cite you for contempt of court. Go back to your seat and be quiet, or go to jail."

Denton stepped out of the witness stand and stomped to where she'd been sitting before the prosecuting attorney called upon her.

Emerson said, "Members of the jury, you all heard Ms. Denton disparage the defendant's Fifth Amendment rights. It's considered an egregious abuse of constitutional rights. I've received a motion for a mistrial, and I hereby grant that motion. The state will dismiss this case with prejudice, and the defendant cannot be tried again due to the double jeopardy clause. Case dismissed. Court adjourned. The jury is free to go home."

Judge Emerson left the bench and headed for a door behind the clerk's station.

Denton stood up in anger, clenching both fists and glaring at the judge.

Emerson turned and witnessed her acting in a threatening manner. "Bailiff, guard this door from any potential attack."

A uniformed deputy sheriff stood post in front of the door and said to Denton, "Are you crazy? Intimidating a judge is a felony. Get out of here."

Denton stormed out of the courtroom as media reporters shouted at her and took video for the evening news.

Jake sat at the defense table with Tammi and Bart until almost everyone had left.

Bart said, "Well played, counselor. I'm pleasantly surprised."

"Thank you, Bart."

Tammi asked, "What was all of that talk about how Denton swore to uphold the Constitution she didn't understand?"

Jake said, "Preparing the judge and jury for when she disparaged your Fifth Amendment rights, as I believed she would."

Bart stood. "I'm off to enjoy dinner at the Bohemian Club. Sorry I can't invite you both. It's for members only."

Jake had never been to the ultra-elite, all-male club on Taylor Street. "Oh, sure. I guess Tammi and I will grab dinner at a taco truck in a parking lot."

Tammi smiled, rose to her feet, and gave Bart a hug. "Thank you for standing beside me, kind sir."

"You're most welcome. Be careful out there, Officer."

When Bart left the courtroom, Tammi put on a wicked smile. "So, you're finally asking me out to dinner?"

Jake realized she'd taken his joke seriously. "Uh, did you like those tacos at Clancy's Pub?"

"Loved them. It's a date."

"Yes, we'll have to plan a dinner party there soon to celebrate your victory," Jake said carefully. "You, me, Sarah, Cody, Vito, Terrell, Alicia . . . everybody who likes Clancy's."

He gathered his papers and noticed the playful twist of her lips when she said, "I'm disappointed. I thought it would be an actual date with only you and me. What a letdown."

"Hey, a group taco party isn't so bad."

"What could possibly be more disappointing?"

He tilted his head, as if giving it deep thought. "Maybe a honeymoon hand job?"

She burst out laughing. "Speaking from experience?"

"Nope. Never been married."

"Probably for the best."

"You're right."

The tension passed, and they walked out of the court building together to find Vito waiting by his shiny black limousine with the back passenger door open. "Big Mo wants a meeting with Tammi."

Tammi slid onto the seat, closed the door and put down her window. She looked at Jake, and her eyes softened. "Thank you, Jake. I owe you."

"You're welcome. My fee is one dollar, and I'll expect that invoice paid on time and in full."

It had been a long day, and the sun began to set as Jake drove toward Sarah's clinic. They had dinner plans.

Upon arrival, he found a parking spot but then received a FaceTime call from McKay.

"We have an emergency," she said. "A catastrophic threat to the city that involves xylazine."

CHAPTER 60

Jake gazed at McKay's worried face on the video call. He dreaded hearing what she was about to say. "Sitrep?"

"We have intel that suggests the terrorist group we're hunting might dump xylazine into one of the city's water supply lines."

Jake cursed. "When and where?"

"Tonight, at Sunset Reservoir."

Jake's dashboard display lit up with a map. "I've walked my dog at the reservoir park."

"You'll enter through a rooftop service gate at Twenty-Seventh and Quintara Street."

"On my way. I'll have Beppe deliver Cody to me there. And I need help from Lieutenant Terrell Hayes on this mission."

"Agreed, along with Agents Easton and Greene. At the moment, we've classified this threat as top-secret. It could terrorize the population."

Jake let out a breath, took a sharp corner with tires squealing, and stomped on the gas pedal. "Dear God. The water supplies."

McKay said, "In a computer simulation of this terrorism scenario, a large percentage of a targeted city's residents wake up in the morning and use drug-tainted water to brush their teeth, make coffee or tea, cook oatmeal for their children, refill their dog or cat bowl, and take a shower."

Jake gritted his teeth. "Not on my watch."

"General Clemens has always feared that terrorists could poison the water supply of a US city or military base. They'd wipe out most of the population within twenty-four hours, leaving everything else unharmed and intact to be seized."

"Seized by whom?"

"Russian sleeper cell agents and mercenary operatives. We've finally discovered the tranq supply mastermind is a Russian SVR hard-liner named Nikolae Stepanovich Koval, who recently found out he's dying and only has six months to live. Koval decided to go out in a blaze of glory, and Xylazine became his weapon of choice."

Jake knew the SVR was Russia's version of the CIA. He ranted some creative profanity as he circled the reservoir that covered several city blocks. It felt surreal to know a mass murder weapon was about to be deployed at the beautiful antique cistern, with its manicured park, and trails to walk dogs while enjoying a breathtaking view of the Golden Gate Bridge.

He turned onto Quintara Street, raced up the steep hill, and arrived at the cross street of Twenty Seventh. A tall cyclone fence circled the top of the reservoir, but at this spot a gate hung open. Jake turned left and drove through it, onto the flat round top of concrete that covered the tank installation. Green and white city water department trucks sat parked in a row, and there was a building along the fence to his right. He parked near it. "I'm at the reservoir."

"Terrell and my agents will arrive shortly."

"Rules of engagement?"

"Do whatever it takes to protect lives." McKay ended the call.

Jake got out of his rig and opened the back hatch. He grabbed the MAC-10 submachine gun, and wore it across his back using the sling. He put the Marshals badge on his belt and sent a quick text to Sarah. *McKay says I'll be late for dinner.*

Sarah replied. *Watch your six. Come home safe.*

Beppe drove up in his sports car, and let Cody out of the backseat.

"Thanks, Beppe. You can't mention this reservoir to anyone. Is that clear?"

"Crystal clear. You have my word." Beppe shook Jake's hand, said "Good hunting," and drove away.

Cody barked at Jake, who patted him on the back.

"Good dog." As Jake placed a bulletproof vest on Cody, a police SUV arrived. Terrell stepped out, holding his city-issued tactical shotgun.

Jake raised his eyebrows. "Gonna get some?"

"Blast 'em," Terrell said. He moved toward the building.

"Run and gun." Jake and Cody followed Terrell as they jogged in the dark and found their way to a partly open steel security door with a CCTV camera above. Someone had smashed the camera lens and the doorknob. A sledgehammer was lying on the concrete.

He took a picture and texted it to McKay. *Perimeter breached.*

He noted how Terrell stared in dread at the stairs that led down into the depths. The man was brave and tough but suffered from claustrophobia because of a mission he never talked about.

"I'll clear the way for Cody." Terrell gritted his teeth, went inside, and charged down the stairs.

"Roger." Jake followed his former commanding officer down under the surface. He would follow that man anywhere, at any cost. They shared a brotherhood forged in battle and blood.

At the bottom of the stairwell, concrete passageways veered off to the left and right. Fresh air from outside blew out of a vent above their heads.

Terrell whispered, "Clear."

Cody raised his nose to breathe in new and unusual scents, then whined and held his tail down.

"What do you smell, Cody?" Jake held out a zip-top plastic bag with one pill inside marked "ASPRIN."

Cody huffed in recognition of a chemical he'd smelled before, turned his head and pulled on the leash.

"Seek, Cody. Seek. Seek. Seek."

Cody moved left, following a scent cone as Jake held the leash in his left hand and drew his pistol in his right. They moved as a team, with a special energy running up and down the leash between man and dog.

Terrell took up the rear. "I'll cover your six."

"Roger." Jake and Cody hurried along the hallway, with Cody tracking scents that Jake knew may include the drug, a weapon, or a person. Most likely all three.

Cody passed a door, stopped, and put his nose close to the bottom gap. He let out a low growl as his hackles stood up.

Jake turned the doorknob. It was unlocked.

Terrell held up his hand to signal stop. He went in first, shotgun up. A moment later, he quietly said, "Clear."

Jake and Cody entered and found themselves in another hallway. This one had a male employee lying on the floor, dressed in a security guard uniform. Cody sniffed the man's face and pawed at his chest.

Jake checked his wrist for a pulse. "Alive and breathing. Blood on the back of his head."

Terrell nodded. "Knocked cold from behind, I'd bet."

"I'll let McKay know someone is injured." Jake sent a text. "Hope that goes through. I barely have one bar."

"Let's keep moving," Terrell said.

Jake spoke to Cody and pointed at the man's bloody wound. "Smell that, Cody." The K-9 followed orders, then raised his head, sniffed the air, and pulled on the leash.

"Find him," Jake said.

Cody now had the scent of fresh blood to follow. He trotted ahead confidently, sure of the direction. Jake jogged along, with Terrell covering their backs. They came to a steel hatch in a wall featuring a wheel that turned to lock or unlock. It reminded Jake of something out of a submarine. A sign warned "No Unauthorized Access." Jake turned the wheel and pulled the door outward.

Moving in first, Terrell looked around and silently waved Jake forward, then put one finger in front of his lips to signal no talking. Cody walked a short distance and barked in warning.

In front of them were a dozen large duffel bags next to an open hatch on the floor. A tall, bald man with broad shoulders knelt beside the hatch, unzipping one of the duffel bags.

Terrell stepped forward and aimed the shotgun. "Police. Hands above your head."

The man grabbed at a pistol holstered on his belt but never got off a shot. Terrell blasted his hand and holster with a cloud of double-aught buckshot pellets, taking off several fingers and wounding his thigh. As the man fell down screaming, Terrell ran toward him, bringing the fight to the enemy.

The look on Terrell's face told Jake that the claustrophobia was torturing his mental state. "Let's take him alive, Grinds."

Terrell held the barrel end of his shotgun in front of the terrorist's face. The temperature was cool, but sweat glistened on Terrell's feverish forehead. He swallowed hard, regained his composure, and tossed his handcuffs to Jake.

Cody stood on his hind feet and caught the cuffs in mid-air, then dropped them into Jake's outstretched hand.

"Cody, guard." Jake holstered his pistol, let go of his K-9's leash, and took a knee beside the wounded terrorist. He rolled the man onto his stomach and handcuffed his wrists behind him. "Secure."

Terrell said, "Take a picture of his face, and send it to McKay."

Jake pulled out his phone. "I don't have any bars."

"Did you hear me? Take the photo, boot."

"Yes, sir." Jake shot several photos.

Cody sniffed the air, cocked his head, and trotted back the way they'd come.

"Cody, no." Jake ran after him.

The dog barked in the tone he used to greet a friend.

Agent Greene's voice was thick with worry. "Where's your handler, Cody?"

She sounded upset. He and his dog were rarely apart. "Agent Greene, this is Jake. We're in here. Cody, to me. *Heel.*"

Cody trotted back to Jake's side.

Jake scolded him. "You know better than to run off."

"Tell me the name of an island I mentioned to our boss in Napa," Greene said.

Jake thought for a moment. "Nantucket."

Agent Yvonne Greene of the US Secret Service walked in. "Easton is guarding the entrance. Who is this?"

"Unknown, but I'd bet he's either Russian or Albanian."

Jake looked down through the hatch and saw a vast cistern of water that went on and on. He took pictures of the duffel bags and the open hatch that accessed the water supply. "Cody found him as he unzipped that bag full of xylazine."

Greene's face paled. "Whew, that was a close one."

Terrell handed his shotgun to Greene with a challenging look, then closed the hatch. "Jake, help me drag this guy outside for medical attention so he can be interrogated." He placed an extra tight zip tie on the wrist of the man's injured hand to act as a tourniquet, then another on his thigh.

Jake knew Terrell desperately needed to get outside and leave that place at once. "Roger. I'll grab his ankles."

Standing near the duffel bags, Greene said, "I'll remain behind and guard the hatch and drugs."

Terrell said, "That's the plan."

As Jake helped carry the wounded man, he said, "Grinds, this guy has big feet. You don't suppose it's possible..."

CHAPTER 61

Once Jake and Terrell came outside, they dropped the prisoner. Terrell walked to where he could see the Golden Gate, then lit a cigar.

Jake said hello to Agent Easton and watched as Cody sniffed the agent's holstered handgun—a familiar weapon he'd smelled many times. Easton stood guard, trained eyes watching for threats, unfazed by the dog.

Jake received a reply text from McKay. *Medical help will arrive shortly.*

Now that he had a strong phone reception on top of the reservoir, he sent the photos to McKay.

Returning downstairs, Jake attached Cody's leash to his belt, picked up the security guard, and hefted him over his shoulder in a firefighter's carry, then hiked upstairs to the roof where a plain-clothed paramedic took over.

"Navy corpsman?" Jake asked.

"Former Army medic. The feds keep me busy."

Jake received a video call from McKay. "Your orders?"

"Load the duffel bags into the back of Easton and Greene's

Suburban," she said. "It's a federally owned and registered vehicle."

"Roger that."

"Ride along with the agents on the drive to Camp Parks Army Base, located on the eastern side of the San Francisco Bay Area." McKay sent him the GPS coordinates. "You'll meet a soldier from the Western Army Reserve Intelligence Support Center."

"What next?" Jake said.

"Hand over the contraband to the Army. They'll transport it to nearby Lawrence Livermore National Laboratory, where it'll be safely destroyed by the lab's High Explosives Applications Facility team."

Jake raised his eyebrows. "They'll blow it up?"

"Yes, in an underground weapons testing chamber at remote Site Three Hundred, using what they describe as optimized explosives with custom characteristics."

"Sounds like jargon for massive heat and flame that can incinerate anything without a trace. I've often wondered what they do at that lab."

"Important work on issues of global security," McKay said. "They recently invented ELITE, the Easy Livermore Inspection Test for Explosives. A pocket-sized high-explosive detector used at airports to find residue on luggage."

"A pocket-sized detector dog nose." Jake glanced at Cody, who quirked a brow.

"The laboratory also invented the Mechanical Safe Arming Device, which prevents accidental or unintended detonation of a nuclear warhead, especially any potential activation from outside sources."

"The Marine Recapture Tactics Teams will be glad to know about that," Jake said.

"Get to work bringing those duffel bags topside." McKay ended the call.

Jake led Cody over to Terrell. "McKay said to have her agents carry up the duffel bags while you guard topside and I guard the access hatch."

Terrell appeared both doubtful and grateful. "She's in charge." He put out his cigar and followed Jake to the door.

Jake repeated the spiel to Easton, who followed Jake and Cody downstairs. The dog quickly led them to the access hatch Greene sat on top of with Terrell's shotgun across her lap.

When they entered the area, Easton grabbed two heavy duffel bags, then headed back the way he'd come in.

With Easton gone, Greene stood up, set the shotgun aside, leaned into Jake, and kissed him on the mouth.

Jake held still, caught off guard and not sure what to do. He took a step back and held up one hand to signal stop. "Wait. What was that for?"

"Sorry, I know you're dating Sarah," Greene said. "But when I saw Cody alone, my heart did a flip. I thought you might be dead."

Jake chose his words carefully. "It was a great kiss, but we all have our boundaries and you crossed mine. I'm dating Sarah—and *only* Sarah. You can't kiss me again. I mean . . . never."

Greene smiled, grabbed one duffel bag and hoisted it over her right shoulder. "I like your suit. You look infuriatingly tall, dark, and sexy." With a toss of her auburn hair, she was gone.

Jake watched her go. He looked down at his courtroom suit and tie. *Infuriatingly?* She was an amazing woman in so many ways, but now he felt guilty, as if he'd been unfaithful to Sarah for a moment.

When Easton returned and grabbed two more duffel bags,

Jake teased his overly-serious friend, as he often did. "Do you even lift, bro?"

Acting as if the bags were giant dumbbells, Easton did a bodybuilding exercise of a biceps curl and overhead lift. With that done, he headed out.

"I'm impressed," Jake called out after him.

Agent Greene walked back in, gave Jake a smile about their secret, grabbed the last duffel bag, and hefted it over her shoulder. She spoke to Cody, "Come on, golden fur ball. Let's get out of here."

As Jake carried the shotgun and followed her out, he noticed she'd removed her suit jacket, and he could see both her pistol and shapely derrière. He wondered if she'd done it on purpose, and he tried to look anywhere but there as she climbed steps and flexed her glutes.

Once outside, they met up with Terrell, and everybody moved toward the Suburban.

Terrell said, "McKay's sending me home."

"Thanks for your help, brother," Jake said. "We should get together for a barbecue this weekend. Grill some steaks and drink fine wine."

"Sounds good. What's the occasion?"

Jake told him about his liver and the three-month break from booze. "I wanted my last drink before abstinence to be a glass of rare juice from Dylan's collection."

"Alicia will be happy to join you. Some of those aged bottles you have could sell for a thousand dollars each nowadays. She'd never get to taste them if not for you."

"We have Dylan to thank for that," Jake said.

"Did you know corn is bad for your liver? Not as bad as alcohol, but your taco habit isn't helping."

Jake blinked. "What? You dare to suggest I give up tacos? That's blasphemy."

Terrell chuckled, got into his police SUV, and drove away.

Jake wished he could be on his way home, too. "Why am I going along on this road trip?"

Greene pointed at the MAC-10 he carried on his back via a sling. "You and Cody are added security. A war veteran K-9, and an infantry Marine armed with a submachine gun."

"All right." Jake opened a door on the Suburban and let Cody hop into the back seat. He slid in beside the dog and put his arm around him.

Greene sat behind the wheel and drove east toward the Army base.

Jake said, "Easton, can we swing by a Super Duper Burger on the way?"

Easton exhaled loudly and finally spoke. "You always ask me that, and I always say no. Give it a rest."

Jake shrugged at the overly-serious agent. "Hope springs eternal."

Greene turned on the flashing lights and broke the speed limit.

They arrived at Camp Parks Army Base and stopped at the gate. A soldier from Army Reserve Intelligence checked their IDs.

As a Marine, Jake wanted to make a typical military rivalry joke about how Army Intelligence was an oxymoron like jumbo shrimp. He held his tongue for once.

After everyone had passed inspection, Greene drove inside the base.

The soldier directed them to a parked armored vehicle. "Back up to that MRAP," he said, referring to a Mine-Resistant Ambush Protected vehicle.

Jake kept Cody safe inside the Suburban as Easton helped the man transfer their deadly cargo into the MRAP.

The soldier shook hands with Easton. "Thanks, we'll take it from here."

Easton returned to the SUV, and Greene drove back to the city, winding her way to Quintara Street and up the steep hill.

On arrival at the reservoir, Jake said, "Thank you both for your help to protect the water supply."

"Where are you off to now?" Greene asked.

Jake raised his eyebrows. "Super Duper Burger, of course. I can't let Easton deprive Cody of an organic vanilla ice cream cone."

Jake and Cody exited the SUV.

Greene lowered her window. "He definitely earned a treat." She looked Jake in the eyes and drove away.

Jake removed the MAC-10 he'd had slung across his back and placed it in the Jeep's cargo area. He opened Cody's automatic K-9 door and snapped his fingers. Cody hopped in, and Jake took a seat behind the wheel.

His phone buzzed with a text from McKay. *Sitrep?*

Jake texted the initials for mission accomplished and exfiltrating. *MA. EX.*

He received the same reply as he did after the Key West mission. *Copy MA. EX.*

Jake thought of texting Sarah to ask if she still wanted to have dinner. That made him remember Greene's surprise kiss. He flipped down the visor to look at his face in a mirror and make sure she hadn't left any lip gloss on his mouth. No, he wasn't "tagged."

He texted Sarah. *We're free now. Have you eaten yet?*

Sarah replied. *No. I waited for you.*

Jake thought about the burger place. He couldn't go there

because Greene might show up. He texted again. *I can bring takeout. What are you in the mood for?*

Sarah replied. *Surprise me.*

Jake called a restaurant Sarah loved, and placed an order for takeout. It was ready by the time he stopped by. He could have had it delivered but wanted to personally hand it to her.

When he walked into Sarah's apartment carrying her favorite pizza, she kissed him on the lips. Hers tasted like the cold beer she'd been sipping.

He covered his awkward feelings with humor. "Yum, you taste like Modelo Especial. Gonna grab one outta the fridge." He fetched a beer and took a long drink. "Ahh, that's what I needed."

"Tough assignment?"

Jake poured kibble for his dog. "It was a nightmare, but Cody saved the day."

"He's gifted. Can you tell me anything?"

Jake thought about the terrorizing fear of being killed by your own tap water. "No, sorry. McKay ordered me to keep it secret."

Sarah grabbed two plates, added a slice of pizza to each one, and then hesitated. "I have a scary memory attached to this pizza."

"Tonight, you'll replace it with a pleasant memory."

"So, how about some Netflix and chill?"

He smiled at the reference that meant watch TV and then have sex. "Love to."

She returned his smile with one that promised good things would happen later that night. "I read in *Cosmopolitan* magazine that the cure for insomnia is making love at bedtime."

"I'd bet *Cosmo* says that's the cure for just about every situation in life."

CHAPTER 62

Tammi Martinelli waited until after midnight and then drove to former Sheriff Corrine Denton's house. She cruised past it and pulled over at the construction site of a partially built condo complex. A sign offered two-bedroom, one bath townhomes with solar panels. The so-called "Pine Ridge" community didn't feature any pine trees and wasn't on a ridge.

She switched off her car's headlights and checked an anonymous GPS tracking device to confirm Denton had parked her car at a repo company. She now worked the night shift using a tow truck to steal cars and trucks from the owners who were late on payments.

Exiting her vehicle while keeping the dome light off, Tammi walked to Denton's front door in the dark, gloved up, and used a battery-powered lock pick to gain entry.

Once inside, she conducted a quick but thorough search, starting in the main bedroom, where she looked through dresser drawers, the closet, and under the bed. The master bathroom medicine cabinet contained typical items, along with many bottles of prescription meds and a pill splitter.

Acting on a hunch born of experience as a cop, Tammi picked up a ChapStick-style of lip balm and removed its cap. She pulled out a small piece of facial tissue and found several pills imprinted with the misspelled word "ASPRIN." Denton had cut one of them in half.

Tammi recognized the tranq from an evidence photo of what Cody found on Gerald Oliver's yacht, the *Tiburon*. She put the hidden items back and closed the cabinet.

The second bedroom was set up as a home office. She searched the desk, file cabinet, and closet. Moving on, she combed the kitchen, a walk-in pantry, the living room, and the guest bathroom.

In the garage, Tammi found a row of gray plastic storage tubs stacked three high along one wall. She dug through them until finding a black duffel bag with its zipper held closed by a padlock.

Using her lock pick gun, she opened it and discovered scores of vacuum-sealed plastic bags full of pills that were also imprinted with the misspelled word "ASPRIN."

The large quantity of bootleg animal tranquilizer in Denton's possession was enough for her to be charged with the intent to distribute. Tammi had learned from Jake that the drug itself was not illegal, but dispensing it without a veterinarian license was against state and federal laws.

But Tammi didn't have a search warrant. She'd violated Denton's civil rights protection against illegal search and seizure, and the evidence wouldn't be admissible in court. None of that mattered because she had other plans.

When she removed the bags and set them on the concrete floor to take a picture, she found a small .22 pistol. It was the type of cheap, older, well-worn handgun referred to as a

Saturday night special—the kind used in a drive-by shooting at Jake Wolfe. The gun smelled as if someone had fired it recently, and the magazine was one round short of a full mag.

After taking a few more pictures, she repacked the duffel bag, locked it, and arranged the tubs back in their proper order.

Tammi returned to the front door, looked through the peephole, then exited Denton's house and hurried in the dark to her car.

As she drove away, Tammi thought of all the crimes Denton had committed against her fellow law enforcement officials. She'd shot Tammi, a cop in uniform, using a sheriff-issued pistol. And the small .22 handgun suggested Denton might have shot Jake Wolfe as he was helping the US Marshals and carrying a badge. In fact, Denton might have been aiming for Cody, the city's favorite K-9. And now Denton had a large amount of tranq in her garage—enough to be a major dealer who could disrupt the city and put every LEO in danger.

Tammi tried to think of a way to have Denton arrested or fired that wouldn't involve the sheriff's department or the police. Tammi could never rat on a fellow cop to internal affairs. She would be shunned and ostracized, her career would end, and her life would be ruined.

Denton was one of the rare bad apples that could harm the reputation of their upstanding coworkers. A needle in a haystack. If Denton lost her job due to misconduct, she would simply move away and get hired by another city or county.

Maybe an anonymous tip to the drug enforcement agency could do the trick.

Tammi drove home, sat at her computer, and used a VPN to go online and visit the DEA's website. She found their page for reporting crime tips and filled out the form, writing it in the amateur way a citizen would, not a trained police officer filing an official report.

With that done, she deleted her web browsing history, ran a cleaner software, and went to bed.

Staring at the ceiling, unable to sleep, Tammi wondered how long it might take for the DEA to investigate and whether the tranq would still be in Denton's possession if the feds searched her garage.

CHAPTER 63

The next morning, Jake received a text message from McKay that canceled his plans for driving Sarah to work.

He told Sarah, "McKay wants to debrief me in her rig."

Sarah put on a pair of sunglasses. "No worries. I'll ride the cable car with Clarence and Gus." She kissed him goodbye and walked away.

"Tell them hi for me." Jake stood outside the Victorian house until Agent Greene pulled over in her Suburban and popped the hatch. Jake led Cody to the cargo area, closed the door, and slid into the back seat next to McKay.

Greene drove through the city as McKay said, "Once we discovered it was Russian hard-liner Nikolae Koval deploying xylazine as a weapon against the US, we were able to track down the people he's paying to import this aspirin pill form of tranq from Venezuela into our country. The drug mules belong to the ruthless Albanian criminal network Ali Demi Bishat, that murdered and tortured their way to control much of the cocaine trade in Europe."

Jake said, "Looks like now they want to repeat that plan in the US, but with xylazine."

"Yes, and the gang is also involved in human trafficking and murder for hire," McKay said. "They're a TCO—transnational criminal organization."

"What's the English translation of Ali Demi Bishat?"

"Ali Demi is the name of a prison in Albania, and the word bishat means *beasts*. The founding members of their network had all done time at Ali Demi for violent crimes."

Jake turned to her. "So, the Russian, Nikolae Koval, is using the cartels and the Albanian gang as mercenaries in his secret war on America. What's the answer to these criminal partnerships?"

"The only hope so far is a United Nations program that helped thousands of South American farmers stop growing illegal coca for cocaine, and replace it with cocoa for chocolate."

Jake raised his eyebrows. "Thousands of farmers? That's impressive."

"The farmers are no longer oppressed by violent drug criminals, and they've planted over a million trees to restore the rainforest ecosystem."

"Ingenious." Jake thought it over. "So, the hostile foreign nation you heard rumors about is Venezuela?"

She nodded. "The rogue communist regime of Venezuela."

"And the Russian, Nikolae Koval, is manipulating them." Jake said. "If we take down Koval, we cut the head off the snake. Is he currently in Moscow? Send me there."

McKay drank from a to-go cup of coffee and set it down in a cupholder. "Rumor has it Koval is running the tranq attack from his super-yacht that's always at sea and on the move. Koval is a billionaire who amassed an illegal fortune over his career."

Jake looked out at the bay as the Suburban crested a hill and drove down toward the water. "You find the yacht. I'll take Koval out of play."

McKay rubbed the back of her neck. "The CIA and the NSA are both searching for the yacht as we speak. They have top analysts and super-computers combing through satellite imagery, cell phone calls, wire transfers of funds, and large purchases of diesel at marinas."

Jake paused, deep in thought. "Ask if they're tracking oil tankers. Russia sold crude oil to North Korea despite an embargo by meeting on the ocean and pumping it from one tanker to another. The yacht could refuel with diesel in a similar way and never buy any in port."

McKay said, "I'm sure they're on top of that, but I'll mention it, just in case."

"Does Koval have another motive besides wanting to kill Americans?" Jake said.

"Yes, to weaken the US using xylazine as a weapon, and then spark World War Three, which ends with Russia occupying America," McKay said.

Jake frowned. "Russia and China want our farmland, but Koval might also be a war profiteer, who bets money on commodity futures of gold and oil. Both skyrocket in price during wartime."

"Venezuela has the largest oil reserves on the planet. Their current rogue communist leaders stand to profit from a world war. They and Koval could use insider trading to buy futures at the right time."

They rode in silence for a while as Agent Greene continued driving an evasive and unpredictable route through the city.

Finally, Jake said, "I feel sorry for the common working-class people of Venezuela."

McKay met his eyes. "An innocent person gets murdered every twenty-one minutes there by cartel *sicarios*."

Jake shook his head in dismay. "I'd imagine the police and military are overwhelmed."

"Yes, and the country's prison system has a capacity for fourteen thousand people but currently holds over fifty thousand."

"No wonder their regime is releasing thousands of criminals and sending them here."

"The police in this city are overwhelmed, too," McKay said. "That's why the state government recently called upon the California Highway Patrol to help solve the fentanyl crisis. The CHP is the largest state police agency in the nation."

Jake looked out his window at a passing Highway Patrol car. "How are CHP officers helping?"

"The state government changed CHP jurisdiction to include city streets, then deployed officers to the Tenderloin district."

"The government did something smart for once?" Jake said.

"So far, CHP officers have seized over five point two kilos of fentanyl in the Tenderloin and surrounding area. Enough to potentially kill two point four million people. The entire population of San Francisco three times over."

"That's an encouraging success story," Jake said. "My friend Randy works for the CHP. Hopefully, those fine people can help get xylazine off the streets, the way they're doing with fentanyl."

McKay pulled out her phone and checked a new message. Her eyebrows went up. "We may have a lead on Koval's yacht. There's a chance that Gerald Oliver met with our mission target."

"Why Oliver?"

"He was a lobbyist with contacts in the state capital and could guide contributions toward local, state, and national politicians of both parties to favor Koval's agenda. Trickery, lies, blackmail, and bribery can do wonders."

Jake said, "Do we know if Oliver flew to a far-away location to meet Koval, or was the yacht here in our sector of the Pacific?"

"I'm waiting for more intel but hoping beyond hope the yacht is somewhere within striking distance."

"Cody never got his chance to search Oliver's house," Jake said. "Why don't we do that and maybe find your answers?"

McKay looked at him with a question in her eyes. "I thought you searched it."

"No. Roxanne made a fake photo of Cody in front of the house to frighten Oliver. A police dog searched, but it wasn't Cody."

"Does right now work for you?"

"Yes, let's do it."

McKay consulted her phone and read the address out loud. Agent Greene tapped on the dashboard GPS and headed for Gerald Oliver's house.

CHAPTER 64

Upon arrival at the deceased lobbyist's house, Greene parked on the street.

Jake let Cody out and attached a leash to his collar. They moved toward the front door, where Jake gloved up and tried opening the lock by sliding a credit card in between the strike plate and latch plate next to the doorknob. The latch bolt slid away, but the deadbolt above it held fast. Jake owned a KRONOS lockpick gun, but it was in his Jeep at the moment. "Let's try plan B."

He led his dog around back and found a sliding glass door. Someone had removed the wooden dowel from the track and forgotten to put it back. "Thank you, Officer." Jake lifted the door by its handle and rocked it up and down until he worked the latch free and pushed the sliding glass to the side.

Greene stood behind him. "Looks like you've done that before."

Jake shrugged. "I might have fractured a law a time or two, but my memory is hazy on the subject." He led Cody into the kitchen.

Greene followed them inside. "McKay is keeping watch on the front of the house, and Easton will cover the back."

"Roger." Jake removed Cody's leash. "What do you smell?"

Cody lifted his head and gave the house a deep sniff. His nostrils flared, then he huffed and trotted to the kitchen trash can. After giving it a curious inspection, he moved on, walked slowly down a hallway, turned around, and trotted back to the living room.

Jake ejected the mag of rounds from his pistol for Cody to smell. "Seek, Cody."

The scent dog slowly closed in on a fireplace, sniffed all around it, and sat down.

A small box of wooden Strike Anywhere matches were on the mantle.

Jake wondered if Cody was only smelling the sulfur, potassium chlorate, and phosphorus sulfide. He opened the matchbox and checked inside, then set it back on the mantle. "Good dog. Keep searching."

Cody pawed at the brick hearth in front of him.

"Oh, I see." Jake grabbed a shovel with a long, slender handle from the fireplace tool set. As he dug through the thick blanket of dry ashes in the firebox, he asked Greene, "Can you grab a bathroom towel?"

"One second." She ran to the hall and returned with two of them.

Jake laid a towel on the floor and began dumping shovelfuls of ashes onto it.

Cody watched him intently.

After several scoopfuls, Jake unearthed something small and rectangular that plopped onto the towel.

Cody sniffed at it and growled.

Jake picked up the item in his gloved hands and dusted it

off. "Another matchbox." It was unscathed by fire, only buried in the cold, dry ashes. He opened it to find matches, and under them a shiny, nickel-plated key. "Good work, Cody."

The dog sniffed the key and huffed.

"Where's the *lock*?"

Cody looked at him and quirked a brow at hearing the new word.

"You know." Jake walked to the front door and pretended to use the key. "Where is the lock?" He tapped the key on the lock three times, then held it under Cody's nose. "More? Same?"

Cody took several deep sniffs of the key, walked back and forth in a search pattern, and moved his nose high and then low.

Greene stood alongside Jake. He held up his hand to signal stop, and they both quietly observed the dog at work. Finally, Cody returned to the fireplace and sat down again.

Unsure what to think, Jake moved to Cody's side. "What?"

Cody stood on his hind legs and pawed at a painting above the mantle.

Jake pulled on the painting, and it swung open like a door on hinges to reveal a hidden wall safe. "You are a genius dog."

Jake took a picture of the safe and texted it to McKay. He used the key to unlock it and found a variety of items inside. "Grab that other towel."

Agent Greene held it in both hands as Jake emptied the safe's contents and Cody eagerly sniffed everything.

Jake led Greene and her towel to the dining room table, and she laid it down. He took a picture of the loot and sent it to McKay.

"Now, what can we find out?" Jake sifted through the jewelry, papers, credit cards, cash, gold coins, and such items until he found Gerald Oliver's passport. He turned on his phone video, handed the device to Greene, and then slowly flipped through the pages while she used the phone to record each one.

He noticed a stamp from Mexico. "Oliver flew to Cabo San Lucas."

Greene took video of the stamp. "That was recent. If he met the yacht, it could still be off the coast of Baja or San Diego."

Jake held out his hand to retrieve the phone, wrapped up the towel full of items, and headed for the door. "Cody, heel."

The trio walked outside, and Greene drove them away in the Suburban.

McKay put on a pair of nitrile gloves.

Jake gave her the passport, open to the page stamped in Cabo.

McKay studied it for a while. "Could we be this lucky for once? Please God, let us catch a lucky break. I thought Gerald Oliver was a lowly pawn on the chessboard."

Jake said, "Every chess piece matters." He made a phone call and spoke in halting Spanish to the woman who answered. "Si, señora. Mi nombre es Jake Wolfe. Estoy con los US Marshals. Quiero hablar con Agente Lourdes Benitez de la Policía Federal."

There was a pause, and an English speaker came on the phone. "Who's calling? Identify yourself."

"Yes, ma'am. My name is Jake Wolfe. I'm with the US Marshals. I want to talk to Agent Lourdes Benitez of the Federal Police."

"Give me your ID."

He recited his US driver's license number.

"One moment, please."

Greene said, "You speak Spanish now?"

"Not much, but I'm working on it." Jake turned to McKay. "You introduced me to Lourdes Benitez."

McKay nodded. "One of my best contacts in the area."

"Hello. This is Benitez."

"Lourdes, it's Jake Wolfe. We met at the hospital in Cabo. I'm up north with Agent McKay. We're tracking a man who landed in Los Cabos airport on the following date and time." He recited details, along with Gerald Oliver's name and passport ID.

"I remember you, Jake," Lourdes said. "Hold on while I check the computer." Soon, she came back on the phone. "We flagged Oliver as, how do you say . . . suspicious. He met with a known criminal named Collazo, and went on board a Sea Ray 370 Sundancer Coupe model boat with a hardtop and three outboard engines. It's popular with drug runners. The boat cruised onto the ocean, and when it returned, Oliver was no longer a passenger."

"We think he met up with a yacht," Jake said.

"I can give you the transponder tracking of the Sea Ray," Lourdes offered. "You could match it up with other boats it went close to and the travels of your suspect's cell phone."

"Yes, please," Jake said.

"How's Sarah doing? Okay now?"

"She's good. I'll tell her you asked."

"Here's the data. I'm sending it to your phone."

Jake received a file. "Thank you, Lourdes."

"You owe me one. Oh wait, that's two."

"You're right. Take care, my friend."

"You too, amigo." Lourdes ended the call.

McKay said, "Jake, forward that file to me, and send a copy to Roxanne Poole."

"Roger."

McKay received the file. "Now, hopefully, either the Secret Service or the SFPD senior tech officer will find a yacht that met up on the ocean with that Sea Ray motor boat and Gerald Oliver's phone."

Jake nodded. "No offense, but my money is on Rox Star."

CHAPTER 65

At the end of a long day, Sarah turned the sign on her veterinary clinic's glass door from open to closed. She asked Madison, "How are you and Beppe getting along?"

Madison's eyes sparkled. "We're madly in love. Tell Jake he's a matchmaker."

Sarah smiled. "That's wonderful. I'm happy for you."

Beppe pulled up in his sports car, Madison left to hop in, and they drove off.

Sarah grabbed her purse and reached inside for her keys to lock up. Suddenly, a client appeared in the doorway holding a cat carrier. Sarah recognized the tall and shy client named Pax.

Pax looked at the purse in her hand. "I'm sorry to stop by at closing time, but Simon was in a fight, and he's limping."

Sarah glanced at the plastic crate, but Pax was holding it backward. She couldn't see his cat through the crisscross bars of the front door. She also noticed he held the crate as if it was lightweight. It couldn't be empty, could it? "Sorry, Pax, we're closed, but the twenty-four-hour veterinary hospital will take good care of Simon."

Pax had a strange look on his face, and sweat on his brow. Sarah felt a premonition. She hadn't really thought about how Pax was tall and had big feet. Lots of people fit that description.

Pax wiped his wet eyes with one hand. "My heart is breaking. Please help us, Dr. Sarah."

When he reached up to his eyes, the movement lifted his sport coat which revealed a red-handled knife in a sheath on his belt, in the spot where people holster a gun.

An ice-cold trickle of panic ran down her spine. Instead of taking the keys from her purse, she reached for her handgun. The .380 pistol wasn't a large caliber, but a hollow-point round fired at close range could kill.

Pax dropped the empty cat crate, charged at Sarah, and tackled her to the floor, lying on top of her and pinning her arms in his tight embrace. "If I can't have you, nobody can."

Sarah saw her purse and gun on the floor, close-by, but out of reach. She gave Pax a vicious headbutt to his nose. He cried out in pain and reflexively reached up to his face with his right hand, releasing her left arm. Sarah used Jeet Kune Do to hammer his throat with a classic straight-lead punch she'd practiced endless times at the gym. Keeping her left elbow up, she struck him with a devastating blow to the windpipe.

Pax rose to his knees and brought both hands to his throat, desperately gasping for air as he sat straddling her thighs.

Sarah sat up straight and threw both fists in repeated strikes, using his throat as a punching bag.

He wheezed through his injured throat as he pulled the red-handled knife out of its sheath, stabbed at her face, and missed.

Sarah bucked him up like a bronco, rolled on the floor, grabbed her pistol, and leapt to her feet. "Stay back. Drop the knife."

Pax came at her, sucking in shallow breaths, with the knife pointed up and threatening.

Sarah held the pistol in both hands and took aim at center mass. "Stop, or I'll shoot. Final warning." Her hands were shaking, palms sweating.

Jake and Cody appeared in the doorway, and Jake shouted, "Cody, disarm."

Cody ran to Pax and bit down on the wrist of his knife hand, causing him to scream and drop the weapon.

Cody picked up the knife handle with his teeth, ran to Jake and dropped it.

Jake moved toward Pax, holding his pistol up and wearing the star on his belt. "US Marshal. You're under arrest. Put your hands behind your head."

Sarah continued aiming her handgun at Pax's chest. Her heart was racing. "Did you kill that rave dancer who looked like me?"

Pax sneered at her. "Yes, but no one will ever be able to prove it. My alibi is bulletproof."

Sarah felt anger burning inside her chest. Pax's alibi could keep him out of prison. He'd continue harming women who looked like Bianca. Her throat tightened. She couldn't breathe. Blood roared in her ears. The gun suddenly went off, to her surprise, shooting Pax once and putting a bullet into his evil heart.

Pax crumpled to the floor, lying on his back and dying from a chest wound.

Jake was shocked that Sarah had executed the killer. He holstered his handgun. "Whoa there, girlfriend. Lower your weapon. Easy does it."

Sarah lowered the pistol as tears rolled down her face. "I didn't pull the trigger. The gun misfired or something."

"Your hands were shaking pretty bad," Jake said. "It was an accident."

"Maybe my subconscious mind caused my finger to pull the trigger because I was so upset that animal kept trying to kill my sister over and over again."

Jake held out his hand. "Sarah, please give me your gun. Trust me, and everything will be okay."

Sarah did so, appearing dazed.

Jake stepped to where Pax lay and shot him three more times in the chest. The .380 hollow-point rounds didn't go through the body and into the floor. He set her gun on the counter. "Now, give me your lab coat."

She took off her white coat and handed it to him.

"Go wash your hands and forearms as you do before surgery," Jake said. "Scrub them extremely well. Do it three times."

Sarah nodded silently and wandered down the hallway like a lost soul.

Jake hurried to the back room with Cody following him, put Sarah's lab coat into the washing machine, and turned it on. He added detergent and poured bleach into the automatic dispenser.

Jake then checked on Sarah, who was still rinsing off at the sink.

She held up both wet hands in front of her, used one elbow to close the faucet handle, and then dried off with paper towels.

He guided Sarah to her private office. "I'm going to erase part of the security video."

She looked at him. "How will you explain that?"

"The lights flickered and tripped your surge protector." He pointed at the device on the floor.

Sarah sat on the couch. "I feel dizzy."

"Cody, comfort Sarah."

The dog leapt up to lie across her lap. She patted him on the back and watched Jake with vacant eyes.

At Sarah's desk, Jake tapped on the computer keyboard. He kept the video of Pax assaulting Sarah, and her fighting him, but erased everything after that, including where she rolled free and grabbed her pistol. He then turned off the surge protector, and the computer went dark.

"You won't say anything to the police," Jake said. "Not one word. Your attorney, Bart Bartholomew, will speak for you. Understood?"

"Yes, understood. Not one word from me. Only Bart."

Jake moved to the door. "I'll be back in a minute. Cody, stay. Protect."

Sarah held onto the dog's collar as Jake left the office.

He hurried outside to the Jeep, took off his pistol and holster, and placed them inside the center console storage compartment. He returned to Sarah's office unarmed and pulled out his phone.

CHAPTER 66

Jake made a call, and Terrell answered on the first ring. "What's up, boot?"

"I have trouble and need your help at Sarah's clinic."

Terrell let out a long breath. "How bad?"

"I shot the guy who's been attacking every woman who looks like Sarah."

"You're sure it's him?"

"Sure enough to shoot him dead. He tried to kill Sarah with a red-handled throwing knife like the one that hit her apartment door."

"I'm on my way."

"Ask Wilson to join us."

"Roger."

"Thank you, brother." Jake ended the call.

Soon, two vehicles arrived outside, and Terrell came in the door, Wilson following him.

Jake pointed at the body and at a pistol on the reception counter. "I shot that dirtbag with Sarah's gun."

Terrell stared at him in doubt. "Where's Sarah? Is she okay?"

"Lying down on the office couch, in shock from almost being stabbed to death. Cody is by her side."

"I'll need a statement from her later," Terrell said.

Jake shook his head. "No, sorry, Grinds. She won't be saying a word unless her attorney, Bart Bartholomew, tells her to."

"That'll never happen." Terrell glanced up at a television on the wall. "Let me see the security video."

"Sure thing, I have to go turn on Sarah's computer. Be right back." Jake entered the office, clicked a switch on the surge protector, and the computer came back to life.

He returned to the waiting room, swiped on his phone, and paired it with the TV and security system. He rewound the video until it showed Madison leaving, and Pax arriving. The man attacked Sarah. She fought back. He pulled a knife, and the screen went blank. "That's where the surge protector clicked off. Cody and I arrived, and, well, we did what Marines do best."

Terrell looked at the body. "At what moment did you enter this room?"

"When this man Pax was sitting on Sarah and holding a knife," Jake said. "I arrived to find the door wide open, hurried inside, and saw them fighting. Sarah's purse and gun were on the floor. I identified myself as a US Marshal and displayed my badge, but the man leapt to his feet and came at me. He said he'd kill all of us. Left with no choice, I picked up Sarah's pistol and shot him in self-defense."

"Why didn't you use your own handgun?" Terrell glanced at Jake's waist.

"I'd left it in the Jeep because I was off duty and we were going on a dinner date."

"It looks like Cody bit the perp's wrist," Terrell said. "Why'd he do that if you'd shot the man?"

"He was frantic to protect me and Sarah," Jake said. "Even though the perp was down, Cody did his job and disarmed the threat."

Wilson studied Jake a moment, then nodded. "It makes perfect sense to me."

Terrell's eyes bored into Jake's. "Your hands and shirt will test positive for this pistol's gunshot residue?"

"Yes, sir."

"Your fingerprints and DNA will be found on the gun?"

"Yes, sir."

"Sarah's hands will be clean?"

"Yes, sir."

In the silence that followed, they could hear the washing machine chugging in the back area used for dog grooming.

Terrell looked at Wilson. They held each other's gaze for a moment.

Wilson said, "I believe the deputized US Marshal has given a true and accurate statement of events that transpired."

"Give me the timing of these events," Terrell said to Jake.

Jake nodded. "I'll play the video again and walk both of you through it while you take notes for your reports."

Terrell noted Pax's large shoes, and the throwing knife on the floor. "All right. Let's do this."

Jake explained each sequence of events as a lawyer would in a court of law. "And then I had to double-tap him twice with hollow-point rounds. The four shots ended his life."

"Nice and neat and complete," Terrell said, studying the four wounds on Pax's chest in a tight grouping.

Jake pointed at the body. "Compare the perp's shoes to those from the rave club security video."

Terrell played the video on his phone. "Disguised face. Same shoes."

Jake nodded. "The footprint found in the mud outside that one lady's window had a horizontal line across the ball of the right foot."

Terrell swiped on his phone and magnified a photo. He held his phone next to the sole of the man's right shoe. "Well, look at that."

Jake said, "It's a match."

Terrell let out a breath. "Have your fed boss call my city boss."

"Will do, and Agent McKay will remind Chief Garcia that I'm a privateer, operating under admiralty and maritime law," Jake said. "This city is on a peninsula, surrounded by ocean. Every edge is coastal. I'm also empowered to mete out judgment, as in hunt down and shoot a beast."

"Thank God Sarah and Cody are both okay." Terrell's phone buzzed. He glanced at it and said, "Scooter is here."

The lights shone on Homicide detective Beth Cushman's red hair as she walked in and stopped at the dead body. "The big foot perp?"

Jake nodded. "I shot him. Did you get a text from Sarah?"

Beth didn't answer, but walked into her friend's office and closed the door.

Jake heard Cody woof at Beth in greeting. He called out, "Be friends, Cody."

The CSI van pulled up outside. Two team members came in, and Jake recognized them from when he'd found the body on Fort Funston dog beach.

Terrell said, "This is the perp who threw that rave dancer off a cliff."

The female CSI officer scowled at the body. "Who shot him?"

"I did," Jake said. "Four times."

"Thank you for your service," she said.

Jake had paused the video on the TV where Sarah was punching the killer's throat with both fists as he sat on her thighs holding a knife. "I had the easy part."

The CSI cop looked at the TV and then back at him in understanding. "Is she okay?"

"Yes, Scooter is talking to her, and she has my dog by her side."

"That's an amazing dog you have."

Jake said, "And an amazing girlfriend."

CHAPTER 67

Former Sheriff Deputy Corrine Denton left the house after midnight and headed to work at her new job. She enjoyed the thrill of driving a tow truck and repossessing cars at night.

However, her anger flared up whenever she thought about the reasons for her career change. First, Chief Deputy Sheriff Leslie Ritter had called Denton into her office and showed her an orange juice jug full of xylazine pills. Second, she'd played a security cam video of Denton tying the jug to the *Far Niente*'s anchor. Third, she'd asked for Denton's resignation.

On top of that, Chief Ritter showed her a printed copy of an anonymous complaint against Denton with the Commission of Peace Officer Standards, the state's law enforcement accreditation panel.

The commission was investigating Denton's alleged crimes. If they found her guilty, they'd invoke a one-year suspension of her license to carry a badge in California.

Denton was sure Jake Wolfe had sent the complaint.

"Let's make this easy," Chief Ritter had said. "Turn in your badge and gun right now, and go find another job. Otherwise,

I'll make sure the commission goes through with your suspension due to possession of xylazine with intent to distribute."

Denton had resigned, turned in her badge and gun, and walked out of Chief Ritter's office as an unemployed civilian. The repo job was a temporary paycheck until she could get hired by another sheriff or police department in a city nearby.

"I'm going to make Jake Wolfe pay for screwing with me," Denton said to herself. "A tragic car accident caused by brake failure will do nicely, and getting rid of that evil dog will be a bonus."

∼

Half an hour before sunrise, Tammi Martinelli once again approached Corrine Denton's house in the dark. This time, behind the wheel of a stolen car.

She drove past, turned off the car's headlights, and pulled over near the same lot of new condos under construction.

Checking an anonymous GPS unit, she noted the tracking device on a map that revealed the target car's location as it moved. Denton would arrive home soon.

"I don't get mad—I get even," Tammi said. She was also acting on orders from Anselmo, head of the Family. She was duty-bound by the omertà.

Tammi grabbed a rucksack, exited the vehicle, walked to the target's house, and opened the front door with her lockpick. Closing the door behind her, she walked through the living room and into the kitchen.

She heard the garage door rumble as it rolled up and then down. Tammi quickly hid in the kitchen's walk-in pantry, closed the white louvered wood double doors, and peeked out the slender open ventilation gaps. She could see out, but the other person could not see in.

Denton walked into the kitchen, set her purse on a counter, and poured herself two fingers of straight gin in a highball glass. After drinking it down in one gulp, she poured another, but left it there as she walked toward a bathroom.

Tammi waited until she heard Denton relieving herself, then moved quietly to the glass of liquor and used a tiny bottle with an eyedropper to add a strong dose of tranq. She'd previously ground up several pills and dissolved them in water, creating a bottle of tasteless and odorless knockout drops. Tammi returned to hide in the pantry closet just in time.

Denton came back into the kitchen and drank down her gin. She grabbed the bottle and empty glass, moved to the couch in her living room, poured a third drink, and thumbed a TV remote.

Tammi remained still as the television blared a morning news station. She waited until Denton leaned her head back and fell unconscious, then approached, opened her rucksack and withdrew a bedsheet that she laid on the carpet. Gripping Denton's shirt front and belt, she eased her onto the sheet and laid her on her back before carefully dragging her across the carpet and through the access door that led into the garage.

Back inside the house, Tammi fetched Denton's purse off the kitchen counter and reached inside for the car's key fob. Returning to the garage, she unlocked the car and leaned the driver's seat back. Tammi then held all four corners of the sheet in both hands and grunted with effort as she raised Denton's unconscious body and set it down. She removed the sheet, dropped it on the ground, and set Denton's purse on the front passenger seat.

Denton remained asleep, her breathing slowing down from the tranq. If left alone, she might or might not wake up.

But Tammi followed the Family's orders.

She put the key in the ignition, started the engine, and dropped a folded sheet of white printer paper onto Denton's lap that spelled out a written confession of her drug-dealing crimes.

She'd made the printout with an untraceable inkjet printer, the same kind of printer Tammi had seen in the house on her first visit. As a cop, Tammi knew color laser printers had secret codes embedded to ID the devices and prevent counterfeiting, but black-and-white inkjets did not.

Tammi lowered the driver's door window an inch, opened her rucksack one last time, stuffed the bedsheet inside, and pulled out a length of garden hose. She placed one end of the hose into the open inch of the driver's window and closed the door. Then she moved to the back of the car, pushed the other end of the hose into the car's exhaust pipe, and stuffed one of Denton's kitchen towels in there to hold it in place.

Stepping away to observe her handiwork, she noted how the car engine continued idling as the hose filled the vehicle's interior with exhaust. It wouldn't take long for a fatal dose of carbon monoxide poisoning to turn Denton's cheeks a bright cherry red—the sure sign of CMP.

When police found the suicide note and confession, they'd have no reason to suspect murder. A coroner would agree it was obviously a suicide.

Eventually, news reports would say the deceased had used liquor and tranq to numb her fear of dying. Then she'd passed out in her car while the exhaust provided an easy, painless death to a criminal suffering from guilt and shame.

Tammi moved to the stacks of plastic storage tubs,

extracted the locked duffel bag containing tranq pills and handguns, and placed it on the back seat of Denton's car.

Lastly, she reached into Denton's purse and took out her iPhone to call 9-1-1. The device would allow her to make the call without unlocking it, but that might leave a clue. She used Denton's right thumb to unlock the screen, opened the phone app, and typed three numbers. When the operator answered, she ended the call and set the phone in a center cup holder.

"Wash me thoroughly from my wickedness and cleanse me from my sin," Tammi whispered, quoting Psalm 51. She made the sign of the cross, seeking forgiveness as much for herself as for Denton.

She quietly exited the house, drove her stolen car away in the dark, and headed back to drop off the vehicle where she'd borrowed it.

On the way, she told herself it had to be done. She'd had no other choice. Denton was a threat to the community. And Tammi deserved to be avenged. Last but perhaps most of all, in her opinion, the innocent dog, Cody, needed to be protected from a psychopath who wanted him dead. When Tammi reported back to Anselmo, she knew he'd say, "The Family thanks you."

CHAPTER 68

On the *Far Niente*, Jake sat at the stern deck patio table drinking a cup of coffee when he received a phone call.

McKay said, "Roxanne found Nikolae Koval's yacht. She created an overlay of Gerald Oliver's past phone travels and the Sea Ray Sundancer's transponder history off the coast of Baja California. They both converged with the transponder of a yacht named *Solar Eclipse*. The Sea Ray returned to Cabo, and Oliver's phone remained on the yacht as it cruised up the coast."

"How far up the coast? To Northern California by any chance?" Jake said.

"Yes. We're on the side of the angels, and they've given us a gift."

Jake set down his coffee and stood. "Current location of Koval's yacht? I'll go there immediately."

"Easy, Tiger. Here's the plan." McKay filled him in.

Jake ended the call, gazed at the ocean, and shouted some blistering Marine boot camp profanity.

Cody looked at him and quirked a brow.

Jake paced back and forth on the sidewalk in front of Juanita Yacht Harbor as he waited impatiently for Agents Easton and Greene to arrive.

Detective Flynn walked up to him carrying a to-go cup from the Sausalito Coffee Company across the street on the other side of the park. He wore the same gray slacks, blue shirt, and navy sport coat as always. "Wolf Person, our security cams recorded somebody in a mask tampering with your vehicle last night."

Jake raised his eyebrows. "What did they do, boss?"

"Crawled underneath for a few minutes and then walked away," Flynn said. "I looked just now, and it appears they cut your brake fluid lines." He showed Jake a picture on his phone.

Jake blew out a breath. "A masked person with breasts. Thanks for telling me. I'll have my mobile repair guy stop by and fix that." He sent a text message.

Flynn showed Jake another picture on his phone. "Our K-9 has a vest now. Thank you."

"It was my pleasure to help the SPD K-9 unit."

Flynn took a sip of coffee. "Watch your back. Gotta keep Cody safe."

Jake shook hands with his friend.

Flynn walked toward the coffee shop as a black Suburban drove into the parking lot and stopped near Jake. Easton, Greene, and Sarah stepped out. They waited until Flynn was across the street, then Easton lifted the back hatch to display a large Pelican case containing a weapon.

Jake recognized the M249 Squad Automatic Weapon as the same kind his Marine platoon's SAW gunner had carried on patrols overseas.

The agents also brought along three predator backpacks.

Each was loaded with a box of ammo belts holding 750 rounds of linked ammunition in the main compartment.

Jake had seen them once before. He could adjust the regulator to fire 750 rounds per minute, or faster or slower.

Lastly, Easton showed him a wireless signal jammer similar to the one mounted on the drone in Key West. It would block cell phones, Wi-Fi, Bluetooth and most security cameras for 100 meters.

Jake put on a backpack and carried the SAW in its Pelican case as he made his way down the dock. Following him were Greene with a backpack and Easton also wearing one. Sarah carried the jammer. The four of them set everything down on the *Far Niente's* stern deck.

"Thanks for the SAW," Jake said, "but I specifically requested a six-barrel Gatling-style mini-gun that fires two to four thousand rounds per minute."

"There are two thousand two hundred fifty tracer rounds here," Greene said. "I'm sure you'll make do somehow."

Cody sniffed the weapon and rounds and let out a low growl.

"Leave it, Cody." Jake patted the case with one hand. "My gun." He patted a backpack. "My ammo."

Cody relaxed his shoulders, accepting the new weapon as part of Jake's ever-growing collection.

Covering it all with a gray tarp, Jake tied the corners down so it wouldn't blow away. He briefed his team. "McKay ruled out any collateral damage. There are no innocents on the targeted yacht. The captain gets visits from prostitutes, but none today."

Sarah took a deep breath and let it out. "I can do this."

Jake nodded at her and said, "Cody, heel." He led his dog inside to the master stateroom, where he dressed Cody in a bulletproof vest. "Get in the crate, boy."

Cody growled in protest but went into the Kevlar-protected dog crate. The air vents and door were made of slotted steel that slanted downward like partially open Venetian blinds.

Jake secured the door. "It won't be long. I'll be right back."

Returning to the stern deck, he said, "Okay, everybody change clothes and stand by."

He untied the lines, headed up to the bridge and piloted the *Far Niente* across two bays and onto the ocean. Jake then navigated toward the mission target—Nikolae Koval's luxury super-yacht named *Solar Eclipse*. With luck, when the two vessels passed each other, Jake could use the SAW to reach out and touch someone.

Jake turned off the *Far Niente*'s transponder and began broadcasting a spoofed signal. Any other boat captains who checked their Automatic Identification System would ID Jake's yacht as *Jezebel*, denoting a tempting seductress.

After traveling many miles on the sea, Jake spotted the yacht. There were currently no other boats nearby. As Jake cruised on approach, he saw armed men on the yacht watching *Jezebel* through binoculars. They couldn't see the name *Far Niente* painted in back on the stern.

Jake told Easton, Greene, and Sarah, "It's go time." He tapped a control on the dashboard and played a mix of dance club music at high volume.

Easton sat in the second seat next to Jake. He'd changed from his suit and tie into jeans and a T-shirt, along with a ball cap and sunglasses. The man of few words said, "Ready?"

"Affirmative," Jake said. "Take the helm and maintain course."

Easton stood so he could be seen by people on the *Solar Eclipse*, and placed both hands on the wheel, acting as helmsman.

"Try smiling and nodding your head to the music," Jake said.

Easton's stoic expression didn't change.

Jake returned to the stern deck as Sarah and Greene stepped out through the sliding door, barefoot and wearing bikinis. The music was their cue to get into position. They hurried forward to the sun pad at the bow, where they planned to dance to the music and put on a distracting show for the narco boss target.

Jake waited to turn on the wireless signal jammer, slid under the gray tarp, attached a backpack feed to the SAW, and gazed through the machine gun's ACOG scope over the gunwale. Several bodyguards on the *Solar Eclipse* appeared to go on high alert regarding the passing yacht until they saw it was a "party boat" with hot babes in skimpy swimwear. The next song to play was "Buttons" by the Pussycat Dolls. The female singer's lyrics teasingly invited a lover to please help her get undressed.

He spotted his target standing inside the armored, enclosed fly bridge and looking out a window of bulletproof glass at the alluring ladies.

Jake couldn't see Sarah and Greene on the sun pad, but he knew when that song began Greene would take off her bikini top and give the Russian an eyeful as she danced brazenly to the provocative music, lip-synched the lyrics, and stared at him with a challenging look. She served as a femme fatale and honeytrap on any missions that required such.

Finally, the mission target, Nikolae Stepanovich Koval himself, stepped out of a door on the bridge and stood there with a big grin on his face while using binoculars to watch the women. The multi-millionaire waved a fistful of cash money at them and spoke over the PA system. "Take it all off, ladies. I'll buy those bikinis from you. Name your price." The laughter of a man drunk with power boomed over the speakers. Koval set down the binos and pulled a phone out of his pocket, tapping on the screen as if preparing to take a video.

Jake turned on the wireless signal jammer, took aim and pulled the SAW's trigger, firing rounds at Koval in a controlled burst. It only took twenty seconds and approximately 250 of the M856 red hot tracer rounds to obliterate the Russian warmonger's body.

Jake poured another third of the tracer rounds into the open door of the bridge, where they ricocheted back and forth, ping-ponging off the bulletproof glass windows, ravaging the three crew members piloting the yacht, and starting a blazing fire.

With the bridge taken care of, he now had the rest of the yacht and full crew to deal with. He strafed the yacht's port side with the remaining rounds, taking down many of the bodyguards on deck and causing multiple fires and buying time to reload.

Sarah, Greene, and Easton had plans to take cover immediately when they heard Jake firing the SAW. Easton would drop out of sight, and Sarah and Greene would step inside a tall bulletproof locker and close the door.

Jake remained prone below the gunwale and switched the empty backpack for a loaded one. Several narco guards returned fire at Jake, but he aimed over the gunwale once more and raked the targeted yacht from stem to stern with a full 750 rounds, slaying bodies and tearing the upper decks to flaming shreds. When his second burst ended, he felt the *Far Niente* increase speed as Easton bumped the throttles to gain distance between yachts before Jake's third and final attack.

On the yacht, an armed man came out of a passageway leading belowdecks and fired a rifle-launched grenade from a tube mounted below an M4 carbine.

Jake was out of ammo when he saw the shooter. This was his worst-case scenario. He ducked his head and lay next to the third backpack of 750 tracer rounds. If the grenade landed there, Jake would die a horrific death, and the *Far Niente* would sink, taking all souls onboard down with it.

CHAPTER 69

The grenade sailed past behind the stern, barely missing its target, and splashing into the sea. Easton's increase in speed had saved them.

Jake hurriedly connected the third backpack before his enemy could reload and fire another grenade. He blasted additional tracer rounds, killed the guard, and set more of the yacht ablaze. He then focused a barrage of rounds on an access hatch that covered the gas cap for taking on fuel, above decks of the fuel tank itself. The burning tracer rounds ignited the diesel, which exploded and turned the vessel into a floating structure fire.

A blast of heat and the smell of burning diesel washed over Jake as he set down the SAW and felt the *Far Niente* increase speed again and rise up on plane. He left everything hidden under the tarp and hurried to the stateroom so he could reassure Cody. He guessed that to his dog, the SAW made a unique sound from a remembered nightmare about another life in sunbaked deserts far from home.

"It's all good, Cody," Jake said as he entered the stateroom. "Sorry I smell like war."

Cody barked and scratched at the dog crate until Jake opened its door, then rushed out and stood on his hind legs to paw at Jake's chest and lick his face.

"Okay boy. That's enough dog slobber," Jake said with a smile.

Cody dropped to four paws and pressed his head against his handler's stomach, almost knocking Jake off his feet, but Jake stood his ground and patted Cody on the back.

Sarah and Greene, dressed in blue jeans and T-shirts, came into the stateroom.

Sarah put her arms around Jake and hugged him. "I was so worried about you."

Jake refrained from telling her about the grenade that barely missed.

"You were right, Jake," Greene said. "Narcos won't shoot at women in bikinis. They'd much rather take us captive. We're worth more than gold."

Jake tried to avoid looking at Greene. Sarah had only agreed to do this if Jake wouldn't see the other woman performing like a dancer at a topless club. He said, "Thank you both for your help with the mission."

"It was teamwork," Greene said. "Thank goodness the security cameras were off and the jammer was on." She patted Sarah on the back with a coconspirator's smile and headed to the sliding door.

Jake noticed Greene turn her head before exiting. He carefully ignored her, took a knee, and focused on removing Cody's vest.

Sarah opened a porthole window and looked back at the burning yacht. "How many men died?"

"Dozens."

"How much money was that yacht worth?"

"Millions."

"It's shocking." Sarah said.

Jake closed the porthole. "Yes, but sometimes, in order to have a breakthrough, you need to break something."

Sarah nodded thoughtfully, went to the head, and closed the door behind her.

Jake realized he'd been so focused on destroying the yacht, he'd forgotten to turn off the *Far Niente*'s cameras. His weren't wireless and the jammer wouldn't block them. He used his phone to access the boat's security system and turn off the cams. He then tapped on "Erase By Date," and deleted the entire day's video from midnight forward without looking at Greene's segment.

Sarah returned to him and saw the security system controls app. "There's no video, right?"

"No video of today at all." He showed her how the feed ended at midnight and the cameras were off.

"The reason I asked is, uh, well, I don't know how to tell you this, so I'll just blurt it out."

"You know I'll always listen to anything you have to say without judgment."

She took a breath. "When Agent Greene showed off her topless body, the target didn't open his door."

"What changed his mind?"

"I removed my top when Greene urged me to help." A pink blush rose up her cheeks.

Jake was surprised. "Wow, I'll bet that's when he finally came out of the bridge."

She put both hands over her face for a moment. "Yes, Greene said one babe was good, but two were twice as good."

"*You* were the reason he came outside," Jake said. "You're irresistible."

"Thank you for the compliment. And I'm sorry you missed my debut at topless karaoke."

They both laughed, relieving stress.

"That's just wrong," Jake teased. "Maybe you could perform a topless karaoke encore for me tonight."

"Hmm, I'll have to give it some thought."

"Give it plenty of thought... I know I will."

The intercom crackled, interrupting their repartee. Easton said, "Jake, report to the bridge, and pilot this vessel."

"Roger." Jake was amazed Easton had spoken a complete sentence. He made his way up to the bridge with Cody and Sarah following him.

He found Greene in the black leather second seat, where she tapped controls on the dashboard, trying to access his security camera system.

"Need help with anything?" Jake asked her.

Greene said, "McKay ordered that all cameras remain off during our mission in order to maintain operations security."

"Right, so they couldn't record me blasting the *Solar Eclipse* and its crew straight to hell. Might be hard to explain that if a hacker put it on the internet."

"I wanted to double-check the cam feeds," Greene said.

"Good idea." Jake leaned over and tapped a password on the laptop keyboard. "You're in."

"Thank you." Greene reviewed the security videos and appeared relieved at her findings.

Jake turned to Easton. "You did some excellent piloting of the *Far Niente*, but I'll take the helm now."

Easton didn't know about Jake's protocol. He simply stepped back and gestured at the wheel.

"Captain has the helm." Jake turned off the extra transponder, causing the spoofed ID of *Jezebel* to vanish from the Automatic Identification System. He kept the *Far Niente*'s transponder off and traveled as an unknown vessel for a while.

With a bump of the throttles to increase speed further, Jake turned the wheel and changed course, racing away from the scene of destruction and the last known heading of *Jezebel*.

Far behind them, the *Solar Eclipse* was engulfed in flames as it burned to the waterline and sent up a plume of smoke visible for miles in all directions.

His phone buzzed with a call from McKay.

"Situation report?" she said.

"Mission target down. No casualties on our team. We're doing a quick exfil."

"We have an incoming Coast Guard cutter, and this mission is on a need-to-know basis," McKay said. "Alter your course to a new heading." She gave him the coordinates.

"Aye, altering course." Jake turned the wheel again, bumped the throttles further and rocketed across a cobalt ocean topped with whitecaps.

"One last thing," McKay said. "Leak a news story to your reporter friend. The yacht was a floating meth lab that exploded."

Jake thought of Linda at the news station. "Roger that."

"Thank you all for your service." McKay ended the call.

Jake said to his team. "Good work, people. The world is a safer place now, thanks to you."

CHAPTER 70

The next day, Jake's life felt surreal as it settled back to normal. At noon, he swam in the marina at Juanita Yacht Harbor using a dive mask, snorkel and fins. He slowly circled around a beautiful sailboat, completing a presale inspection for two clients of Bart Bartholomew's law firm.

Cody dog-paddled alongside his handler, bright eyes watching Jake in curiosity.

Taking a breath and holding it, Jake dove underwater and studied the hull. Cody dove, too. Jake encouraged him to do so because it helped the dog avoid separation anxiety when his handler vanished beneath the surface and left him behind. Few people understood how hard it was for dogs to shut off their noses and not smell the world around them.

After Jake made a few more quick dives to inspect the keel and rudder, he finished his appraisal, climbed onto the dock, and then grabbed the handle on Cody's vest and helped him up. While Cody shook his fur and sent water drops flying, Jake removed his snorkeling gear and stood there in board shorts and bare feet.

A retired couple, Gordon and Rita, waited to hear Jake's opinion. Rita stared in amazement at the many scars all over Jake's muscular body, and then focused on his latest—a fiery red round scar at the top left side of his chest.

Jake told the couple what they didn't want to hear. "I'm sorry, but I don't recommend you buy this particular boat."

Gordon appeared surprised. "Really? We had it inspected by a surveyor. He said this is a seaworthy sailboat with everything in good shape."

Jake shook his head. "I respectfully disagree with the surveyor. In my opinion, he missed several problems. For example, the rudder stops are bolted to rotting wood that needs to be replaced. You could lose steering and end up drifting rudderless toward a ship or shoreline."

Rita turned and stared at the sailboat as if imagining a frightening scenario. "How much would that cost to fix?"

"It's not cheap," Jake said. "A shipwright would have to raise the boat out of the water and keep it in dry dock while under repair."

Rita sighed. "What else did the survey miss?"

"The wires and connections to your bilge pump are rusted. If the bilge fails, you could have a flood aboard. Possibly at night while you're asleep. A flood might cause water damage, mold, and dry rot."

Rita said, "Mold can harm your lungs and nervous system."

"And there are a lot more problems that make this boat a fixer-upper."

Gordon let out a long breath. "Thanks for saving us a lot of time, trouble, and money."

Jake nodded. "You're welcome. And don't worry, I'll help you find your dream boat. There are plenty of used, high-quality vessels for sale, and I'm not on commission."

"I wish we hadn't already paid that surveyor," Gordon said.

"Bart will file papers and get you a full refund," Jake said. "Next time, hire someone who belongs to the Society of Accredited Marine Surveyors."

"Do they have an online directory?" Rita asked.

"Yes, and I know an accredited married couple here in town you can trust to do it right. They'll insist on having you over for dinner while you look at boats on their large screen TV."

Rita smiled. "I'd like to meet them."

"And they'd like to meet you," Jake said. "The first consultation costs nothing, and you'll enjoy a delightful meal with new friends."

Gordon shook Jake's hand. "That sounds great."

Jake made a phone call and set up an appointment.

After Bart's clients left, Jake walked back to the *Far Niente*, and Cody trotted along with him. Jake's left shoulder still hurt from the bullet wound, and his left arm felt weak. He had to favor his left side, and that made him impatient, but he faithfully continued doing daily PT exercises to regain his strength.

He stood on the stern deck. "Cody, heel."

Cody trotted to his handler's side.

Jake reached down with his left hand and grabbed hold of the dog's vest handle, then slowly lifted him up and down in ten exercise reps as he grunted with each painful effort.

Setting the dog on his feet, Jake said, "Thanks, buddy." He removed Cody's vest, used a beach towel to dry his fur, and then brushed him.

His phone buzzed with a text from an unknown number. There was no message, only a link to an obituary.

Corrine Denton Has Died

Corrine "Cori" Denton died Tuesday at the age of 43. Initial reports have not yet specified a cause of death, but confidential sources claim it's being ruled a suicide by carbon monoxide poisoning. Rumors that Ms. Denton was battling severe depression after losing her job at the sheriff's department have not been confirmed. The former deputy will be buried at Redwood Meadows Cemetery in Colma.

Jake felt mixed emotions, but mostly relief that Cody was safe from harm. "Rest in peace."

A black limousine pulled up to the marina docks and stopped. Vito stepped out and opened a back passenger door for Beatrice, the fortune-teller. They walked down Jake's dock, and Vito unlocked the gate using a key Jake had given to him.

Vito led Beatrice to the *Far Niente's* boat slip and called out, "Permission to come aboard?"

"Yes. Welcome aboard," Jake said. "Be friends, Cody."

Beatrice embarked and looked around in wonder. "I had to see this 'horizon' of yours."

Jake nodded. "The horizon and boat from tarot card number thirteen."

Beatrice glanced at Cody. "And the protective animal. I heard you were shot and wounded."

"Cody warned me, but I didn't duck fast enough."

Beatrice observed his bare chest with a worried frown. "May I lay hands on you?"

"Be my guest."

She put her hands on the entry and exit wound scars, closed her eyes, and spoke a healing prayer in Italian.

Jake said, "From your lips to God's ears."

Beatrice took a step back. "Vito tells me your sports bet won twenty thousand dollars."

"Yeah, I gambled a thousand dollars at twenty to one odds," Jake said. "Please donate my winnings to your favorite charity, as we planned."

"A nun at church is fundraising to buy meals for hungry people and families," Beatrice said. "It's an endless task, growing more difficult every day. Father O'Leary's food bank keeps running out of food."

"Sounds like Sister Mary of Perpetual Motion."

Beatrice smiled. "Yes, and Sister Mary told me you'd call her by that silly nickname."

"We're old friends," he said. "Last time I talked to her, she was handing out brown bag lunches to homeless people. A criminal shot her, but a thick Bible stopped the bullet. She's one lucky nun."

"It wasn't luck," Beatrice said matter-of-factly.

Jake looked at the alleged clairvoyant, who appeared utterly sure of herself. "If you say so."

"Does that donation meet your approval?"

"Yes, of course. Please give my winnings to Sister Mary of Perpetual Goodness." Jake pulled on a dry T-shirt. "I received my thousand back, too. I could bet it again if you want."

Beatrice said, "So far, I'm not feeling any loss of my gifts."

Jake noticed Vito hanging on every word. "You copied my bet, didn't you, Vito?"

Vito acted innocent. "What?"

Beatrice shook her finger at him. "Don Vito, you have to donate your winnings from that bet to charity."

Vito groaned. "C'mon... you're kidding me."

"Beatrice gives you plenty of winning tips," Jake said. "This one is for me only, and the money will help Sister Mary feed hungry people."

Vito scoffed. "And you think that'll keep you out of Hell?"

"No, not really." Jake looked up at the rolling hills dotted with houses. "I'm simply collecting money from rich people who voluntarily gambled and lost by betting on sports. And I'm donating it to a nun who once gave me a D in religious studies on my fourth-grade report card for doubting everything she said and asking endless questions about the Virgin Mary's immaculate conception."

Vito threw his head back and laughed. "It probably didn't help that the nun was also a virgin named Mary. Okay, I'll donate my winnings to feed families and never copy Jake's bet again."

Beatrice held out her hand. "Your word of honor?"

Vito gently shook hands. "Yes, my word of honor."

Jake gave Beatrice a nod. "Vito's word is absolute."

"Thank you, Vito," Beatrice said.

A uniformed deputy sheriff walked down the dock toward them. She opened the gate with a law enforcement master key. "I'm here to see Captain Wolfe."

Jake recognized the jail detention deputy. "Sheriff Moore. How are you, ma'am? Please come aboard."

Moore embarked, and Cody woofed at her.

"Be friends, Cody." Jake introduced Moore to Vito and Beatrice. "What brings you here, my friend?"

"I stopped by to thank you personally," Moore said. "The chief deputy reassigned me from jail duty to the department's new speed boat, *Patrol One*. I'll be working with Captain Yoshida."

Jake smiled at seeing how excited and happy Moore was to get out of jail and onto the water. "Yoshida is an excellent captain, but that boat was a sausage fest and needed a female influence."

"They were short one seasick deputy who'd transferred,

and I accepted the position. Chief Ritter told me you put in a good word on my behalf."

Jake shrugged. "You were kind to Officer Martinelli in jail when she needed a friend. Thank you, Moore."

She hugged him impulsively, and then turned and walked away, calling over her shoulder, "I'll see you out on the bay."

"Yes, see you out there," Jake said.

Vito told Jake, "We're going to the restaurant for lunch. Care to join us?"

"I'm having lunch with Sarah."

"She's invited, too, along with Red Rover."

Vito and Beatrice walked up the dock, returned to the limo, and drove away.

Jake took a quick shower, dressed himself, and led Cody to the Jeep. He looked underneath to make sure his mobile repair guy had fixed the brake lines, then drove across the Golden Gate to Sarah's veterinary clinic.

When he and Cody arrived and stood out front, a black Suburban pulled up and stopped. The darkened backseat window buzzed down to reveal Agent McKay. Her daughter, Aspen, sat next to her with their newly adopted guide dog, Faith, across her lap.

"We're off to Travis Air Force Base and a flight home," McKay said. "Aspen wanted to say goodbye."

Jake was reminded of how McKay tracked his location via the phone she'd given him.

Aspen spoke up, wearing dark sunglasses and facing in his general direction. "Jake, thanks again for Faith. She means everything to me."

"You're more than welcome, Aspen. I know you'll take good care of each other." A lump formed in Jake's throat, and he had trouble saying anything more.

McKay studied his face and gave him a nod in

understanding. "I can't thank you and Cody enough for this guide dog."

"The happiness of Aspen and Faith are all the thanks we need."

"I hope you take time off to heal and recuperate," McKay said.

Jake reached up and rubbed his hand over the wounded area. "Cody and I went for a swim this morning, and now we're off to have lunch with Sarah."

"Have a good one. Take care." McKay patted Agent Greene on the shoulder, and the Suburban drove away.

Sarah came outside, and Jake told her about Vito's invitation.

"Yes, of course. I love Amborgetti's. And we can take our time. My substitute doctor is working all day."

Jake drove to the restaurant and parked. He opened the SUV's center console and pulled out a sub-compact 9mm Sig Sauer P365 pistol. "This is for you. Loaded with XTP hollow-points. Now we have matching pistols, mags, and rounds."

Sarah accepted the handgun. "His and hers pistols. Such a romantic gift," she teased as she stashed the gun in her purse. "Thank you."

"I know, right?"

Jake led them inside.

The Italian hostess said, "Welcome, *Giacobbe il Coltello*. Please come with me." She led them to Vito's table.

Jake said, "Sarah, this is my new friend, Beatrice, who can read palms and tarot cards. She told me it was fate that Cody brought you and me together."

Sarah smiled at Beatrice. "I like her already."

Beatrice observed Sarah with a curious gaze.

Jake and Sarah took their seats, and Cody lay on the floor

in-between them. A waiter stopped by and asked, "May I start you off with a cocktail, wine, or beer?"

Jake's phone buzzed with a text message from Leena. *Friendly reminder. Please enjoy alcohol-free drinks at lunch. You can do it.*

He sighed and told the waiter, "Pellegrino water for me," then he showed the text to Sarah, who smiled and chuckled.

Leena sent a follow-up text. *My mom got hired by the hospital!*

Jake replied. *Congratulations!*

He shared that text with Sarah as well, because it had been her idea to help Leena's mother get hired.

Jake noticed Beatrice had never taken her eyes off Sarah. She said, "Sarah, may I please read your palm?"

Sarah appeared doubtful, but played along and held out her hand.

"I see you're considering possible futures and how to spend your time." Beatrice spread tarot cards on the table. "Please pick a card."

Sarah reached out and flipped one over.

"The lovers card," Beatrice said. "The sixth card of the major arcana represents choices. You and Jake have been making choices that keep you apart. Maybe you could both choose to meet halfway."

Sarah reached for Jake's hand. "You asked me if I'd like to spend my weekends in Sausalito. Now that I have an assistant working for me again, my answer is yes, I'd love to. Let's try that and see how it goes."

Jake squeezed her hand. "Sounds good. And I can dock the *Far Niente* at Pier Thirty-Nine on a weeknight or two, so we can enjoy what the crazy big city has to offer."

Beatrice nodded wisely and put the cards away in her ornately carved wooden box. "All's well that ends well."

Jake agreed. He'd been through Hell on Earth and almost died, but the stars aligned and everything turned out well for himself and so many of his friends. He was both grateful and relieved. As the waiter set down plates of gourmet food and a bowl of plain meatballs for Cody, Jake said, "Amen to that. Let's eat. *Mangia, mangia. Buon appetito.*"

The group dug in and enjoyed their delicious meals and lighthearted conversations.

All was right with the world—for now.

— The End —

DEAR READER

Dear Reader,

Thank you for reading Mission Target. I do a lot of research while writing novels for you, and I try to include interesting tech, gadgets, and weapons for your reading entertainment.

Quite a few readers send emails asking me which things in my books are real. To answer that for everyone, I've put together a quick list pertaining to this book.

Please note, the following list contains spoilers, so if anybody skipped to the back, I advise them to please read the book before reading this list.

First, what is *not* real.

As in every book, names, characters, places, events, incidents, and dialogue are all products of the author's imagination or are used fictitiously. Any resemblance to actual persons living or dead, businesses, organizations, events, or locales is entirely coincidental. For example, there are many boat marinas in Sausalito, but none of them are named Juanita Yacht Harbor.

Second, what *is* real.
 The following things really do exist but are used fictitiously in this novel. Noted in order of appearance.

Xylazine (pronounced ZAI'-luh-zeen) is a veterinary tranquilizer drug used on horses and other large animals. People have started taking the animal medicine to get high. On the street it's known as tranq. A slight overdose can easily kill a person by slowing down their breathing and heartbeat to deadly levels. Xylazine isn't an opiate and it doesn't respond to Naloxone (Narcan). There are no known antidotes. In humans, it can cause the side effect of terrible flesh wounds.

Some big tech companies really do use your phone apps and browsing history to create a profile of you and your life, which is unofficially known as your "voodoo doll." I won't mention specific names of giant corporations with teams of lawyers, but if you're curious you can read about it in the book *Stolen Focus* by Johann Hari. For example. Why are maps and GPS free to use on your phone? They're free so that your voodoo doll can include details of where you go every day of your life and keep the data forever in your permanent record.

I once met someone in Maui who claimed to be a palm reader. A skeptical tourist couple paid the fee, and the husband said,

"Guess what I do for a living." The palm reader only took a moment to reply, "You exercise good judgement." The wife smiled and said, "He's a district court judge."

I observed a woman panhandling by using a dog and an empty red plastic gas can as props. Her cardboard sign said she was stranded and only needed enough money for gas to leave town and drive to her mother's house. I lowered my window, handed her some dollars and mentioned that I'd seen her in that same spot for months and months. Would she tell me her story? She laughed and admitted earning more money from panhandling than she'd made at her previous employer before being laid off.

A United Nations program helped thousands of South American farmers stop growing illegal coca for cocaine, and replace it with cocoa for chocolate. The farmers are no longer oppressed by violent drug traffickers, and they've planted over a million trees to restore the rainforest ecosystem. You can support this farmer co-op by enjoying an organic Alter Eco chocolate bar. It costs more because you're also planting a tree.

It's true that in a recent sweep of San Francisco, the Police found most drug addicts arrested were people from other states. Only three out of 45 people listed San Francisco as their address. That means roughly 95% had come from elsewhere for the purpose of using recreational drugs on the friendly city's streets, taking advantage of local residents' kind hearts.

. . .

MISSION TARGET

Many years ago, a dog named Roselle, a golden retriever—Labrador retriever mix, graduated from the Guide Dogs for the Blind school in San Rafael, California. Roselle was adopted by a blind man named Michael in New York. On 9/11 a hijacked plane flew into the World Trade Center's North Tower where Michael worked. The plane's fuel exploded with a force equal to 480,000 pounds of TNT. In the chaos that followed, Roselle remained poised and steady, totally focused on Michael, doing her job. Ignoring the flames, smoke and falling debris, she calmly led her blind best friend away from the 78th floor and down a stairwell's 1,463 steps in the burning skyscraper to safety, while many other people followed them. The guide dog and her blind handler saved countless lives. This is the unbelievable but true legacy of retriever dogs. In this novel, Cody and Faith are patterned after these real-life K-9 heroes. After a long and happy career and retirement, Roselle passed over the rainbow bridge. Rest In Peace, special dog. You will always be remembered.

The Lawrence Livermore National Laboratory near San Francisco really does have a High Explosives Applications Facility team, and an underground weapons testing chamber in a hidden location named Remote Site 300. Lab scientists conduct tests there on what they describe as optimized explosives with custom characteristics. LLNL teams invented a pocket-sized high explosive detector that is now used at airports. Lastly, the lab also invented the Mechanical Safe Arming Device which prevents accidental or unintended detonation of a nuclear warhead, especially any potential activation from outside sources. Thank you, lab scientists.

. . .

The California Highway Patrol is the largest state police agency in America. California recently changed Highway Patrol jurisdiction to include city streets, and deployed CHP officers to the besieged Tenderloin district of San Francisco. So far, the agency has seized over 5.2 kilos of fentanyl. Enough to potentially kill 2.4 million people. The city's entire population three times over. This team effort by the fine officers of the SFPD and the CHP is making history in a city that appreciates an assist from the state. We can only hope the other 49 US states may learn about this successful collaboration and follow their example.

The M249 Squad Automatic Weapon is carried by a Marine platoon's SAW gunner. They are also mounted aboard US Navy patrol craft. The M249 can fire ammo belts of 200 linked rounds loaded in machine gun boxes, but Marine SAW gunners on foot carry a smaller belt pouch of rounds humorously referred to as a "nut sack." While rare, there really are bigger SAW machine gun boxes loaded with ammo belts of 750 linked rounds, which will fit inside a large predator backpack.

Sports betting involves mind-boggling sums of money. Reuters estimates around 50 million Americans bet over $8 billion every year just on the March Madness basketball tournament. According to the Statista website, last year the global sports betting industry reached a market size of $242 billion US dollars. Larger than the GDP of over 100 nations.

ACKNOWLEDGMENTS

Thank YOU for reading my books. Thanks for letting me entertain you. Your readership helps me keep doing what I love, and living my dream of being a novelist. Writing is hard work, but I'd rather do this than anything else. I appreciate you for coming along on the journey. I hope you enjoyed reading *Mission Target*, and you might consider leaving a short review. Word of mouth is really helpful to an author. Thanks so much.

Thank you to my talented team of editors, proofreaders, early readers, beta-tester readers, fact finders, cover artists, and more who worked hard on this book and spent long hours going through the story, page-by-page to make it enjoyable for you. These fine folks are all so valuable to me they'll remain a trade secret for now.

Last but not least, thank you to every dog I ever loved, who made me a better human. As I've often said, I'm just trying to be the person my dog thinks I am.

ALSO BY MARK NOLAN

Here's a list of my novels, in order, that feature Jake and Cody.

If you enjoyed reading this book, would you consider leaving a short review? Word of mouth is really helpful to an author.

Thank you!

Dead Lawyers Don't Lie

Vigilante Assassin

Killer Lawyer

San Diego Dead

Deadly Weapon

Key West Dead

The Girl Who Escaped

Mission Target

"The Girl Who Escaped" is a spin-off action novel where FBI agent Reynolds asks Jake and Cody to help her with a dangerous case.

Please subscribe to my reader newsletter at marknolan.com and I'll send you an email when I publish another book.

ABOUT THE AUTHOR

Mark Nolan is the Amazon bestselling author of the Jake Wolfe thriller novel series. Right now, he's busy writing the next story about Jake and Cody. If you'd like to be the first to know about upcoming books, please join Mark's reader newsletter at:

www.marknolan.com

To be notified by Amazon when a new book is available in the Kindle store, visit Mark's author page and click on the "Follow" button under his photo:

Amazon.com/author/marknolan

Made in the USA
Middletown, DE
04 December 2024

66140898R00232